Between The Holidays

BOOK ONE

AMANDA BRYK

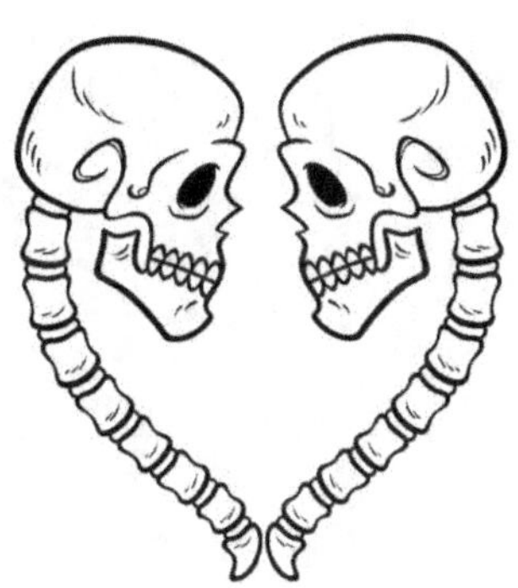

Beloved friends and Cherished family
This book is not meant for you.

NSFW

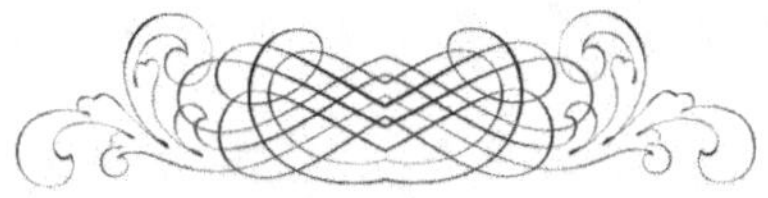

There are a minimum of two sides to every truth. In the case of this hexagonal love story, it's more like half a dozen, but only two or three you need to be overly concerned with. As so often is the case, love is a messy business, sometimes testing the bonds between friends and family. But to deny a love as inevitable as theirs would be a tragedy, and I am not here to rewrite Romeo and Juliet.

CHAPTER 1
Val

Halloween is by far and above my absolute favorite holiday. I've spent the last two weeks curating the perfect treat baskets overflowing with candies, stickers, and toys, even though fewer than two dozen kids call this apartment building home. Tonight is the one night of the year when it is socially acceptable to give gifts to strangers without any expectation of reciprocation.

As someone who shies away from the spotlight, I've never been comfortable opening presents in front of people. There's too much pressure to act surprised and happy, and overall, I don't enjoy it. The only thing worse than getting a gift, if you're someone like me, is receiving a compliment. The thought of it sends a shiver down my spine. However, the act of unconditional gift-giving warms my cold, dead heart in a way that little else can. Plus, I love seeing people embrace their inner monster.

My neighbors were kind enough to inform me that the kids in the apartment usually roamed the halls early, so I was sure to be prepared. It makes sense to go door to door in the building first. Then, they can drop their first load of candy at home before meeting with friends who live in the development across the street. Before Trick or Treat officially starts, the kids from the building have already collected a month's worth of sweets.

I dream of being able to afford a house like the ones across the street, but for now, I'm here, gluing together the remaining pieces of my shattered existence. Thankfully, I have the world's greatest french bulldog puppy to keep me company. Otherwise, my slow descent into madness might have been a much quicker trip.

By 5:30 pm, I've seen nearly everyone, and I'm about to slip Christmas out of his black skeleton hoodie when there's a knock at the door.

"Trick-or-treat. Smell my feet. Give me something good to eat. If you don't, I won't be sad." I open the door as Samuel finishes the last line of his well-rehearsed holiday poem. *"I'll just make you wish you had."*

The masked goblin I know to be my eight-year-old neighbor stands with arms outstretched, bag open at the ready, waiting for his bounty of sweet treats. I drop a full-size chocolate bar into the cotton pillowcase and hand his mom one of the skull-shaped baskets.

"Don't eat my toes! I have candy!" I say, with a tone of false terror.

"Might as well drop this off before we head out. Aunt Val outdid herself, per usual." Tracy gives him a second to peek through the basket's contents before allowing it to fall away to her side. "You spoil him."

"Christmas and I don't eat chocolate, so I have to spoil someone. I'm surprised to see you two getting a late start. I figured you would've been my first visitors of the night." The smile on my face slips when I notice, for the first time, the look of exhaustion worn by Samuel's mother.

Tracy is recently divorced and struggling to balance work and home. We bonded almost instantly over a shared dislike of men and have developed a sort of friendship over the last ten months. She was one of my first and maybe only friend here in Ohio, and I appreciate all the times she has listened without judgment. Hopefully, the feelings are mutual.

"These double shifts at the hospital are kicking my ass, and Sam was supposed to go out with his dad tonight, but here we are..." Her voice trails off.

I can tell there's more to the story, but this isn't the time for details. Tracy is good about holding her tongue in front of her son. However, once he's out of earshot, look out! She's talked my ear off until sunrise on more than one occasion. Not that I mind. When she needs someone to listen, I'm happy to oblige. Honestly, the more she talks, the less I have to say, so it works out in my favor.

"I'd be happy to blow off my plans for the night and take this little monster out if you need to kick your feet up and relax. Christmas never passes up a chance to go for a walk, and he's already dressed." My offer, while genuine, will ultimately amount to nothing. If I know one thing about Tracy, she prides herself on being a great mom. She isn't going to miss an opportunity to create a positive memory with her son, especially since I'm assuming his dad canceled again at the last minute.

"Sweet of you to offer, but we'll be fine. You go have fun and text me when you get home later." She manages a half smile as she places a hand on Samuel's shoulder. "We better get out there before all the good candy is gone. Say goodbye to Aunt Val."

"Mom, can I give Christmas the treat I brought before we go? He's dressed in a costume but doesn't get to go trick-or-treating. It's not fair." Samuel lifts his mask and beams at the small white dog pressed against my leg. Once the pumpkin-shaped biscuit is in full view, Christmas begins to pitter-pat his feet, struggling to contain his excitement.

"Only if Aunt Val says it's okay." Tracy and Sam cast their eyes in unison, searching my face for a response.

"Of course, you can give it to him. All kids deserve a treat on Halloween, especially the furry ones." I watch to make sure Christmas takes the treat gently from Samuel's tiny hand, then say my final goodbyes. I still need to finish getting ready for my date, and I'm running low on time.

I'm not entirely sure what the plans are for tonight. Where we're going and whom we're meeting remains a Halloween mystery, though, for the record, I'm not someone who enjoys surprises. All Allen told me was, *"Be ready by 5:45 and do NOT wear a costume."* He was sure to say it in his stupid fucking condescending voice that always makes me want to choke the life out of him.

His comment rubbed me the wrong way, and I had half a mind to paint my face like a skull and wear my rib cage t-shirt because I knew it would ruffle his feathers. But I'm feeling generous tonight, so I settled on a black shirt, jeans, light makeup, and a messy bun. I may not be the wild and crazy girl I was in my 20s, but I haven't retired completely. As for Allen, his 30s seem to have brought him to a screeching halt, and I wish I could have met the guy he claims to be in stories.

He constantly talks about playing sports in college, pledging a fraternity, touring with his band, all-night video game sessions, and late-night bar crawls. Sometimes, I feel like I'm dating the idea of a guy instead of an actual person. Like one of those catfish, only his face matches the images I first stumbled across online.

We met, like most people do these days, on a dating site. And that's fine. The part I regret is allowing myself to be manipulated. He used my kindness against me and talked me into dating him when I knew we didn't have a real connection. Don't get me wrong, Allen and I are capable of having fun together, and he's nice enough to be around for the most part. He isn't even hard on the eyes, if you know what I mean. But our personalities don't align as perfectly as he initially claimed, and as time passes, I've been feeling slightly duped.

Then again, this may be what dating in your thirties is supposed to feel like. People get older, and they settle down. In fact, *settling* is the perfect word to describe our relationship. Neither of us seems overly impressed with the other, but who wants to be single? The never-ending cycle of swiping left and swiping right, excitement over a potential match, first date butterflies, disappointing conversation, and the inevitable rejection. It all gets pretty old, really quickly.

I don't love Allen, and I'm confident I never will, but I'll stay with him until he gets tired of me and moves on. Fingers crossed, that happens sooner rather than later.

Kold

It's been three years since I've heard a peep from Allen Cuttler, and suddenly, he's reaching out, acting like meeting is an urgent matter. A decade ago, he didn't exactly leave things on the best of terms when he bought a guitar with my credit card and disappeared before the first bill came in the mail. Since then, he's kept his distance, hiding behind his parents and his fake importance. Maybe he's finally planning to pay me back the $2,800 he owes me, or maybe he's looking to screw me over again.

In hindsight, my brother and I should have kicked the shit out of him when we had the chance, but I was too worried about the long-term consequences. I was being too nice for my own good. Thankfully, it was a deficiency I learned to overcome.

I read through our conversation again, looking for any excuse to cancel.

> Allen: I ran into Corey P the other day, and he mentioned you guys are still in a band together. We should get together and play an old set sometime. Have you heard anything from Silver lately? That guy was such a wreck after what happened with Sarah. He probably ended up banging on plastic buckets for quarters on the streets of California.

: Yeah. Corey mentioned running into you. As for Silver, he's perfectly happy and doing quite well for himself. He moved back to town a year ago with his wife and daughter. We get together once a week and tour when we feel like it. As for me, I'm doing great. Thanks for asking. What do I owe for the trip down memory lane?

Allen: I didn't mean any offense by it. Forgot how close the two of you used to be back in the day. I'm glad to hear everyone is doing well. As for my reason for reaching out, I wanted to see if we could meet up, for old times' sake. I have someone I want to introduce you to, and there's something I've been meaning to give you.

: Where and when?

Allen: How about we get chicken wings and beers around 6:00? We could meet at that bar near the movie theater. The one that Corey's sister used to work at. Do you know what place I'm talking about?

: Yeah, that works.

Allen: Not sure how many women you're currently dating, but feel free to bring one along. The more, the merrier. See you at 6:00.

After all these years, why I let this guy get under my skin is beyond me. Worse than that, I'm meeting him for drinks, and I don't know why. Though, I doubt it's anything life-threatening. Knowing Allen, this is all some flimsy excuse for him to show off whatever girl he's dating and brag about some fake promotion he was handed at work. I've never hated anyone more and allowed them the privilege to live. Allen Cuttler tells more fish stories than a sea captain, and I'm all out of Dramamine.

As for the women in my life, there's no one worth mentioning. Maybe I'll go out after and drown my sorrows surrounded by girls in synthetic neon wigs and skin-tight corsets. It is Halloween, after all. Then again, the girl I'm looking for would be casual and comfortable. There's something incredibly sexy about a woman willing to go out for the night in a t-shirt and jeans with her hair pulled back. Maybe because the ones who get all dolled up are a dime a dozen.

In my twenties, I was content to sleep with any vapid one-night stand who glanced my way, but these days, I'm looking for more than a painted-on pretty face. I need someone who can make me feel something. Otherwise, what's the point? I'm not getting any younger, and my options dwindle with every year that passes.

Staring at a future set in stone, I frequently wish for a bolt of lightning to strike and blow the whole thing to pieces.

CHAPTER 2

Val

I've been ready to go for what feels like ages, and the nagging voices at the base of my skull have begun pestering me to finally see reason. I swear, I have the patience of a saint in line at the grocery store, but when it comes to sitting on the couch at home, dressed and ready to go, I start crawling out of my skin and second-guessing whether or not I want to leave the apartment.

You're wasting our time with this guy. He's a joke! Everything that comes out of his mouth is a lie.

"And what would you have me do? Go on first dates for the rest of my life and die miserable and alone? He's not that bad."

Not that bad? At best, he's insecure about his life and feels the need to make himself sound more interesting, which, you have to admit, is pathetic and tiresome.

"Okay, so he inflated the truth and most likely customized his background to match mine. I'm sure loads of people do that."

So, you acknowledge he's a human chameleon. That's a start. More than likely, he's a pathological liar and a cheater who is playing you for a damn fool. What kind of guy takes his girl-friend to a hotel when he owns a house? You've been dating for three months and haven't met any of his family or friends. He's always on his phone texting or sneaking off to talk in private. And you know he's never actually at work past 4:00, or on the weekends when he claims to be. You've driven past to check more than once, and he's yet to be there. Wake up, girl! The guy is probably married.

"I'll make you a deal. If you're right and Allen is married, I'll let you out, and you can revenge fuck his wife. Fingers crossed, for all our sake, she's good-looking."

And then you let me destroy him.

"Fine. But we do that part together."

Fabulous! I love it when we can reach an agreement.

By the time Allen arrives, I've gotten myself into quite the mood. For whatever reason, he started texting from the car instead of parking and ringing the buzzer. We've been seeing each other for months, and he's been inside my apartment exactly twice for less than an hour. Maybe I'm overthinking things. Where he chooses to park and how he elects to meet me feels mildly insignif-icant in the grand scheme of things, but I'd like to see him make more effort, not less.

> Allen: Move that sweet ass of yours. We're late.

> : I'm coming.

Slipping on my shoes, I give Christmas one final scratch on the back and a kiss on the top of the head. "Please be a good boy, and don't be sad. I'll leave the TV on so you don't get lonely, and I promise to be back soon." I swear, no one has ever loved me as much as this dog does, and I'm not sure if I should be grateful or depressed by that realization.

> Allen: Well, in that case, I'll be right up.

> : Ha! Very funny.

I roll my eyes, shake my head, and allow a small laugh to slip out. I enjoy our time together when he's in a playful mood, but those moments have been few and fleeting. Still, it's nice to hope things might continue on this track for the rest of the evening, even if it is unlikely. Perhaps if he plays his cards right, he'll get lucky, though that may require a drink or three on my part and a miracle on his.

Before moving to Ohio and diving head first into the online dating swamp, I tried the whole *Marry the Person You Love* thing, but it was an epic failure. John filed for divorce six months into our marriage after getting another woman pregnant. So yeah, sometimes, I think love is bullshit. Other times, I miss the idea of happily ever after. The best I can hope for these days is a guy I don't hate, with a job, who won't cheat on me. Allen has a job, and I wouldn't say I *hate* him, so that's something. As for the final requirement, it's too soon to tell.

I can see his black jeep through the glass side door of my building as I jog down the hall. Stupid me, I got so twisted around with internal debate that I forgot to grab my hoodie. Thankfully, we'll be inside tonight, and it's been unseasonably warm this year. As I climb into the passenger seat, I sense he's already annoyed.

"Is that seriously what you're wearing?" His words fall heavy into my lap, too stern to be taken as a joke. And like that, he's already killed any hope I had for a fun evening. "Whatever, we're already late."

I look down at my dementor t-shirt and swallow my feelings. When I was out earlier, I came across this shirt at the mall and thought I'd never seen anything more perfect. It's a nerdy Harry Potter shirt that looks rock and roll as fuck. Allen, who claims to be a metalhead and a nerd, should have loved it, in theory. Yet here we are.

Honestly, I thought it was ideal for tonight. It looks as Halloween as I could get without wearing a costume, but I should have known better.

Just once, I wish he would relax and play along. I'll never understand how he's lived this long with a cactus shoved in his ass. Or maybe that's a new thing. I wonder if they make a cream for that. Perhaps I can add it to his Christmas list if he's still around. I'm nothing if not thoughtful in that way.

As we pull into the parking lot, he places his hand on my leg and attempts to smooth the tension between us. "I'm sorry I snapped at you about your shirt. I wanted you to make a good impression on my friends, and I thought you would have dressed nicer or tried to look cute." His backhanded apology hits me where it hurts, and I feel myself shrinking in the seat.

"I'm sorry to disappoint you. Maybe next time you could convey your expectations more clearly so I might make every effort to accommodate." My statement is punctuated with a strained smile as I pull the rubber band from my messy bun. Maybe with my hair down, I'll appear more ladylike and socially acceptable. Maybe even cute. Whatever it is, I find myself wishing I had stayed home.

Allen is an asshole and a fool.

In a bar full of people on Halloween, there's bound to be someone who finds me mildly attractive. I have half a mind to hunt that person down, buy them a drink, and disappear out the backdoor, never to be seen again.

"It's fine. Let's not allow it to ruin the night." Allen speaks as if he's being gracious.

I open the door and jump out without uttering the response currently banging around my head. Accepting that my options are limited, it's best to smile and play along until I can find another ride home. I swear, if he pulled away right now and left me standing here, I wouldn't cry a single tear. Come to think of it, I wish he would, but I doubt he'd be so bold. Allen wouldn't risk looking bad unless he could find a way to blame it on me.

Surprisingly, he catches me at the back of the jeep and wraps his arms around me. Rocking me gently in his arms, he kisses my neck. Allen knows this is my kryptonite.

"Baby, let's not fight. You always look beautiful, and I'm sorry for being an asshole." His words whispered like a lullaby against my skin. "It was a stressful day at work. Seeing you tonight has been the only thing keeping me going."

He kisses my neck one final time and softly bites into my shoulder, wrapping his arms tighter across my chest and waist so I can't arch away. "If you forgive me, I promise I'll make it up to you later when I take you home."

At this point, I'm not sure what options I have. I could try calling for a ride, but it's a small town, and Uber isn't a thing out here. Someone in the bar might be willing to take me home, but those rides usually involve sexual favors, and that's pretty much the last thing I want to deal with. Alas, the most direct path forward is forgiveness, so I suppose I'd better start accepting his half-ass apologies if I want to salvage the night.

"Okay."

I've been in this position with guys before, red flags in full view, and I'm smart enough to know I should walk away. Yet I stay. Seeing the good in people has always been one of my biggest downfalls. That, and the fact I've never broken up with anyone. I stick it out until they reject me, which usually only takes six months to a year. Maybe my midnight wish for the New Year should be to find my resolve. And my spine.

Allen positions himself half a step in front of me as we approach the door and glides his hand down the inside of my arm, stopping at my palm. I lace my fingers into his as we enter the restaurant, hand in hand like a happy couple.

I'm still not sure who we're meeting, so I let him take the lead. Guiding me through the crowded restaurant tables toward a chorus of drunken battle cries, there's a group of men at one end of the bar causing quite the scene. My heart sinks at the sight of them overreacting to highlights from last night's game, and I wonder if there's still time to run. I hate interacting with large groups of people, especially when they all know each other and I'm the fresh meat.

No part of me craves the spotlight. I much prefer the dark.

Allen passes behind the large group without so much as a nod and proceeds toward a light-haired man sitting alone.

"This guy is cool, and he has his shit together, so try not to be weird." His words cut in ways he's incapable of understanding, so I keep the explanation to myself.

Looks like I'm in costume after all. This year, I'm pretending to be the perfect girlfriend for Halloween.

Kold

I recognize the greeting immediately as Allen slaps his hand down forcibly against my shoulder blade to overcompensate for his size with false bravado. Already off to a great start, I consider how satisfying it would feel to punch him square in the face. Before turning, I drink in the idea with a swig of beer and swallow the impulse to swing. What the hell am I even doing here? I've been sitting on this bar stool for ten minutes, surrounded by belligerent assholes, waiting for a guy I can barely tolerate.

Standing to face him with my jaw clenched and a snide remark at the ready, I have half a mind to finish my beer and leave. However, the urge escapes me when I turn and find my future placed directly in front of me. This girl is the image of perfection, even as she glances down nervously at her shoes. Yet to meet my gaze, I rake my eyes over her body, eager to memorize the curves of her form.

Waves of long hair, highlighted in chestnut and gold, frame her heart-shaped face. And once she looks at me, there's no going back. I can see it all right there in the depth of her crystal blue eyes. She is my greatest adventure, my undeserved forever, my lost love. I want to lick, kiss, and nibble every inch of her until she begs me to stop. I want her squeezing her thighs against my head and screaming my name. If I could, I would hide her in my pocket, steal her away, and hold her close for safekeeping.

I all but forget who I came here to meet until I notice her hand in his. My eyes land on Allen, and every muscle in my body reflexively tightens, disgusted by the sight of him claiming what is so clearly mine.

Talk about a kick in the dick. I've been single for six months, after a decade of garbage relationships, only to find the girl of my dreams standing hand in hand with my worst enemy. Of all the bullshit things I expected this night to bring, I never considered this.

"Hi, I'm Val. It's a pleasure to meet you." She looks at me for the first time, extending her free hand into the space between us.

Pleasure? Seriously? This girl has no idea how much *pleasure* I want our meeting to be. The things I would do to her right now if given the chance. Staring at her lips, my mind races with possibilities. And I'm not talking about some sweaty, one-night stand in the backseat of my SUV or bending her over the sink in the bathroom. She deserves better than that, certainly better than the joker she's arrived with. I would devote the rest of my life to her every happiness if she were mine. Hell, I might do it anyway, even if I can't have her.

Taking her hand, I brush gently along her fingertips before marrying our palms together, and I'm surprised by the confident handshake that greets me. There's a buried strength in her, but something or someone is holding her back. I want so badly to fuck her until that strength comes barreling out. The idea of her soft hands pressed against my chest while she grinds out the stress of her day on top of me makes the words catch in my throat. I want her shaking and clenching as I pull her body against mine, filling her with every last drop of my obedience. I already belong to her, and she doesn't even know my name.

"I'm Kold," I announce, nearly shouting it at her.

"Well, I guess you should've worn an actual coat." A cheeky smile lights her face. Pleased with her cleverness, she draws my full attention, casting all others in shadow. "I'm kidding. Although you do have a bit of a Jack Frost look about you."

"Seriously?" Allen says, shooting Val a look soaked in disgust.

I'm prepared to torture him. I want to watch him bleed out as he pleads for the life I'm no longer willing to spare. Fucking me over financially was one thing, even if I didn't need the money. Darc thought we should've responded out of principle, but it wasn't worth the risk. However, seeing him disregard Val's feelings is a crime punishable by death, and I am currently less concerned about the consequences. I don't care who his parents are, what elbows they rub, or what palms they grease. My family name carries as much weight in this area as his, if not more, depending on the time of day.

"Sorry about that, man. She likes to think she's funny." He attempts to keep his tone firm but friendly, with a hint of annoyance rising towards the surface.

The dismissive way he says *she* instead of using her name sets my teeth on edge, and I watch as his comment wipes the smile from her face. One more word out of his mouth, and I'm at risk of ending his life right here and now, in front of everyone.

Dropping her head, Val redirects her gaze back toward the ground. Her hand falls away from mine, her shoulders round forward, and her body shrinks. I've seen Allen do this to women in the past, but for some reason, it didn't bother me back then. If he chose to treat women like possessions instead of people, that was his business. However, this isn't three years ago, and Val isn't anything like those other girls. Remaining silent doesn't feel like a viable option when my possible future happiness feels eternally linked to hers.

I need to be smart. I have to protect her in a way that doesn't take away her options. It's not for me to decide what kind of relationship they have based on one interaction and a few lines of dialogue. For all I know, they fought on the way here but are otherwise happily in love.

She doesn't look like she's in love. She looks broken and perfect, all at the same time.

The thought of her being in love with anyone, let alone this douche canoe, sets my blood to boil. So much for being smart. I need to take a deep breath and calm down. If I allow myself room to think about him touching her, I'll wind up back in jail, and then I'll be useless to her.

"Val, you're welcome to make all the jokes you want. I assure you I can handle it. Why don't you take my seat and order us a round of drinks? I need to sort something out, but I promise I'll return before you miss me." What the hell am I even saying?

"Don't make promises you can't keep." She says under her breath as she slides onto the tall wooden seat. Allen takes the stool next to her, seemingly unaware of her comment.

Reaching forward to grip the bar beside her, I lean in as close as I dare. She smells like honey and almonds, and it's fucking torture. I take a deep breath and linger for a moment before saying. "I wouldn't dream of it."

I have no choice. I've got to walk away and collect my thoughts, chill the fuck out, and regroup. But I can't leave Val's side until I see her smile. "By the way, I'm obsessed with your shirt. Where can I get one?"

She turns slightly, and I can see the corner of her perfectly shaped lips pull into a smile as she whispers against my cheek, "I'll add it to your Christmas list."

CHAPTER 3
Val

Whether or not Kold meant what he said about my t-shirt is irrelevant. This flawless specimen of a man could tell me I look *nice*, and I'd be putty in his hands. When he leaned into my personal bubble, filling the space around me with his presence, I swear time momentarily stood still. The lights around us went dim and hazy, the noise of the surrounding crowd died away, and the atmosphere was sucked from the room. The only thing keeping me alive was the breath shared between us and the realization that he saw me.

His sharp features, squared jawline, and kissable lips make him a sight to behold. I have no doubt that every woman in this place has ventured to sneak a peek. Somehow, Kold smells like he stepped out of a hot shower and has yet to cool, leaving me jealous of each drop of water that's ever touched his skin.

Even his hair is a photoshopped image of perfection. Cut into a fade. I desperately want to run my fingers through the length at the top and over the stubble at the back of his head as I dive into his lips and find myself lost in the depth of his stare. I want to run my hands over his chest and back as he buries himself inside me. I want to call out his name while I'm conquered by hedonistic pleasure and left twitching and boneless beneath the fully collapsed weight of his exhausted frame.

The intensity of his bottomless, Mariana trench, blue eyes

drag me deeper into his abyss, and I can feel the immense pressure of his presence as my makeshift existence collapses around me.

It took every ounce of my diminishing willpower not to kiss him when my lips were an inch from his chiseled jawline, and I'm quite certain I may have died and gone to heaven.

Kold's white blonde hair, piercing blue eyes, and broad shoulders are enough to make him look like a Norse god on loan from Asgard, and I'm very much obsessed. Wherever he's going, I want to sneak away and follow, stalking from darkened corners. My heart and head are frantic to fill in each piece of the puzzle before he walks away for good, and I never see him again.

In all my years of dating, I've never wanted a guy to break up with me as badly as I do now. Allen has been running hot and cold all day, and I'm tired of smiling through his bullshit apologies. I should have ended things with him before they began, but then I wouldn't be here. Change one thing in the past, and it alters the future. Without the boyfriend I never wanted, I might not have found the living embodiment of every fantasy I've ever had.

I don't know a goddamn thing about this tall, blonde-haired man beyond what I see, and I'm already throwing my chips all in. My hands ache with the need to touch him again. The second he looked at me, I could feel my heart beating between my thighs, and I already knew I'd fall asleep tonight saying his name. Whispering. Screaming. In his bed. Or at home alone. Wherever this night takes me, my thoughts will all lead back to him.

Isn't that the way life goes? You finally meet the one person you can't imagine your life without, and he's the only guy in the bar who's off-limits. Even if I were suddenly single, it wouldn't matter. They're friends, and I'm sure they adhere to some sort of bullshit bro code.

Why would Allen bring me to meet a man like this, knowing I'd spend the entire evening drowning in my drool? Is this some sort of test of my loyalty? Are they both playing a game, waiting to see if I'll crack?

Most likely, Kold's got a gorgeous supermodel wife, a couple of kids, and a family dog at home waiting for him. That's probably who he stepped out to call. And here I am like some starry-eyed idiot, thinking he might be experiencing even a fraction of what I'm feeling.

A year and a half ago, when I met John, there was a tingle in my chest, and in my desperation to feel less alone, I convinced myself it was fate. Of course, that was all bullshit and beer goggles. But whatever I felt back then pales in comparison to the shock wave resonating within me now. This guy lit me up with ten thousand volts and walked away like he didn't even notice what he was doing to me.

Whatever this is, I need to be clever. I'm not some disloyal cheater who hops from one bed to the next. If Allen wants to test me, so be it. Challenge accepted. However, if this isn't a test, and Allen accidentally introduced me to my soul mate, I need to gather information and play my cards in the right order.

If I find myself in bed with Kold at some unknown point in the future, I'm going to owe my ex-boyfriend a fruit basket and an invitation to the wedding.

"You're shaking." Allen's voice is concerned and judgmental as he rubs his hand over my thigh. "Are you getting sick?"

I don't know, Allen. Maybe it has something to do with the Kold front that blew through, leaving me frozen to my core!

"I think it's just a chill. I probably should've grabbed a sweatshirt on my way out the door." If I want him to break things off with me, I have to stop being polite. But rudeness requires a new driver, and the one itching to take the wheel can be a bit temperamental.

The bartender stops in front of us, looking annoyed, though I'm not sure why. I order the round of drinks as requested and vow to be on my best behavior for the remainder of the night. Still convinced this is all some elaborate Fred Jones trap, I'd like to avoid mindlessly stepping in with both feet, but that might require a minute of damage control.

I reach over, placing my hand on Allen's arm, making sure to connect physically before speaking. "My intention was never to make you look bad, so I am sorry if you felt like that's what I've been doing. And I apologize for joking with Kold about his name.

I can see where that comment would be inappropriate since I'm meeting him for the first time."

My inability to be tough in the face of struggle is unsettling. Allen doesn't deserve my apology because I didn't do anything wrong, yet here I am, pretending to be perfect. I hate when people are mad at me, even when I don't particularly like them.

"I'm sorry I've been in such a shit mood all day. Most of it wasn't your fault. Let's reset and move on. I'm glad you're here with me." He leans forward, expecting me to meet him halfway, but I remain unmoved. With a sigh, he closes the lingering distance between us and kisses me. Then pulls back, uttering "I love you" for the first time, catching me off guard.

I don't know how I feel exactly, but I can say with certainty that there is nothing resembling love in my heart. Not for him. Sitting in stunned silence, I wait for the moment to pass, regretting each word of my apology.

Making matters even worse, I can feel Kold standing next to me before I see him, and I'd give anything to disappear.

Kold

Well, fuck! I step outside for three minutes and return to find these two snuggled together at the bar, playing kissy face and professing their love for one another. It seems I misread the situation and allowed past anger to cloud my judgment. This woman is out for an enjoyable evening with her boyfriend, and I'm over here stewing and plotting like the jealous ex.

I'm usually spot on when it comes to reading women, but tonight I find myself oblivious. A few minutes ago, I could have sworn Val's feelings aligned with mine, but maybe it's nothing more than the usual sexual chemistry.

No. I'm used to women looking at me with lust-filled eyes, and that isn't what's happening here. The playful way she quips and teases isn't her attempt at getting laid. But she also hasn't shied away from my touch, which denotes a level of interest.

Val might lack my certainty, but there's no denying that this woman belongs by my side. I can feel her in my bones. The second I laid eyes on her, I knew. I have loved her for a thousand lifetimes, and tonight is the beginning of a thousand and one.

"Here. Lemme get out of your seat." Val moves, but I pause her motion with a touch.

"What's mine is yours, and you look better sitting there than I do." I shouldn't keep touching her, but Allen isn't brave enough to stop me, and the urge is too great.

Her reaction to every hint of contact feeds my need, so I'll press my luck until she asks me to stop. At the slightest brush of my skin against hers, her breath catches, her body twitches, and her cheeks flush. She's turned on, and I want to tease her until she explodes.

"Cheers to that. I appreciate the lie." Val pulls the drink to her lips, smells it, wrinkles her nose, and takes a sip. Her eyes close, and her lips screw up at the ends as she forces herself to swallow the initial taste. "Oh, that's so gross."

When she opens her eyes and reads Allen's disapproving expression, her tune quickly changes. "Sorry, I meant to say, Mmmm. Delicious!" Her declaration capped off with an over-emphasized smile faker than Allen's last promotion.

"Is it not what you ordered?" I can't help but laugh. From where I'm standing, it looks pretty good, but the woman likes what she likes, and that's precisely what she shall have. Judging by his face, her date doesn't seem to agree with my sentiment, but to hell with Allen. I doubt he knows the first thing about satisfying a woman.

"Oh, it's fine. The bartender used the wrong vodka, but it's no big deal. I'm fine with whatever." Val's going to great lengths to convince me that everything is *fine* when it's anything but. So, she's a people pleaser? That makes sense. I can see how that might be an easy characteristic for someone like Allen to exploit.

There are times when it's prudent to avoid conflict and times when it is not. Tonight, I'm willing to set my peaceful demeanor aside should a need for violent solutions arise. Seeing Val has unlocked the base animal urge that lives inside of me, and I'm unsure how to cage the beast in her presence. I want to ravage her seven ways to Sunday until she forgets Allen Cuttler exists. But only if she asks me to.

"Can I try it?" I ask, sliding the glass through her fingertips and draining it in three gulps before she can respond to my question. "Vodka and Red Bull, huh? Good choice."

I catch the bartender's attention, which is easy enough since she's been staring at me since I arrived. "I need two more of these, only this time I need them with..." I turn my face to Val, inviting her to finish my sentence.

"Umm. Three Olives Cherry. And thank you."

The bartender rolls her eyes at the request, registering her earlier mistake. She turns with a huff, mumbling something under her breath. For her sake, I'll pretend that attitude was directed at me and me alone. Otherwise, her tip is going in the toilet, and her job is getting handed to someone else. I might not own *this* bar, but one call would tell me who does.

"Here, try this one." Allen pushes his drink toward Val, but she doesn't take it.

There's a look of concerned hesitation on her face, and I'm not sure why. Allen isn't exactly a stranger offering her a drink, but I can't help but wonder if she's had a bad experience in the past involving cocktails. Something beyond your standard hangover.

I've seen firsthand the deplorable tactics some men enlist to get what they desire. Not many women come into my bar, but when they do, my no-nonsense bartenders have been trained to keep a close eye out. I have zero tolerance for predatory sexual behavior that undermines the concept of consent.

"No, thank you. I appreciate the offer, but I can't drink that. I'm allergic to rum, remember?" She waves off the suggestion, uninterested in sharing the drink, and her response piques my interest.

"That's not a real thing. Stop being dramatic and take a sip." Allen takes his drink from the bar and places the glass in her hand, unwilling to accept her polite refusal.

Now I feel guilty for polishing off her beverage. Here I am, thinking I'm being chivalrous, and all I did was throw her into harm's way. I'm certain she'll surrender the drink and stand her ground, especially if an allergy is involved. I get the feeling she's used to handling herself.

Unfortunately, I couldn't be more wrong. Val isn't combative. She's a peacekeeper. She's the type of person who will put her well-being aside to defuse the tension. When my brain finishes overthinking the information and I realize I need to speak, it's already too late.

She brings the glass to her lips, takes a sip, and hands it back. "It's not bad."

A minute later, she begins rubbing her shoulder with a vacant expression that reaches her eyes. I've never heard of someone being allergic to rum, but there's no denying that it has affected her. I can see a change in her demeanor and feel the shift in her concentration. To avoid reacting to whatever discomfort she's feeling, Val has retreated inside herself and left us with only a shell.

Remorse floods my senses as I drape my arm across the back of her chair, trying to offer a small comfort. I could have saved her, and I didn't. I failed her when she needed me, and I'm helpless to absorb her pain. For some reason, I can't think straight when I'm next to her.

When the new round of drinks finally arrives, I study the details of Val's appearance, scanning for any lingering uneasiness. It seems she has returned to her former self, or maybe she's hidden her discomfort someplace deeper. Taking a hesitant first sip, a wave of calm washes over her. "Perfection." She says before licking her bottom lip.

Yes. You most certainly are.

And with that one little, unintentional move, she has the beast within me, ready to pounce. I tuck my waist behind her chair, out of visual range, as I wait for my erection to subside. In my thirty-five years on this Earth, I've had my fair share of women flirt with me, and it hasn't been all bad. But I've never had a woman turn me on so completely by merely existing in my presence.

I'll bide my time if I have to. I'll stand back and wait my turn. I'll become friends with Allen if that's what it takes to see her. But I won't steal her away, and I won't force her to choose.

When Val and I are finally together, it'll be because she had every option available in the world and chose to be with me.

CHAPTER 4
Val

Another chill rocks through my frame, pulling my shoulder blades together as goosebumps freckle my arms. I try to force my body to behave, but nothing works. I'm not even looking at Kold, but he's all I see. The tenor of his voice and the heat from his body fill the gap between us, making him impossible to ignore.

As the shiver subsides, Kold presses his arm against my back, pretending to lean on the bar as he talks to Allen. I'm not sure if his actions are deliberate or unintentional, but he seems to exert every effort to touch me as covertly as possible. If I didn't know better, I might think Kold was flirting with me.

More than likely, he's unstable on his feet after another round of drinks and steadying himself with the nearest chair, which happens to be the one I'm sitting in. Perhaps he was here for a while, drinking alone before we arrived. I'm sure that's all it is.

I'm starting to feel the tingle of alcohol in my veins as well, or maybe it's something else.

Allen dips in and out of the conversation, only half listening, checking his phone for the millionth time since arriving. His detachment from the moment annoys me even more than usual, and I'm unsurprised when he abruptly slides off his chair and offers some bullshit excuse to escape.

"I need to take care of something for work. Hopefully, this

won't take long, but you might want to leave me out of the next round." He steps away without so much as a glance in my direction, echoing his true feelings. At this point, I'm wallpaper. He can't be bothered to notice, let alone care, and it should hurt, but it doesn't.

Once he's out of range, I say under my breath, "Good riddance to bad rubbish," then catch myself, remembering his friend is within earshot.

Kold removes his black hoodie and hands it to me, sliding himself into the now-empty slot beside me. "That's twice I've felt a chill run through your body. Now, who's the one who should've worn a coat?"

The well-defined lines of his muscles are evident through the slim-fit shirt he's selected, as his broad shoulders and thick arms stretch the material to its limits. I drink in the sight of him, wanting to run my fingers over his exposed forearms and impressive biceps.

Without the sweatshirt, I can see some of the black and grey photorealistic images inked into his skin, like the sprawling pages of National Geographic. Whoever did his tattoos is a true artist and master of their craft. Every part of me yearns to discover more.

Biting my bottom lip, I can't help but wonder what else he's hiding under his t-shirt and jeans as my mind spirals off into the nearest fantasy. I need to remember the details while I have him in front of me, in case this is the closest I ever get to making him mine.

"I'm not sure it's temperature related, but I appreciate the gesture. It's mostly my hands that are cold." Slipping into his hoodie, I allow the warmth lingering within its cotton fibers to bleed into my skin as I press my fingers into my palm.

"Here, let me see 'em. I'm always warm." He lifts my hands to his lips, blowing a warm, steady breath into our conjoined hands. As he exhales into me, I forget how to breathe. "If you were mine, I'd put your hands under my shirt and press them against my chest. Then you'd be warmed up in no time."

Oh my god. Please, yes. Do all of that, and don't stop.

"I'm sure that would do the trick," I say, slowly pulling my hands away. "Do you have plans after this?"

"Not unless you intend on staying out all night. I'll probably head home, watch a movie, and hang out with my dog. Was there something you had in mind that we could do together? Because I'm certainly open to suggestions." Kold's words are quicksand, and I'm tempted to step in, knowing full well he'll consume me.

As my thoughts wander down several pathways at one, I begin quietly singing along to the music overhead. It helps to calm the voices and recenter my racing thoughts. But all hope is lost when I catch him looking at me with a deliciously playful smile stretched across his face. "Sorry. You can ignore me," I say, blushing.

His eyes narrow, and he wets his lips before speaking. "That's not going to happen, Val. Any man who could ignore you is a goddamn idiot, and I'm not stupid enough to miss what's right here in front of me. I only regret that it took me so long to find you."

"Well, everything lost is always found in the last place we think to look."

His eyebrows pull together, and he smiles as though my response amuses him. "Because once we find it, it's no longer lost."

"Exactly." I take my drink from the bar and hide my smile along the lip of the glass.

There's something incredibly natural about our interaction. The way topics weave together like macrame. Nothing is forced or surface level. It's as though we're old friends separated by time, falling back into step without missing a beat.

As the evening progresses, I'm surprised to discover how much we have in common. Unlike Allen, Kold can authenticate his claims with an impressive wealth of knowledge. He isn't pretending to be anyone other than exactly who he is, and he isn't the least bit insecure.

I'm four drinks in when I find out that Kold has a black frenchie named Midnight. Because, of course, he does. We spend the next fifteen minutes scrolling through each other's phones, *Oohing* and *Aahing* over dog photos, and exchanging fun facts about sharing a bed with a miniature farting furnace.

While digging through my personal space, Kold comes across two of my go-to music playlists and a list of my top ten, all-time favorite movies. He airdrops all three to the phone in my hand, which I accept. "Is there anything else you plan on stealing from me while you're perusing through my life, performing your impromptu FBI background check?"

"Sorry, I can stop if you want. I got excited when I saw Alien 3 on your movie list, even though I can't entirely agree with your choice. Aliens is by far the best film in that series and definitely in my top five."

"Game over, man. Game over." I retort in my best Bill Paxton impression.

The look on his face causes laughter to bubble in my core and a small snort to expel from my lungs. I bring my hand over my mouth, trying to hide my embarrassment, but he pulls it away with a smile. As he holds my wrist, I think he might kiss me, but he doesn't.

Even without the kiss, I have my answer. Kold is unquestionably flirting with me, and I can't get enough.

"Thus, proving my point. Can you quote me a single line from the third movie? Probably not. Plus, Paxton is the only person in history to be killed by a Xenomorph, a Predator, and a Terminator." He continues to hold my wrist while his eyes decipher what remains of me.

"What about Lance Henriksen?" My tone is matter-of-fact as I give him a look that says, *I know shit about movies too.* I bite my lip, anxiously awaiting his reply. When it comes to movies, I typically know my stuff, and I'm hoping this won me more points than I've lost, but maybe I should tread more carefully.

Allen rarely plays along, and is quick to display his annoyance anytime I dare to know anything. I'm hoping Kold isn't the type of guy to get mad over someone challenging his overarching authority, especially when that someone is being playful. Thankfully, he shakes his head and smiles, almost as if he's pleasantly surprised and maybe even slightly impressed.

We argue the ins and outs of Alien lore and end our lively debate with a handshake and a vow to hang out and watch the trilogy together soon. I agree, under the condition that I'll be allowed to cover my eyes during the scary parts.

"Deal. Now, back to our previous topic of conversation. How are you going to have a dog named Christmas and hate the holiday he's named after? Make it make sense, Val." Kold's face is adorned with a playful grin as he hands me back my phone.

"In all fairness, I hate most holidays, except for Halloween. But now, I can tell people I *love* Christmas without lying through my teeth. It all makes perfect sense when you think about it from my perspective." I can't help but mirror his expression whenever I look into his endless blue eyes. This night is nothing like what I expected and so much more than I ever could have hoped for.

I've spent the last four hours fantasizing about the man beside me and regretting the kiss I shared with the wrong guy.

Allen is the wrong guy, isn't he? Haven't I known that since we met? And now I'm here, talking and laughing with someone who seems to enjoy engaging with me, and I don't know if I'll ever see him again.

Dating is so stupid.

"All right. Then tell me why you hate Christmas so I can fix it. I know there's a story, and I want to know everything about you."

His innocent prying shouldn't upset me, but it does, and the unwanted emotion flashes across my face before I can catch it. "I didn't always hate the most beloved holiday in modern times. It's sort of a recent thing. But it's not worth talking about. Not tonight. I don't want to ruin the conversation." I attempt to shovel dirt onto the bodies Kold threatens to exhume, but it's useless. My eyes well with tears as I turn away.

"Hey, Val. I'm sorry. We don't have to talk about it." He turns my chair and cups my face in his hands, wiping the falling tears from my cheeks with his thumbs. "I'll never forgive myself if I'm the reason for your tears."

"I promise you aren't. Someone else beat you to it." I swallow the lump in my throat and let my head fall against his right hand. I want Kold to kiss me, but I'm in no position to ask for anything, which reignites the burning in my chest. "I think I might be drunk."

He leans close as if conducting a field sobriety test with his mind. "What makes you say that?" His voice suddenly laced with concern.

"Because there's two of you."

A hiccup interrupts my thoughts as I melt into Kold's touch. His eyes never avert from my face, even as the other man settles at my side. It's rude not to greet him, but I'm too lost to further acknowledge his arrival. As my body falls forward, I tuck my face into Kold's chest.

"I wish you were real."

Solid steel that's warm to the touch, Kold is strong and confident but also considerate and kind. The conversation flowed like water all night, and my cheeks are sore from smiling. I wish he were mine so I could spend the rest of my life laughing with him. I haven't had enough time to appreciate his other impressive features, being as consumed as I was by his personality. But there were hints dropped along the way.

When he removed his hoodie, the bottom of his shirt lifted, and I got a sneak peek at the body he'd been hiding underneath. Dear god. He's got the torso of an underwear model and a cock sizable enough to see the outline of it through his jeans.

And in case there was any room for doubt about my feelings, his tattoos ensured I was hook, line, and sinker. They're a detailed mosaic of various scenes played out in nature, leading me to believe he might be even more complex than I initially gave him credit for. I want to tear his clothes off and set out on an adventure to discover the rest.

In singularity, the man sitting in front of me is beyond comprehension, so the sudden appearance of an exact copy convinces me that this entire night has been a dream. And if that's the case, I hope it's a sex dream because I'm starting to understand the twin fetish.

"Heads up, I saw Allen outside as I was coming in, and I got the feeling my presence was enough to catch his attention. I suspect he'll be returning any minute." The face and voice are the same, but this new Kold isn't Kold at all, nor is he a drunken delusion.

I straighten my spine and right myself on the stool, pretending the last couple of hours haven't completely changed the trajectory of my future.

I can't trust my feelings on this one. I have to think through it.

"How've you been, man? Long time no see," Allen says, greeting the newest male addition to our group in his go-to fashion.

The abrupt reappearance of his voice sets the tension back into my shoulders, and I realize how long he's been gone. "Where have you been this entire time?"

"I had a few phone calls I needed to take and some issues at work to sort out. No big deal. Why? Did you miss me?" Allen's tone is smug. It's a side of him I've never seen before, and I get the feeling he's putting on an act for his friends.

I can't help but feel like the toy in the sandbox that all the boys fight to play with, but no one takes home at the end of the night.

"I'm just surprised you bothered to return at all. Thankfully, your friend was kind enough to indulge me in conversation. Otherwise, I might have felt abandoned and drank myself into oblivion. But now you've returned, and all is well. Thank goodness." I know I'm being a sickeningly sweet smart ass, but the vodka has given me liquid courage, and I also feel myself playing to the audience. For the first time, I realize the pair of men standing on either side of me seem to like Allen as much as I do, if not less.

"Seems like you're pretty well there, so perhaps we'd better call it a night." Allen's cold eyes lock on mine as he extends his hand, and I hesitate to accept. "Sorry to cut the evening short, but we'll have to do it again sometime. Maybe a boy's night out."

Boy's night out, meaning I'm not invited because I'm such an embarrassment. How would he even know since he spent the entire night on his phone, ignoring me? I don't think Allen said two words to me since walking in here, aside from correcting my attempts at humor.

I sit frozen, waiting for Kold to speak on my behalf. He could say anything, but he doesn't. He glares at Allen, vacant of the joy that previously highlighted his features. Perhaps I've misjudged not only the conversation but also the man. Reading too much into a situation is pretty on-brand for me. So, I shouldn't be surprised.

"It was nice to meet you both. I hope you enjoy the rest of your night." My eyes lock on Kold's chiseled expression before falling to the floor. There are infinite hairline cracks in my armor, threatening to leave me in pieces, but now is not the time or place to break. In a last-ditch effort to appear indifferent, I attempt to return the borrowed hoodie.

"Keep it. I'll get it back next time I see you." The weight of his hand falls heavy upon my arm, not in anger, but in what feels like defeat. Or maybe I'm projecting.

I follow Allen out to the jeep without a backward glance.

My souvenir from the night, still bathed in the scent of its previous owner, is coming home with me, and there's a good chance Kold will never see it again. Not because we won't hang out. I'm going to make my best effort to ensure that happens. However, this piece of him, I consider keeping, whether he likes it or not.

As the street lights pass in a blur, I rewind my thoughts and review the details of our interactions. All Kold had to do was ask me to stay, and I would've never left his side. He must have known that. But why would a guy like that want someone like me when he has every option in the world available?

CHAPTER 5

Kold

The shock of what happened burns inside me like rage while my brother's words fuel the fire. "Why would you let her leave with him? That guy's a fucking asshole. Did you get her number? Her last name? Where she works? Anything? Do you even know what Val is short for?"

I nod my head, indicating a resounding *No.*

"What the fuck did you talk about for four hours? You called me twenty minutes after leaving the house and told me you had found the one girl you couldn't live without. Then you let her walk away? And you don't even know how to find her? I showed up here thinking, finally, you'd let me end that guy once and for all. Instead, you let him walk away with our girl. What the fuck are you doing, bro?"

"I didn't know what to say, all right! I thought I had more time. How did I know he would walk in here and they'd be gone two seconds later?"

I play back the last few hours in my mind, sifting through the details for clues. We talked about everything that makes a person interesting, but none of the boring stuff that would help me find her. And Allen's a dead end for the time being. He isn't on social media. I know because I already did a search before they arrived.

"We'll find our girl, but it might take some time. Are you

going to be okay with that?" Darc attempts to console me by patting my shoulder.

Glaring at the door I let her leave through, I ball my hands into fists and dig my nails into my palms. "Looks like I don't have much choice, do I? And she isn't *our girl*. She isn't even *my girl*. Apparently, she's *Allen's girl*, and I'm a fucking idiot!"

My voice rises as I run through the list until I'm nearly shouting. The people around us turn to look but quickly realize it's probably unwise to stare. This conversation is pissing me off, and I need a shot. Or, more likely, a dozen shots and a time machine. I need to drown myself in her drink until I figure out how to find her.

The idea of them together, and him touching her. "I want to break something. Or someone."

Darc laughs. "Now you're talking. Let's put that temper to good use."

Val

The clock in Allen's jeep reads 10:47 pm, but I'm not sure how that could be possible. Somehow, it felt like I was in that bar for three weeks, yet everything transpired in less than five hours. A series of unanswered questions plague my consciousness as I vividly recall the details.

If I want information from Allen before he drops me off, I need to choose my wording carefully. Am I even competent enough to charm him after a night of imbibing? How much did he see? Is he angry or indifferent? I wish I knew where we stood so I might know where to begin and with which foot to start.

"Thanks for taking me out to meet your friends. They seemed a bit... Oh, I don't know. Intense." An awkward laugh passes over my lips between sentences. "I'm not sure I even caught how you all know each other."

"Kold and I toured together in a band after college. I guess he still plays with some of the guys. He asked me if I wanted to get together to jam sometime, and I thought it might be wise to catch up first. I hadn't heard from him in years, so I wasn't sure what to expect going into the evening. Oddly enough, I hadn't anticipated him flirting with my girlfriend the entire night, nor did I expect her to entertain his advances with such enthusiasm." Allen's tone is dismissive, as if he can't be bothered to care, but his body gives him away. He appears to mind considerably, although I'm unconvinced it has anything to do with me.

"I don't think he was flirting, so there were no advances for me to entertain. We talked about our dogs, movies, music, working out, and preferred vodka brands. Nothing I would consider risqué." I try to brush aside his assumptions by making light of the interactions he was absent from.

A sound of exasperation expels from his lungs, but when he speaks, his tune has changed. "It's possible I read too much into the conversation. You seemed happy, and I can't say I've ever seen you that way before."

"You asked me to make a good impression, so I tried to be friendly. I'm not great in social situations, but maybe you haven't realized that. Next time we're around your friends, I'll sit back and let you lead the conversation. Okay?"

"If there is a next time!" This is the last thing Allen says on the matter. The rest of our drive passes in silence.

This is what I expected and feared. I know nothing useful about Kold. No social media handle. Marital status. I don't even know if he's local. Other than his incredibly unique first name, he's a mystery. Even that could be a nickname. Or maybe his last name. He mentioned playing football in college, but I didn't ask which school he attended. One thing I remember from high school was all the jocks calling each other by their last names, so perhaps I'll look for a Mr. Kold. I don't know, that doesn't feel right, somehow.

Allen did mention touring in a band together. He also let slip that Kold still plays music. I'd imagine there has to be some lingering trace of that old band online, which could potentially lead me to any information about his current group. Maybe I could attend a show and randomly bump into him.

Even if I could find him, what would I say? When he had the opportunity to speak and extend the evening, he sat there, the image of perfection, silently crushing my dreams. Maybe that's too harsh. I was there with another man. A man who's allegedly his friend. A man that I left with. Did I truly expect him to duel for my hand in the parking lot by the light of the setting sun?

Besides, it's the middle of autumn. The sun was a distant memory when Allen announced our sudden departure.

I'm being ridiculous, and I know it. But when I close my eyes, Kold's face is the only one I can picture, as if the image of his smile is permanently burned into my retina. I need to be around him again. For a moment. For a weekend. For a lifetime. It's not even an option. To my heart, this man is essential.

"Did you want me to come in for a few minutes, or are you tired of looking at me?" This is Allen's way of trying to get laid without committing to spending the night.

I hadn't noticed until now that we were parked in front of the doors to my building and not in a parking spot. Guess he's expecting me to say *No*. "I need to take Christmas for a walk. You're welcome to join us if you'd like. Then maybe you could tell me where you were all night."

"It was work issues, and I should probably get back to them. I'll text you later. Be careful walking. Lord knows how many weirdos are out tonight, and your dog isn't exactly tough." He leans over to kiss me, then reaches past to open the door. "Brunch on Sunday at the usual place?"

"Sure." My response is as distant as I feel.

Would my twin delusions still exist if I got into my car and raced back to the bar? Did they ever? Maybe I hit my head getting out of the jeep and dreamt the whole thing up. Perhaps they were a figment of my overactive imagination, franticly searching for a reason to feel less alone. Or maybe someone laced my Red Bull with acid. The way I've been feeling, if someone dosed me, it was with a drop of ecstasy.

No, I don't think I was drugged, and I don't think it was caused by a bump on the head or debilitating loneliness. Incredibly enough, I believe my perfect man exists, and by god, there are two of him.

I exit Allen's jeep, questioning every decision I've ever made.

CHAPTER 6
Kold

Everyone I talked to this week said the same thing. Allen Cuttler is a smug piece of shit who thinks he's important because his parents handed him a V.P. title and a paycheck. Besides that, no one's kept in contact, and none of them had heard of Val. How exactly does a guy like that land a woman who radiates so much humor and intelligence? She's too good for him. Hell, she might be too good for all of us, but I can't get her out of my mind.

When I got home that night, I jerked off thinking about her perfect little mouth and how her symmetrical features were accented off balance when the left side of her lips pulled into the most adorable smirk. Whenever she was playful or quiet, I wanted to know her deepest thoughts so that I might be the one to fulfill her every fantasy.

I could see our entire future in her icy blue eyes and perfectly crooked smile, like a dream I didn't remember having until she ushered me awake. And now I'm doomed to a life where I can't live without her. I should've kissed her when I had the chance. Then, she could've shot me down, and we could be done with it. But I didn't kiss her, and she didn't shoot me down, and now I'm left with an urge my hand is unable to satisfy.

I want to go back and live in that moment forever with her, like Groundhog's Day. If given enough opportunities, maybe I could get it right. There's got to be a version of Halloween night where Val falls asleep in my bed, but how do I get there?

The muscles over my stomach tighten as my hand involuntarily rubs the length of flesh swelling in my shorts. I close my eyes and imagine her riding on top of me. The way her nipples harden as her body arches. A cascade of hair falls down her back like well-earned beads of sweat. My girl is the picture of desire, and my balls ache with the need to please her. Moving my hands to her hips, we rock together, falling into one synchronized rhythm. I can feel the walls of her pussy tighten around me as she bites into her bottom lip, and a shiver ripples through her body. She moans with pleasure as she begs for my release. And I'm close. I'm so close. I want to pump her full of every last drop of this unquenchable desire now and for the rest of my life.

"Fuck, Val. You're gonna make me cum."

No longer holding back, I expel the sticky spray through my fingers. Half of it clings to the inside of my shorts while the rest greases my palm. "Goddamn, I fucking love you."

Rather than try to walk, I lay there in my embarrassment, feeling like a teenager with his first crush. Last night's fantasy is in a discarded shirt on the floor next to the bed, and now my shorts are headed that way. "This girl is gonna be the death of me."

I've tried everything I can think of. Even went so far as to join a local dog park group online specifically for people with french bulldogs, but no sign of Val or Christmas. How can one woman be so hard to locate in a day and age where everything can be found online?

There's only one option left if I wanted to see her, but I swore he would be my last resort.

> : Meeting Val was highly entertaining, but you took off before we had a chance to catch up. Do you two have anything going on this weekend? Maybe we could meet for drinks.

Allen: Hopefully, she wasn't too annoying. I'm swamped with work for the next couple of weeks, but maybe sometime around Thanksgiving.

: Sure. Let me know.

Thanksgiving? That's three weeks away. There has to be some other way to track her down. I type **Val Christmas** into the search bar and cross my fingers, hoping for a holiday miracle. Top on the list is an IMDb for Val Christmas, an actress known for her role in the 2016 film Cast Adrift. Whatever that is. Next, we have *Val does Christmas*, a holiday décor related Instagram. Not the Val I'm looking for. I scroll further down the list, but nothing jumps out at me.

Next, I search through images. Everything from an album cover for Val Doonican's Christmas Gold, Christmas in Vail, handmade holiday cards on Etsy, and Val Selasi's appearance on the Great Christmas Bake Off litter my screen. I even found an image of Val Kilmer in a Santa hat, but no white frenchie puppy or photos of my girl.

Evil Twin: Breakfast?

: Only if it's brunch at Valentine's.

: Fuck! On second thought, I'm never eating there again.

Evil Twin: When you were seven, you told Mom it was the only acceptable place for breakfast within a 100-mile radius and refused to go anywhere else. Now get your ass out of bed and shower.

: Chicken and Waffles aren't going to take my mind off this girl.

Evil Twin: Maybe we can ask Conrad to change the name to Balentine's so it won't trigger you. He's divorced. I'm sure he'd understand.

: Fuck off!

Midnight remains content, snoring under the blanket like a lump when I get out of bed. I wonder if all french bulldogs sleep like this or if mine is broken. How do they breathe under a heavy comforter? She's like a mini furnace at night and insists on touching me, even if it's only with the tip of one paw.

Midnight is better than I deserve, which reminds me of someone else I know.

Val

The air is crisp this morning, and it burns my lungs as I encourage Christmas to pee and be done with it. Of course, he's hell-bent on sniffing each branch on the property before settling on a final selection, only to make a beeline back to where we started. "Will you hurry? I'm about to freeze to my death out here."

It's not his fault. I'm the idiot who stopped to put a coat on her dog but didn't bother to grab one for herself. After my shower, I was so rushed to get outside that I blatantly ignored my desire to grab Kold's hoodie from the bedroom. In hindsight, a foolish decision. One I intend to correct as soon as we can get back inside.

My thoughts are a million miles away, attempting to track down my heart. No. Not a million miles, more likely down the street, in a direction I wish I knew. I dug around online and found some information about Allen's old band, including a list of members. Allen Cuttler, Corey P, Silver, and Kold Jakobsson.

"Silver and Kold." I laugh aloud to myself as the joke finally dawns on me. "That should've been the name of their holiday album."

The next three minutes are spent orchestrating a punk rock version of Oh Holy Night in my head while Christmas kicks his feet into the air, twisting and grunting, attempting to scratch his back in the dried grass. "Come on, buddy. Let's go inside, and

Mom will cut the tag out of your coat. I probably missed one." He bucks himself around in another half-circle before getting onto his feet.

"Why are you so weird?" My question causes his head to cock to one side as if to say, "Well, isn't that the pot calling the kettle black." I laugh, realizing I've been having a full-on conversation with a dog out loud in public. The neighbors will think I'm a loon or a pathetic woman who can't hold onto a man. Either way, I check for witnesses as I unlock the door and scoot inside. Thankfully, the coast is clear.

I haven't lived in many apartments, but this place is the nicest on my list. I moved in on December 26th last year, a week after my husband informed me our marriage was over.

I've always loved deeply. So, when John asked me to marry him, I thought I was set and my life could finally begin. Of course, there were red flags by the dozens, but I *loved* him. Surely, that had to be enough. Passion, we had in spades, but his anger towards me far outweighed any delight.

One week before Christmas, after less than six months of marriage, he turned to me and said, "I want a divorce." Matter of fact and to the point, completely out of nowhere, he uttered the words as if they weighed nothing. All while sharply dressed men on television recapped the greatest sports moments in history.

Shock morphed into disbelief and anger as I struggled to accept his request. I didn't know what to say, so I pulled out my phone and booked the first flight to Las Vegas.

"You can take me to the airport tomorrow morning. I'll be back on Christmas." My words were cold and unwavering. Maybe if I left, he would realize how stupid he was being. Or perhaps the lights of Sin City would illuminate my shortsightedness, marrying a guy I barely knew after only dating for two months. Either way, I was running away, and he didn't seem bothered.

On the flight out, I spoke with the guy seated beside me. A blonde-haired man in his late 20s who drove a race car, of all things. According to my new friend, the lack of snow made Vegas the ideal place to drive over the winter months. And just like that, you learn something new every day.

He was good-looking and interested, so we exchanged numbers and met the next day. Bowling, drinks, and a make-out session pressed against a slot machine were what my ego craved in the moment. The next night, it was casual sex with some random, attractive, dark-haired Finnish man whose name I didn't bother to ask. His accent alone was enough to get me into bed. Then, there was the 23-year-old emo boy named Chi and a bartender from the Bellagio.

With four little words, John had broken me, and if I had to glue myself back together with sweat and semen, I would give it my full effort. After all, loving someone with everything I had wasn't enough, so what was the point of involving my heart in any future decision-making?

Numb and no longer burdened by the crushing weight of love's embrace, I would fly back home to face what was coming without feeling a goddamn thing. Or rather, that was the plan I concocted while eating oxtail soup at a restaurant in the California. If John didn't want to be married to me, fine. I didn't need him.

Unfortunately, even best-laid plans crumble in the face of reality.

My week in Las Vegas changed everything and nothing. John met me at the airport and drove me back to his place, silence being all we exchanged that Christmas morning. He hadn't changed his mind about ending our marriage, a fact I discerned from his actions and continued lack of communication. And my resolve to remain detached slipped the second he parked at the curb. I wanted to beg, plead, and fight for him, but it would have changed nothing, so I cried silently as the world outside passed without notice.

There was only one way I could think to hurt him, the way he was hurting me, and it wasn't with my absence. John didn't care if I was gone. Heck, that's what he wanted.

After an hour of silent separation in our tiny apartment, I snapped and emerged from the bedroom with an arm full of presents, dropping them in his lap. "I want you to open these before I return them to the store." The words expelled from my lungs like fire, wearing the wings of hate.

No. I guess that's not entirely true. I never really hated John, not then or now. Last Christmas, I was wounded and hurting. Today I'm scarred.

Watching him open the gifts that would leave with me in the morning wasn't as satisfying as I had hoped. He was as detached from that moment as he had been from our entire marriage, and it was then that I finally realized nothing I did or said would ever mean anything to him because I had never meant anything to him. I made him my everything. In hindsight, a careless decision. He was the point in space and time that I orbited around, and to him, I was insignificant.

Love is a lie we tell ourselves so life won't feel so pointless.

CHAPTER 7
Kold

Darc and I find our usual table reserved in the corner and order without glancing at the menu. My brother's right. I could never abandon this place. The food is bar none, and it's the only place in town that allows dogs inside at the tables. Midnight loves this restaurant as much as I do, and I can't break her heart because I'm having a soul-crushing relationship crisis with a woman who doesn't even know how I feel.

"So, I take it from your overall brooding demeanor that you couldn't track down any leads?" Darc fiddles with his watch to avoid making eye contact. "If no one knows who she is, we can probably assume she's new to town. Allen most likely met her online. Is it possible they live together?"

"I doubt it," I say, reaching down to scratch Midnight on the top of her head. "I got the feeling they've only been together a couple of months, at most. He doesn't know a goddamn thing about her."

"What makes you say that?" Darc's eyes focus on my face as his brows pull together. It's as though he's trying to watch the memories playing in my head.

"There was this whole thing with a drink at the bar and a rum allergy. He either didn't remember or didn't care. Either way, he pushed the issue even after she said no."

"Seriously? And you sat back and let it happen?" Darc wears a disapproving expression, seeming to question my fortitude and protective instincts. "I would've never..."

"Yeah. Well, I'm not you, okay? I'm not the kind of guy who swings first when there are witnesses and never worries about the consequences. I was trying to walk a fine line and not overstep. I want her to choose me. So yeah, I backed off when I shouldn't have. More than once." Having my mistakes repeatedly pointed out to me is getting a little old.

"You act like I don't know who you are. You've always been the more controlled twin. But I've never known you to be weak. I'm surprised, is all. So, what happened? Did she drink it?"

"She took a sip, and within a minute, I could tell something was wrong. Allen was sitting there so she wouldn't say anything, but after he walked away, she said it felt like someone was stabbing a knife through her shoulder and twisting. The pain seemed to subside after a few minutes, but I imagine it would have lingered had she consumed the entire drink."

"Shit! I've never heard of anything like that, but people have allergies to all kinds of stuff. Guess I'd better polish off that bottle of Bacardi at the house before we find her. Just make sure your girlfriend knows we're a package deal."

Thankfully, the owner arrives with our breakfast, pausing the conversation. In the past, Darc and I have occasionally swapped girls. But those were one-night stands, nothing more. If he thinks I'm sharing Val with him, he's severely mistaken.

"Quick question, Conrad. My brother and I were wondering if you'd be open to changing the name of your restaurant?" Darc probes nonchalantly as if he's asking for a refill on his coffee.

The man sets down our plates, giving us a questioning glance.

"He's joking. We would never suggest such a thing." Sometimes, I hate my brother.

"You boys have grown up here, and I think of you like family, but this place is named after my daughter, so good luck convincing me to change it. Enjoy your breakfast, and tell your parents I said hello!" Conrad gives us each a nod before turning and walking back into the kitchen.

I wait for the man to be out of earshot before smacking the

shoulder of my lesser half. "I can't believe you said that. And I didn't know Conrad had a daughter, did you?"

"I knew he had an ex-wife he left back in Indiana. She died a year and a half, maybe two years ago. That's about it. Why?" Darc begins stacking eggs on the prongs of his fork by stabbing at them a bit too aggressively.

"No reason," I say as my mind wanders down far-fetched tracks, each bringing me back to her face.

This girl has corrupted my hard drive and rewritten my programming. At this point, I'm so determined to find her, everything feels like a lead. The next three weeks are going to be hell if I can't catch a break in this case.

Val

Tracy is knocking on the door to the apartment as we emerge from the stairwell. "Nobody's home," I say, jokingly, as Christmas and I close the distance.

Turning to face us, I can see that she's been crying. "Hey, Val."

"Where's Sam? Is everything all right?" My heart jumps into my throat as I fear the worst.

"Sam's fine. Greg's worthless ass finally materialized in my doorway a week late, and I didn't have the heart to send him away. That man is as thoughtless as he is arrogant, but a son's love for his father is unconditional, it would seem. I was hoping we could have a drink and talk."

"It's kinda early for drinks, don't you think? Maybe some coffee? We could go for brunch?" The lingering effects of last night's libations are still present and accounted for, so I'm not exactly looking to add insult to injury.

"Is it okay if we stay in? I haven't seen you all week, and you still need to tell me about your date." Tracy manages a smile.

"On second thought, it's five o'clock somewhere."

"Oh lord, I take it Allen put his foot in his mouth again?"

"Girl, that's not even half of it." I push open the door and unhook the leash, stepping aside so Tracy can follow us. "Allen

50

was in a mood about something before he even arrived, but that's nothing compared to what happened at the bar."

I walk into my bedroom and grab Kold's hoodie before joining Tracy in the kitchen. "The options are coffee, tea, or mimosas. You pick."

"Did you and Allen finally call it quits for good?"

"No. I don't think so. Who knows? I haven't heard from him since he dropped me off that night." A fact I hadn't bothered to register until now.

"Hmmm. Did you guys get into a fight?"

"Not exactly. He left me with his super-hot friend at the bar, then went outside on his phone." I want to be angry, but the memory of Kold and I alone at the bar gives me tingles, pulling my lips into a smile.

"Umm, excuse me? Who is this super-hot friend, and does he have a brother?"

"Oddly enough, he does. An identical twin I was momentarily convinced was a very attractive drunken delusion, but it turns out he's a real person."

A delusion I've used every night before bed to blow off steam.

"You've got to be messing with me, right?" Her eyes are wide and mouth agape as she teeters on a knife's edge, waiting for more. Not so much as a hint of a tear remaining. "You aren't kidding, are you? Holy shit! I need details, and we need mimosas."

I pour the drinks, and we settle on the couch, ready to exchange stories. My eyes scan the room and locate the lump snoring atop the oversized dog bed in the corner. Between last night and this morning, Christmas has heard enough of my stories and tucks himself neatly under his favorite blanket.

"You came over because you wanted to talk. Why don't you go first?"

"Are you crazy? Do you think I intend to waste one more second of this morning crying over my asshole ex-husband when I can sit here and live vicariously through you? I don't fricken think so, woman. Now spill. Who is this new guy, and how do I get one?"

It's funny watching my friend get excited over the mere

mention of a man. I love it. She'd explode if I ever managed to get the two of them over here. Hell, I don't think I'd be too far behind her. I never understood the whole *having sex with twins* fantasy until I met Kold and his brother. Even now, my forearm still hurts from the masturbatory beatings I've inflicted on myself, thinking about them coming home with me.

"Val! Don't leave me hanging over here. Who is this mystery guy?"

"He's one of Allen's friends, although they didn't seem overly chummy. They used to be in a band together."

"Allen was in a band? The way you describe him, he always seems so strait-laced and boring. I'm shocked to hear he might have been fun at one point."

"Okay. For the record, we have been known to occasionally have fun together. He's not always a horrible person. Last month, when we were in Chicago, he let his guard down for three whole days, which was nice. Before that, we stayed at that bed and breakfast for the weekend and ordered takeout. There was also that time we went to a show downtown and out to dinner, and I think he might have even laughed at one of my jokes." I hate myself for trying to justify a relationship that isn't working. "I don't love Allen, and I never will, but he's safe, and that's good enough. I don't want to be hurt again."

"Trust me. I understand that better than anybody. After what you've been through, I give you credit for even attempting to date." Tracy reaches forward, placing her hand on my arm. "But you deserve to be happy, Val. You deserve to be loved and cherished, and most importantly, respected. I know you don't want to believe anything I'm saying for some reason, but it's true."

"Yeah, I know, and I appreciate you saying all of that, even if it is hard to hear. But he's just some guy. I'm sure I'll never see him again. So, what did Greg have to say for himself when he came to see Sam?"

"Don't do that. Don't deflect and redirect. That smile looks good on you." She lifts her glass, clinking it to mine. "Now tell me about this guy who's got you lit up like a Christmas bulb, and don't leave anything out."

"I don't know what to say. Kold is observant and considerate. He looks like he could kill a guy with his bare hands, but he's also incredibly sweet. He gave me his sweatshirt when he saw me shiver, and he stole my drink when the bartender made it wrong. He didn't hesitate to suffer in my place. Or maybe he was hot and thirsty and I read too much into it. All I know is, being with him felt comfortable. Like it was meant to be. Like I was free to make wrong choices, and he'd stick around to glue together the pieces." I sip my drink, hoping it might buy me a second to organize my thoughts. "Maybe that doesn't make sense. I don't know. It felt like he was listening to what I had to say. Taking it all in as if he was going to be tested on the information later. And he's funny, like really funny. And you wouldn't expect it because he's tall and muscular and devilishly handsome, but the guy is hilarious. We played off one another as if we'd spent a lifetime building a banter, chalked full of inside jokes." My voice trails off while my thoughts continue to check off boxes in his favor.

"Holy shit! You're in love with Kold Jakobsson?" Tracy's hands come to her face, blocking her joker's grin.

"We spent like five hours together. Hardly enough time to fall in love." *Right?* "Did you say Kold Jakobsson? How did you... Do you know him?"

"The Jakobsson twins graduated from the same high school Greg and I went to, but they're older, so I never met them. However, I have heard about them. High school football stars, business owners, social media eye candy. The girls at work follow them online, and I've heard stories... But don't change the subject. You're head over heels for this guy, and I'm slightly jealous. When are you seeing him again?"

"I'm not." My smile fades at the realization. I won't see him again because I'm not looking to have my heart shattered into ten billion pieces. I don't want to fall in love, get cheated on, and be left like trash on the tree lawn. Nothing good can come from getting my heart involved and falling in love with this guy. I already know I can't love him halfway. It's forever and always or nothing.

"What are you even talking about? You have to see him."

"I'm dating Allen. Period! You know how I feel about cheaters. I'm not about to turn myself into the kind of person I despise."

"So, end things with Allen, track down Mr. Perfect, get married, have babies, and live happily ever after. And while you're doing that, introduce me to his brother so we can get matching houses and be neighbors forever. Unless you plan on keeping them both for yourself?" Tracy attempts to lighten the current mood with a playful wink.

"I think that drink is going to your head."

"And I think this guy has gone to your heart, and you're afraid to lose him."

"He's not mine to lose."

Is he?

"Sounds to me like he could be."

I drain my glass and retreat to the kitchen to pour another. I wasn't expecting a therapy session this morning. Normally, Tracy is the one spilling her guts, and I'm the one offering tough love. Now that the shoe is on the other foot, I'm not sure how much I like it. The next time she comes to me for advice, I'll keep my ears open and mouth shut.

"Tell me you'll see him again so I can die happy."

"Fine. I'm seeing him again. His band is playing a show downtown on Christmas Eve, and I already bought my ticket."

CHAPTER 8

Kold

Val has officially invaded every part of my life, and I've spent the last two weeks obsessing over minute details and fantasizing about what-ifs. This next week will be torture if I can't get my mind off her for at least five minutes. Everything reminds me of her and the conversation we had. It probably doesn't help that the playlists I airdropped to my phone have been on shuffle nonstop since that night. I've added all of her favorite movies to my Vudu account. And I've searched every possible combination of words and descriptors I can think of on the internet in hopes of finding her, but I keep coming up empty. When I typed in **white french bulldog puppy named Christmas,** I thought I would find something useful, but she's a ghost, and so is her dog.

Darc is convinced that Conrad's daughter and Val are one and the same, but it doesn't seem possible. We've been eating at that restaurant once a week for most of our lives. I'm sure I would remember meeting her, even if it happened 20 years ago when we were still kids. Valentine's has become a staple in this community, so the idea of its name-sake living in obscurity somewhere in town seems unlikely.

I heard something potentially interesting while playing private investigator, but I've yet to confirm the information. However, if true, I will dump Allen's body in the lake and let the fish eat him.

My heart begins pounding at the thought of Val in pain and the image of her walking away. I rack my weights and sit forward on the bench. Working out has always been my go-to escape, but even here, she haunts me.

"What?" I remove my earbuds and shoot Darc a look.

"I said, are you good?'" His voice indicates only a hint of concern.

He's been annoyingly intrusive all day, which isn't helping to take my mind off things. "Not everything is about her." I shoot back a defiant glare. Although, even I don't believe the words coming from my mouth.

"Are you sure? Because it seems like it might be."

"Fine. If you must know, I was thinking about the look on her face as she fought back the tears and how her eyes pleaded with me to speak in her defense." My failure to protect her might be my greatest sin, which is saying something, considering my past.

"For fuck's sake! Why do you insist on torturing yourself? Valentine is fine. She isn't in danger. She's lost. We'll find her eventually."

He's right, of course. Deep down, I know Val is fine without me. But my hands ache to touch her again. To feel her face pressed against my chest. I want to kiss her, bury myself inside her, and call that place home. This isn't some fleeting desire I can stifle with booze and cold showers. Val is the poison and the antidote.

"You don't get it. I have five hours' worth of memories I live in, obsessing over two and a half minutes of regret. Each time I could've opened my mouth in her defense and didn't. I watched that fucking asshole break her spirit, and I didn't protect her."

"You were in a tough spot."

"No, that's the thing, I wasn't. Val was the one in a tough spot." I stand and pace across the area in front of me, unable to remain still. "If I'm lucky, I'll see her again sometime this week. Maybe? You saw the way Allen reacted. There's a good chance he might never let me see her again."

"You don't know that for sure. We could run into her anywhere. And since when do *we* wait for permission from a fucking nobody like Allen Cuttler? I'm starting to worry that you've forgotten who we are."

"I haven't forgotten. I've been distracted. And you seriously expect me to find comfort in the off chance that we could randomly cross paths in the dog food aisle of the grocery store?"

If only.

"Well, there's two of us, so if you think about it, the odds of her running into one of us are twice as good."

I laugh, sitting on the bench, as I replace my earbuds. Before the music can resume, I hear Darc mumble under his breath, "Maybe whichever one of us finds her first should get to keep her."

Val

Tracy stopped by last night for drinks, and to discuss some new guy she's been talking to online. I'm happy for her, even if the thought of returning to the online dating cesspool gives me the creeps. Our conversation left me with a lot to think about, and all night, I questioned what kind of future I truly wanted for myself.

The last two years have been unfortunate, and for some reason, I convinced myself that settling was better than trying.

When my mom died, I married John so I wouldn't have to deal with my grief. Then, when John left me, I ran away and convinced myself he would find me and win me back. However, when he found me, it was to deliver divorce papers and a court date.

I hated Allen when I first met him. I still remember telling him on our first date that we could be friends but nothing more. But he kept calling and texting and eventually, he broke me down.

Who am I kidding? I was broken when he found me. That's the only reason we're together. Ultimately, Allen is a convenient distraction and an excuse to further delay my mourning. Not only the loss of my mother but also my career, a failed marriage, and the life I spent thirty-five years cultivating in Indiana.

I know what I have to do, and it isn't only about Kold. Although, I do wish I could talk to him. The last thing I need is a new boyfriend, but I could use a friend.

Allen: I'm downstairs.

: Getting my shoes on. See you in a minute.

I click the leash into place and make my way to the elevator. Maybe I should tell him it's over in a text and be done with it. If we ride with Allen to the restaurant, and I end the relationship there, Christmas and I will be stranded. I've never been the one to break things off with someone, and the thought of saying *I'm leaving you* gives me anxiety. Typically, those words hurt people, and I'm not in the habit of doling out pain.

When we get downstairs, Allen is parked in his usual spot by the door. He seems to be a creature of habit, and his practices are generic at best. Tracy wasn't wrong about him being strait-laced and uptight. The guy is wound tighter than a top.

"Why do you insist on bringing him with you for brunch?" His attitude is already on full display.

"Because I can." Maybe breaking things off with Allen won't be as difficult as I'm making it out to be in my head.

Christmas is the sweetest puppy in the world, and he pretty much saved my life after I moved here. Having him gave me a reason to get out of bed when I didn't want to face the day and a reason to come home at night when being out would have gotten me into trouble.

I'll never understand why Allen disapproves of me having a dog. That alone should have been enough reason for me to break things off before they started. Yet here we are. Every time I've told him I'm exhausted, he finds a way to pull me back in.

"Baby, all I'm saying is, it's a restaurant. No one wants dog hair around their food." Allen reaches for my hand and releases it all in the span of a few seconds.

"And yet seventy percent of people in the U.S. have pets." I remember looking for that statistic after a previous disagreement that looked much the same as this one.

"Fair point. I was thinking about grabbing drinks with Kold again next weekend. Would you be interested in joining us, or should I make it a guy's night?"

The sudden change of topic throws off my entire plan. If I

end the relationship now, I'll miss an opportunity to further explore the potential situation with Kold. However, if I keep showing up on Allen's arm, does that send the wrong message? I have a ticket for the show, so I know I'll see him again, eventually. But next weekend is a hell of a lot closer than the day before Christmas.

"Yeah, of course. I'd love to go with you."

We pull into the parking lot of Valentine's, which is the only worthwhile brunch spot in town, according to everyone I talk to. Even Allen insists on eating here, but that has more to do with the fact that we never receive a bill for our meal.

I hop out near the door and head straight to my usual table in the back corner. The one with the sign that permanently reads "Reserved." I've tried sitting at other tables, but nothing else feels quite right. I know it sounds silly, but something about this chair feels like home. It's like we belong here. And for some reason, Christmas is obsessed with how the carpet smells in the corner next to my feet. He seems to experience the calming energy of this exact spot the same way I do.

"Only the two of you this morning? Finally, get rid of that *boyfriend* of yours?" Conrad sets down my usual cappuccino and feeds Christmas a strip of bacon. "Wasn't sure if you were coming in today."

"Well, I'm here, and the *boyfriend* is parking the car."

Conrad looks displeased as he watches Allen pass through the tables on his way to where we're sitting. Everyone has such strong opinions about my dating life, yet where were they all the times my life was falling apart? Don't get me wrong. It's great that he wants to act all paternal, but it's about thirty-five years too late.

I started coming in here once I moved to town, hoping to get answers, but all Conrad had to offer back then was food. As the owner, he doesn't take orders, pass plates, or bus tables unless you're sitting here. He told me once that this table was reserved for family. I've never seen anyone else sitting here, but it seems odd that he'd reserve a table for thirty years on the off chance I might come walking through the door one day.

Then again, I suppose it worked. I am here, aren't I?

"Can you make mine a double? I'm eating my feelings this morning." I drop the end of the leash and wrap a hand around my coffee. The warmth of the cup feels nice on my fingertips.

"I'll let the chef know." Conrad strolls back into the kitchen, not bothering to take Allen's order.

CHAPTER 9

Kold

I'm halfway through the fourth movie on Val's list, trying to distract myself from the fact that Allen blew off our tentative plans to meet, when I hear the doorbell ring. It would be easy to hide in my room until whoever is there gets tired of waiting and goes away, but Midnight is already halfway down the stairs and losing her mind. What kind of person rings the doorbell? There's an unwritten rule between dog owners that a quiet text to alert one to your presence is adequate. Anything more than that, and you're an asshole. No need to wake the family and startle the pets because you decided to stop by. Not that I have a family to wake.

After my workout, I showered and threw on shorts but nothing else. I suppose if I'm going to answer the door, I might want to cover myself. For all I know, it could be my 90-year-old neighbor stopping by with pumpkin pie. Wouldn't want to give the old girl a heart attack and miss out on Christmas cookies. There's a gray hoodie on the chair by the door that'll have to do.

Between the dog barking at the window and wrestling into my hoodie as I speed down the stairs, I catch myself on the fifth step from the bottom and nearly tumble to my death. Thankfully, my fingers have enough grip strength to keep that from happening.

"Well, that would've been embarrassing," I say to myself

before scooping Midnight from the floor and answering the door without bothering to check who it is.

Darkening my doorstep is the absolute last person I was anticipating, and behind him, still sitting in the car, is the one person I can't stop thinking about.

"I wasn't expecting to see you today. What a pleasant surprise." Everything inside me wants to knock him into the bushes and run to the driveway to get my girl, but I know I need to play this cool.

"Val and I were at breakfast, and I remembered you lived somewhere around here. Saw your SUV in the driveway and thought we'd stop by. Hope we aren't interrupting anything." There's something he's not saying, but I can figure out his motives later, after releasing Val from his clutches.

"Do you want to come in?"

Midnight stopped barking when I picked her up, and now a low growl is coming from her belly. Turns out dogs *are* a good judge of character.

"Maybe we shouldn't. I don't trust Val's dog alone in my jeep."

He seems to be testing me somehow, though I can't quite figure out his angle. The Allen I knew years ago was a habitual liar and a mediocre manipulator. He consistently looked for ways to pit people against one another to take the heat off himself, but it rarely worked. Most of us were quick to see through the bullshit and kicked him out of the band after six months. He only played one live show with the group before scurrying away.

After that, he'd reach out every so often when he wanted to show off his latest fling, as if anyone would be impressed. And I don't mean that as a knock against any of those women. They were all dating a man who didn't exist. Once the blinders came off, they would head for the hills, and he was on to the next. He fell off the radar a few years ago, and I didn't hear from him. No real loss, so I didn't think much of it until recently.

"Give me one second." I jog past him, skipping the stairs in a leap, and head straight for the passenger side of the jeep. Her face is a vision being burned into my memory. Regardless of what comes next, Val will leave here knowing my feelings for her.

I knock on the window, and she looks equal parts stunned and stunning. The sound of the knock alerts her miniature protector to my sudden appearance, and the alarm bells begin ringing. Midnight joins in, taking sides, and the battle is on. All I can do is read Val's lips as she whispers, "I'm sorry."

I motion for her to roll down the window, but the car's off, so she moves to get out. As the door swings open, I project my voice over the chorus of barking, "I swear she's nicer than she looks." As if on cue, the yapping subsides, and both dogs stretch and strain in an attempt to sniff one another.

"Are you kidding me? She's adorable. I want to rub my face all over her, change her name to New Year's Eve, and take her home with me." Val's playful excitement makes my heart thunder as I clutch my chest. "Are you okay?" Her tone changes from gleeful to slightly concerned. "I don't want you dying on me."

How are you so goddamn cute?

The words are on the tip of my tongue, but an unwelcome addition to the conversation pulls me up short. Where is my brother when I need him? I have to find a way to get Val alone long enough for me to get my number into her phone. If Darc were here, he would know to act as a well-timed diversion, though he has been known to lack a certain subtlety. With my luck, Allen would end up gutted in the kitchen, and Val would be traumatized.

"We should probably let you get back to whatever you were doing. I forgot you had a dog. Didn't mean to cause a commotion."

"You're here now. Might as well come inside."

Allen can backpedal all he wants, but this girl in front of me isn't leaving my sight until she knows, in no uncertain terms, that there are other options on the table, especially when she's standing in my driveway wearing my hoodie.

Val

I'm not sure how we got here, especially after the argument Allen and I had over breakfast. Exchanging hate-filled glances and silence over coffee and avocado toast has become our new Sunday tradition. He keeps manufacturing arguments and accusing me of outlandish indiscretions while increasing the distance between us. Last night, we were supposed to go out, but Allen canceled at the last minute, claiming Kold changed his mind about getting together. Brokenhearted, I cried myself to sleep, which likely prompted my vulgar mood this morning.

Seeing Kold after three weeks of missing his smile feels like any number of candles on my birthday cake, and my heart swells with possibilities. If I had one wish, he's all I want.

Now that I know where the man of my dreams is resting his head at night, I could potentially come back alone. I wouldn't have to bide my time continuing this charade with Allen. Let's hope Christmas behaves himself and doesn't ruin this for me. However, at this point, I worry more about Allen ruining things for me than the dogs.

Kold leads the way, and I can't help but smile at the sight of him barefoot, in gym shorts and a hoodie, trotting across the grass carrying a dog. This right here is everything my heart needed today.

If I let myself, I could love him beyond measure, the way love was always meant to be given. Unconditionally. But having him temporarily and watching him slip through my fingers is the kind of loss I would never recover from, the sort of failure that could ultimately destroy me. And there's the rub. It might be for the best to keep feelings out of it altogether. My own happiness included.

I'm not sure what I expected the inside of his house to look like. Maybe more of a frat house or bachelor pad vibe with mismatched couches and dirty cups on the table. But I'm pleasantly surprised to see it's quite the opposite. It feels like a home, unexpectedly clean and well-decorated.

Allen's house is half empty, like someone moved out in the cover of darkness and took half the furniture with them. I'm not sure if that's what happened, but if it did, he never bothered to replace anything. In the four months we've been together, I've only been to his place once, for less than an hour. I sensed I wasn't welcome, so I never returned, and he never invited me.

The stark contrast between the two men is reflected clearly in their homes and hearts.

I shut the front door behind me and slip out of my shoes. Allen, however, steps off the mat, still wearing his boots, which I find to be the height of rudeness. The more time I spend with him, the more I hate him.

Since meeting online, I've caught Allen in lie after lie. Initially, those half-truths and embellishments seemed harmless. I thought maybe he was self-conscious and telling tall tales to make himself appear more interesting, but over time I realized it was more than that. He seemed to be customizing his backstory to align with my personal taste, and his stories never added up, lacking detail and proof. If I dared to ask questions, he pushed me away. Then, when I stopped corresponding, he pursued me relentlessly.

I'm not sure the flags he's waving could get much redder, but somehow, over the last few months, he's found a way to convince me I'm colorblind. That all ends now. I don't need him anymore, nor do I want him. I wish this unintended boyfriend of mine would go away and never return.

"Do you feel comfortable letting the kids play together while we hang out?" The wording of Kold's question causes my thoughts to race. I don't even want kids. But for him, I'd be barefoot and pregnant, cooking dinner in the kitchen with a spatula in one hand and a toddler on my hip.

"Yeah, I'm sure they'll be fine. Do you mind if I take this one out for a quick pee break in your backyard? I'd like to avoid any accidents." I hold my squirming puppy like he's the prize-winning piglet at the fair.

I've fantasized about this man for weeks, and when I'm finally granted another opportunity to see him, I'm talking about dog pee. Seriously? Sometimes, I wonder how I've ever been able to attract men at all, let alone impressive ones.

"Good call. I'll let Midnight lead the way." He sets the jet-black frenchie down so gently that her paws kiss the floor before she takes off running. "Come on, New Year's Eve, let's go outside."

I laugh, setting Christmas down in front of me, still holding on to his leash. He pulls against the nylon lead, raring to make the acquaintance of this new friend. Following Kold's path through the hallway and into the kitchen, I catch up with him at the open backdoor.

"Don't worry. The yard is fenced in. You won't lose him." The combination of Kold's playful grin and the wink he tops it off with has me weak in the knees.

It's not the dog I'm worried about losing.

That's what I want to say, but I'm still holding back for some reason. Maybe it's Allen standing ten feet away, craning his neck to see us. Or perhaps it's the crushing fear of loving someone so deeply who might never love me back. I consider the risk of airdropping my number to Kold's phone, a move I wish I had made weeks ago while sharing playlists and playful banter, but Allen is watching me like a hawk, scrutinizing my every smile and gesture.

When the dogs finally come running back into the house, we move into the living room. There's a lightness to the moment and a corresponding tension. Allen's caught me off guard. An intentional move, no doubt, but I've had plenty of time to learn from my previous mistakes, and I don't plan on fucking this up again.

"I hate to ask, but do you mind if I use your restroom?" I don't actually have to pee, but I figure a second alone to regroup couldn't hurt, and if Kold shows me where the bathroom is, maybe I can say something.

"Make yourself at home. I would happily give you a guided tour if you'd like. Or would you rather peruse alone while conducting your impromptu FBI search and seizure?"

Kold seems to be joking, but now I'm not sure if I should leave the couch. I don't want to give him any reason to think I'm here under false pretenses or with ill intent. To be honest, I had no idea we were coming here. Until I saw him at the door, I wasn't sure where Allen was taking me.

"If you're offering a guided tour, I'd happily buy a ticket."

CHAPTER 10

Kold

Allen joins the procession, taking my mood from thrilled to annoyed. He keeps talking like we're best friends, and the implication sets my teeth on edge. I don't want anyone associating him and me, especially not the woman currently positioned between us. Although I shouldn't be surprised he insisted on tagging along. If Val were mine, I wouldn't trust anyone else around her either.

Whatever game Allen is trying to play, I'll figure it out eventually. I haven't talked to this guy in years. Then he messages me out of the blue and introduces me to the woman tailor-made to be my wife, saying he has something he wants to give me. Did he mean her? Because he sure as hell didn't offer to pay back the money he owes me. Not that I even care. Fuck the guitar. Fuck the money. All I need is *my* girl. And here he is, delivering her to my doorstep. I'm not sure if I should shake his hand or push him down the stairs.

"This is my room, so you can use the bathroom through that door if you'd like. Just don't write me off if there's a wet towel and some sweaty clothes on the floor. I swear, I was going to clean while I did laundry." Suddenly self-conscious, I look around the room, wishing I had made my bed.

Val laughs lightly, as if to herself, and presses the back of her hand to my forearm with a whisper's touch. "Your house is basically spotless, so I'm sure I could overlook a set of clothes on the floor. Plus, the movie paused on your television wins you more points than you could ever lose." Flashing me half a smile, she crosses the room and disappears into the bathroom, leaving me teetering on the edge of insanity.

She absorbs into my personal space, replacing the hollow masturbatory images that stood in substitution as the scent of honey and almond lingers beside me like a ghost. If we were alone, I would lay her across the bed and drown between her thighs. But we're not alone. A fact Allen's persistent jabbering won't allow me to overlook. The guy still thinks he's the authority on everything, even going so far as to comment on the crown molding the builder used in the house. This arrogant asshole is about to lose his girl and is too oblivious to notice.

The door across the room opens, revealing my once and future queen, and even before she speaks, Val has my full attention. "Right, because it's not creepy at all, having you both standing there waiting for me to come out. You might want to be careful. Your weird is showing."

Feeling exposed and wondering if my previous thoughts about taking her on the bed could be seen from across the room, I move my hand in front of my crotch.

"I said weird, not wiener, you dork." Val giggles and walks over to my bed, sitting in the place where I spend my nights dreaming of her.

Slipping the hoodie over her head, she sets it beside the pillow and smiles at me. "Thanks for letting me borrow that. I would've returned it sooner but I didn't know how to find you. I did, however, find a bunch of new albums on iTunes, and I officially have a new favorite band. So, thanks for that. My current *dog walking* playlist is comprised entirely of Our Last Midnight songs." Her enthusiasm fills the room like laughing gas as her hand mindlessly brushes back and forth over my bed sheet.

Holy shit! She's been thinking about me.

The reality of the moment has me dumbfounded.

The girl of my dreams is sitting on my bed, touching my sheets as if she's absorbing what lingering traces of me remain there, and she looks happy. Not like someone pretending to be happy because everyone's looking, but truly and honestly at peace in the moment. Or maybe that's how I feel for the first time in my life, and she's acting as a mirror. It wouldn't be the first time I saw my image reflected back at me.

Val admitted to looking for me online when she acknowledged finding the band. Which means she most likely browsed through *all* of my personal social media pages. This could be problematic.

My looks have opened several doors, professionally and personally, and I've gotten good at manipulating the masses by accentuating certain assets. If I'm being honest, I look like a fuckboy online, and Darc makes quite a bit of money via video prostitution and dick pics. Thankfully, nothing about how Val looks at me indicates disappointment, so maybe she understands the game.

I'm more than who I pretend to be online. True, she didn't friend request, follow, or even add me to her favorites. I know because I've been combing through everything, relentlessly searching for any trace of her. But she did look for me, and that's something. Maybe my girl doesn't have profiles on any of the usual apps. That would explain why I haven't been able to find her, but that doesn't address the issue of me looking like a whore online. Given the chance, I can explain. I can take it all down if I have to. Darc and I have several revenue streams that keep the cash flowing into our accounts, and social media is nothing more than a mask.

Over the last few weeks, I never let myself consider that Val might also be looking for me. Content like that would have felt too much like wishful thinking, and I both love and hate the thought of her missing me as much as I miss her. I want to be the reason she feels good, not sad.

To hell with Allen. Darc and I can sort him out later. Right now, I have to tell Val how I feel.

I'm on the verge of spilling my guts when I hear my brother shouting downstairs. "Kold, help me! The dogs just ran out the front door."

My heart stops as Val and I head for the stairs. This can't be happening. If Christmas or Midnight is injured because I was distracted and didn't keep them safe, Val will never forgive me.

Darc is already three houses down when we get out the front door. Racing across the street in his direction, I can see both dogs getting further away. Before I'm out of breath, I stop and exhale an ear-splitting whistle.

Midnight halts in her tracks and turns to run back with Christmas following behind like a love-sick puppy.

"I am so sorry that happened. I had no idea that was you in the driveway, and I wasn't expecting..."

Darc trails off as he retrieves the white puppy, kisses him on the head, and places him in Val's arms. "When I opened the front door, they shot past my legs, and I was afraid I couldn't catch both of them on my own."

I pick up Midnight and press her into my chest. "You're in serious trouble, little miss. Now apologize." Stepping towards Val, I can see the making of tears twinkling in her eyes.

"Babe, it's okay. They're fine, and we'll know to be more careful next time." I pass Midnight to my brother and wrap my arms around the girl whose heart we've nearly broken. She's shaking, on the verge of tears, and this time the blame falls squarely on me and my slightly irresponsible half.

I pull off my hoodie and slide it over Val's head, covering her and the white puppy in her arms. Kissing the top of her head, I fix her hair and tilt her chin towards me. "There's something I need to tell you. Something I should have said three weeks ago. Val, I..."

The horn of Allen's jeep sounds from the street beside us, stealing my spotlight. Late to the party yet again, and in time to ruin everything. He opens the window and shouts for Val to get in, banging his hand authoritatively against the metal door.

Every part of me wants to pull him through that window and beat him to death in the street. Who the fuck does this guy think he is, barking out orders in my neighborhood as if he's the one calling the shots? If Val weren't standing next to me, this would all be playing out differently, but she still hasn't chosen me. Not yet.

"I look forward to hearing what you want to say, but I should get this little escape artist home. Call me later?" Her statement turned up at the end like a question.

Once more, I am painfully aware that my girl is electing to leave with another man. This can't be happening. Not again. I had her in my bedroom. I held her in my arms. All I had to do was speak. Now I'm standing, half-naked, in the middle of the road, watching her disappear.

"What did she say? Is she pissed at me?" Darc joins me in the street with Midnight still tucked under his arm.

"She said, 'Call me later,' and walked away."

What is she even talking about? If calling was an option, I would have done it weeks ago. Does she not realize that she's impossible to find? It's not like Allen is going around writing her name and phone number on the bathroom walls at the bar.

"Bathroom walls." The words hang in the air behind me as I take off toward the house. "Maybe she left her number in the bathroom upstairs."

Val

How do I keep messing this up? Why didn't I stay? The most gorgeous man I've ever seen was holding me in his arms, and I left him alone in the cold. Well, not alone exactly, but close enough. The image of him, damn near naked, will live rent-free in the front of my mind from here until eternity. And for a second, I thought my life could be different.

Maybe it could be if I stopped allowing everything else to get in the way. Allen included.

"We need to talk." My words hang, suspended in the air like a guillotine, threatening to bring about the end.

"Baby, I'm just glad Christmas wasn't hurt or killed. You would have been devastated, and I couldn't bear the thought of that. Some things never change. Those two assholes are as thoughtless as they come, and I'm sorry I ever introduced you to either of them." Allen's tone is absent of its usual sharpness.

"It was an accident, and thankfully no one was hurt. Had one of us been downstairs when Darc came in, the dogs wouldn't have gotten out. Sometimes, unfortunate things happen, Allen. It doesn't always have to be someone's fault."

I've always despised the blame game most people insist on playing. As if pointing the finger at others somehow absolves them of any wrongdoing. So long as someone else is more to blame than they are, they're in the clear. But blame isn't something you assign. It's something you accept.

Christmas wouldn't have been left unattended had I not been so eager to get Kold alone. I wasn't even thinking about the dogs. When I was upstairs in the bedroom, I couldn't see anything except for him. There was no one else who mattered at that moment. Kold was the beginning, the end, and everything in between.

"I doubt you'd be so diplomatic if Christmas had gotten hit by a car, and we were racing to the vet instead of driving home." Allen is laying it on thick, filling the jeep with his false concern.

"I hear what you're saying. I do. But they both apologized, and no real harm was done. Let's learn a lesson, be thankful nothing bad happened, and move on." I press Christmas tightly against my chest and tuck his head under my chin.

Doesn't this furry jerk know how important he is to me? I'll need to keep a better eye on him the next time we visit with Midnight. If Kold ever invites us back, that is.

I've made a point to wear Kold's black hoodie every time I leave the house, with my phone number tucked into the front pocket. I thought if I saw him or his brother out somewhere, I could slip them the note, even if Allen was around. At the house, in his room, I panicked. Deciding the least obvious thing was to return the hoodie altogether and hope for the best. Now that I take a moment to think about it, I'm afraid Kold might throw the sweatshirt into the laundry without checking the pocket, and my whole plan will be washed away with yesterday's dirt.

"I'm leaving tomorrow and going out of town for a few days. You should come with me. We could order room service, go for a swim, flirt at the rooftop bar, and try out some new role-play. I feel like it's been ages since I've had you all to myself. I want you in a hotel bed, naked and ready to please me." Allen's sudden change of topic and complete tonal shift causes me to squint my eyes and shake my head.

"What are you even talking about? I have to work the next three days, and Thanksgiving is on Thursday. You told me we were going to your sister's house for dinner because you wanted me to meet your family. If you meant for me to go out of town for the week, why are you telling me now? Allen, I can't do this anymore."

"The trip was scheduled last minute, and I thought you might like to get away. If you can't go, then you can't go. No big deal. I'm sure I'll see you when I get back, and we can make up for the lost time." He pulls next to the door and parks. "Unless you want me to come upstairs so I can take care of you one last time before I leave."

My resolve crumbles once sex is on the table. A button easily pressed. After all, a woman has needs, and I can only accomplish so much with my hand.

Despite all of Allen's faults, I'll give him credit. He's persistent and not entirely terrible in bed. Regarding sex, I've had better, but I've also had worse. Right now, it doesn't matter. I'm turned on, and the only dick I want isn't mine to have. So, fucking Allen is going to have to be good enough.

Christmas jumps into the backseat, retreating in time to avoid being squished.

"Don't make me beg." Allen allows his hand to move along my thigh as he bites into my shoulder.

"I... Umm. I don't know if we should." My body heats as my legs part slightly, allowing him one step closer. Images of Kold and his brother flood my mind as reality mixes with fantasy.

"Come on, baby. I'll let you say his name while I'm inside you. I know you want him." Allen's words melt into my skin, making my back arch.

This is something we've played with before, so I'm not surprised when he offers. Normally, the names belong to actors or tattooed underwear models. I relish the suggestion of being shared, and I think Allen enjoys the idea of seeing me with other men. That's probably why he introduced me to Kold in the first place. He knew how strongly my body would react and enjoyed watching me squirm.

What he hadn't planned for was Kold's physical reaction to me.

"Maybe you should've let him have his way with me while I

was sitting on his bed. Then you could've scrutinized his performance later at dinner. Or taken the memory with you on your business trip. Either way, we both would've gotten something we wanted." The more I think about Kold touching me, the further I'm willing to let this go.

"We're going upstairs. Now!" The direct order comes out with a force that reaches my core. Allen is prepared to punish and reward me for being a flirt, and I'm about to let him.

I grab Christmas from the backseat, unlock the door to the building, and ascend the flight of stairs with hurried steps. I'm out of breath when Allen presses himself against me outside the apartment door.

"If you don't hurry with that lock, I'm going to fuck you in the hallway. And if you're lucky, all your neighbors will come out to watch as you cum on my dick while you're screaming his name."

Twisting the key, the deadbolt gives way, and the door swings open as Allen begins kissing my neck. We spill into the living room as I drop the leash and lock the door, needing to avoid further close calls. Once secured inside, we alternate between kissing and removing articles of clothing as we make the short trip to the bedroom.

Allen pushes me onto the bed, aggressively clear in his intentions, but it isn't difficult for me to picture myself in another room with a better man. I shut my eyes tight and allow the fantasy to take over.

"Tell me what you want him to do to you. In detail. I know you've been thinking about him," Allen's voice echoes beside my ear, passing me off to the man in my head.

I find my way back to Kold's bed and imagine being alone with him. Pulling away the corner of the comforter and rubbing my hand across the smooth cotton, I feel his sheets beneath my fingertips. I smell a hint of his cologne on the sweatshirt I carried into the bedroom with me. And I hear his voice singing my new favorite songs.

"I want him to kiss me and mean it." I feel Kold's lips as they press gently to mine and then disappear. Why does he tease me?

Doesn't he know I need more? More time. More attention. More inside jokes and stolen glances. Doesn't he know I need *him*?

"Keep going." His words urge me forward, clawing the truth from my bleeding heart.

"I want him to tease my lips with his tongue while his hand glides over my body, making my hips roll. I want him to start at my neck, kissing his way past my collarbone and over my nipples." I allow my body to move along with my wishes and find that I am rewarded with the touch I'm describing.

"He's going to love your perfect little tits and the way your nipples harden against his tongue. You're being such a good girl for him." He licks and sucks between sentences. "Fuck! You've got my cock so hard, baby. Don't stop."

"I want him to brush his fingers over my panties while I beg him to fill me." My legs part slightly at the request of his touch.

"He wouldn't make you beg. I bet he's jerking off thinking about you spread open on his bed, wishing he could have you." Sliding my panties to the side, he pauses. "What do you want him to fill you with? Tell him so he knows how you like to be pleased."

"I want his fingers first so that it won't hurt as much when he gives me his cock." Seeing the outline of Kold's dick through his jeans and examining it further in the photos he's posted online, I know he could hurt me if he wanted to.

Allen pushes two fingers inside. "Oh, goddamn. You're so wet for him, baby. Does he know how badly you want him to fuck you?"

"No." I grip the sheets as my muscles tighten.

"But you do want it, don't you? You want his cock inside you."

"Yes," I imagine Kold's defined muscles, his tattooed skin, and the way his eyes lighten when he smiles at me.

"You want him stretching you out and filling you up?"

"Yes," I call out, biting back tears. The escalating pleasure threatens to overtake me as he positions himself on top of me.

"Oh, come on. You can do better than that." The head of his cock teases at my opening for an extended second before plunging inside. "Tell him how good he feels. Tell him how badly you've wanted him."

"I can't." My senses are lost in the tidal wave of emotion. I'm on the edge of euphoria, about to take flight. "I'm scared."

"Oh, you should be scared. You have no idea what he's capable of. He's going to fuck you so hard you'll be begging him to stop, and then he's going to break you for the fun of it." His strokes intensify as he slams into me. "Now, tell him everything you've been holding back."

"No. It's not that. I want him to hurt me." I squeeze my eyes shut tighter as the pounding continues.

"Stop holding back. What are you afraid of?"

"I don't want to lose him." I turn my head to the side before opening my eyes, unwilling to recognize the other person in the room. It's me and Kold in this moment together, and reality will not convince me otherwise.

"He's already yours. Can't you see that?"

The walls of my pussy tighten as I reach down to rub my clit, fully submitting to the fantasy Allen has created.

"Now claim him!" Hurried strokes suggest that the end is near for both of us as his fingers press into my flesh.

"Oh god. You're gonna make me cum. Fuck! Don't stop." The convulsion starts in my core and ripples out my fingers and toes. I can hear my voice bouncing off the empty walls of the bedroom as I scream his name.

"Kold, I love you."

CHAPTER 11
Kold

I looked everywhere, tore the bathroom apart searching, but there was no sign of her anywhere. I even checked the pockets of my gym shorts for a slip of paper in case she tried hiding the phone number from Allen's view. It doesn't make sense. She specifically said, "Call me," knowing full well I didn't have her number.

Finally admitting defeat, I drop onto the bed and pull the black hoodie to my nose. The scent of honey and almond is woven into the fabric, stabbing at my heart and making my cock twitch. "Goddammit, woman! How the hell do I find you?"

I take the movie off pause in an attempt to distract myself, but my every thought is with Val. Nothing makes sense without her. Every song reminds me of the girl I've let slip through my fingers. Every movie, I imagine watching with her in my arms. This girl has become the center of my universe, and she doesn't even know it.

Feeling determined, I do another deep dive through my phone, searching for hidden meaning in the songs on her playlists. Why didn't I memorize her number while I was holding her phone in my hand? Or I could have typed my info into her contact list. This would all be so simple if I could go back to Halloween night and do it again, knowing what I know now.

Who am I kidding? I knew she was meant to be mine the

second I saw her. How long is it going to be now until I see her again?

With a total lack of options at my disposal, I message the man with information on the only person who matters.

> : Could you tell Val that Darc and I feel terrible about what happened earlier? I hope they're safe at home and no worse for the wear.

> Allen: Yeah. She was pretty upset on the ride home, but I tucked her into bed and left her feeling relaxed. Don't be surprised if she doesn't want to hang out again. My girlfriend can be a bit over-sensitive, especially when it comes to her dog. I mean, I don't blame you for what happened. It was an accident. But she's less forgiving.

> : I understand. Could you send me Val's phone number? I'd like to apologize to her myself.

Fuck my life! There's got to be something I can do to make it up to her. Allen is lying to me. I know it. And I'm about to torture the information I need out of him if he doesn't stop screwing around.

> Allen: I'll give her your number and leave it for her to choose.

> : Thanks.

> Allen: We'll be out of town for the holiday, but I'll get her to calm down. Make sure she forgets about being mad. Hopefully, we can get together again sometime in mid-December.

> : Sure thing.

I read through each line of text individually, scrutinizing every combination of words. He went out of his way to imply that they went home and had sex, which may or may not be true. They are dating, so it's entirely possible. God knows, once she's mine, I intend on pleasuring her every chance I get.

Allen also claimed that Val hates me and never wants to see me again. But he lies through his teeth, so I have to take every assertion with a grain of salt. When she was in my arms, it seemed like she wanted me to kiss her. To hold on and never let go. She would have pulled away if she was pissed off, not melted into my skin like cocoa butter.

Yeah, Val was upset. We both were. But it was our concern that had us shaken, not anger. Once Christmas was back, safely in her arms, she seemed settled. And she told me to call her. Why would she say that if she never wanted to speak to me again? It doesn't add up. Either he's spinning the facts to fit his narrative, or I'm having trouble remembering things correctly.

> : Honest opinion. When Val left, did you get the feeling she hated me?

> Evil Twin: No. If she hates anyone, it's me. From where I was standing, it looked like she was waiting for you to make a move on her, and you didn't. Both times she left with Allen, I'm certain it was to avoid a fight.

I laugh at the insinuation that I couldn't take Allen Cuttler in a fight. Give me a damn break. I'm in the gym seven days a week and have been fighting since I was a kid. I would fucking murder that guy in a heartbeat.

> : Are you kidding me? You know what I'm capable of. He wouldn't stand a chance.

> Evil Twin: Obviously. But our girl doesn't strike me as the type of person who enjoys negative attention. She's playing it safe and keeping the peace because she doesn't want anyone hurt.

: To what end? How long can she stay with a guy who makes her unhappy?

Evil Twin: Normal people stay in shitty relationships all the time. Unless you give her a solid reason to leave, I think she'll stay until he breaks things off with her.

I want to protect Val's heart more than anything, but I can't do that if I don't know what she wants or how to find her. And when it comes to Allen, he isn't making things any easier for us. The guy keeps stringing me along, moving the goalposts, and I get the sense he enjoys the anguish he's inflicting. I get the feeling Allen is fully aware of the feelings between Val and me, and he's using it to fuck with us, which makes me hate him all the more.

There's nothing else I can do today but wait it out. With any luck, there's still a chance Val might drive back over to see me, which is the best I can hope for. Then again, she's probably packing for her trip, eager to put distance between us. Had I known sooner, I could have offered to watch Christmas while she was gone. Not that she would trust me with her dog after what happened.

Fuck! Maybe Val does hate me.

CHAPTER 12
Val

This week has been depressingly quiet. I spent Thanksgiving alone with my dog, watching the Macy's Day parade and the Westminster Dog Show. Christmas had his bug eyes glued to the TV for hours, cheering on the non-sporting group, but an Irish Wolfhound took home the grand prize this year.

All of my go-to distractions have been failing me as I continue to check my phone, willing it to ring, but nothing happens. Maybe Kold never found my note. Or he found it and ratted me out to Allen. I haven't seen or heard from either of them since Sunday, and today is already Friday. Allegedly, it's the biggest spending day of the year, though I wonder if that's changed now that everyone shops online and the stores run the same sale all week. I suppose it doesn't matter since I'm at home wallowing in self-pity, having already completed my holiday gift list.

All morning, I did my best to stay off social media, and I was mildly successful, for the most part. Eventually, I gave up pretending I could live without him and set one of my favorite Kold images as the new background and lock screen on my cell phone. I thought seeing him and hearing his voice in the songs he sings might make me feel less alone, but I think it's made the pain even worse. It will be another disappointing Christmas if I can't get out of this funk.

The presents, wrapped and tagged in the closet, serve as a

painful reminder that he isn't coming back. I've been a fool to think there was something worthwhile between us. Something worth building, nurturing, and protecting. Perhaps if I spent more time shielding my heart and less time chasing after guys who never wanted me, I wouldn't be sitting here in my pajamas on a Friday night, binging reality TV and eating a pint of superman ice cream.

Conrad offered to spend the holidays with me, but I wasn't in the mood for father-daughter bonding time. I'll hear him out when he's ready to talk openly and honestly about the past. But if all he wants to do is skirt around the issues, I'm better off leaving the past buried and our relationship surface-level.

I have enough guys lining up to stab me in the heart this holiday season without adding my deadbeat father to the list. I have half a mind to post my ticket to Kold's Christmas Eve show online and use the money to buy a 90-minute massage, but I can't bring myself to do it. I still want to see him, even if he might not want to see me.

The concert sold out two weeks ago, and I'm intrigued to see what all the hype is about. Maybe they're a bigger deal than I realized. The hordes of women following their social media pages certainly seem to enjoy the shows. Who knew so many twenty-something-year-old girls were into punk music? Can't imagine it has anything to do with the sexy lead singer they drape themselves across in photos.

I place my phone on the coffee table and return the ice cream to the freezer. Constantly staring at the twin images I find online isn't helping my emotional tailspin, but I can't make myself stop. I created a file that now has over a hundred photos saved on my computer, and this week, I've driven past their house after work, on the way to the store, or for no reason at all because I needed to feel connected.

I'm obsessed, and it's pathetic. I've typed two dozen long-winded messages to his personal social media page, but I can't talk myself into hitting send. The guy's got over two hundred thousand followers per app, and I don't even have a profile. Kold is the sun, and I'm the equivalent of a social media blackhole.

Men make women weak. Even Tracy met someone on a dating app who's got her head shoved into the clouds. She's falling for some mystery man named Carter, who'll probably turn out to be a catfish, and I'm crushing on a Greek god who could step online and take his pick. Quite the pair we are. I'm no different from the thousands of women online throwing themselves at Kold. All I lack is a photo for proof.

"Maybe he never was mine." It's certainly possible I invented the connection between us. But how many other women are wearing a hoodie that still smells like him? He should consider selling them on his only fans page because he'd make a fortune. I'd buy a new one every month just to pretend like he was with me.

I wrap my arms across my chest, falling back into the corner of the couch, and allow the tears to fall freely onto my waterlogged cheeks.

"I hate this time of year."

Kold

The minutes tick by like days as hope fades. Tomorrow will be one week since I saw my girl. I thought she might magically appear at the front door, but it's possible she may not even be in town. She's probably busy fucking Allen in some overpriced hotel, paid for by the company expense account. Too distracted by her real life to bother with thinking about me.

No. That's not fair. It's not Val's fault I'm crushing on someone I can't have. She never lied to me about being in a relationship, and she never promised me anything. She was genuinely friendly, ridiculously funny, and unbelievably thoughtful. I consciously fell in love with her, knowing she had a boyfriend. She didn't lead me on or string me along. That girl gave me half a smile and made a crack about my name, and I was hooked. This entire thing is my fault.

Not like I had a choice.

I can't keep dragging my body from one day through the next. At this point, I'm so annoyed with myself that even if she did come around, I doubt she would stay. I need to get it together. My only hope of winning her over is to be the best version of myself. Eventually, Allen will fuck up, and I'll make sure I'm there to collect the pieces. Given his track record, it shouldn't be too much longer.

87

: I'm going to shower. Then we're going to Valentine's.

Evil Twin: Glad to see we're using the V word again. Seems like a step in the right direction.

: Fuck off and get ready. I'll be down in ten.

The warm water feels like needles piercing my skin when I first step in. I like it. Something about a hot shower feels like a fresh start, and that's exactly what I'm looking for right now. Lord knows, the cold water I've been dousing myself in the last month has done nothing to stamp out my desire for the one person I need but can't have. I have to find a healthy way to love her and still function.

It's been more than a few days since I've shaved, and if I'm being honest, it doesn't look half bad. I never considered how I might look with facial hair, but if the internet is to be believed, flannel shirts, tattoos, and beards are all the rage these days. All I need now is an ax and some logs to split. Surely, then Val would be impressed.

Or maybe she's already impressed, and I don't have to change.

Darc thinks Val is with Allen, not because she loves him, but because she doesn't want to hurt his feelings by ending things. Optimistic thinking on his part, which isn't usually my brother's style.

Darc isn't one to take feelings into consideration, his own or anyone else's. However, I've noticed some slight changes in him lately. At first, I thought he was being supportive, but that's not it. He seems invested, as if he wants to find her as badly as I do. And I heard him on the phone, the day after Val was at the house, telling the cleaning lady she needed to start coming once a week instead of twice a month.

For fun, I pull a flannel shirt from the closet and look at myself in the mirror. All right, I suppose I can see the appeal. A hoodie over a button-down is uncomfortable, so I grab a vest and head downstairs.

Midnight is in the kitchen, dancing by the door, waiting for someone to notice. This is her way of saying, "I need assistance from someone over a foot tall. Now, will you help me or what?"

I lean against the door frame, watching her run circles around the yard. There was a moment last weekend when Val was here, and the dogs were playing together, that everything felt perfect. The stars aligned, and I found my reason for existing. Then my brother opened the front door, and everything went to shit.

"Come on, let's go! You take any longer, and we'll be eating brunch tomorrow." My shouts out the back door do little to persuade her. Midnight takes her time, sniffing each blade of grass along the fence, testing my patients.

"I'm gonna leave you at home and eat breakfast without you." Still nothing. She seems to be putting her selective bulldog hearing to good use and ignoring me.

"Oh, who's that? I think Christmas is at the front door. Better tell him you don't want to play today." And with that, Midnight comes hauling ass from the back fence, through the kitchen, and straight to the front door, tail wiggling all the way. When she starts whining and looking out the side window, I begin to feel bad for deceiving her.

"I know how you feel, sweet girl. I miss them too."

CHAPTER 13

Val

Tracy has been talking a mile a minute for over an hour, and my brain hurts from trying to process it all. I suppose having her here does make for a nice distraction, and things are finally returning to normal. My only friend is grinding on about some guy, and I'm back to being a listening ear and a shoulder to cry on.

"So, I take it you still haven't heard from him?" The concern in her voice is unnecessary but also unsurprising.

"I'm fine." By this point, I've nearly accepted that the connection wasn't what I made it out to be in my head. Chalk it up to a schoolgirl crush on the sexy rock star and keep it moving.

"Okay, but how do you *really* feel?" Tracy's mouth reiterates the question written across her face as she touches my leg.

"Seriously, I'm fine. Before Thanksgiving, I was cautiously optimistic. I kept thinking he would find the note and reach out, but he didn't. My four-day weekend gave me too much time to think and way too much time to scroll online. When Monday came along, I dove head first into my work during the day, but the evenings were wide open and harder for me to get through. I took a nosedive into my feelings and swallowed my rejection with a few pints of ice cream, but I pushed through and survived to tell the tale." I say this like it's no big deal, jumping straight into over-explanation mode.

"This week, I've officially moved into the acceptance phase."

I'm selling it the best I can. Maybe if I keep saying I'm okay, eventually I will be. I hear myself talking as if I might will the pain to relent with fake stability, but now that the floodgates are open, I can't stop the words from flowing.

"He had to have found the note, right? And he didn't call because he wasn't interested. Five weeks of obsessing over a guy is time enough to realize it's never going to happen. Seriously. I've come to terms with my mistakes, made peace with my demons, and let him go." I lift my glass to cheers with the gods of heartbreak and depression, wishing they would finally come and retrieve me from the agony of this pathetic excuse of a life.

"I was asking about Allen." Tracy suppresses an awkward grin as she takes another sip of her drink.

"Oh." I shake my head, trying to clear my clouded thoughts. "He's reached out a handful of times, but I haven't seen him."

"You haven't seen your boyfriend in two weeks, but you guys didn't break up? And he's still checking in, even though it's obvious that you want to be with someone else. Why not end it and move on? Are you stringing him along because you don't want to be alone, or is he keeping you on the back burner in case you change your mind?"

I don't appreciate her line of questioning, but I hold my tongue and allow her to continue uninterrupted.

"Your relationship with him has never made sense to me, but this seems more complicated than it needs to be. I know you guys were on-again-off-again since the beginning, but why not put a bullet in it and move on?" Tracy begins talking with her hands, and I watch as the waves of mimosa slosh dangerously close to the lip of her glass.

"I would say at this point, whatever Allen and I had has ended, whether we acknowledge it or not. I told him I was in love with Kold while we were having sex. So..." The memory of that afternoon sends a tingle to the one place on my body that doesn't deal in guilt.

"Come again?" Tracy's ears perk and her mood turns on a dime. "You told Allen you were in love with another man. A man he's friends with. While you were naked in bed together, having sex? And you're only telling me about this now? Who are you, and what have you done with my friend?" Thankfully, she sets her drink on the coffee table before bouncing around in her seat like a kid hopped up on cotton candy and Mountain Dew.

I should be mortified. I should be hanging my head in shame, but I can't help but smile. Even if it was Allen in my bed that day, he wasn't the one pushing me over the edge. Kold has my heart, whether he knows it or not. He owns me, body and soul. I'm ruined for all other men except for one.

"It was some role play that got a little too real in the heat of the moment. That's it. I said what I said, and I won't apologize for it. Allen was the one encouraging me to call out another man's name. It's not like I said it out of the blue. If he thought about it later and got mad, that's on him."

"Okay. Well goddamn. I didn't realize my best friend was living in a porno while I was out having the most vanilla sex in the world. Color me surprised, and use green for envy." Tracy reaches across the short distance between us and touches my arm. "I'm going to say something, and I want you to understand that I mean it with all the love in the world. You're being stupid."

"Ouch." I'm not offended by what she says, but I am surprised. She finally gets me smiling and then slaps me with an insult about my intelligence. "And here I thought we were having fun, laughing about my misery."

"Yeah, we are, and that seems kind of ridiculous, doesn't it? Every time I see you, you're wearing his hoodie, like you need that piece of him to get through the day. And if that's how you feel, I get it. I remember what it was like to be so in love with a guy you couldn't think straight. But what's stopping you from getting your shoes on, driving to Kold's house, and telling him how you feel? Why are you wasting time waiting for him to come to you when you're the one who knows where he lives? You just told me Allen is no longer an obstacle, so who's standing in your way now? Stop being miserable for no reason, and go get your guy!"

I take a moment to allow the enormous weight of her words to sink in. Allen wasn't the only obstacle, but he was a convenient excuse for me to hide my heart. I don't want to fall in love. Tracy, of all people, should understand. After all, it was her ex-husband Greg that she couldn't live without, once upon a time. Now, at best, they tolerate each other for Samuel's sake. If Kold is never my boyfriend, then he can't ever be my ex.

"I don't want to embarrass myself." My chest tightens, no longer able to hide behind jokes and false statements.

Tracy lets out an exasperated laugh. "Embarrass yourself? That's what you're worried about?" She gets up from the couch and slips on her shoes. "Three point nine billion men on this planet, and you find the one guy who's meant to be yours. But you're going to lock yourself away in this apartment, miserable and alone, because you're worried that you *might* embarrass yourself!"

"Please don't be angry with me. It's complicated." I hear myself pleading with her to stay, even though part of me is dying to be alone.

"No, Val, it's not. The entire thing is pretty simple once you step out of your own way. You love him. I hear it in every word you say." Tracy flings her words at me from across the room, aiming directly for the heart propped precariously on my sleeve.

"Okay, but what if he doesn't love me back? What then?" My eyes well with tears at the suggestion of his rejection.

"Then, at least you tried. Worst case, he isn't in love with you. But he will be once you spend some more time together. Kold's probably been looking for you this entire time. Maybe he feels rejected and embarrassed too."

"I doubt it!" The muscles in my jaw clench as I straighten my spine. "I doubt he's ever been rejected in his life! Women throw themselves at him."

"Exactly! And how long do you think it'll be until he settles for one of them?" Tracy steps through the door, closing it behind her.

CHAPTER 14

Kold

I'm finishing my last set in the gym when Darc walks in, carrying an unmarked cardboard box and wearing a smile. I'm not sure what he's ordered this time to get himself nearly giddy, but I need to see for myself. I open the top flap and peer inside.

"It's a box of Christmas presents. Are the parents going on a cruise that I don't know about?"

"They're not from Mom. Look at the card." Darc shifts the package so my hand is positioned above a red and green envelope, and I read the simple message handwritten across the front.

Happy Christmas
Love, Val

"She was at the house, and we missed her?" I press the envelope to my nose and inhale, searching for that familiar scent. The honey and almond hand cream is faint but evident. "How is that possible?"

"Midnight was sitting by the front door crying when I got out of the shower. Otherwise, I wouldn't have even looked out there. I'm guessing our girl dropped off the box and left without ringing the doorbell." He sets the box on the bench and starts reading name tags. "Jack Frost, New Year's Eve, and Pitch Black. Okay, that seems pretty straightforward. This one says, Open immediately to Remember Forever. Whatever that means."

"Give it to me!" Taking the gift-wrapped square, I turn it over in my hands. If Val means for me to open this particular gift posthaste, that's exactly what I'll do. Waiting until Christmas morning feels impossible, and anticipation gets the best of me within seconds. "I have to know what it is."

The holiday wrapping falls to the floor as I pause before opening the box. Whatever it is, I already love it. This cardboard treasure chest of presents is enough to renew my lost hope. Val was here, and she hasn't forgotten about us.

Removing the lid, I unfold the tissue paper and laugh. Inside is a folded black t-shirt I recognize immediately. In red lettering across the top is the word Dementor with a Ministry of Magic logo in white. True to her word, Val bought me the shirt she was wearing the night we met and dropped it off this morning.

I'm on such a high that I feel like I'm floating. "She doesn't hate me."

"Obviously. Why would you even waste your time thinking that? You know, we still aren't any closer to finding her." Darc pulls out his phone and starts typing.

"I've tried searching for her online. It's no use." The excitement is still evident in my voice. Nothing will wipe the smile off my face right now, not even reality.

"Yeah, I know. I'm ordering a camera for the doorbell. So the next time Valentine stops by, we can see her coming." Darc slaps me on the arm and picks up the box.

"I need to go out and do some last-minute shopping. If there's any chance I could see Val for the holiday, I want to make sure I have something for her. Maybe I can get her to hate Christmas a little less."

Darc stops dead in his tracks, turning to face me. "What are you talking about? No one hates Christmas. Why would she name her dog after a holiday she hates?"

I shake my head and shrug. "It's a long story. One I haven't heard yet."

"Well, if I'm Pitch Black, then she's the Grinch," Darc says, holding the package meant for him and giving it a shake. "Can't we open them all now? I mean, we're grown-ass adults, and nothing on here says we have to wait."

"We've waited this long. What's another week and a half? Also, consider this your one warning. If you even jokingly call my girl The Grinch on Christmas, you and I will be fighting in the driveway."

"All right, easy there, Jack Frost. I still have time to come up with an acceptable nickname. Now let's go shopping so I can get our girl a more elaborate gift than you do."

"Game on."

My thoughts hop, skip, and jump from one store to the next as I try to imagine the perfect gift. Val has a specific taste, which means there are things I know she'll love, but it might also mean those are items she already owns. I've never been to her place, so I'm going into this gift-giving holiday completely blind.

Last week, when I was neck-deep in my unhealthy obsession and beginning to lose confidence, I made Val a playlist. Fifteen non-traditional love songs to suit her liking and convey my feelings. Buried in the tracklist is a song I wrote and recorded for her. It took me a month to finish, but it had to be flawless.

During my workouts, I listen to her playlist, fiddling with the arrangement, making sure everything is perfect. I picture her safe in my arms, happy and loved. If only I had known that while I was in the gym today, thinking about her, she was standing outside the front door thinking about me.

From the start, Val and I meeting felt like fate, and I've been at a loss the last six and a half weeks, trying to understand how two people destined to be together can remain apart. Perhaps I needed to realize a few things about my life so that I could get my priorities straight and be the man she deserved when our time finally came.

I haven't always been boyfriend material in the past. I'm not exactly terrible or anything, a solid eight and a half out of ten, but still room for improvement. Between work and the band, there's a never-ending supply of temptation lying around. And while I'm not a cheater, the accusations never seem far off once photos of me with other women get posted online.

Darc and I have carved out a pretty nice life for ourselves, thanks to our parents, a black book of under-the-table dealings, a bit of talent, and some good looks. But at what point do we leave the party and settle down? I would never want Val to have any reason to doubt me, and I'm not willing to risk losing her once she's mine.

Val

My heart feels lighter since dropping the wrapped packages off on Kold's front porch on my way to work. Even if I was too much of a chicken to ring the bell and stick around. I'm not entirely ready to face the truth, not when the fantasy is so delicious. Baby steps. The concert is one week away, and I'm going to see him there. Hopefully, in a venue of a couple thousand people, I can disappear into obscurity if he isn't interested.

However, seeing Midnight's adorable face behind the glass was nearly enough to break me. I left with a wave and a promise to bring Christmas for a play date again soon. Maybe that should have been my excuse for stopping by. Or is that weird?

I'm two seconds away from convincing myself to drive back over when I receive a text. My heart flips in my chest as I fumble with my phone. Please let it be Kold.

Allen: I'd like to see you tonight. It's important. Please don't say no. Come to dinner with me so we can talk.

: I thought we were past all of this make-believe bullshit. Stop pretending like you care.

Allen: I was never pretending with you. I do love you. I've been busy as fuck with work, back and forth from one site to another. I haven't been home in weeks. I got back into town this morning.

: I don't feel comfortable being alone with you anymore. But if you're looking for closure, that's all I have to offer.

Allen: Kold will be there with some other people, so you'll have backup. And I promise I'll be on my best behavior.

Allen and I are done. Finished. Kaput. Story over, close the book and put down the pen. I have zero interest in listening to any more of his half-truths and excuses. The only reason I'm leaving this house tonight is because the undisputed love of my life will be there, and I can't pass up an opportunity to see him. This is my punishment for not ringing the doorbell.

Being at Kold's house, standing at the front door alone, was too much pressure, and I cracked. However, I can assess the situation in a restaurant without fully serving myself up on a silver platter. The fact that he's willing to show up at all means he wasn't creeped out by the gifts. So, that's a plus.

: Fine. What time and where? Who else is coming?

Allen: I'll pick you up in an hour. Thanks for doing this, baby. I can't wait to see you.

"Okay, first things first." I grab the leash by the door and take Christmas out for a quick run around the side yard. When five minutes begin to feel like an hour, I drag him back inside. My usual routine will need to happen in overdrive if I want to walk out the door looking good enough to catch the eye of a man who could have any woman in the room. I'm going to need makeup, a miracle, and a goddamn fairy godmother.

"No," I say aloud to the reflection in the mirror. "Selling myself short ends here and now. I deserve to be happy."

I couldn't agree more.

"Why shouldn't I be with him? I have as much to offer as anyone else."

Maybe even more. All you lack is confidence.

"I'm confident he's the one."

Then, give him a chance to prove himself. Go get your guy, and while you're at it, get the other one for me.

"Deal."

I wink back at my reflection and laugh at the ridiculousness of it all. Having one of them for a night seems an impossible feat. Wanting both is greedy, and I love it. My body tingles at the thought of their hands on me, but there's not enough time for a release.

I check my phone every few minutes as the seconds race in time with my heart. Tonight is the night I tell Kold what I want, for better or for worse.

CHAPTER 15
Kold

And with that, I have officially finished the last movie on Val's list. This week has been especially busy, between my job, band practice, workouts, and near-constant obsessing over the girl of my dreams. Despite the lingering high from receiving an early Christmas present, I'm physically and mentally exhausted. At this point, I'm almost looking forward to a quiet night alone.

"There's only one person who could get me out of the house," I say, giving Midnight a scratch along the length of her back. "But that feels like a long shot."

When my phone lights up on the nightstand, I nearly throw myself off the bed, reaching for it.

> Allen: Anything going on tonight? I need to get
> out of the house.

He keeps talking to me like we're friends, which we're not. Everything about him, I find incredibly off-putting. However, he could ask me to be the best man at his wedding, and I'd agree if it meant seeing Val. Of course, in that hypothetical situation, he'd need to be marrying someone other than *my* girl. Otherwise, objections would be raised.

My heartbeat quickens at the thought of seeing her in a white dress, gliding towards me down a flower-lined aisle, escorted by a monochrome pair of ring-bearing dogs. This week, I've found myself playing out every possible scenario of our life together, but this is the first time I've imagined our wedding. When exactly did I turn into some sappy oversized teddy bear? What the fuck is wrong with me?

Back to the annoyance at hand. Maybe he wants to go out and drown his sorrows after breaking up with my future wife. If nothing else, maybe I could steal her number out of his phone.

: What did you have in mind?

Allen: Double date? I'm sure you've got a few on the back burner.

: You must have me confused with my brother.

Allen: No worries.

How the hell am I supposed to respond to that? Is he saying, bring a companion or don't come at all? Now, I have to hire an escort to be my fake date for the evening so I can flirt with the woman I'm obsessively in love with while she sits beside her boyfriend. This shit is getting out of hand. I have to find some way to talk to Val without him around. I need a phone number, address, social media handle, gamer tag, something, anything. Christ!

: I'm sure I could find someone to bring with me, if necessary.

Allen: Perfect. How about we meet for dinner tonight at the hibachi place around 7?

: Wasabi?

Allen: That's the one.

: See you then.

This guy is so transparent that he might as well be made of glass. Allen wants me to break her heart, and that isn't going to happen. Is he planning to get up and make her leave if I show up without a date? Or does he think I'll play along because he told me to? Allen doesn't know me like he thinks he does, and he doesn't seem to be paying attention. This works in my favor on both counts.

My contact list is full of women I could ask to be my pretend date for the night, but there's no way I would disrespect Val and risk upsetting her, even if I could explain it later. It's time to stop playing nice and get the job done.

: You're coming out with me tonight. I need a date.

Evil Twin: Hope you're taking me someplace nice.

: We're getting our girl.

Evil Twin: Well, Hello Dolly! It's about time.

Val

My hands are shaking so badly that I'm about to lose an eye with this mascara. For weeks, I've been dodging Allen's calls and delaying my responses to his text messages, having fully accepted that things were over. And now this. The only reason I didn't tell him to fuck off tonight was because he dangled the golden carrot in front of my face. But this is the night everything changes. No more excuses. I'm dressed and ready to go, looking about as good as I can make myself without a filter, and I'm going to tell Kold how I feel even if I have to shout it across the table.

Allen sent a text while I was in the shower informing me that dinner is at 7:00, so we have an hour to talk over drinks before anyone else arrives. I've already changed my outfit a dozen times, curled my hair, fixed my face, and tried to breathe through the anxiety. But my heart is in my throat, and I can't get to the restaurant soon enough.

> Allen: I'm here. Unlock the door so I can come up.

During the entire span of our relationship, Allen put forth a bare minimum effort. I would ask him to park and come in, but he couldn't be bothered. And now that I've stopped begging for his attention, he blows up my phone with, "*Baby, I love you. Baby,*

I miss holding you. Baby, I can't live without you." More bullshit lies from the snake oil peddler, and I'm done buying it.

I can't even be bothered to care anymore. I'm not sure why I ever did. Even if it means I'm alone, so be it. I refuse to continue going through the motions with a guy I can't stand while my heart beats for another. And even though I don't think Allen gives a single fuck about me, it's unfair to string him along.

Regardless of what happens with Kold, Allen and I are finished. I can't allow him to drag me back in. Not this time.

"It's over, and I'm done," I say to myself as I kneel to kiss Christmas on the top of the head. "We deserve better, don't we, buddy?"

Christmas looks up at me, waiting for a string of words he knows, but I have nothing further to offer. This next part of the evening, I have to do by myself.

The weather has finally begun to turn, so I grab a warm coat and head out the door. For a minute, I think about wearing Kold's grey hoodie, but I want to look sexy, not obsessed.

Allen and I meet in the hallway near the elevator. "Wow. You look beautiful," he says, leaning in to kiss me.

I turn in time to give him a cheek and step through the still-open metal door. All I have to do is get through drinks. Then, the chips can fall where they may.

Tracy and Samuel are about to walk in as Allen and I are headed out, so I swing open the door and tussle the boy's hair. "Hey, little man, if you aren't too busy tonight, maybe you and your mom could check on Christmas for me. There may or may not be an entire container of cookies on the counter baked fresh today."

I look up at Tracy's face for approval and realize she's angry. Like tears in her eyes, about to stab me in the chest, angry.

"Sorry." I mouth, suddenly feeling uncomfortable. "On second thought, buddy, don't worry about it."

Allen tugs at my arm, offering me an excuse to walk away. I hate to leave my friend standing there upset, but clearly, a larger conversation needs to take place away from Samuel's listening ears. I wonder what happened. Tracy was so excited when she got my message about the early morning Christmas delivery I made to Kold's house that she responded in all capital letters. And then, when I saw her a minute ago, she looked pissed off and ready to punch someone in the throat.

I can't worry about it now. Whatever's going on in her life, she'll have to tell me later. This night requires my full attention to avoid messing everything up for a third time.

"I like your coat. Is it new?" I say, settling into my seat. Allen isn't a bad-looking guy, and he knows how to put together an outfit. However, he isn't good-looking enough to be as arrogant as he is. And once you factor in personality, he's about as ugly as they come. I don't know. Maybe some women enjoy being lied to. If that's the case, he needs to find one of them and lose my number.

"Yeah, I bought it while I was in Chicago, and I was hoping you might like it. You were on my mind the entire time I was away. I'm sorry, baby. I should have flown you out for the long weekend. I could have taken you shopping and spoiled you." He reaches over, trapping a lock of my hair between his fingers. "You know how much I enjoy taking care of you."

"Why are you doing this?" I sit frozen in place as I contemplate jumping out at the next light.

"I like it when you curl your hair for me. It makes you look more refined." His compliments are still laced with insults.

"Thanks." I roll my eyes and push his hand away, leaning closer to the door. "Are you going to tell me where we're going and who we're meeting? Or is it a surprise?" He has been intentionally cagey with the details all evening. He mentioned Kold by name but kept saying *they* and dodging my questions. So, it's a group of people, or Kold is bringing his dog to dinner. In which case, I'm about to be upset I left Christmas at home, alone, with the TV.

"I can't remember her name, and Kold didn't say it. When he asked me if I wanted to get dinner, he suggested making it a double date. Said he wanted to bring his girlfriend along. Thought you'd enjoy meeting her. Now you won't feel like the odd man out, being the only girl in the conversation." His words strike like daggers into my chest.

His girlfriend? Yeah, that makes sense. I wrote my number inside the Christmas card in case he hadn't found the slip of paper in his hoodie, and I was surprised he hadn't texted me. As it turns out, there's nothing surprising about it. I'm such an idiot. He's probably bringing his girlfriend, so I know to stop showing up at his house.

"Oh, that's cool. Have they been dating long?" I try to keep my voice steady, but it's proving difficult. Thankfully, it's dark, and Allen's eyes are focused on the road. Makes it easier to hide my emotional disembowelment.

"Pretty sure they've been together off and on since high school. I never met her during the band days. Think she was still in college at the time, getting her Master's. But I do remember seeing photos, and she's gorgeous. They look perfect together, and he seems happy. I'm glad they found their way back to one another and rekindled the romance."

"Everyone deserves to be happy," I say, feeling broken.

Especially him.

Allen drops me off at the door as a text comes in on my phone.

> Tracy: We need to talk.

Walking into the crowded restaurant alone, I take a moment to dry my face, fix my makeup, and pull my hair up into a nest on the top of my head before sliding into an open bar stool.

"Three olives cherry vodka, and Redbull. Make it a double, please, and keep 'em coming. I appreciate it." My credit card is already on the counter when I order, so the bartender knows it's that kind of night. All he has to do is keep my glass full, and he can be my new best friend.

> : It's not a good time, but I promise we'll get together tomorrow. I'm sorry I couldn't stick around to talk.

I hit send, silence my phone, and slip it into my back pocket. As much as I love my heart-to-heart talks with Tracy, my shattered ego can only handle so much, and Kold has yet to show up with his perfect girlfriend. I can't risk my emotions getting the best of me because I'm upset about every man I've ever met. If I talk to Tracy now, I might say something I don't mean, and when tomorrow comes, I'm going to need a friend. So, she's a bridge I would prefer to remain unburned.

By the time Allen locates me, the bartender is back with my drink. At this point, my fake date is irrelevant. I'm going to drink myself into oblivion and choke on the truth I can no longer say aloud. My relationship with Allen is over. Fine. Good. About damn time. But I can't tell Kold how I feel. It would be unfair of me to say something stupid and ruin his *happily ever after*. If I'm destined to be miserable and alone, so be it, but that doesn't mean everyone else has to join me.

In my twenties, I was quite the party girl, known to overindulge. But the day my mom told me she was sick, everything changed. She wanted me to focus less on the present and more on the future, so I did. We had some good years and some bad years, and then she was gone. But that drunk little demon inside me never died. She was hibernating. And now, she's thirsty.

Between rounds, I check my watch as the numbers blur together. I don't know how many drinks I've had at this point, but they keep tasting better and better. I want to go to sleep dreaming of his face and never wake up.

CHAPTER 16

Kold

Before running down the stairs to meet Darc, I throw on the black hoodie that used to smell like Val. The one from the bed that has felt like her ghost sleeping next to me. This is the first time I've worn it since she left it behind, and I'm hoping that if I show up with it on, she'll be reminded of the night we met.

Upon arriving at the front door, I smash my hands into the front pocket, bracing for the wind. There's a chill in the air tonight. It's the first hint that autumn days are about to turn into winter nights, and I intend to spend those nights with my girl in front of the fireplace. I need her in my arms. Val is my first, last, and only chance at living a full life, and I can't afford to let her slip through my fingers again.

"Are you fucking kidding me?" Exasperation laces with elation. Pulling a scrap of paper from the pocket and holding it up to the light, I can't help but shake my head. "Her goddamn phone number was in my bed this whole time!"

A smile stretches across Darc's face as he holds out his hand. I can almost feel his ambition. The chase is on, and this is not a race either of us aims to lose. "Give me your keys, and I'll drive. Text her now! Let her know we're coming to get her."

I sprint to the SUV and throw myself into the passenger seat. Typing her number into my phone, I try to think. We'll be at the restaurant in fifteen minutes, but I know Darc is right. I need to

109

text her now. Val is precious to me in a way that I can not describe. She is essential. Her happiness is my happiness, and I'm willing to give her anything.

My thumbs type out the words faster than my brain can process its racing thoughts. It's time for me to take a risk and say what I should have said on Halloween.

> : I'm an idiot! But I'm hoping you can overlook that fact and hear me out. I finally found your phone number in the hoodie. If it's too late, you can tell me. Otherwise, I'm coming to get you. And I'm not leaving until you know how I feel about you.

Staring at the phone, we arrive at the restaurant with my text still unread. I should have known. Val is the type of girl who gives people her undivided attention. She wouldn't allow herself to be distracted while on a date with her boyfriend.

A boyfriend who's about to disappear.

Walking into the restaurant, I'm not the least bit surprised when women break their necks to steal a look in our direction. People tend to notice us wherever we go, but I'm not here for them and don't care what they think.

The look on Allen's face, when he catches our twin reflections in the mirror behind the bar, is priceless. He turns to look at us, and he's pissed. I love it. My girl, however, is a different story. She looks droopy, like a flower in need of water.

I shoot across the room with hurried steps and steady myself by her side. "Val, look at me. Are you okay?" I place my hand on her shoulder and move in closer. The energy she's giving off is unmistakable, and I need to repair whatever damage has been done before she shatters and disappears, but she won't even look at me.

Her head hangs to the side like it's too heavy for her neck to support, and she keeps staring at her half-empty glass, wiping beads of condensation from the side. I slip the beverage from her fingers and drain what remains. When the bartender promptly arrives with a refill, I take the drink from his hand and swallow it in three gulps.

"She'll have water from here on out. And if you serve her one more drink, I will get you fired." My tone reinforces the seriousness of my words, so there's no confusion.

Finally, Val turns her head to look at me, tears pooling in her eyes. She isn't drunk, merely deflated. Taking a deep breath, she fills her chest with air and brings herself back to size. It's as though she's slipped back into her armor and prepared herself to face the enemy.

Am I the villain in Val's story?

She steadies herself against the bar and turns in her chair, arm outstretched, but stops short when her eyes land on my lesser half. "Oh! You're not the person I was expecting." Her hand falls with a half-hearted laugh, but Darc catches it and presses it to his lips.

"It's nice to see you again, Valentine. I'm sorry we were never properly introduced. My name is Darc, with a C instead of a K. Consider me, fully and unquestionably, at your service." He tops it off with a wink. Darc is laying it on thick to distract Allen, giving him a new target.

"Let's go! We're leaving! You're so drunk, you're probably seeing double." Allen reaches for Val's arm, but she pulls away.

"Well, I have two guns." She says in a distinct cadence as she motions to the pair of us. I recognize the line immediately and nearly quote the rest along with her. "One for each of you."

Darc and I look at each other and erupt in twin laughter. This girl is amazing, and I'm about to make her mine.

"What the hell are you even talking about?" Allen seems to be getting angrier by the second, clearly the odd man out. He isn't in on the joke.

Allen doesn't understand her references and isn't capable of complimenting her humor because he's only pretending to like what she likes and know what she knows. When it comes time to deliver, he's lost.

"Val Kilmer! Tombstone! In Vino Veritas." She lifts her hands in an exasperated motion. "Seriously? Nothing?"

He attempts to grab her arm again, but I'm faster than he is. I pull Val from the side of the chair and press her against my chest. "Touch her, and I'll break your arm."

This time, I will protect her. This girl is a treasure. She's the crown jewel. No. She's more than that. She's the meaning behind the crown, that which gives it significance. Without her, the kingdom falls.

"Who the hell do you think you are?" Allen delivers the words with as much false bravado as he can muster, but even someone with his arrogance knows when they're defeated.

"Oh, Allen. Don't play stupid." Darc and I take half a step forward, shielding Val from harm but not blocking her from view. "You know exactly who *we* are."

Val

The vodka fuels my rage, burning off my buzz as the loudest voice in my head fights to come out. If I relinquish control, she will tear Allen to shreds. Which I long for as much as she does. But I can't risk losing my restraint in front of them. Our twins won't stick around for long if Valentine is the one sorting out the current situation.

"You lied to hurt me, didn't you? You knew how I felt, and you used it against me. Why couldn't you leave me alone?" My voice rises as I run through my list of questions, daring him to lie to me one last time.

Allen ignores me as if I'm not even there. Only I am there, and the other two men, standing in a flanked position at my side, have no trouble acknowledging my existence. They remain stone silent as the three of us await Allen's response.

"Even though you've been hell-bent on overlooking me the last few weeks, I thought I'd be nice and give you exactly what you wanted. Honestly, you should be thanking me instead of standing there with that ungrateful look on your face. Now you get to fuck 'em both."

Allen's words resonate as both men drag him through the restaurant and out the front door. Once they pass through the glass entry, the entire restaurant looks in my direction. Panic wells inside me as I nervously tap my credit card against the top of the bar.

"Can I please clear the tab?" My hand trembles as the bartender snickers, returning seconds later with my card and the receipt. I tack a $20 tip onto the $80 tab and scratch my signature onto the paper before making a beeline for the side door. I'm nearly through the patio gate when someone grabs me from behind.

"Running out on the bill, huh? Ballsy move." His arms halt my forward progress while his words extinguish every trace of my previous anger.

I spin on my heels, distressed and desperate to explain myself. I wasn't running away from the bill or him, even though it might appear that way. I needed air and space and a fucking second to think without everyone judging me.

"I wasn't. I swear I paid for everything. Everyone was looking at me." My voice cracks as I melt into his arms. "I completely embarrassed myself in public."

In public is what I say, but I'm mortified that I caused a scene in front of him and his brother. As much as I thought I wanted to nail shut the coffin of my previous relationship, I wasn't interested in having it play out in front of a bar full of strangers.

"It's okay. I can fix this. We'll stop at an ATM and I'll cover whatever bar tab he stuck you with. Then, we'll take you wherever you want to go, and I'll make sure you're safe. Allen is an asshole, and he's the one who should be embarrassed. You know you can trust me. Right? You didn't do anything wrong." Kold lifts my chin and penetrates my soul with his gaze. "If it makes you feel any better, every woman in that restaurant wishes she was you."

"Why? Because you're so unbelievably attractive?" I speak without reservation.

This is the first time Kold and I have truly been alone. The patio is empty this time of year. No crowd of people looking on with sideways glances. No Allen standing in the background, threatening to ruin everything. It's Kold and I and no one else.

"Nah, my brother's the devilishly handsome one that women

fall all over themselves to get to." Kold moves his arms across my back, pulling me into his chest.

I can't tell if he's being serious or making a joke, which makes me laugh harder.

"You look the exact same."

CHAPTER 17

Kold

She feels at home, laughing in my arms like she was always meant to be there. For the longest time, I thought Darc was my other half, being made from the same stuff and all. But right now, with Val pressed tightly to my chest, I feel whole for the first time. And when she kisses me, my fate is sealed.

Val lifts on tiptoes and rests her arms atop my shoulders as her hand rubs the back of my head. Even here, in our first kiss, she's meeting me halfway. Something about this moment feels like a metaphor for the future we're meant to have, or maybe I'm still dreaming.

I twine my fingers into her hair, unraveling the strands of her messy bun, as my tongue plays at the opening of her lips. Her kiss is sweetened with vodka and Red Bull, and I want to drink her dry. Without thinking, I press my erection into her as she lets out the most delectable moan.

"Do you have any idea how many times I've thought about kissing you? How badly I've wanted you?" There's so much I need to tell her, but this is only the beginning. Words could never do my feelings justice. I'll have to show her and pray she feels the same way.

"I'm starting to get the idea. But we can't do it here."

She pulls the rubber band from what's left of her bun and allows the thick waves to fall freely around her shoulders. Then she takes my hand and rubs it across her lips, down the curve of her neck, and between her breasts, guiding me straight down the front of her jeans. "I need you inside me."

Her verbal confirmation is all I need to make my move. I grab her ass, lift her off the ground, and head straight for the backseat of my SUV with her legs wrapped around my waist. Once inside, I lock the doors and pull her onto my lap. "I don't wanna stop, but I will if you ask me to."

"Please don't." She moans against my neck while unzipping my pants. "Don't ever stop."

We both fumble to remove our pants before settling back into position. With one final kiss, she slides down the length of my swollen appendage, taking me inside.

"Goddamn, you look good sitting on my cock. I wanted to do this with you on Halloween." I kiss through her shirt, teasing the parts of her that remain covered. "Would you have let me?"

"Yes." Her breathy whisper sends shock waves through my skin as I rock her hips back and forth.

I thrust, burying myself as deeply as possible while pulling her body closer. If she's going to take me, then she will have all of me. I'm no longer willing to deny my desires or her wishes.

"You deserve so much more than I can give you right now. I need you in my bed tonight and tomorrow and the day after that." I'm doing everything I can to hold back, but the more she squeezes, the closer I come to exploding. "Fuck! You're gonna get me off already. You need to slow down."

Her hips move faster as she arches her body back, using the gap between the front seats to modify her position. "Stop holding back. I want to feel you cum for me."

Her request breaks my resolve, and I release everything I have inside her. On the final thrust, I pull her forward and growl into the side of her neck. "I need you to be mine."

With my body shaking and my cock still twitching inside her, I feel exposed in a way I've never experienced before. Here I am, secretly hoping I impregnated a girl, and I don't even know how she feels about me.

Val leaves a breathless kiss on my jaw before leaning back to meet my eyes. Tucking her fingers into the neck of my hoodie, she comes forward to kiss me but stops short of my lips. Then whispers sweetly. "I've been yours from the start."

Val

Hot holy hell! Did I actually do that? I detach myself from Kold and begin searching for my jeans. "I need to find my phone."

"Val, stop for one second and look at me." The deep timbre of Kold's voice fills the dimly lit space between us. "Did I do something wrong?"

I shake my head no, unable to commit my response to words. This man has no idea what he does to me. I could listen to him say my name for the rest of my life, but right now, I don't want him to see me. Not the way he's looking at me as if my secrets are on full display. If I don't leave soon, I never will. The moment I looked into his eyes, I knew. The way he talks about tomorrow, he means forever.

"Let me text my brother and tell him we're leaving. I'll take you home if that's what you want."

"No. Please don't. I'll find a ride. It's no big deal. Stay out and have fun. Forget you ever met me." I'm not sure why I said that last bit. I imagine I'm offering him a way out without complications or excuses. We can chalk this up to a drunken one-night stand and go our separate ways, even though he's probably sober.

My insecurities are about to ruin the best thing that's ever happened to me, all because I'm afraid that forever might last one night at worst and six months at best. Or maybe I'm afraid everyone who came before him was right about me, and I'll never be enough. Meaningless sex is always a good time, so long as you leave before the rejection comes.

"You don't mean that." He picks up my phone from the seat and hands it to me. "I only came here to see you. So, if you're leaving, I have no reason to stay."

I light up my phone and read the text I missed earlier as an amused smile spreads across one side of my face. "You seriously never thought to check the pocket?"

"I've been looking for you everywhere." He grips my waist and pulls me closer. "Had I known the key to finding you was reserving your place in my bed, I would have reached out a hell of a lot sooner."

I want to kiss him and never stop, but having sex has shaken my insides, and I don't trust my stomach to hold onto its contents. "Would it be okay if we went back inside, real quick? You can find your brother while I grab my coat from the bar and use the restroom."

"Whatever you need. But tell me something before you walk away. Are we good?"

"Yeah, of course. I think you and I are great." And with that, I can feel an hour's worth of self-induced poison about to come spilling out. I'm not going to make it anywhere near a toilet. I'll be lucky if I make it out of the backseat of his car.

Thankfully, I'm able to hide in front of his SUV before losing my dignity all over the parking lot. Kold slips the rubber band from my wrist and pulls back my hair while I continue to heave. This is the most embarrassing thing that's ever happened to me, and that's saying a lot. So much for looking sexy and making the best impression possible.

Kold leaves momentarily and returns with a napkin and a bottle of water.

"You really know how to hurt a guy." His joke is meant to defuse any of my hurt feelings. "I've had women complain about my performance before, but this is next level."

"I find that entirely inconceivable." I swish another gulp of water in my mouth before spitting it onto the pavement. Can I possibly embarrass myself any more tonight? I don't think so. I might as well post my concert ticket for sale online because, after tonight, he's never going to want to see me again.

Kold leads me over to the side of the vehicle and presses me against the door. I'm caught off guard when he kisses me, and my knees nearly buckle. He doesn't hold back, so neither do I. Everything about him feels too good to be true, and it's too late for second-guessing. I'm in love with him, and there's no going back. This night has been a roller coaster of emotions, and it's not even eight o'clock.

I feel myself melting into him, wanting more than is legally allowed in public.

"I think I'm okay to leave now," I whisper into his chest, still searching for sure footing on unstable ground. "If you don't mind giving me a ride."

He sends a quick text and slips the phone back into his pocket. "Darc has your jacket, and he's good to take us to your place. Then you can change into something comfortable, and we can go from there."

"Us? That's quite presumptuous of you." I let my face fall away into shadow in case the street light threatens to reveal how flush my cheeks are.

"Val. I'm not leaving you alone. You're far too important to me." His hands cup my face, lifting it to meet his. Kold pauses to gauge my reaction before continuing. "You don't have to invite me in if you don't want to, but I will be there to walk you to your door. I'm going to pet that adorable dog of yours, and then I'm going to beg you not to kick me out. If you let me stay, I'm willing to sleep on the couch."

I don't know how to convey the warring thoughts in my mind. I want to invite him in, but I'm scared. I want to keep him, but I don't know how. I was with Allen because I never wanted to fall in love again, and now here I am, drowning in it.

"You can come over under one condition." I reach for his hand, braid our fingers together, and squeeze. "You're never sleeping on the couch alone if there's a bed we can sleep in together."

CHAPTER 18

Kold

The ride to Val's apartment passes in blissful silence.

After giving Darc the address, she promptly curled up on my lap in the backseat and closed her eyes. I've been playing with her hair and watching her sleep for the last ten minutes, making peace with my place in the world.

So, this is what real pleasure feels like.

The extended quiet offers me an opportunity to slow down and reflect on the series of events that landed us here. In my excitement, relieved to finally have Val in my arms, I forget to consider the toll this evening must have taken on her. Whatever happened with Allen before our arrival seems to have exhausted her emotionally. And then I walked in, cocksure and ready to go, carrying her off to the backseat of my car like some teenager, absorbing what remained of her physical reserves.

My girl is drained, and I'm partially to blame. The more I pour over the details, the more guilt I feel. Normally, I have a strict policy about sexual interactions and inebriation. The policy being, I don't fuck drunk girls.

Taking Val in the backseat and finishing in under five minutes was not by design. I've had months to pour over the details. Planning out cute dates and romantic, candle-lit evenings. More than anything, I want to make sure she feels seen and heard. I want her to think of me as someone she could build a life with, not some guy you screw around with and throw away.

"Am I dropping you both off, or…" The second half of Darc's question remains unsaid.

The last month and a half have felt like an eternity, always waiting for some unknown date when I might get the chance to see her again and having zero control over the planning. Allen outdid himself this time, fucking with the hearts and minds of those around him. I wasn't expecting to be included among the victims of his manipulations, but I'm glad he thought of me first. As much as I hate him, he's the reason I found Val, and I don't want to go back to the life I had before she was in it.

"You can drop us off. I'll call you if anything changes."

My voice is enough to rouse my sleeping beauty, and she sits up, taking in our location.

"I feel rude if I don't invite you both in, but if I'm being honest, I'm in no fit state for entertaining. Rain check?" She sets her hand on Darc's shoulder with such tenderness that, for a moment, I feel a twinge of jealousy. "I promise I'll make a better impression the next time you see me."

"You, my dear, have made a lasting impression, and I wouldn't change a thing. I look forward to seeing you tomorrow at break-fast. But if you need me before then, for any reason, don't hesitate to reach out."

Val's phone lights up as she accepts the airdrop request. Right in front of me, after everything that's happened, my brother is not only trying to charm the pants off my girl, he's going so far as to embed himself in her contact list.

Note to self: Thirty-five years with an evil twin brother is long enough.

"Let Midnight out when you get home, and let her sleep in the bed with you. Otherwise, she'll be up all night looking for me." I open the door and slide out, offering Val a hand. Her soft, confident touch sends an electrical current from the tips of our fingertips to the base of my groin.

"You two have fun. I'll be at home cuddling with the dog," Darc's snarky tone makes me grin as the door closes.

I smile as he drives off, knowing he'll be grumbling under his breath the entire way home. Not that he'd ever get any sympathy from me. If he had a mind to, my brother could make one phone call and have a girl naked in his bed before the hour was up. He's not hurting for playmates. What he lacks is a connection. Until now, I don't think he minded, but something in us has changed since Val stepped into the picture.

"Sounds like my kind of night. Not sure what he's complaining about." The sugary sweetness in her voice makes it impossible to keep my hands to myself.

I spin Val around, catching her in my arms. Her head falls to the side, leaving her neck on full display. She's giving me an open invitation and pointing me in her chosen direction, and I'm nothing if not accommodating. It's not for me to deny the needs of my queen.

I kiss the base of her neck, moving slightly to caress her again. "I'm going to kiss you once for each time I've thought about you over the last forty-seven days." My lips brush against her skin, planting a row of kisses along the length of her neck. "But it's going to take me all night, and I'm going to need you out of these clothes."

The electric lock on the building door clicks, and she pulls me inside. Leading the way, Val escorts me down the hall and into the stairwell, where she stops and turns, standing one step higher than I am. Face to face, I'm in awe of her beauty.

"This is the one place I can kiss you without you looking down on me." Her eyes give away the fact that she's only half joking.

"I'm guessing you haven't noticed the pedestal I've got you on. But there will be no more talk of me or anyone else looking down on you. Not tonight, or ever. Are we clear?"

I seal my vow with a kiss and silently dedicate my remaining years to her every happiness. Val doesn't know it yet, but I will give her the world even if I'm not the one she wants.

"I can feel you overthinking things. Maybe if I brush my teeth, it'll help." She says with a laugh, pulling me up the remaining stairs and onto the floor I'm assuming is hers. When we stop in front of 202, she turns to face me. Only something has changed. "If at any point you wanna leave, I can take you home. Don't feel like you're stuck here with me."

By the end, her voice is so quiet I can barely make out the words.

"Do you think I'm being dishonest when I flirt with you?" My question comes out more forcefully than I intend. "Because I'm not in the habit of lying to the people I care about."

It's interesting watching the two halves of Val's consciousness grapple for control. One minute she's this confident woman with a devil-may-care attitude who wants to get fucked in a parking lot, and the next, she's this sweet little girl who doesn't want to hurt anyone's feelings. At this point, I want to fuck them both and call it a night.

"I don't think you're a liar, but I do think you're a lot like me. You want people to feel important when they're with you. Like they're the center of everything."

It's easy to forget that Val doesn't know me in this lifetime. She hasn't met the man I was forced to be until now. For her safety, I hope she never picks up a shovel and begins digging through the dirt for details. The man she'd find buried beneath boxed corpses could never deserve the life she has to offer.

"That guy you're talking about. The one you see when you look at me. He only exists for you."

Val

I'm still thinking about the words we've shared since entering the building as I watch Kold roll around on the floor, laughing until he's red in the face. Christmas is attacking him with puppy kisses, in a scene that would make even the Grinch's heart grow.

Allen wouldn't so much as pet Christmas, let alone wrestle with him on the floor. If I hadn't insisted on taking him to brunch with me every Sunday, there's a good chance my ex might not have ever met my furry soulmate.

Begrudgingly, I walk away from the lively display unfolding on the living room floor, but only because I need to brush my teeth and change out of these clothes sooner rather than later.

"Do you want me to take my new friend for a walk while you get changed into something I'm going to enjoy stripping you out of when I get back?" Kold shouts from the other room as I dig through my dresser for something casual yet sexy.

"Has this whole night been some clever ruse so you can steal my dog?" My question is meant in jest. I don't expect him to respond, but when he does, it comes in the form of arms around my waist and his breath in my ear.

"It's your heart I'm interested in stealing."

"Ha! That broken down 'ol hunk of junk, you can have. My dog, on the other hand, is worth more than all the gold."

"All right, that's the last one you get for the night." He says, kissing the top of my head. "No more disparaging comments about yourself in part or whole until tomorrow."

"It was meant to be a joke." Even though I know it wasn't.

"Irregardless. I'm gonna take the dog for a quick stroll in the grass, and when I get back, I want you on the couch, under a blanket, waiting for me, ready to watch a movie. Deal?"

"Yes, sir," I say with a smile. From my thoughts to god's ears, nothing is sexier than a man who knows what he wants. I can only hope he's this assertive in the bedroom, as well. When I scoot past to get into the bathroom, he grabs the back of my neck and smacks my ass.

"Good girl."

Now, when I tell you I've had an array of sexual experiences in my day, quite a few stemming from my time away at college, I fully mean to imply that I was a bit of a whore. But not in the derogatory way that men insinuate when they're angry at you for shooting them down. And not in the way the dictionary would describe it since I certainly never got paid for my good time. I mean to say, when presented with an opportunity, there was a 99.9% chance I would end the night on my knees begging, "Please, sir. May I have another?"

Allen had only recently stumbled upon that side of me, but he wouldn't have known what to do with her had *she* come out to play for real. I'm not always a submissive, although that is the role I frequently find pleasure in. Sometimes, with the right person, I crave control.

Similar to the duality within me, the man currently consuming my fantasy also comes in good and evil. The only difference is that his opposite sides reside in two physical bodies.

Give a girl the world, and she'll still ask for more.

I finish brushing my teeth and take a long look in the mirror.

"Stop doing this!"

I'm not doing anything, babygirl. You're the one in control.

"You're trying to make everything about sex so it doesn't hurt when he leaves, but it doesn't have to be one or the other. I want to love him and please him."

No one's stopping you. I see you, and so does he. The man has been counting the days since he met you. So, either he really enjoys doing mental math, or he's as obsessed as you are. Now get your cute ass out there, and do what you were told.

I'm on the couch and under a blanket when Kold comes in carrying Christmas. He's quickly making this apartment feel like home in a way it never has.

"Little man and I have officially bonded, and he's given me the go-ahead to date his mom. So, that's settled." Kold unhooks the leash and hangs it on the peg by the door before setting Christmas on the couch beside me. "Now I need to hear it from you."

You know how there are two kinds of people in the world, those who feed your soul and those who feast upon it? Well, Kold is the kind of guy who nourishes the soul, and everything he's offering is delicious.

"Take off your clothes, slowly, and look at me when you do it." I'm not asking, and this isn't up for debate. Kold is either the sort of guy who plays along, or he's wasting my time. Either way, I'd rather find out before I'm fully invested.

Too many times, I've gone into situations judging people on their potential instead of grading them on the faces they chose to wear. Look deep enough, and you can find the layers, but don't ignore what's right in front of you. My ex-husband was deceptively endearing until he wasn't. Red flags by the millions, the facade crumbled shortly after the marriage, and I think we were both keenly aware of the mistake. Only I didn't quit, and I didn't cheat. I didn't throw away everything and then lie about the reason. I didn't destroy him, rather than own up to my infidelity. I could have forgiven the sex. The part that broke my spirit was all the goddamn lies.

Kold starts by removing the black hoodie, revealing a gray t-shirt underneath. The fabric hugs his arms and chest, hinting at the impressively sculpted body beneath. I've seen him with his shirt off before, but the image playing out in front of me is enough to get my heart pounding and my panties soaked.

He takes his time, giving me what asked for while teasing in a way that has me ready to beg for more. Once freed from his shirt, he drops it on the floor with a playful grin.

Sitting on the edge of the armrest, he slowly removes one sock and drops it in the pile of discarded clothing. Then removes the other, never breaking eye contact. I wouldn't have considered socks or feet erotic before tonight, but Kold makes sure each part of this strip tease is a show. Finally, he stands and unhooks his belt.

It takes every ounce of my self-control to remain seated. I want so badly to be the one unzipping his pants. Sliding them down his muscular thighs until they find a new home on the floor. It should be my hands brushing against the front of his boxer briefs, accidentally on purpose.

"Do you want these on or off?" The tips of his fingers play at the waistband of all that remains.

"What I want is for you to start paying up on all of those kisses you owe me."

My teeth bite into my bottom lip as I allow the blanket to fall aside, revealing the form-fitting sheer tank top and matching panties I chose for tonight's ensemble.

The low moan reverberating from his chest is all it takes to break me. I lunge forward, reaching for him, but he catches my arms and pulls me from the couch.

"I'm going to make you cum with my tongue, and then I am going to fuck you. Is that what you want?" His gravelly sex voice has me purring.

"Yes," I say, feeling the warmth between my thighs spreading.

"Then get in the bedroom, and stop acting like you're in control."

CHAPTER 19

Kold

Who knew the love of my life would be hiding in the body of a kinky little sex kitten? I half expected to find restraints on the four corners of the bed, unlocked and at the ready. She's primed and very much willing, but do I risk spoiling the mood by telling her I came here for more than her body? I suppose we could always talk after.

Teasing her when she's already so close to the edge is an exquisite form of torture. One I intend to inflict mercilessly. I play through the invisible fabric barrier before pushing it to the side, diving head-first into the center of her pleasure.

Having her trembling beneath me and hearing the soft whimpers as they escape past her lips invites the inner animal out for supper. Even as she arches her back and screams for me to stop, *he* continues. With my tongue and lips glazed in her sweetness, Val is the one thing I will never grow tired of tasting.

"I need you to stop. Before I disappear."

Now, what kind of monster would I be if I denied a request as cute as that? I stand at the edge of the bed to remove my boxer briefs and use the swatch of cotton to quickly dry my face. She's gone and made a mess of me, and we're only getting started.

"Are you finished for the night?" My need to fuck her only matters if she is prepared to be an enthusiastic recipient. I will play the dominant and pretend to hold control because it pleases her. However, she is the one who ultimately has the final say.

"No. I can keep going. I want you to get off in whatever manner you prefer." Her voice sends a quiver of desire through my body.

"So be it! Roll over, put your hands above your head, and lock your ankles together."

Kneeling over her with her wrists locked in one hand, I guide the head of my cock past her swollen lips and slide myself inside, allowing her time to adjust. Despite how wet she is, in this position, she's squeezing down on me like a vice.

"Goddamn, you're fucking tight! I'm not out to hurt you, babygirl, but I am going to fuck you really, really hard. If it gets to be too much, you need to tell me."

"I understand."

With her pussy constricted and her body willing beneath me, I doubt this is going to take long. Hopefully, the round we went in the car will extend my performance. Otherwise, I fear I might embarrass myself. Figures, the one day I don't jerk off in the shower thinking about her is the day I finally get to bury myself inside her.

Please, lord, let seven minutes feel like half an hour.

I turn off my brain and get to work, pounding her into the mattress. Forcing her to take every inch of what I have to offer. Pinning the length of her body with my own. This is what she wants from me, to be taken care of sexually, and then what? Are we finished once I am?

She must sense my shift in mindset because her body makes an effort to redirect my attention back to the action. Squeezing her thighs together and clenching down on me, Val has me about to blow past any and every internal distraction.

"Show me how much you love me." Her words are a breathy invitation to succumb. And succumb, I do. "Please, Kold. I need to know."

I blow a phalanx of tiny soldiers inside her, like cannon fire, before crumpling down on the bed at her side. Rubbing my fingertips over the tattoos on her back, I attempt to catch my breath. I want to make her cum again, but I'm not sure I'll get the chance.

"Thank you." She says, stretching her neck out to kiss me, and then she's gone.

Seconds later, I hear the shower turn on and debate my next move. Do I give her a moment to herself, or does she want me to join? The thought of holding a freshly cleansed version of the woman I love while I'm still a sweaty, sticky, defiled mess doesn't sit right with me. So, I decide to join her.

If my presence in the shower is unwelcome, she certainly makes no indication. Her arms come up around my neck, and she's on her toes to kiss me. Not forcefully or even playfully, but a mix of gentle passion. The kind of kiss that conveys feelings beyond those of a one-night stand.

"Do you mind if we skip the movie and stay in bed? I'd rather talk. Maybe fall asleep in your arms. Unless you're headed out?" With her overconfidence exhausted, Val's more timid side seems back in control.

"I'm here as long as you'll have me." These words are a promise I intend to keep. Leaving her now, after everything that's happened, is inconceivable. Thankfully, it's the weekend, so we have time to spend together uninterrupted by the day-to-day of our 9-5s.

Her response comes in the form of a single kiss, and I love her all the more for it.

Val

I grab a clean set of sheets from the closet and the oversized sweats I recently bought for lounging. "Here, you can wear these," I say, tossing the bottoms to Kold, whose current wardrobe consists of a wet towel.

What is it about a guy in grey sweatpants and nothing else that's so sexy? Is it the fact that he's exposed, but only slightly? Comfortable, but still making an effort? Or is it because you can see the outline of his dick in a way that teases the taste buds? Whatever it is, Kold looks delectable, and I want to keep him.

Peeling off the sheets still damp with sweat, I pile them on the floor and begin remaking the bed. Hopefully, fresh linens will mean a clean slate and a new start. Or maybe it's too late for that. I don't regret having sex with Kold since that was going to happen one way or another, but perhaps I should have slowed things down a smidge. I need to give him a reason to stick around past the morning.

I'm on the last corner when his arms catch me from behind. In the past, physical touch from a man has been nothing more than a means to an end. But the way Kold touches me, he isn't looking to get off. He's trying to connect. I lean back into his embrace, allowing it to consume me.

"Would you believe me if I told you I've thought about you nonstop since the night we first met?" His tempo mirrors the swaying of our bodies in time together, like cradling palms in a tropical midnight breeze.

"I've been thinking about you too." For a half second, I considered deflecting with a joke and responding with an *I'm sorry,* but I figured, with him, maybe it's safe to be honest.

We finish making the bed together and cuddle up under the comforter. Alternating between spooning and facing each other, our conversation picks up right where it left off. After imagining him next to me for so many nights, having him in my bed feels like a dream. And a part of me wonders if it might always feel that way.

The tips of his fingers trace over invisible patterns on my arm as we speak, and the sound of his voice in a set played only for me, is my new favorite album. "I know it's short notice, and I realize you might have other plans for the holiday, but if you aren't doing anything next week Saturday, would you be interested in going to a concert with me?"

It's adorable the way he asks the question as if it isn't his band headlining the show.

"I would love to, really I would, but I'm already going out on Christmas Eve. My friend's band is playing a show at Club After Darc, and I'm trying to be supportive of his musical aspirations."

His eyes narrow as he studies my face.

"I can't tell if you're messing with me or not. I'm mentally running through the list of guys I know in the other bands, trying to sort out who you could be talking about before I respond. Please tell me you're joking." The look on his face is a mix of tortured optimism and uncertainty.

"I'm joking with you. Obviously! I'm going out that night to see *your* band. I bought a ticket after we met, in case it was my only opportunity to run into you again. At the time, I didn't know how else to find you." I reach across the six inches of space separating us and press the palm of my hand against his chest. "Since then, the days have felt like a countdown to Christmas Eve."

"Babe, those tickets were over $100, and that's if you got one before it sold out. Why didn't you ask me to put you on the list?"

"Well, for one, I didn't know that was an option. And for two, I would've spent ten times that, so long as it meant seeing you again." I scoot my body closer until we're nearly touching. "There's nothing special to me about money. I can go to work on Monday and make more. That being said, I'd love to go to the show with you. Or I can meet you there. Whatever works, I guess. I know you'll be busy, and I don't want to be in the way. I'm more than happy to fan-girl out in the audience and leave you to do your thing."

"Sell your ticket and come with me as my guest. I'm certain we can upgrade you to our VIP package since you're such a valued and loyal customer." The muscles in his arms tighten, pulling me into his chest.

"That sounds like a line you guys use at the club to pick up women. In which case, I think I'll hang onto my ticket and view the show the old-fashioned way."

I don't know why I'm getting in my head about this and picking a fight over nothing, but I need to give it a rest. Especially since I made a joke about going to the show to see a different guy's band, and he played along. Kold is being cute with me, and I'm jumping into my negative feelings like they're my safe space. I need to stop with the push and pull before I push so hard that he doesn't bother to come back.

My inability to accept his offer slapped the playful smile from his face, and I need to correct my mistake while there's still time. "Okay, wait. Before you respond, let me take a second to rephrase. I appreciate what you're offering, and I would love to spend any amount of time with you that I can. But I would also like to use the ticket I paid for, for sentimental reasons. It's important to me."

"I appreciate your rewrite. Thank you." He leans in for a quick kiss. "And I'm sorry if I implied something I didn't intend."

"No. You're fine. I love the way you joke and play with me. Please don't ever stop. That was just some of my insecurity coming out, trying to ruin a perfectly lovely evening. In the past, I've walked away from my relationships feeling like I was never good enough to be permanent. My exes made it clear that I was there for a good time, not a long time, and I'm pretty sure I've been cheated on by every guy I've ever dated. As a result, if I find myself in competition with another woman for a guy's attention, I tend to concede and walk away relatively quickly."

"Fuck, not me. I was willing to fight Allen to the death for you."

I laugh before leaning in to kiss him. The more we talk, the more I realize I don't have to use jokes and sarcasm to deflect my feelings. Kold values my honesty, and he's willing to hear me out. He isn't half listening, simply waiting for his turn to talk. Kold is actively engaged in the conversation, as though he hangs on my every word. It's different from what I'm used to, but a welcome change.

"A part of me would've liked to see that." I pull back, looking into his eyes. "Hey, Kold."

"Yes, dear." I feel like he knows what's coming and isn't the least bit bothered.

"I love you." The words roll off the tip of my tongue, and I'm ninety-seven percent certain that it's way too early to admit feeling the way I do, but I've already held it in longer than I thought possible.

"Say it again."

"I love you," My voice barely above a whisper. "I do. I love you. I know it's ridiculous, and you don't have to say it back, but I needed you to know."

"Are you kidding? Babe, I've been dying to say that shit to you all night. I nearly blurted it out while we were having sex. Both times."

"Well, it doesn't count if you say it for the first time during sex."

"Good to know. Honestly, if I weren't afraid of scaring you off, I'd ask you to spend the rest of your life with me."

My body stiffens in his arms, and I feel myself about to shut down.

Not now. Please don't do this.

"Judging by your reaction, I fucked up, and that was the wrong thing to say."

"No. I'm sorry. You didn't fuck up," I say, attempting to reassure him and myself. Taking a deep breath, I can see him waiting for the *but*.

We pass the minutes in silence until my thoughts go cloudy, and I forget why we stopped talking. He keeps smiling and playing with my hair, putting me into a trance-like state. His touch feels like paradise.

When I finally speak again, my voice sounds like it's coming from far away, as if I'm on the verge of sleep.

"Maybe I should've waited to tell you how I was feeling. Those words carry a great deal of weight when spoken properly, and we haven't spent much time together. Don't get me wrong. I'm not looking for a take-back. I meant what I said, but I don't want to race to finish. I want this to last as long as possible. Can we just enjoy our time together and see where it goes?"

"Absolutely."

We share a kiss before I roll over in his arms and sink back into him. I drift closer to the edge of sleep, secure in his embrace. Clearly, I'm already dreaming when I hear Kold's words carried on the backs of butterfly wings.

"Hey, Val. Just so it doesn't go unsaid. I love you too."

CHAPTER 20

Kold

I'm so used to waking up early that my body won't allow me to sleep in, despite my comfort. Most days, I'm at work before 8:00 and home by 3:00. Then I work out for an hour or two, get cleaned up, make dinner, and fall asleep halfway through a movie. Of course, all that sounds pretty standard. If I didn't have to factor in tours with the band, photo shoots, traveling, making and uploading content, and the occasional nighttime outing for family business, I could be any old nobody.

Val is still in bed, sleeping peacefully, soI take the dog out and text my brother. I'm not sure I could get used to apartment living, but I could easily grow accustomed to the role of a devoted husband and doting father. All I have to do now is convince my girl that I'm worth the risk. Easy enough if she doesn't look too deeply past the surface.

As I'm coming back in with Christmas, I hear a distraught woman shouting and banging on one of the doors on the second floor. Someone must have thoroughly messed up last night because this woman sounds pissed, and I can't wait to sneak a peek on my way back to the apartment. Except, when I get to the second floor, I'm shocked to see the angry stranger standing outside 202, screaming and hitting the door.

"GET YOUR ASS OUT HERE AND FACE ME! I KNOW YOU'RE IN THERE!"

Christmas tucks himself behind me as I walk toward the apartment door. In all the commotion she's making, the woman doesn't hear me approaching, and I catch her off guard.

"Excuse me. Is there something I can help you with?" I ask in the nicest way I can.

"Oh! Um. No. I don't think so." Her voice trembles with nervousness, like a child caught in the middle of doing something they shouldn't have been.

"I think you might be knocking on the wrong door."

"I most certainly am not! I know exactly who lives here, and I saw her with my boyfriend. Then she turned off her phone and spent the night having sex with him. Some friend." By the end of her rant, she sounds sad rather than angry.

"Look, I don't know you. But I can assure you, I've been the only man in that apartment with her all night. So, whoever your boyfriend is, he didn't sleep here."

"You're lying." She says, but the shaking in her voice highlights her uncertainty. "I saw her leaving with him."

"Is it possible they were walking out of the building at the same time, and you simply mistook the situation for something else?"

"No! I watched her get into his jeep, and they rode off together." Her voice sounds hollow, like she's far away and reliving the details still vivid in her memories.

"Are you talking about her ex, Allen? Yeah, he picked her up and drove her to the restaurant, but then he took off." The woman looks confused by my words. "He's not in there. Like I said, I've been with her all night."

I'm not sure what else to say at this point. Reaching past the woman, I turn the knob and step through, giving her a half smile before closing the door in her face. I can hear Val in the shower singing, nearly drowned out by the music. Guess that explains how she missed all the excitement.

I make sure to lock the doorknob and the deadbolt before stripping out of my clothes, turning down the music, and joining Val in the shower. The idea of telling her about the strange woman at the door is in the front of my mind until I see her naked. Then, all I can think about is touching her.

Taking the loofah from her hand, I wash her shoulders and back before moving down to her ass. It doesn't take long before my dick is hard, and I have her pressed into the wall, kissing her neck.

"Do you see what you do to me?" I push my erection against her soft flesh so she can feel how hard she makes me. "This is all for you, anytime you want it."

"I want it now." She says, dropping to her knees and taking me into her mouth. Her hand works the base of the shaft while her mouth takes care of the rest.

Looking down, watching her take the length of me like a seasoned pro, makes me harder still. "Goddamn, you're so fucking good at that. I don't care what you say. I'm wifing you up as soon as possible." My fingers knot into the hair at the back of her head as my hips thrust forward.

This woman is about to swallow our potential family if she doesn't ease up.

"Val, get up! I need to fuck you."

Like a good girl, she stands, leans forward, and spreads her legs, using the wall for support. But there's no time for playful praise. I'm on the verge of exploding and need to be inside her. I guide the head of my cock into her opening and push myself inside, feeling her squeeze against me.

"I need to slow down, or that tight little pussy is gonna make me cum." I grab onto her hips, but there's no stopping her. She works me over until I can no longer hold back. Squeezing her hips tighter, I thrust into her as hard as I can, over and over, until she's crying out my name.

"Mmmm! Kold, I can't take much more."

I turn off the shower and grab a towel from the hook.

"Let's go to the bed." My words are half question, half command. I'm too out of breath to play the dominant convincingly, so I don't bother to try.

Lying on the bed, I motion for her to get on top of me. This is the way I want to finish, looking into her eyes. And I'm so close. When she leans forward to kiss me, I wrap my arms across her back and drive my hips up, resulting in the final blow.

"Fuck! You're beautiful."

The full weight of her frame collapses onto me with a breathy laugh. "You're too much."

"Am I?" I ask, suddenly self-conscious and still trying to catch my breath.

"No. Not really. The audio is my favorite part, so keep doing what you're doing. It's sexy."

Moving to lay beside me, Val begins touching herself. "Are you offended if I take care of myself? You have me right on the edge."

"By all means. Would you like some assistance with that?" I tease the inside of her thigh with my fingertips and begin kissing her breast.

"Keep doing that. I'm so close for you." Her eyes close, and her head drops to one side while her hand methodically circles her clit.

Watching her, I feel like I'm getting a master class on *how to properly satisfy a woman*. It's incredibly sexy and informative. I make a mental note to save the image of her in my mind for later, in case I should ever find myself horny and alone for the evening.

"Do you want to make me happy?"

Despite how much I enjoy watching, my dick is still hard, and I need to be inside her. I know she's close, so I stand and wrap my hands around her ankles, pulling until her ass reaches the edge of the bed.

"More than anything." She gasps, returning to rubbing her clit.

I lift her pussy to align with my swollen cock and push inside. "Then be a good girl and hold your breath while I count down from five. And when I get to zero, I want to feel you cum all over me."

"Five."

Val nods in agreement, sucks in a steady breath, and closes her eyes.

"Four."

Holding onto her hips, I pound into her repeatedly with

uninhibited force, causing her to grip and twist her free hand into the sheets.

"Three."

Her fingers circle faster against her clit as she tightens around me.

"Two."

The rose of her cheeks spreads as her body begs for new air.

"One."

Driven to the point of orgasm, Val's stomach convulses wildly until her pleasure is exhausted and her body begins to twitch and relax.

She lies still for a moment, and then sits up to kiss me. "Thank you."

"For what? I should be the one thanking you."

This woman blew my mind, in more ways than one, and she's expressing her gratitude toward me. It doesn't make sense. How can one person be so incredible, and how is it that she's mine? She can't be real.

I'm about to drop to my knees and worship at her feet when my phone goes off on the nightstand.

> Evil Twin: Your ride is here, and I brought you clean clothes.

"Tell your brother I'm unlocking the door so he can get in."

"Val, wait." I motion for her to stop, but it's too late. She slides the bar on her phone that unlocks the outside door. Maybe I'll get lucky, and he's still parking the car.

Before I can retrieve my pants from the bathroom and slip them on, Darc is at the door to the apartment that Val is answering wearing only her robe.

"Looks like I came at a good time." He toys, eyeing the pair of us.

"Sorry. You missed all the fun. Maybe next time." Val jokes before walking away. "Make yourself at home while I get dressed."

"I'm taking that as an official invitation, Valentine." He calls after her.

"No. You aren't! Now give me my clothes before I forget

you're my favorite brother and kill you." I take the bag from his hand and join Val in the bedroom, where she's already half-dressed.

"Hurry up, you two. My date is in the car, waiting."

Val

The only one waiting in the car when we get to the parking lot is Midnight. Her paws pitter-pat against the door as she watches out the window, overcome with emotion. Once she sees Kold and Christmas, she begins howling and whining, eager to play. Kold gets Christmas into the back before opening the passenger door and telling me to hop in.

"I'll sit in the back with the kids and make sure they behave." He kisses me with such passion that it makes my toes curl.

Kold certainly seems to know what he's doing. Tens across the board from the American judge.

On the way to the restaurant, I catch myself staring at Darc as he drives, studying his facial expression. It's uncanny how identical the two brothers are. I thought for sure I would have an easier time telling them apart, but with clothes on, I'm certain they could switch places without me catching the change. Something I'm sure they've done in the past.

"Do you see something you like, sweetheart? Or is it the novelty of having both of us at once the concept that appeals to you?" Darc's confident and cocky tone gives him away.

"I'd be lying if I said I hadn't considered it." Maybe I should lie, or bite my tongue to keep from speaking. I can't imagine Kold is interested in hearing this conversation play out any further. And as if on cue.

"Take your seat belt off and get your ass back here right now!" The voice coming from the backseat is firm and direct.

I do as I'm told, climbing over the center console between the seats, and land in the back with a thud. The dogs bark excitedly at my arrival before disappearing into the now-empty passenger seat.

Kold gets up on one knee and presses me against the window. His mouth is an inch from my ear when he whispers, "Have I not been taking care of you in the bedroom?"

"You have." I keep my voice low before biting my bottom lip.

"Then why are you playing games with him? I'm more than happy to satisfy your needs at any time. In every way possible. All you have to do is ask."

"Be careful. Or I'll make you prove it." My heart bangs wildly against my ribs as I toy with the man who's taken over my fantasies. A small part of me is afraid I've pissed him off, and the rest of me is certain I've turned him on.

"I would happily prove it to you right here and now. But if I make you cum in front of him, he'll never stop pursuing you. Is that what you want, babygirl? You want to see which of us can fuck you the hardest?"

Oh my god, yes. Yes! A thousand times, yes.

That's what I'm thinking, but I don't dare say it.

There's playing with fire for fun. And then there's dousing yourself in flames and burning the world to ash. I need to put down the lighter fluid and rein it in before I wake up in a hotel room with my future ex and his soon-to-be-dead brother.

"You're already more than I can handle. If you fuck me any harder than you did last night, you'll break me." My whispered admission might not be the truth he's seeking, but it's a truth nonetheless.

Kold licks up the side of my neck, sending a shiver through my body. "Hmm. Maybe I should. Or would you rather I let someone else do it?"

"I'm sorry I said what I did. I only want it to be you." I seal my agreement with a kiss, which quickly evolves into making out.

Before I know it, we're pulling into the restaurant parking lot, and I'm hotter than a cat on a tin roof. In theory, having them both is fun until jealousy is considered. No sense in creating issues where there needn't be any.

"We're here. And for the record, I hate you both. I'm taking your Christmas presents back after we eat." Darc's annoyance is comical for some reason, though I know he doesn't mean it to be.

Kold and I look at each other and laugh, but my joy is short-lived when I see the scowl on Darc's face. Immediately, I remove the smile from my lips and drop my eyes toward the pavement. If Kold's twin brother decides he hates me, this relationship will be over before it even has a chance to begin.

Grabbing Christmas, I hurry towards the restaurant, eager to disappear. It feels strange to be at Valentine's on a Saturday instead of my usual Sunday. Once inside, I notice that my regular table is empty and head straight for it. Christmas and I grab our spot in the corner and wait for the guys to join us.

"Excuse me, miss. I believe you're sitting in my seat." Kold teases, taking the chair next to me.

"I doubt it. This is my seat, thank you very much. I sit here every Sunday for brunch." My retort is delivered in pretend defiance.

"Every Sunday, huh? Well, I sit in that chair every Saturday, so today is technically my day."

I stand and motion for him to take the seat. "My apologies, sir. How exactly do you get away with sitting at this table? I thought it was reserved for family. Dear god, you aren't related to Conrad, are you?"

My heart jumps into my throat, and I feel like I'm about to throw up. If Kold tells me Conrad is his uncle, or worse, his father, I will drown myself in the lake. I never thought to ask if I had additional family in the area, and Conrad never offered much regarding personal information about the past. He told me once. "Best to leave it buried." To which I responded, "Like Mom." And that was our first and only conversation about life before my move to Ohio.

"Conrad is like family, but we aren't blood-related if that's what you're asking," Darc responds, eyeing me suspiciously. "Why? Are *you* related to Conrad?"

"Not in any way I own up to!" I turn back to Kold, who's petting the dogs. "I should've brought something to change into if we're going to have a movie marathon. Why didn't you remind me?"

He leans forward, placing his elbows on the table. "Because I want to see you in my clothes or nothing for the rest of the weekend."

I swallow hard, thinking about the possible situations ahead of me. Am I willingly walking into the lion's den with only a fifteen-pound puppy to protect me? Even his loyalty appears questionable at the moment. The second Kold walked into the apartment, my dog took one look at him and said, "Mom, who?"

Kold takes my hand and presses it to his lips. "Naked is preferred."

When Conrad comes out carrying two cups of coffee, he looks at me and stammers. "Val, I didn't see you there. Are you staying and eating?"

"Looks like it," I say, my hand resting atop the table, fingers woven into Kold's.

As I study the older man's face, it's easy to see how uncomfortable he looks. Whenever Allen came in with me, Conrad always wore the same judgmental grimace, but this is something else. He appears concerned instead of disapproving, though I can't be bothered to care about his reason.

"Can I talk to you in my office for a moment?" His eyes dart from one brother to the next. "It'll only take a minute."

"I'm good," I say, narrowing my glare.

"It's important!"

Whatever he has to say, I'm not interested. This conversation might as well end now before it even begins. If Conrad wanted to have a say in my dating life, maybe he should've stuck around. When I respond, my tone is cold and unforgiving. This is the last thing I will say on the matter, and I will hear nothing further.

"Best to leave it buried."

CHAPTER 21

Kold

After our conversation in the car, Val stopped talking to Darc altogether. She barely said two words at breakfast unless directly spoken to and opted to sit in the backseat on the ride to the house. Her silence wasn't what I had intended when I asked her to stop playing games. I don't want Val to feel like she can't be herself around us, and I'm afraid that's what I might have implied. When it comes to my brother, it's a no-win situation. If she's playful, Darc will keep seeing how far he can push her, but if she ignores him outright, he'll hunt her to the ends of the Earth.

My brother enjoys the chase more than I do. Most girls are easy, and he loses interest before they can finish finding their clothes. But I get the feeling that something about this girl is different, even for him. If I want him to stop flirting with Val, I'll have to be the one to put my foot down.

I'll let it play out for now and see what happens. Before my earlier comment, she seemed to be enjoying the idea of having us both, and if that's the case, it's a wish easily granted. I'm willing to give her anything. All she needs to do is ask.

Standing in my bedroom, I watch her from the corner of my eye as my mind wanders. Val is in the bathroom, with the door open, changing into a pair of sweats and a t-shirt so that we can spend the rest of the day cuddled together in bed. The first Alien movie is queued and at the ready, and the bedroom door is locked. All I need now is my favorite girl in my arms. Then I can die happy.

When given a choice between the living room and the bedroom, Val elected to have our movie marathon in the bedroom so we could be alone. I can't say I'm disappointed. Even the dogs are peacefully sharing Midnight's bed, each chewing on a bone from the basket of toys.

Looking adorable in my clothes, Val walks toward the bed. She has to hold the waistband of her borrowed sweats to keep them from falling off, adding another layer to the cuteness of the moment. However, as lovely as she looks, all I can think about is how badly I want to take the outfit off of her. Maybe I should have given her a t-shirt to borrow and nothing else.

Since we've each seen this particular cinematic masterpiece no less than a dozen times, we decided to open the floor to comments, dialogue, and jokes instead of the standard watching in silence. Sort of like our own Mystery Science Theater, except we'll be watching good movies.

Laying in front of me, ready to cover her eyes for the scary parts, my girl is perfection. She fits against the front of my body as though we were crafted to be part of a matching set, and the conversation flows with the ease of decades. We talk and joke like a couple who's been together for years instead of people who are still getting to know one another. It's strange in a comfortable way, or maybe comfortable in a strange way. Either way you want to think of it, I know I've found my person, and I'm happy to finally have her all to myself.

"Um, did you want to pause the movie and address this situation, or am I supposed to ignore it?" Val laughs, scooting back into my semi-erect penis. "Because I'm happy to do whatever. Seeing Sigourney Weaver in that tiny tank top and panties is sort of doing it for me too."

"You're hilarious," I say, raising my hand to cup her breast. "I can't help it if having your sexy little body pressed against me gets my dick hard, and I won't apologize for it." I should probably be embarrassed, but the more she teases me, the more I want to fuck her clear into tomorrow.

"Nor should you apologize." She rubs her ass against me, making me harder still. "I like that you get turned on by me. It's flattering."

With my arms across her chest, I pull her closer. Don't get me wrong. I want to have sex. Clearly. But I also want to spend time not having sex. Too often, my relationships have been solely about physical pleasure or monetary gain, leading them toward a swift conclusion.

Since high school, sex has been easy to come by. As a senior, Darc got a blowjob from our math teacher in exchange for a passing grade. I studied and got a B. After college, we started making some real money of our own, giving the women another reason to pursue us. My surface-level relationships have always felt transactional, and in most cases, that's because they were.

With Val, it's different. Sure, we're having sex, and I'm dying to spoil her rotten, but I get the feeling she intends to stay by my side no matter what. Money or no money. Val is more interested in my other slightly atrophied assets. She's in love with my humor and my caring nature. The sides of my personality that usually only Midnight gets to see are the characteristics my girlfriend places with the highest value. Val is the first woman to spend more time looking at my eyes than my abs, and both times I insisted on refunding the money she spent on drinks or a concert ticket, she graciously refused to accept my offer.

"I want to take you on a proper date. Anywhere you want. Name it, and I'll make the reservation." I can appreciate that Val isn't looking for me to prove my feelings with money, but it's kind of the only thing I know how to do.

"I don't need you to blow your savings on me. My attention and affection aren't priced by the hour. Being here with you, watching a movie, and sharing a few laughs, this is the best date I've had in a long time. Why can't we normalize free dates?" She says, without a hint of humor. Val is serious and wants her words to be taken that way.

"We can have all the free dates you want, but there are also places I'd like to take you that cost money. So, how about a compromise? I'll give you all the free dates you want if you join me on two paid outings a month. It can be anything: movie, concert, mini golf, bowling, batting cages, rock climbing, ax throwing, dinner, luxury vacation... What's the best first date you've ever been on?"

"Oddly enough, I've been on a plethora of good first dates, but those evenings didn't result in a relationship or even a second date. So, I'm not sure spending money is the same as making an effort. I'm more interested in an investment of time than I am in money."

"Fair enough. I hear you loud and clear, and I intend to invest as much time and effort into you as you'll allow. But for now, indulge me and tell me about the best first date you've ever been on, and don't fudge the details trying to spare my feelings. I can handle it." At least, I think I can handle it. I do my best to sound confident, but the more I think about Val with another guy, the more I wish I had access to a time machine.

"Fine," she says with a laugh. "If you want to know, I'll tell you, but you're the one who brought it up. I didn't choose the topic of conversation, so you can't hold my answer against me after the fact." She shifts her position in my arms so that we're facing one another and begins her story with a kiss.

"Understood. For the record, I would never do that to you."

"Okay. So, one of my favorite dates happened about five or six years ago when I was living in Indiana. I met a guy online, you know, as people do, and we exchanged messages. He asked me to go to dinner, and I agreed to meet him at the restaurant. Figured that was safer than having him know where I lived. We met at a Chinese restaurant I frequented and had a nice meal. When the check came, he asked what I wanted to do next. Said he was having a great time and wasn't ready for the night to end. Suggestions were made on both sides, but somehow, we settled on taking a spur-of-the-moment road trip to Michigan to go to the casino in Detroit."

I want to interrupt because I have questions. So many questions. But I don't want to ruin the moment by seeming judgmental. When I remain calm, quietly waiting for the rest, Val continues.

"He followed me to my house so I could drop off my car and pack a quick overnight bag. Then we started driving. I had known the guy for less than two hours and had agreed to leave the state with him. Of course, things could have gone horribly wrong. I know that. I would ground my future daughter for a lifetime if she were ever so reckless with her life, but back then, I didn't care enough about myself to worry." For a moment, Val sounds distant, like she's fallen back into a mindset she worked hard to forget.

"You don't have to tell me the rest if you don't want to. I expected your best first date would be a happy memory, but maybe I was wrong to assume that." I'm starting to feel bad for bringing it up. Sometimes, I forget that Val and I don't fully know each other. We're only beginning to scratch the surface of the thirty-five years worth of joy and pain that made us who we are today.

"I'm fine. It is a happy memory. For a second, it just reminded me of something else... So, I was responsible for our driving playlist and directions, and he was in charge of getting us there in one piece. We did amazingly on our assigned tasks and got to the casino ready to have fun. I remember taking $200 out of the ATM and not giving a single fuck if I lost it all, which thinking about now, seems ridiculous and gives me anxiety. But that's neither here nor there. At the time when this happened, I was much more liberal with my safety and my finances."

As she talks, an image forms in my mind. Val, smiling and happy, standing on the floor of a casino. Surrounded by the flashing neon lights of a thousand slot machines, she draws my undivided attention the way no one else could. I wonder what it might have been like to know her when she was younger and carefree. The Val lying in my arms is incredible, and she maintains full ownership of my heart, but I'm curious to find out what prompted her changing priorities. Was it the knowledge and maturity that comes to us all with age, or something else?

"So, you know how some guys like to show off, pretending to know everything? Well, this guy was one of those show-off types. He was trying to impress me by playing poker and lost all of his money in five minutes, turning a fun evening into a bit of a downer. The more I won playing slots, the worse his mood got, so I suggested leaving."

"Okay, so then what happened? Did he give you the silent treatment the whole way home?" I can tell she's leaving something out.

"We didn't drive home until the morning."

"So, you got a hotel room and spent the rest of the night in bed together?" I can feel the jealousy rising in me, even though I promised I wouldn't get upset. The idea of another man touching her, using her, disrespecting her makes me sick.

"Let's just say the evening ended on what I thought was a high note. In the morning, he drove me home, told me he had an amazing time, said he would call me later, and kissed me goodbye. That was it. End of date. He left and I never heard from him again."

"Babe, that guy was an idiot who got in his feelings about losing money he probably couldn't afford to spend, and he let that cloud his opinion. That was a flaw in him, not you. Unfortunately, some people are like that, but you can't take it personally."

"Sure. I mean, it was a long time ago. I don't even recall the guy's name. I just remember having a great time and then feeling rejected. It was confusing. I couldn't understand what men were looking for. If a guy had a good enough time to continue the evening and was attracted enough to sleep with me, why wasn't that worth enough to warrant a second date? As a man, I need you to make it make sense."

"I can't answer for that clown. Had you gone to that casino with me, you would have heard from me. I would've called you on my drive home simply to hear your voice, and I would've made plans to see you again that night. Some guys don't know a good thing when they have it. That's why they're cheating on the woman they've got or crying about being alone."

"Have you ever cheated on someone you were dating?" Her eyes narrow as she studies my face.

"I've never gone out of my way to cheat on someone, but I can think of one instance where the girl I was dating cheated on me, and I found out. The relationship was clearly over but not officially ended. I went out and made myself feel better by accepting the advances of another girl. Looking back, I know it was a stupid decision. So, I guess technically, I cheated, but I didn't think of it that way at the time." Watching Val's expression closely, I can tell she's making a concerted effort not to react. I attempt to reassure her, but the damage is done.

"You know I would never be unfaithful to you, right?" The last thing I want is to paint myself as a cheater, especially after she confided in me about her past. I already know Allen was unfaithful the entire time they were together, but I don't have the heart to tell her.

"The only thing that tells is time. So, maybe we'll find out, or maybe we won't." Val rolls over and practically throws herself off the bed before I have time to react. "I'm gonna take the dogs out, and then maybe I should get going. Don't want to overstay my welcome."

She scoops up Christmas off the dog bed and is out the door, with Midnight following close behind. What the hell happened? One minute, we're staring into each other's eyes, having a pleasant conversation, and the next, she's running out the door, talking about leaving altogether.

I get up and head downstairs, where Val is leaning against the wall near the back door. She's not crying, but it's obvious she's upset and avoids making direct eye contact when I approach.

"I really don't want you to leave. Can we talk about it?"

"You know I have to go home eventually, right? At some point, you have to be willing to say goodbye." Her words are a realization I'm not ready to face.

"But does it have to be right this second? Can't we slow things down? I'm not interested in racing to the finish with you. I want this to last."

"Using my own words against me, huh? How's that working out for you?"

"What?"

"Being clever."

For a second, I'm confused about what she means until I recall a similar exchange of lines in Fight Club, movie number seven on her top ten list. The two sides of Val, yet again at war, fighting for control of her mouth. I'm starting to see the deeper meaning behind some of the movies on her list, and I wonder if Val has a side hustle making soap.

"Please stay with me until Monday morning. We can go back to your place if you would rather, or we can stay here. The location doesn't matter so long as you're next to me. Please don't ask me to let you go. I'm not ready." For the first time in my life, I feel like I'm begging a woman to love me, even though she was the one who said it first. "Give me a chance to prove that I'm willing to put in the effort you deserve."

"And what if, after all of that, I never hear from you again?"

Now, it makes sense. Val isn't afraid of being with me, and she isn't upset about any shared information from the past. She's worried that regardless of how much fun we have together, how good things feel, or how many times I say I want it to last, once we part ways, she'll never hear from me again. And she doesn't want to invest her weekend or her heart into someone temporary.

The multiple first dates, full of potential, that ended where they began have her questioning my intentions to the point where she's willing to walk away rather than risk being rejected.

"I don't know how to convince you with words because the men who came before me fucked up your ability to trust. They said things they couldn't stand behind, and I'm sorry they didn't respect you the way they should have. I'm sorry they didn't love you how you deserve to be loved. But I'm not them, and I'm not going anywhere. If you let me love you, I can back up my words with a lifetime of actions. So, stop trying to push me away because it isn't going to work."

Before Val can say something she doesn't mean, I push her against the wall and kiss her neck. The way her body welds to mine whenever my lips contact her skin tells me everything I need to know. As much as she might try to build impenetrable walls, this woman is as much in love with me as I am with her. Deny as she may, her body gives her away.

If I have to prove myself, so be it. I was going to do that anyway.

Val

We're about three-quarters of the way through the second movie when I allow my body to give in to the overwhelming desire my mind has been attempting to hold at bay. Kold's teasing touch has broken down my defenses one layer at a time until I no longer have it in me to fight. Everything with him is a losing battle. He sees past all the bullshit and continues to look straight into the heart of who I am. Fully accepting the woman I keep locked away for safekeeping.

When his hand slips past the waistband of my pants and brushes over the soft skin between my thighs, I stop attempting to watch the movie.

"Why are you doing this to me?" My words are a breathy plea, begging for my surrender.

"Because for two months, I could only dream about touching you, and now that I have you in my bed, I can't get enough. Do you want me to stop?" His fingers tease at the gates, awaiting an invitation for entry.

"No. I want you to show me some of the things you were dreaming about." As much as I'm attempting to protect my heart from the inevitable downward spiral that will follow the end of this relationship, I know I can't deny him. Loving Kold might be my death, but it shall be a glorious demise.

I pull off my shirt and pants, leaving myself on full display. No sense in playing coy. I want him inside of me, and I'm not wasting another second on silly self-doubts.

He's quick to join me in baring flesh, no longer existing behind a barrier of clothes. Our hands move over muscle and sexually appealing pillows of fat, exploring one another with fingertips and palms. Mapping out all the places our lips will soon follow.

This dance we've been rehearsing gets better each time as we learn each other's reaction to touch. My hands seem to pique Kold's interest, but my mouth garners his full attention. And the harder he gets for me, the more turned on I become.

"I want you to sit on my face." His request stops me dead in my tracks, and I feel my body freeze into a solid block of ice.

This particular position is something I've seen in videos, and I understand the mechanics of his request, but I've never actually tried it with anyone. I'm terrified by the mere suggestion.

"I don't. Don't. I don't. What? I don't know how to do that." My words hitch like a scratched record. A long-forgotten childhood stutter that only comes out when I'm overly excited about a topic of conversation or terrified of saying the wrong thing. In this situation, I'm assuming the latter.

"I promise you'll like it. Put your knees by my shoulders and lay on my chest. You don't have to do anything else except enjoy yourself." He pulls my hips towards his head. "Now giddy up."

The awkwardness of the situation is enough to make me run out of the room screaming, but I endure and push through. After all, somewhere inside me is a girl who was willing to take a road trip with a stranger, get married to a guy after a few weeks of dating, and have sex in a parking lot full of cars. Sitting on a guy's face should be a piece of cake. Come to think of it. I'm surprised I hadn't attempted it sooner.

I'm barely into position when Kold grabs onto my ass and buries his tongue inside of me. Once the sensation of pleasure reaches my brain, I forget how to be embarrassed and begin rocking my hips back and forth above him.

In front of me, within licking distance, is a perfectly hard cock, and I can't, in good conscience, ignore it. That would be rude and unfriendly. Two things I tirelessly try to avoid being in and out of the bedroom. A kindness he's quick to reward.

Despite how closely he's got me to the edge, I know I'll never fully get out of my head enough in this position to finish. A feeling Kold must pick up on because, after five minutes, he taps out and repositions himself on his knees behind me. Now, this is a pose I am well acquainted with, and I should have no trouble enjoying myself.

Pounding into me, deeper with each stroke, he doesn't waste time being nice. Kold is on a mission, and my orgasm is the fortune he seeks.

Being the caring and capable lover I am, I decided to help him reach his goal faster by fingering my clit while he rails me.

"Stop trying to get yourself off, Val." His arms link through mine, pulling me back at the elbows. "You either cum for me, or you don't cum at all."

I'm not sure I can obey his request, but I'm willing to try. It isn't an issue of his performance. When it comes to dicking down a girl, he knows what he's doing. A skill I'm sure he's honed over two decades of practice. Although, that's not something I want to spend too much time thinking about if I have any hope of finishing for him.

"I'm trying." I let out, catching my breath between thrusts.

"Stop overthinking everything, or I'll shove my cock in your ass." His words offer no hint of playfulness. "Or maybe that's what you want. The way you're clenching down on me, I think you might enjoy getting that tight little hole stretched out."

The threat alone is enough to send me hurling over the edge, my body convulsing against him as he continues his attack. Thankfully, he isn't far behind, and we crumble onto the bed in a sweaty, breathless heap.

I slap his arm and try my best to sound stern. "That's quite the threat you're casually throwing around. Not something one flippantly jokes about in the moment."

"What makes you think I was joking?" He says, kissing my forehead.

"Well, I hate to break it to you, but *that* is never going to fit in there. The downside of having an above-average penis, I guess. Sucks to be you." Collecting my clothes from the floor, I head for the bathroom to clean myself up.

"We'll see about that. Care to join me in the shower before we start the next movie?"

Only now do I realize the credits are rolling down the TV screen, signaling the end of another round.

CHAPTER 22
Kold

It took some convincing, but I was able to talk Val into staying the rest of the weekend. While her feelings never seem to waiver, her resolve to act on them runs like hot and cold. It's cute watching the gears turn behind her eyes, waiting to see who'll come out on top. More often than not, I can sway her in my direction by igniting her passion, though that's beginning to feel a bit cruel.

Val's self-preservation mode takes a back seat each time I kiss her, drawing my lips to her skin again and again. Whenever she so much as hinted at the idea of returning home, I pulled her into my arms and gave her every reason to stay.

Caught in a cycle of needing her with me and never wanting her to leave, the idea of parting ways began to feel like a death sentence, and I think I might be on the threshold of a complete psychotic break.

"It doesn't make sense to take him back to your place when he can stay here. Darc doesn't work during the day, so he's here with Midnight. Christmas staying isn't an inconvenience, and both dogs will be happier with a friend to play with."

I find myself looking for any excuse to get her back here, even going so low as to keep her dog. What the hell is happening to me? Darc and I used to make a game of rejecting the women interested in us. He was better at breaking them quickly, whereas I liked to damage them completely. Val isn't the first woman to believe she's in love at first sight, but she is the only one I've ever loved in return. I need this girl embedded into my life, even though I know letting her in is unsafe.

"I have to go home eventually. Why are you making this harder than it needs to be?" Her fingers comb through my hair as her eyes search my face for answers. "I can't move in here with you after only being together a few days."

"Why not? What's the alternative, you renew your lease? That would be a complete waste of money, not to mention it would mean living separately for another year. I'm not doing that, Val. We're thirty-five years old, not twenty-one. You belong here with us, not living ten minutes down the road."

"I hear you, okay? And I agree with the sentiment of your request, but you need to give me more than half a second to think about it. I want to be with you, but…"

Her words trail off at the same time I actively stop listening. I know I'm pushing too hard. I'm demanding she take our relationship at one hundred miles per hour because that's what I want, and my commands are causing her to pump the brakes. The idea of slowing down when I want to speed up sends me into a frenzy, and all I can do is watch as I spiral out of control.

"What about a shorter lease? Rent month and month until you're ready for us to get a place together. Who's your landlord? I guarantee my dad probably knows him. He knows everyone. We can work something out that would benefit everyone involved."

"Don't overstep, Kold! Please! I promised to think about your offer, and I will. We can get together after work to discuss the details, and maybe you can convince me. I just need to swing by my place to get clothes and my car, and then we can go to dinner." Val's reaction is valid, and her calm demeanor is more than I deserve.

Maybe my overreaction was partly prompted by the story she told me about the first date. How does someone have a good time and then walk away like it meant nothing? I couldn't do that to *her*, but I wonder if she could do it to me.

"I'm not normally this clingy. Honestly, I don't know what's wrong with me this morning. After spending three days together,

I thought I'd be ready for some breathing room, but the thought of you walking away is gutting me. I feel like you're going to disappear again, and I can't go back to how it was before."

"You think I don't understand, but I do. All those weeks, thinking about you every second of every day, not knowing if you were thinking of me. Not knowing if I would ever see you again. It was a fucking nightmare. And now that I'm here, everything's changed. Missing you was painful, but losing you... I don't even want to think about it."

Her voice articulates everything banging around my head, and it's comforting to know I'm not as alone as I thought. My fears, while extreme, fall in line with her own, making them feel less absurd.

I wrap my arms around her waist and pull her in for one more hug before she has to leave. Sitting on the bed, I want to drag her back under the blanket and hide for another three days, but I'd only be delaying the inevitable. Val and I are adults with jobs and responsibilities. It could take years to build a life together, and until then, that means spending time apart.

"So, do you trust me to take care of your miniature best friend while you're at work?" Val loves her dog more than she loves herself, so I'm on the fence as to what her decision is going to be.

"You aren't even going to be home. So, it's not a matter of trusting you. You're asking me to trust your brother."

"You'll come to find we're pretty much the same person."

"Respectfully, I disagree. You two are like night and day. However, Christmas can stay for today, and we'll see how it goes. But you can't keep using my dog as ransom to coerce me into moving here." Her hands glide over my neck and shoulders while she talks. "If I agree to leave him here, does it help to ease the tension? Since you know, I'll have to come back to get him."

"Does it make me sound pathetic if I say *yes*?"

"Does that even matter? I think we both look a teeny tiny bit pathetic." It's nice of Val to include herself, though I don't think she looks pathetic at all. She's holding her ground and remaining level-headed despite my outburst. She reminds me of Darc and one of his more respectable qualities. "I'm gonna miss you, but I do have to go. Text me during lunch if you have time."

"I'm my own boss, Val. I have all the time in the world to text you. And think about you. And worry like crazy when you don't text me back."

"Well, I promise I'll respond as quickly as possible. But I am *not* my own boss, so if there's a delay, I need you not to freak out."

"I'll try my best," I bury my face in her chest. "That's all I have to offer at the moment."

"What more could a woman ask for?" Val squeezes my shoulder before wrapping her arms around my neck and taking a seat on my leg. "Also, I need a ride to work."

Kissing her one final time, I intend for it to be the start and end of this morning's goodbye, but it quickly turns into more. I begin with her top by removing her shirt and dropping it on the floor.

"Call off work and stay home. I need one more day in bed with you." Willing to fight dirty to get my way, I begin kissing her breast and licking my tongue around her perked nipples. Val never says *no* to me when she's turned on.

"And then what?" She sighs. Her back arching as her head falls back.

"Then we get a house together. You marry me. We have a couple of kids. And I spend the rest of my life making your dreams come true."

Val gets up from my lap with an exasperated huff, retrieves her shirt from the floor, and slips it over her head. All I can do is watch in silence. I knew the marriage topic was off-limits, and still, I said what I said. Now, I have to deal with the fallout.

The ride to work is quiet in a thoughtful way. When I pull in front of Val's office, I give her leg a gentle squeeze and park the car to get out. One more hug to get me through the day, and a kiss to last a lifetime, in case I fucked up for real this time.

"I'm sorry about this morning. I didn't mean to sound obsessed. Although, we can both acknowledge, I probably am." At my admission, Val smiles and shakes her head. "Watching you walk away and not being able to find you was devastating. Losing you shattered me in a way I'm embarrassed to admit, and being forced to say goodbye to you is stirring up those feelings even though I know things are different now."

Taking my hand and pressing it to her cheek, Val looks like she might cry. "You're going to see me after work. I promise. Give me a chance to get my bearings, and then it's full steam ahead."

This perfect woman is mine, and all I have to do is respect her completely realistic timeline. Which should be easy if I wasn't standing here losing my mind. If Val walks away and never looks back, I'll have no one to blame but myself.

<h1 style="text-align:center">Val</h1>

Sitting at my desk, I think about Kold more than the stack of papers I'm getting paid to input into the system before 4:00 pm. If we had met two years ago, before my mom died, before my short-lived sham of a marriage, and before the emotional mind fuck that was Allen Cuttler, everything could be different. I would be different.

I'm not sure marriage is still in the cards after everything that happened with John. When I finally found out the truth about his leaving, it broke the piece of me that was willing to trust. All the time I wasted thinking it was my fault, only to find out it was him. And I get it. Kold isn't John, and he sure as hell isn't Allen. Kold isn't anything like the guys from my past. Conrad included. Unfortunately, my rational side hasn't figured out how to fix my damaged heart. So, the perfect guy, who's doing everything within his power to love me, is penalized for everyone else's mistakes.

Everything Kold's feeling, I'm feeling too, only I'm too much of a coward to own up to it the way he does. If I weren't so gun-shy, I'd take him up on the offer to move in. I'd run to the court-house with him and say *I do*. I'd throw away my birth control. Hell, I'd even let him see all the parts of myself I work so hard to keep hidden. I would let him love me, and I would love him back from now until my dying day. I'd stop standing in my own way and place one final bet on happiness.

It isn't fair. John was the one who pushed for the divorce to be finalized so he could run off and get married again, and not even to the woman he impregnated. I hadn't realized there was a line of women wrapped around the block, and all he needed was for me to step out of his way. He moved on at the speed of light like our failed marriage was nothing more than a minor inconvenience.

I jumped into things with Allen after the divorce, not wanting to bother with feelings ever again, but now here I am, feeling everything all at once, and I'm too broken to bear the weight of those emotions alone.

> Kold: I don't want to bother you at work or risk getting you into trouble, but I wanted you to know that I'm sitting here in my office thinking about you, wishing I could kiss you. Also, I checked in with my brother, and the dogs are blissfully content, snuggled up on Midnight's bed in front of the fireplace. He sent me a video as proof. I'll forward it to you. One long message seemed better than sending five short texts, one right after the next. I hope that's okay. Miss you. Love you. Can't wait to see you. Let me know if you need a ride to your place after work. I'll be happy to pick you up.

I have enough time to skim Kold's text when it lights up my screen, but I have to pause my work mid-sentence to read his entire message. Even in text form, he's everything I know him to be. How can a man who is so kind, thoughtful, loving, successful, and unbelievably attractive be single this late in life? It doesn't make sense. I'm surprised some girl didn't poke a hole in the condom or lie about being on birth control as a means of trapping him. If I was younger, the thought might have crossed my mind.

> : I appreciate a long-winded message. And you're welcome to send any length of text you choose. Seeing your name on my screen will be the highlight of my workday. And no worries about getting me into trouble. My office is tucked away in the back, and everyone is on their phones. No one is going to notice me. They never do. Although, if they do happen to see me, they might question the massive smile on my face and worry that I'm having a stroke.

I construct my response, hit send, and pick up where I left off. There's a mountain of files I need to get through this week if I hope to enjoy my holiday. Normally, I would put on some music and zone out, but I find myself distracted by a certain son of Asgard. Even before receiving the text from Kold, he was all I'd been able to think about.

> Kold: I'm hesitant to tell you this because I don't want to risk upsetting you, but I thought you should know. I received a message from your ex, and he's being an asshole. I wanted to check with you before I responded. If you hear from him and he says anything to upset you, I want you to tell me, and I'll take care of it.

Why am I not the least bit surprised? Allen will never leave me alone. He'll find a way to ruin things, even in his absence. The guy is a bad penny, and I have to find a way to deal with him. Kold worries too much as it is, and I don't want him getting dragged into my mess.

> : I haven't heard from him, but if I do, you'll be the first to know. I'm sure he's fishing for information, but I'm sorry that he's bothering you and being a jerk. Please ignore him. He probably wants to find out if we hooked up. As if it's any of his business.

I attempt to work between messages, but it's getting more difficult to focus now that I have Allen invading my thoughts. I'll need to triple-check the parking lot before leaving the building tonight.

> Kold: That would be rich coming from the guy whose side piece was banging on your door, trying to track him down.

Excuse me? What the hell is he talking about? How does Kold know about someone banging on my door when we haven't even been there? Did he set up some sort of surveillance? Also, who the fuck is this side piece, and why am I the last to find out about her? I type out a string of questions and then delete them. Deciding to take a breath and respond in a way that sounds less crazy.

> : Please explain. Who was banging on my door? When was this?

His response comes almost instantly, as though he was typing it out while I was editing my message to him. I guess my questions were rather predictable.

> Kold: I was going to tell you, but then I forgot because you were naked, and I got distracted by your mouth on my dick. When I thought about it after the fact, I didn't want to say anything and have it ruin the weekend. The whole thing happened on Saturday morning before Darc picked us up for brunch.

> Kold: While you were in the shower, I took Christmas outside, and when we came in, a woman was pounding on your door, trying to scream it down. She insisted you had her boyfriend Carter in there, that she had seen you together, and she knew you were hooking up with him. I didn't know who she was, but I assured her I was the only man you'd had in your apartment all night, and she left.

> : Carter? Are you fricken kidding me? My neighbor Tracy is dating a guy named Carter. Shit! That woman totally had the wrong door. I feel so bad for Tracy. She really liked this guy, but it sounds to me like Mr. Carter isn't being honest. If he's cheating on my friend, he's going to have hell to pay. Conrad told me once that if I wanted my ex-husband Taken Care Of, he knew a couple of guys who could do it. LoL. Father of the Year. Maybe I should call him and find out how much they charge.

I'm convinced it's unsafe to meet anyone online. What is with this epidemic of guys who lie and cheat? Has it always been this way? Or have nice guys finished last so many times that they've given up running the race?

> Kold: Did Conrad mention anything else about those guys?

> : Not that I recall. Why? Do you need me to make an ex-girlfriend disappear? I could track her down at the grocery store and hit her car with my shopping cart. LoL.

> Kold: Remind me not to piss you off.

A torrent of laughter erupts from my chest, and I'm helpless to rein it in. Maybe it's a nervous breakdown brought on by all the unaddressed anxiety. Leave it to me to snag the love of my life the weekend before I go crazy.

The misplaced sound is enough to catch the attention of Sandra, my inner office neighbor, who pops her head over our shared cubicle wall to offer me a heart-felt "Shhhh."

> : So you're aware, I'm not in the habit of warning people twice.

> Kold: Understandable. Neither am I.

If I keep reading his messages, then I'll keep responding. It will be 4:00 before I know it, and I will have accomplished nothing besides falling more in love with the man who already owns my heart. And while that sounds appealing on the surface, I think I need to consider the importance money plays in the average adult's life. Probably best not to lose my job.

> : I hate to say it, but I better try to get some of this work done so I don't have to take it home. Thanks for thinking of me. Your texts have given me a lot to reflect on, and hearing from you made me smile. I'll call you at lunch and see what you're up to.

I set my phone face down on my desk and move the button on the side to silent. Working as fast as my fingers allow, I keep one eye on the clock and count the minutes until my lunch break. I can't remember the last time I was this excited about the possibility of talking to a guy on the phone. I can't even be sure that he'll answer.

In college, I dated a guy who lived three hours away, and we could only see each other one weekend a month. Between visits, we would text back and forth during the day and have long-winded phone calls in the evening that would stretch on till morning. That was back when I was younger and could function the next day on less than two hours of sleep. I remember always being excited when he would call and heartbroken when he didn't. Sometimes, it's better not to get your hopes up.

Kold told me he works in finance and mentioned having an office upstairs at Club After Darc, but I'm not sure what all that entails or if he manages other businesses. If I'm considering a future with him, I might want to learn more about all the boring details.

Making up for borrowed time, I get through two-thirds of my to-do pile before my phone begins vibrating out of control. A text and phone call come in simultaneously, pausing my *Work Faster* playlist.

I answer in a panic. Worried something must be wrong. "What happened? Is everything okay? Did the dogs get out?"

"Is that how you answer the phone? I really need to get you on a beach vacation, and quickly." Kold stifles a laugh and attempts to keep his voice soothing, but I can hear his silent teasing. "I called to let you know I'm in the parking lot. I brought us lunch."

"I'm sorry. I was focused on my work and wasn't expecting your call yet. That's my bad. I can be out there in three minutes if you're okay with waiting?" My heartbeat begins to slow back to its standard resting rate, and I drop my head into my hands. Only I could freak out about nothing, always assuming the worst.

"For you, my love, I would wait forever."

And like that, my date with vending machine food and a voice on the phone has turned into a full-on picnic with the man himself. I fix my hair and check my teeth in the mirror beside my desk before grabbing my office sweater from my chair. This day just got a whole lot better.

When I get out to the parking lot, I spot Kold's SUV parked close to the door and see him sitting in the driver's seat, grinning from ear to ear. The sight of him is enough to make me smile. I hurry to meet him, knowing my co-workers will be staring out the windows, and dive into the passenger side, hoping to avoid the curious eyes of those filing out of the building behind me.

"Do you not want people to see us eating together? Because I can leave if you would rather." Kold's offer, while genuine, is ridiculous.

Of course, I don't want him to leave. I've been looking forward to calling him for the last few hours, and now he's here with food. No one has ever surprised me like this.

I lean over, grab him by the front of his shirt, and kiss him. This should alleviate any question of my wanting to be seen with him. Hopefully, my lips can convey what my words fail to communicate.

"You got lunch from Valentine's? But that's on the other side of town." I recognize the calligraphy *V* on the side of the takeout bag sitting on the back seat.

"Full disclosure: I wasn't exactly sure what you might enjoy for lunch, so I went to your dad's restaurant. Figured he might know your eating habits better than I do, and I needed to have a talk with him about something. So, two birds, one stone."

"I hope you didn't go there asking for my hand in marriage because that man has no right to give away any part of me, and I don't like the thought of him knowing me better than you do. However, negative feelings aside, I appreciate you going out of your way. It really means a lot to me."

Sitting here with a container of food on my lap, I'm reminded of a time during my marriage when I ended up in the hospital. I had been in a motorcycle accident and woke up unable to move the right side of my body. The hospital called to inform my husband of my condition, and he showed up six hours later, after work, with a bag of Taco Bell. He didn't even think to bring me a soft taco, let alone a bag of clothes.

After an awkward fifteen minutes of silence, watching him eat dinner in front of me, he got up and left. "Text me later if you want," was all he said on the way out the door. Even now, thinking back on that moment, I'm heartbroken by the lack of primary care I accepted in exchange for my unwavering devotion.

"Is everything okay? You haven't touched your food." Kold reaches over, resting his hand on my arm. "Would you rather have my burger?"

"No. Thank you. What you brought is perfect. I was just lost in thought for a moment, wondering how I got so lucky."

That's not exactly what I was thinking, but the question did cross my mind earlier. Kold is too perfect, and I'm far too flawed to deserve him. Being with him is like winning the lottery, but I don't remember buying a ticket.

If I were to win a lottery, it would probably be more like the 1948 short story by Shirley Jackson, where I get stoned to death at the end.

"I'm the one who's lucky to have you, my dear, but I'm not exactly trying to draw too much attention to the fact. I figure, the longer it takes for you to realize I'm not worth your time, the better." Kold's ability to be self-deprecating makes him even sexier somehow.

"Oh, please. I've spent half the morning thinking about how

much cooler I was two years ago and how I wish you could've met that woman before she was torn to shreds."

I've mentioned the main points of my backstory in passing without delving too far into the details. Since I can't change what happened, there's no sense in dwelling on it, and I don't like it when people pity me. In the past, my sob stories have garnered enough sympathy to keep a greeting card company in business, and that's something I'd like to avoid with Kold.

"I love the woman you are today, and it doesn't take Sherlock Holmes to suss out the fact that you've been through some shit in the last few years. I figured all of that out the first night, and I know that's why you need me to slow down and prove myself. I'm fine with whatever you need, or rather, I'm trying to be. My need to spoil you with affection and attention has existed since day one. Stupidly, I waited too long for the green light."

"We both waited longer than we should have, but what matters is that we ended up in the right place."

Looking back at the timeline of events that led us here, I regret not speaking up on Halloween. I should've given Kold my number before I left, or told Allen to fuck off and stayed at the bar. Worst case scenario, I went home single and alone. Big deal. The whole time I was with Allen, I was alone. The guy didn't give two shits about me.

Hindsight can be a real son-of-a-bitch.

"What time do you have to get back?" Kold squeezes my thigh, making sure he has my attention. "I would ask you to cut out early, but I have a sneaking suspicion you would say *no*, and I'm not sure how many times I can handle being rejected by you today."

Putting my hand atop his, I lace our fingers together. "I haven't rejected you. I merely paused a couple of topics, but I promise you, I'm still considering everything on the table."

"Including marriage?"

How can I say *no* when matrimony seems so essential to him? Do I hate the thought of marriage so much that I'm willing to risk losing him? Is my stance on anything that strong? Sure. There are a few talking points I'm pretty immovable on, but committing to a lifetime with Kold isn't on that list. He could convince me by spring if his actions continue to match his words, but it's not going to happen over lunch.

"Don't buy a ring or anything, but I'm open to discussing it in a few months. For now, I should get back to work. Thanks for bringing me lunch. Would it be a huge inconvenience to pick me up and take me home at 4:00? If it's a hassle, I can find an alternative."

"You've just made me the happiest man in the world. As for the ride, you already know I want to see you as much as possible. I'll be here when you clock out, eagerly awaiting your arrival."

We share one last kiss goodbye, and I walk back into work, feeling lighter in my shoes as though I'm floating to my cubicle, suspended by a string attached to cloud nine.

CHAPTER 23

Kold

When it rains, it pours. I started the day unreasonably distraught over the reality of adulting. My girl needing to leave for work threw me into a panic, and I damn near had a nervous breakdown. I forced myself to drive downtown, and while I was at the office I received a text from her ex-boyfriend. His motives remain unclear.

Then I heard from the woman I love that her father had been saying things he shouldn't. I was supposed to be working at my office, not driving across town, delivering reminders to people who damn well know better. Thankfully, I brought my computer with me, and I was able to connect to the building Wi-Fi from the parking lot of Val's work.

It's not that I don't trust her. Val has my complete confidence, but I don't want to be too far away in case she needs me for any reason. Allen is up to something, and Conrad knows too much. They're liabilities I can't afford, and I'm no longer willing to take chances. Val has made her choice. So, Allen needs to accept her wishes and bow out gracefully, or he needs to disappear.

I doubt my girlfriend would appreciate my stalker-like behavior, but I don't have a choice. Until I know for sure the layout of the board and who exactly my opponents are, I'm keeping a close eye on her shadow from a safe distance. Conrad knows better than to open his mouth too wide, and he's received the only warning he'll get. As for Allen, I'm not sure what he's after, but he's pissing me off.

The thought of leaving crossed my mind, but ultimately, I stayed, and it's a good thing I did. After an hour of working on inventory from the front seat of my car, I received a text from Val.

> Val: Are you still in the parking lot?

> : I guess there's no point in lying since you already know. I swear, I'm working on my computer, not keeping tabs on you.

> Val: It's fine. I'm glad you stayed. I finished everything on my desk and have what I need tomorrow. Told my boss I wasn't feeling well. Might need to work from home for a few days. Mind if we cut out early?

> : I'll have the engine running.

> Val: Lovely. I'll be right out.

My heartbeat quickens at the sight of my girl strolling out the front door, grinning like she's pulled off the heist of the century. I love how easily she finds happiness in the simple things. When it comes to Val, she doesn't have her hand out, expecting the world, which makes me want to spoil her that much more.

She gets into the passenger seat and immediately gives me shit about being here. "It's sort of nice dating a creepy stalker. I was worried I'd have to wait for you to drive in from the city, but you were already here. The ladies in the front office were watching you out the window and called me."

"I figured if I worked in the car, I could get more done instead of driving back and forth. I wasn't trying to be a creep or a stalker." I turn in the direction of her apartment and drive as we talk.

Even though Val is taking my being there in stride, I don't want her to think I'm actually stalking her. Activities like that can go from endearing to terrifying rather quickly. Or that's how it seems in the movies. I want to be the doting husband, not the obsessed ex-boyfriend.

"That's exactly what I told the ladies up front when they asked me if I needed security to walk me out after work." Val laughs, and I wonder if she'd take the situation more seriously if it were anyone but me. "Don't take it personally. I think they just worry about me. After Allen showed up and made a scene in the parking lot a few months ago, people have been more on edge."

How am I only hearing about this now, and why is she telling me like it's no big deal? I might need to make it my life's mission to keep this woman safe since she doesn't seem too worried about doing it for herself. A first date road trip out of state with some guy from the internet, and now this. What else isn't she telling me? I'm going to need a list of names and a kill order.

"Please tell me what you mean by 'Allen showed up and made a scene in the parking lot' before I jump to conclusions." My mind is already tabulating a list of all the ways I'm going to hurt him before the year ends.

"I don't know. It's hard to explain, and admitting that I put up with it makes me look like an idiot. I'd really rather not talk about him, but... You aren't going to let this slide, are you?" She pauses to allow for my response, but I remain quietly waiting.

"Sometimes Allen would accuse me of really random shit and then try to convince me it actually happened. One time, he claimed I was fired from my job in Indiana because I went to work high on drugs. Which, to be clear, did not happen. But he said he knew it for a fact because his parents had paid for some extensive background check on me and that I was a liar. I spent an entire week vigorously defending myself, even though his lies had no basis in reality. After that fight, I broke things off with him, and he showed up at the office, hurling accusations about me and a supervisor. The whole thing was a mess." Val turns her face towards the window and wipes her eyes. "After you and I met, he told me you said I was rude and untrustworthy. I mean, part of me knew it was bullshit. It was unlikely that you left that night hating me, but I couldn't really know for sure. And then, the way you were towards me when we were at your house. He messed up taking me over there, and he knew it, but he quickly found a way to use it against me. Making everything my fault. Once he knew how I felt about you, he needed to destroy my hope in order to keep me under his thumb. So, the night of the restaurant, he told me you were happy and in love. He said you had a girlfriend who was gorgeous and smart and everything I wasn't. Or rather, everything I'm not."

"You and I both know Allen is a liar, but I need you to hear it from me... I've *never* said a negative word against you, and I never will. Regardless of what the future holds, you will always be the best thing that has ever happened to me. And for the record, I do have a girlfriend who's gorgeous and smart, and I love her so much that it scares me. She's everything you are, Val, because she's you."

I enter the apartment's parking lot and find a spot near the side door. Once we're parked, I unhook both seatbelts and pull her into my arms. "I'm sorry I wasn't there to protect you. It won't happen again."

Holding her in my arms, I want to absorb every ounce of discomfort, each moment of grief, every hurt feeling, and painful memory. If I could take it all and feel it for her, I would suffer in her place gladly. Val doesn't deserve the hand she was dealt, and I know that without even seeing her cards.

When the air in the car turns cold, I know it's time to get her inside. "Come on. I'll go up with you. Make sure everything is okay. And then, if you want me to stay, I can. Or I'll head home and give you some space. Whatever you want."

"Whatever I want, huh? The possibilities are endless." She says with a wink.

"Woman! Don't even joke around like that, or I'm gonna take you against the wall in the stairwell." I'm half tempted to follow through. Having her in public that first time was a rush.

The idea of being caught at any moment had me as stiff as a steel rod. Then again, between the thrill of being seen and the excitement of having Val on top of me, I think I lasted about three minutes. Thankfully, my girl's digestive pyrotechnics overshadowed my embarrassment, affording me the opportunity for a second chance later that night.

"You don't scare me," she says with a laugh before jumping out of the passenger seat and taking off for the side door of the building.

I shoot out after her, catching the handle of the door inches before it closes and locks in front of me. Taking the stairs two at a time, I reach her on the landing halfway up the stairwell, and press her against the wall with a kiss. She's laughing and out of breath, so I work on her neck while she squeals and attempts to wiggle out of my grasp.

"Okay, you win!" Still gasping for breath, Val stops fighting for freedom and dissolves into my kisses. "Please follow me upstairs so I can give you your prize."

"I thought having my way with you right here could be my prize." I press her hand against my pants so she can feel what she's done to me.

"There are kids who live in this building, and I'm not about to risk traumatizing any of them because your dick can't wait twenty seconds. So, either take me upstairs in my apartment, or go home and jerk off!" Val uses her, *I'm not mad, but I'm serious as fuck* voice, so I know she means business.

"Yes, ma'am." I unpin her body and take a step back.

As she passes, I can't help myself and slap her ass with one hard crack. Val takes off at a run, up the last of the stairs and down the hall, laughing all the way. At the door of 202, she collapses against the wall, struggling to catch her breath.

"Babe are you okay?" I wrap her in my arms, taking most of the weight off her feet. Before she can answer, her head falls back, and her body goes limp.

"Val, please wake up." My voice sounds hollow, as if it's coming from the end of the hallway.

In a panic, I lay her on the floor at my feet and struggle to get the key into the lock. My hands are shaking, and my eyes are quickly blurring up with tears. Finally, the key slides into the lock, and I'm able to get the door open.

"Oh, my God! What happened? Val, are you okay?" A

woman's voice comes from behind me, and I can feel someone trying to push me aside.

"Back off, lady!" I scoop Val's limp form into my arms and carry her into the living room, laying her on the couch. Then brush the hair off of her face while attempting to coax her back. "Please open your eyes, my love. I can't lose you."

"I'm a nurse. Please step aside so I can help her. She's my best friend." The woman's hand squeezes my shoulder, and begrudgingly I move.

The woman I recognize from our meeting the other day checks Val's pulse and presses a hand to her forehead. "Grab the hand towel from the kitchen and put some cold water on it. I feel a pulse, and she's breathing. She's passed out for some reason, but she'll be okay. What happened?"

"We were playing around, and she ran up the stairs. When I caught her at the door, she went limp, and her eyes rolled back in her head."

I press the cool cloth to Val's head as her eyes flutter open.

"Val, it's okay. You're in your apartment on your couch. Please don't try to get up. You passed out in the hallway, and the guy with you carried you inside. I've done what I can to help, but I think it would be best if you went to the hospital and got checked out by a doctor. Do you want me to call an ambulance?" The woman's tone is calm but direct.

She's used to dealing with these situations and knows how to detach from her emotions. I can respect that. There are times in my life when I have to do the same. When I have to flip that switch and function in robot mode. That would've been useful a few minutes ago, but when it comes to anything involving Val, I'm a fucking wreck. My emotions kick into overdrive, and I forget how to think straight.

"I'm fine," a small voice says. "Please stop fussing over me. I'm embarrassed enough as it is."

I sit beside her on the couch so she can use me as a pillow, and allow her to sink into my embrace. Feeling her warm body pressed firmly to my chest, relaxes me, and I hope that I'm having the same effect on her. Seeing Val so vulnerable and not knowing what you do was a helpless feeling. One I'd never experienced before.

"You scared me." I wrap my arms across her chest and hold her close. "I can't handle the thought of losing you. It would kill me."

"I got light-headed for a second. That's all. I promise you, I'm fine." She sounds like herself again, but her body shivers slightly, revealing her weakness.

Grabbing the blanket from the back of the couch, I do my best to cover her with the soft, lightweight throw.

The woman I'm beginning to think must be Tracy, Val's friend and neighbor, sits on the couch at her feet, fine-tuning the position of the blanket. We sit silently for a moment, ensuring the worst has passed.

Finally, Val breaks the tension by speaking first.

"I suppose I should introduce the two of you. This is my friend Tracy. She lives next door with her son Sam. And Tracy, this is Kold. My, um. Well, my boyfriend, I guess."

"What do you mean, you guess? Are we not together?" I can feel myself getting angry, and I don't think that's the right play, especially after everything that happened a moment ago.

"No, yeah, we are, but we haven't officially defined it yet."

My phone goes off again in my pocket. It's been making noise for the last few minutes, but I wasn't about to check my messages while Val was blacked out on the floor. Now that she's awake and downplaying our relationship, I think it might be a good time to check and see who's trying to steal my attention.

"If you'll excuse me for a moment, ladies. I need to make sure this isn't something that requires my attention." I say, holding up my phone as it lights up again.

Nothing is more important than my girl, but I need to step away and take a deep breath before I say something I'll regret later. I can't believe she introduced me as her maybe-boyfriend. I'm starting to wonder if Val is as sure about me as I thought.

Our undefined relationship status has officially been moved to item number one on tonight's list of discussion topics.

Val

Tracy looks at me like I'm one of her patients, and I wish she would stop. I'm not sure how many more times I can say that I'm fine. It was uncomfortable enough that I passed out in front of Kold, exhausted after running up one flight of stairs. The fact that there's a second witness doubles my embarrassment. I guess it's time to get back in the gym and build up my endurance. Running has never been my strong suit, but I should be able to make it to the second floor in one piece.

"Where the hell have you been? When did you start sort of dating Kold? And where's your dog? What the hell is going on, Val? I've been over here a dozen times looking for you, and you're never home. Are you pissed at me or what?" Tracy's words come out a mile a minute, and it takes my brain a second to process everything she's asked me.

"We aren't *sort of* dating. I don't know why I said it that way. Kold and I are very much together." I've been talking about him for months, so I can't understand why she's acting surprised by his sudden appearance. "You're the one who kept telling me to go for it, and now you're mad at me for being with him?"

"No, I'm not mad about Kold. But I saw you with another guy on Friday. Who was that?" There's a look on Tracy's face I can't read.

"Oh, I forgot about that. Yeah, so Allen and I are over.

Finally! He picked me up, claiming he wanted to talk, but then he tried pulling some bullshit. I got drunk, and Kold and his brother came to the restaurant. It was a whole situation, so I've been staying at Kold's house the past few days."

"So, the guy I saw you with was Allen? Your boyfriend, Allen. The guy you've been dating the last few months?" Tracy's expression still confuses me, and I can't understand her questions. Why is she so concerned with Allen all of a sudden? She's been encouraging me to end things since the middle of November.

"My ex-boyfriend, Allen, the lying, manipulative, mentally abusive jerk you've hated from the start. Yep, that was him. Why?"

I feel like Tracy and I are having two different conversations. No matter which path I walk down, I can't find my way over to her line of thinking. Kold needs to hurry up with whatever he's doing in the bedroom because I'm beginning to regret coming back here. I want to go home and hide in bed under the blanket.

No, wait, that's not right. I'm already home, aren't I?

Kold emerges from the bedroom and walks over to where I'm seated on the couch. Kissing my forehead, he seems distant. Something is off. But my thoughts are scrambled, and I'm struggling to read the room. I usually pride myself on my ability to gauge people's body language, but I can't focus to save my life.

"I need to take care of something. I'll be back for you in a couple of hours. Will you be okay without me for a while?" Kold sounds distant, like he's already gone, and only his body remains.

I'm not okay with him leaving. What the hell is going on? Tracy is acting weird, and now Kold is taking off? The guy who sat outside in the parking lot waiting for me to get out of work is leaving me ten minutes after I blacked out in his arms? It doesn't make sense. Unless he's seen enough, and he's walking away for good.

"Tell me why you're leaving, and then I'll tell you if I'm okay with it." If he's breaking up with me, I want to hear him say it.

I've been on the receiving end of this cold shoulder enough times to know what it means. Guys are always hot and heavy, making grandiose claims and professing undying love, only to walk out the door an emotional robot leaving without explanation. Even worse. Saying they'll be back and then disappearing like it all meant nothing.

"I don't want to lie to you, so stop asking questions. It's better if you don't know." He stares a hole through my chest rather than meet my eyes.

Look at me, you fucking coward! You're exactly like them.

"Fine. Call your brother and tell him I want my dog back, now! Then fuck off and forget you know me." Everything about this moment reminds me of John walking out of that hospital room, not giving a single fuck if I lived or died. It was more important to him to leave and get his dick wet than to stay and waste his time pretending to care.

"Baby, don't say that."

"Don't ever call me that!" I snap back. "A secret is the same as a lie, and I've heard enough of those to last me a lifetime. If you want to leave so badly, go!"

Kold drops to his knees and lays his head on my lap. His arms wrap around my waist, and I feel him vibrating with emotions he refuses to unleash. Any anger inside me melts away once I register how upset he is.

He lifts his head, takes the phone from his back pocket, and places it in my hand.

"0224. Read the texts from today."

I tap the passcode into the phone and open his messages. Allen is near the top of the list under Darc's nickname, but I know which conversation Kold is offering to share.

> Allen: The other night was a total shit show. My girlfriend was wasted, per usual. Did you happen to see who she left with?

> Allen: She's been texting and calling nonstop, begging me to forgive her and agreeing to do ANYTHING. It's hilarious.

> Allen: I kept her around this long for the blowjobs, and because the sex is too good to cut her off. Especially when she begs. Holy shit, is it hot when she begs! I'll probably string her along for a few more months until I line up something better.

> Allen: She told me nothing happened between the two of you, but I figured she was lying. Not that I care. Do whatever you want with her. Everyone else has.

> Allen: You must be caught in the middle of one hell of a day. Let's plan to get together again without my girlfriend. Saw you have a show on Friday, but it's sold out. Can you add me to the list? Hit me up when you're free.

> : I'm free right now. Let's meet up.

> Allen: Awesome. The wing place on 44 in 20 minutes?

> : Sounds good.

"So, what was the plan here? You were gonna kick the shit out of my ex and then come back and pretend like nothing happened? You think that's what I want?" The last person he messaged was Darc, and I imagine he's already on his way to the restaurant. Where there's one, the other is never far behind.

"You can't read those messages and expect me to do nothing! Do you still have feelings for him? Is that what this is? Were you texting him this morning when you told me you hadn't heard from him?"

"Of course not. I don't give a fuck about him! I care about you. Go through my phone if you don't believe me. I don't need you getting arrested for assault because I was stupid enough to date a complete asshole. He's out of my life. Isn't that good enough?" As much as I love his need to protect me, I don't want Kold fighting my battles for me.

"He still thinks you're together!"

"Okay. Well, he's delusional. I've been with you all weekend, and I sure as shit wasn't on my phone. I think you would've noticed if I was calling and texting another guy, begging for his cock." Allen is a perfect example of why women should trust their gut. I knew from the first moment that he was bad news, but I made excuses for his disrespect instead of caring enough about myself to walk away.

"Yeah, that's true. I'm pretty sure I would've noticed that." Kold seems fueled by emotion one minute and detached from them the next. "I don't need him showing up here or at your job, making problems. I can't always be there to protect you. This bullshit with him ends tonight."

"Whatever you're planning, reconsider and stay with me. Please! If you want me to tell him the relationship is over, I will. I'll do or say anything you want." My voice is pleading.

"I'm not suggesting you be the one to fix this. I'm telling you that I will take care of it, and you're asking me to do nothing."

"No. I'm asking you to protect me, but not in the way you're offering. I want you to pull me into your arms and never let go. I need you with me." I can't help but wonder if I'll ever be able to hold on tight enough. Will he slip through my fingers eventually, in spite of my best efforts?

"I would love nothing more than to hold onto you forever. If that's what you truly want, pack a bag for the week and let's go home. You're staying with me. It's the only way I'll know you're safe." He stands and kisses the top of my head. "Tracy, it was nice meeting you. I appreciate you coming to Val's aid, and I'm sorry if I've made a shitty first impression."

"I get it. It can be scary to see someone you care about pass out. I panicked for a second when I saw Val on the floor with you standing over her, but I think you handled the situation well. Even the part where you wanted to run off and kick the shit out of her ex. If Val doesn't accept that offer, I might agree to it for her." Tracy stands and makes her way to the door. "I'm happy you two finally found each other. She always knew you were *the one*, and I can see that you feel the same way about her. Val deserves someone who will fight for her, even though she'll beg you not to."

Tracy leaves without another word, closing the door behind her.

I sit momentarily, attempting to gather my thoughts as Kold makes his way into the bedroom. When I join him, he's already located a duffel bag and has it flopped open on the bed.

"I owe you an apology." I feel awful for getting angry and jumping to conclusions. "I thought you were leaving because I blacked out, and you didn't want to deal with it."

Kold exits the closet with an arm full of clothes and drops everything on the bed before taking my face into his hands. He doesn't speak right away, but I can see he has something to say. We stare into each other's eyes, holding the moment like one holds their breath. When my chest begins to burn, and the words fall to the tips of my tongue, he leans down and kisses me.

"I never wanted to leave you. I wanted to take away your pain." His words wash over me as he holds me in his gaze. "You should know by now that you're everything to me. And if that comes as a surprise to you, I'll work harder to prove it."

"Some things take time." Not *this*, but other things. Tracy was right. I've known Kold was the one since I met him. I fell in love instantly, and I'm not sure anything could change that.

"I understand that, and I'm prepared to give you the rest of my life." Kold's level of commitment always feels like the start of a marriage proposal. "I don't want to be your boyfriend, but since you won't entertain other topics of conversation, I suppose that's the title I'm willing to settle for."

"How gracious of you, kind sir," I grin and stifle a laugh. "Maybe I could be willing to entertain the topic sooner rather than later since I get the feeling you aren't going to quit bringing it up."

Each time he hints at getting married, I move one step closer to giving in and saying I do. But I don't need him to know that.

CHAPTER 24

Kold

I can relax now that Val is home safe, comfortably in bed, surrounded by dogs. This is where she belongs. Darc and I can protect her in ways she'll never know, but I worry that my love for her might be a shield and a target.

It's too early for sleep, so we put on a movie for background noise and discuss the week ahead. She's willing to work from home for a few days, and I've agreed to do the same. I know I'll eventually have to let her out of sight, but I'm not ready.

I offered to make a doctor's appointment or take her to the ER, but she's adamant that everything is fine and I'm overreacting. Arguing with Val gets me nowhere, so I'm willing to settle for keeping an eye on her at home. But if she passes out again, I will call the ambulance and tell them to strap her down. Let the EMTs be the bad guys, and I'll be the loving future husband who brings her comfy clothes to change into and sneaks in her favorite meals when the nurses aren't looking.

Darc was already gone when we got home, and when I tried calling, it went straight to voicemail. Hopefully, when I didn't arrive at the restaurant, he got the idea and left. Then again, this is my brother we're talking about. Darc doesn't shy away from a fight, and he's hated Allen for a decade. Whatever happened tonight was a long time coming.

We're finishing a movie in the bedroom when the dogs hear

the front door open and take off downstairs. "I'll be right back, love. Might as well let them out while they're down there."

"Sounds good. I might close my eyes for a minute." Val sounds like the edge of sleep is within reach, so I kiss her forehead and close the door behind me.

When I get downstairs, Darc is washing blood off his hands in the kitchen. His eyes are brimming with anger and I know he's about to let me have it, so I press my finger to my lips and point toward the ceiling. The last thing I need is for Val to overhear anything he's about to tell me.

"So that's why you didn't show up? You were too busy playing house with your fucking girlfriend while I handled things alone. You send me to take care of the mess *she* brought into our lives, and then you don't even have my back?"

"You're so fucking full of it. You've wanted to erase that asshole for years. When I didn't show, you could've backed off, and you didn't."

"Val owes me for this. And you will let me have her in *any* way I see fit!"

There it is. The real reason for his actions. This wasn't about settling old scores. It was about Val. He wants her to be in *his* debt, and he wants me to agree to the terms.

"You're not going to touch her! Do I make myself clear? Val doesn't owe you shit! I asked you to go, not her." I keep the volume of my voice as low as I can while arguing across the marble kitchen island.

"I am going to fuck her so good. She'll beg me to do it again." Darc's promise cuts like daggers. "And if you deny me my half, I will take her from you."

"If you so much as lay a finger on her, against her wishes, I will put you in the mother fucking ground next to everyone else. You're not the only one of us capable of dark things, and I would suggest you not forget that." I slam my hands down on the counter, ready for this to come to blows.

My mind is laser-focused on the weapons currently at our disposal, calculating the odds of what each of us will choose and who'll come out on top. We've left bruises and broken bones more times than I can count, sparring together in the gym, but we haven't been in a real fight with one another since we were kids. Even then, we played for blood. If he keeps talking about Val, tonight will be no different.

"She makes you weak and sloppy. You know better than to make business personal. If I had left this for you to take care of, you'd get us both caught. Are you willing to throw away everything we've built for this girl?"

"Don't ask questions you already know the answer to. I want more than this," I say, tapping the counter in front of me. "Val is my one chance to have a real life. A wife. A family. The whole fucking thing. Don't you ever get tired of the same old shit? We're not twenty-five anymore. I'm done with it." The more I open up, the more I hope my brother will begin to understand.

"I don't even recognize you. You're a stranger, wearing my face, telling me to fuck off." Darc's hands unclench as he lays them flat on the counter and leans forward. "How many years have we fought side by side, carving out the life we both wanted? And now you think you can walk away on a whim? Without me? It doesn't work like that."

"I'm not trying to walk away from you, but I will if you make me choose. So, either learn to love her or move out because Val isn't going anywhere."

Walking over to the back door, I let the dogs outside. Might as well follow through on what I pretended to come down here for now that the threat of violence has subsided. As I wait for the dogs to come back inside, I hear footsteps coming down the stairs.

"Play nice," I whisper, shooting my brother a look.

One step into the kitchen, Val's eyes fall on Darc as he washes his hands for a second time. "Oh, sorry. I came down to see what was taking so long. I should have figured you were the reason the dogs were barking."

Val walks towards the sink and picks up the towel. Wiping Darc's hands, she takes them into her own. "Please tell me you didn't."

"I did it for you, sweetheart, but it's better if you don't ask questions." Darc kisses the top of her head, freezing her in place.

About to step forward, I pause when she drops his hands and wraps her arms around his waist. "I didn't ask you to." Even across the kitchen, I can see the tears streaming down her face. I'm equal parts envious and frustrated, watching the love of my life fall to pieces in my brother's arms, knowing I should have been the one protecting her.

"You'll never have to ask me to be there for you." He twists the length of her hair around his hand and directs her gaze upward. "I'm already here."

Both dogs run into the house and head straight for Val, jumping on her legs. I shut the door and walk over, touching her shoulder. Having seen enough, I need to break this up before my emotions get the better of me. "Let's go upstairs and lie down, okay? It's been a long day."

Val climbs the stairs in slow motion, allowing her hand to slide across the top of the rail as though she's memorizing the pattern of its grain. Her head bowed slightly in defeat. I worry that my brother has exposed us for the monsters we are. Or worse. Did he make himself the hero by succeeding where I failed her?

"Will you tell me what he did?" She looks at me with sadness marring the features of her face, and I would give anything to take that away. Anything except what she's asking me for.

"No." I can't lie to her, so my only option is to say nothing. Darc didn't tell me what happened, but I know him, and I'm certain I can fill in most of the blanks for myself.

"I think Allen was cheating on me with Tracy." Val sits on the edge of the bed, tears glistening in her eyes, her hands stuffed into the front pocket of her borrowed hoodie.

Sitting beside her, I offer a shoulder to rest her head against. Had I come to her defense sooner, everything would be different now. But would Val still need me if she were slightly less broken? "I think you're probably right."

A soft sob escapes her lips as she tries to bite it back. "I'm never good enough for anybody." Her words stab at my throat like red-hot needles.

"How can you say that when you know I love you more than anything?" I've lied to women in the past plenty of times, but I have no intention of lying to the woman beside me. She's the best thing that's ever happened to me, even if she remains unconvinced. I need to find a way to make her as happy as she makes me.

"Those are only words." She wraps the top half of her body around my arm as I slide my hand up her thigh.

"Then let me show you."

I lay her back on the bed and begin gently caressing her lips. Her kiss sends me to heights previously undiscovered as my fingers tangle into her hair. I've felt the way her body reacts any time I tease along her neck, and I know this is her weakness. Taking my time, I allow her a moment to absorb my touch as I gauge her response.

When she begins lightly moaning, I know she's ready for more. Even through the thick cotton of the sweatshirt, I can feel her nipples harden under my fingertips. I alternate between circling and gently squeezing before sliding my hand under the material and freeing her from the confines of its warmth. Her hips move in waves, grinding against the thigh I've positioned between her legs.

Drinking in the sight of her exposed flesh, I allow my hand to migrate further south, following her delicate curves. My hand slips under the waistband of her pants, where I locate the wet spot on the front of her panties. Her moaning increases as I brush across the damp satin, coaxing the wetness to spread.

"Do you know that I love you?" My question whispered into her neck and sealed with a kiss. I intend to give her the reassuring pleasure she requires in exchange for the answers I seek.

"Yes." Her reply is little more than an exhaled breath. With eyes shut tight, she thrusts her pelvis upwards against my touch. Her body begs to be penetrated.

Pushing her panties to the side, I allow one finger to dip inside. Then, a second. She works her body up and down the length of my fingers, showing me how she wants it. My girl knows exactly how she likes to be fucked, and she isn't shy. With each thrust of her hips against my hand, my cock swells until I feel I'm about to burst at the seams. I slide my fingers out and bring them up to my lips. Licking her off of one and then the other.

"I love the way you taste."

I give the words time to sink in before repositioning myself between her legs and sliding her pants down. Leaving her panties on, I kiss and lick, teasing her through the soft fabric. Whenever Val and I are together, I catalog her likes and dislikes, starring the items that make her body quiver.

It's not enough to rail into her and call it a night. My girl deserves more than a good fuck and a pussy full of my cum. She deserves to be pleased and cared for. She deserves to be satisfied. I move her panties to the side again, this time penetrating her with my tongue.

Pausing to kiss her thigh, I ask, "Do you know how badly I need you to be my wife?" Having her by my side, now until the end, is essential. Of this, I am certain. And I'm willing to do anything to make her mine.

"Yes! Please don't stop." Her whimpered plea is on the list of things I cannot deny.

"Say it. Tell me you'll be mine forever." I need this more than she'll ever know. Marriage is not a piece of paper that can be torn up and discarded, and it's not a contract that can be voided if either party decides to walk away. Marriage is a promise of forever, which is exactly what I am willing to give her.

"Yes. You know I will. I'll be your wife." Her fingers braid into my hair, pulling me back to the only place I long to be. "Show me how much you love me, so that I can show you how much I need you."

It doesn't take long until she's begging me to polish her off, but this isn't about crossing the finish line. We're on a casual Sunday drive tonight, and I control when it's over. Her agreement to marry is not the assurance I require.

I straddle her thighs, rubbing the head of my cock on her swollen clit. "I want to start a family with you. After today, you're done taking your birth control."

"Okay. Whatever you want. Please! I need you." She's so turned on that she'd agree to anything, but these are promises I intend for her to keep.

"Tell me you'll stop taking the pills, then I'll give you what you want."

"I'll throw them away. I promise. I want to feel you finish inside me."

I push the head in slowly, giving her time to open on her own. Then I watch as she accepts the rest of me, all the way down to the base. Seeing her beneath me, knowing she's mine, makes my cock throb. I pull nearly out before slamming back into her. Again and again.

Laying forward, I pin her body to the bed and rub my thumb across her lips before kissing her. "Open your eyes and tell me one last thing. Am I the one you want to be with?"

Her eyes flutter open as she acclimates to the light and the proximity of my face. I watch intently as her eyebrows pull together, and she shakes her head. Reaching to touch my face, she finally responds. "You're the one I want, Kold. You're my whole life." She sucks in a ragged breath, preparing for what's ahead.

"I love you so much." My eyes remain locked on her as my thrusts increase in frequency and power. "I've only ever loved you."

Her hands move to my back as her nails dig into my flesh. "Oh my god, Kold. You're gonna make me..."

We convulse together as she squeezes every drop from me. I fall to the side, still holding her in my arms. Unable to let go. Not until she promises me forever. "Tell me you meant all of that, Val. I need to know those weren't just words."

Her chest rises and falls as she takes my hand and places it over her racing heart. "I'm not in the habit of lying to you."

Once Kold is sound asleep, lightly snoring into his pillow, I slip back into my sweatpants and a tank top. As quietly as possible, I pass through the bedroom door, down the stairs, and into the kitchen. I do my best to walk through the house without the aid of a light, feeling along the wall as I go. Taking a glass from the cupboard, I begin filling it with water from the sink. Without a sound, Darc joins me in the kitchen, scaring me half to death.

"I'm sorry. I didn't mean to wake you. I was trying to be quiet." I sound nervous, and with good reason. Even though Darc is the spitting image of Kold, the two couldn't be more different. Physically, they're both intimidating, but mentally and emotionally, Darc is the kind of guy who would destroy a woman without bothering to notice, let alone care.

He walks towards me, takes the glass from my hand, and spills the water into the sink. Then, he fills it using the water pitcher from the fridge and hands it back. "I was already awake. Kind of hard to sleep when I have to listen to someone else constantly pleasing you. It's infuriating."

I shake my head, taking a step back. "Stop pretending it bothers you when we both know it doesn't. You're playing some kind of weird game with your brother that I don't understand, and I'm not interested in being a part of it."

"And yet here you are. My brother wants you married and

pregnant in a big house with a white picket fence, but that isn't the future you want, is it? I see you, Valentine... You want to be tied to my bed, blindfolded, accepting pain and pleasure as I see fit. You want to submit, and you want me to be the one in control. You don't have to hide who you are with me. I can give you what you need. And I will do whatever it takes to have you. So, stop fucking ignoring me!"

He steps forward, urging me back until there's no place left to go. Then grabs onto my waist and sets me on the counter, pushing my knees apart.

"Please don't. You don't know me well enough to say any of this." Every word is uttered in a whisper as I push my hands into his chest, but he's carved from stone like Kold and impossible to move. "I know you don't care about what happens to me, but you should care about what this would do to your brother."

"Oh please, don't flatter yourself. You wouldn't be the first woman we've shared, and you won't be the last."

"You're disgusting, and I want nothing to do with you!" For a second, I think about slapping him, but I'm not entirely confident he won't hit me back. "If you don't allow me to go upstairs, I will scream."

"Oh, sweetheart, I wish you would. My dick gets hard whenever I think about you screaming for me. I can't wait to be buried inside you."

"Anything above a whisper, and I'm setting off a two-dog alarm in the bedroom where your brother is currently sleeping. What do you think would happen then?"

"If you assume he'll stop me from having you, you're wrong. He'll hand you over willingly. It's only a matter of time. Unless you come to me on your own. When you're done playing make-believe with my brother, you know where my bedroom is." He leans forward, planting a kiss above my collarbone. "Don't keep me waiting too long."

He backs away a few inches, enough for me to slide off the counter straight into his erection. Darc stiffens against me, clearly impressed with himself. When I try to move to the side, he raises his arms on either side of me, hands gripping the counter's edge.

"Goodnight," I say dismissively. My voice trembles, but it's the best I can muster under the circumstances.

"Goodnight, sweetheart. I'll see you in the morning." He kisses the top of my head and steps back, allowing me to pass.

I move quickly but silently, not wanting to wake up the rest of the house. When I crawl back under the blanket, Kold rolls over and pulls me into his arms.

"Where'd you go?" His words become more pronounced the further he distances himself from sleep. "I thought maybe you went down to let the dogs out, but they're still in here."

"My throat was dry, so I went to the kitchen for a drink of water. Then came right back." My statement is meant to sound matter-of-fact, but I can hear a slight shakiness layered into my tone. Darc's words ring in my ears, and his touch lingers on my skin.

"You would tell me if something happened, right?" The weight of his accusation presses down like an atlas stone. Only three days in, and he thinks I would sneak downstairs in the middle of the night to hook up with his brother? Guess it's nice to know where we stand.

"Don't ever marry someone you don't trust. It's not worth it." My words are cold and soaked in venom. But they're also meant as a warning. I learned this lesson the hard way. No reason he should have to repeat my mistake. And as far as I'm concerned, if the trust is gone already, there isn't any point in sticking around.

Darc was right as much as he was wrong. The idea of marriage makes me sick to my stomach. And I'm not one hundred percent on board with having kids, either. But that doesn't mean I'll hop from one bed to the next, even if he does call to a part of me that wants to come out to play.

"My love, I'm not accusing you of anything. My brother is a fucking asshole. It's him I don't trust, not you."

Whatever long-stemming sibling rivalry these two have, I would prefer not to be involved. I get the feeling a girl like me would be collateral damage in under a week. I'd disappear into the void while they moved on to the next, never bothering to look behind at the trail of broken bodies left in their wake.

"I get the impression he doesn't like that I'm here. It would probably be in everyone's best interest if Christmas and I left first thing in the morning." Darc seems to want to hate fuck me, though I have no idea what I've done to merit his ire.

Kold sits up in bed and pulls back the blanket. "Tell me exactly what he said."

CHAPTER 25
Kold

It isn't difficult to read Val's body language. When something is bothering her, she wears it like a winter coat. The woman doesn't have much of a poker face, for one, but even in the dark, her body gives her away. As my hand glides over her skin, I feel the tension twisting her shoulder muscles into knots.

I get out of bed, pulling her up with me. "Alexa! Shuffle playlist Valentine's Day."

The first song that comes on isn't what I have in mind for the moment. "Skip!"

"What are you doing? I love that song." Val touches my chest, causing my heart to pick up the pace, matching the beat of the next song. "Ooo, this is a good one too. What is this playlist? I like this."

"Damnit, Alexa! Play, Lost Letter to My Valentine." As the music starts, I wrap one arm across the small of her back and take her hand into mine. We begin to sway with the beat, dancing together in the dark.

"I don't know this song. Who's it by?" Val is overthinking again. I can feel it in her stiffened movements. She's half in this moment with me and half in the kitchen with him.

"Shhh. I want to dance with you." It took me a month to write and record this song. I started it the night we met, but it wasn't until weeks later that I found the chorus. From the beginning, I knew it had to be as perfect as the girl it was written for. Someday, this song would serve as a record of the night I fell in love, and the days I spent dying without her.

"This guy's voice reminds me of yours. I want to fall asleep listening to him on repeat."

I've never sung for a girl before, but there's so much inside of me that needs to come out, and I'm choking on all the swallowed feelings. When I begin to sing along with the recording, Val rests her head against my chest, and her body relaxes.

By the end, I could feel her tears on my skin. "Are you okay, my love?"

"Yeah, that was a beautiful song. I'm a total sucker for sentiment, and I know what it's like to love someone you can't have." Val wipes her cheeks and comes up on her toes to kiss me. "Can you send me this playlist so I can listen to it on repeat until my heart breaks into dust?"

"Why would I want that? That sounds terrible. Did it make you think of someone from your past?" The lyrics didn't have the effect I was going for. Further proof that punk rock guys who listen to metal music shouldn't write love songs.

"No. It's more current than that, like a heartbreak that hasn't hit me yet. The kind of truth that takes a minute to sink in once denial has worn off."

"I'll be honest, dear, you've kind of lost me. I'm not exactly sure who you're thinking about, and I'm kind of new to the whole *Love* thing."

"Well, from what I've gathered, there are three kinds of love. There's a love that takes up time. It fills the moments with stuff that doesn't matter, and when it's over, you leave wishing you had valued yourself more from the start. Then, there's the kind of love that speeds up time. It forces you to cling to memories as they fade slowly away. Reminding you that nothing is permanent. And there's a love that stops time. The sort you might find once in a lifetime. There aren't necessarily lessons to be learned, but there is a price to pay. You get to live as a whole person in one suspended moment, but when it's over, there's no going back to who you were before. You leave hollow, wishing you had known to cherish the seconds you had and the person you held dear. The first kind will test you. The second will break you. And the third will shatter you beyond repair."

"Well, goddamn, babe. I'm sorry. I didn't realize your marriage left you feeling that way." The more Val opens up, the more I want to be the glue that holds her together. But I worry she'll keep me at arm's length and eventually push me away, claiming it's for my own good.

"Oh, it didn't. I wasn't talking about him. John was more of a level one love." She says with a laugh, confusing me even further.

I'm not sure if I'm still half asleep or a complete idiot, but I have no idea what my girl is talking about. She conducted an entire semester course on the levels of Love, compacted into one 68-second speech, all while dancing around my questions about her impending devastation. She said *a heartbreak that hasn't hit me yet,* and I find it hard to believe she was talking about Allen if her marriage falls under level one.

"Is there something you want to tell me? Something about us? Something that happened downstairs? You're saying a lot without answering my questions, and I feel like you're going out of your way to spare my feelings, but I don't know why." There's an entire conversation happening at the fringe of what is being said, and I need her to start being straight with me before I walk downstairs and do something irreversible.

"I think, maybe, we should try being friends."

"What the fuck are you talking about?!?" I grip her arms, careful not to squeeze too hard. "Before I fell asleep, you looked me in the eyes and told me you were in love. Then you came back from the kitchen, tense as fuck, talking about heartbreak and denial and love that leaves you dead inside. And now, all of a sudden, you want to be friends? But I'm supposed to believe nothing happened downstairs to make you feel this way." I pull her into me, wrapping my arms around her, vowing to myself never to let go. "Tell me what he did!"

"Nothing, okay! I'm scared."

"Of me?" I take a deep breath and calm myself before saying anything further. I let go long enough to click on the lamp beside the bed. If Val intends to take a wrecking ball to my dreams, I want to watch her do it. Tears stream down her face as she stands before me, shaking.

Sitting on the bed, I extend my hand to her, and she takes it. "Please talk to me. Whatever I did to make you feel this way, I didn't mean for it to happen."

"This competition with your brother is not one I'm willing to engage in, so I give up." She sits on my lap and tucks her head between my neck and shoulder. "I do love you, but I don't want you to resent me if I'm the reason you lose the life you built before me."

"Fuck that! You're my priority. If you're telling me right now that I have to choose between you and my brother, I'm choosing you. Okay? I don't want to go backward. I don't want to be friends. If all the talk about marriage and kids is making you take a step back, I understand, and I won't bring it up again."

"It's not that. I love the idea of having that life with you someday. But at the same time, I'm scared. If I let myself believe everything you say during sex, and we split up before we make it to that point, I'll have to mourn the loss of you and the future we never had. I can't handle the thought of losing a lifetime with you."

While she's talking, Val touches her hand to my chest and holds it there. I wonder if she's monitoring my heart rate or my breathing. Or maybe she's trying to connect. I take a few more deep breaths and find my control before opening my mouth. I thought I was about to lose her, but she wasn't as ready to give up as I feared.

"Love, I need you to understand, and this is in no particular order." I reach behind me and grab the quilt, wrapping it around us. Now that the intensity of the moment has resolved, I'm starting to get cold, and Val isn't exactly in warm clothing.

"The future we talked about is what I want our life to look like, but it wasn't something I prepared for. Before you came along, I never thought I'd find someone worth sharing it with. You've asked me to prove myself over time, and I intend to do that, but you can't cut me off at the knees each time someone else interferes. That being said, I will have a discussion with my brother as soon as we're finished talking. Whatever he did or said to upset you, I'm not okay with. If you still want to leave, we can. Tonight, in the morning, whenever you want. We can go back to your place and stay there, but I need you to tell me that you're not giving up!"

Val spins on my lap so her legs and arms are around my torso, sinking deeper into the hug. Waiting for her answer, I can't help but smile, thinking she reminds me of a koala bear climbing a tree. I play with her hair until her face comes level with mine.

"I'm sorry I suggested being friends. That isn't what I want. I mean, I would like to marry my best friend, but I don't want you to *only* be my friend. And I'm going to stop saying *friend* now. Honestly, nothing crazy happened downstairs, I swear to you. Please don't go down there assuming the worst. Your brother said something that triggered my flight response, and I should've slept it off and reevaluated in the light of day. That song you put on had me pretty deep in my feelings, thinking about what it was like to miss you every second of every day. I'm afraid to love you as much as I do, so I find myself pulling back one second and giving in the next. It's confusing and frustrating to me, so I imagine it's equally so, if not more, for you. I'm not giving up on us. I'm sorry..."

I kiss her before she can say the rest, finally hearing everything I need for the moment. The conversation with my brother is going to have to wait. Right now, all I want to do is hold her in my arms until we both fall asleep or until it's time for breakfast. Whichever comes last.

Val loves me, and she isn't giving up. Beyond that, nothing else matters.

CHAPTER 26

Val

As my body begins to awake from sleep, I have a heart-stopping moment when I realize the sun is up and my alarm has yet to go off. Grabbing my phone from the nightstand, I check the time and throw back the blanket, racing to the bathroom to drain my bladder and find clothes.

While washing my hands in the sink, I catch sight of myself in the mirror and remember that I'm working from home today. Now I can relax. It takes a second for my body to regulate, having jumped directly from sleep to sheer panic and back down to relative calm. I take a deep breath and step back into the bedroom, realizing I'm alone. I wonder where everyone is. The bed I came from seconds ago is painfully empty, along with the oversized dog bed on the floor.

"I guess they're downstairs already," I comment to myself aloud. "Nice of them to wake me up for work."

I reset the alarm on my phone so tomorrow morning isn't a repeat of today, and head downstairs to find the family. The passing thought makes me smile to myself. I suppose I do think of Christmas as my child. And oddly enough, I've begun including others in my domestic equation without a conscious effort.

Kold and Midnight fit into my life like they were always meant to be there. Even Darc, with his brooding sex appeal and piss-poor attitude, has taken up residence in an abandoned section of my withered heart. But that's for me to know and for him to find out, never rather than sooner.

It's been a while since I was part of a family, and it's nice to feel like I belong. Although, I need to check with everyone to ensure I'm welcome.

The sound of the TV in the living room has me turning left at the bottom of the stairs instead of right toward the kitchen.

"Good morning."

The sound of his voice, in combination with the sight of him on the couch, cuddled up with both dogs, pulls a response from my heart instead of my brain. "I had hoped you'd be in bed with me this morning when I woke up. I had something I wanted to give you."

Quickly, he jumps up from the couch and walks toward me with fire in his eyes and a smirk on his face. Before I can utter another word, he tangles his hand into my hair and kisses me. The passion sets my body ablaze. As the intensity of his kiss increases, I can feel him backing me toward the wall.

While continuing to kiss me using a delectable amount of tongue, he grabs my ass and lifts me off the ground, pressing me into the wall as my legs settle around his waist. Everything within me craves more. He feels like a fantasy come to life, and I don't want it to stop. Thankfully, neither does he. When his kiss moves to my neck, my lips tingle as though he's still there, and I want his mouth on me for the rest of the day.

"Mmmm. You're getting me so turned on right now. I hope you intend to follow through." I want to beg for his cock, even though I'll never have to. Feeling the parts of my body that yearn for his lips aching beneath his touch causes my need for him to deepen.

I pull down the front of my tank top, exposing my hardened nipples. There have been times when I considered getting larger breasts, but being on the smaller side has meant a life free from the confines of a bra. Occasionally, I'll wear something lacey when I want to be sexy, but for daily life, I go without. And my B cup has remained perky even as I've aged into my mid-thirties, which I am immensely thankful for during moments like this.

He looks down at my offering and licks his lips. "Oh, sweet girl. You have no idea. I intend on taking excellent care of you for a *very* long time. You're all I can think about. Now tell me you love me, so I can bend you over the arm of that couch and fuck you until your body gives out."

"Ohh. Yes, please. I need to feel you inside me." I kiss him again as the wetness pools between my legs. "I love you. Today, and for the rest of my life." I love this man with every fiber of my being, even if I struggle to fully accept that he loves me back.

"Hearing you say that makes me so fucking hard." He allows my body to lower a few inches, aligning the parts of us that desire a connection. Even through our clothes, I can feel the ridge of his cock as it rubs over my clit.

"I can see why my brother likes it so much." His words catch me mid-moan, strangling the sound as it sucks back into my lungs.

The realization of my actions hits like a truck as I struggle to free myself from his arms. But he pulls me back up, locks my legs in place with his arms, and presses me into the wall with his chest.

"What the fuck, Darc! Put me down. Why the hell would you do that?" At the sound of my whispered distress, both dogs begin barking from the couch, finally taking notice of my presence.

"Calm down!" His words are an order I follow without question. Maybe it's the confidence in his tone when he speaks, but I find myself ready to obey, unafraid of what he'll ask of me. "I have every intention of burying myself inside of you, Valentine. But I needed you to know I was the one pleasing you."

"You know damn well I thought you were Kold. I can't fricken tell you two apart when you're wearing long sleeves." The lingering effects of the previous moment are still pulsing in my core, suspended dangerously close to the instrument of their release. I need him to put me down before we get caught by my actual boyfriend.

"Despite your intentions, *we* are not having sex this morning.

But if you put me down, I will keep this between us." Secrets and lies are one and the same, but I've convinced myself that this one is for the benefit of us all. Knowing Kold, he'll be more upset with his brother than me. I don't know what it is with these two, but they seem on the verge of killing each other one minute and back to being best friends the next. Maybe it's a twin thing.

Darc lowers me from the wall and returns me to my feet before pressing his erection into my torso. "I'm going to need a minute, woman. You're fucking killing me with this shit."

Walking away toward the kitchen, I'm not sure that I should follow, but the dogs chase after him like he's the pied piper. So, I fix my tank top and trail behind, tethered to him with secrets and a desire to better understand who he is beneath the surface.

Opening the back door, I call for Christmas and Midnight to take a lap around the yard. I lean against the wall, watching Darc from the corner of my eye, pretending not to notice him. After a few minutes, Midnight races inside, with Christmas prancing close behind. Seeing them bond so quickly is cute, but it makes leaving that much harder.

"I'm sorry about what I said last night." Darc joins me at the door, handing me a fresh cup of coffee. "I was being jealous and petty. I wanted to hurt you the way your rejection hurt me, but I realized after you walked away that I was being unfair. And when I spoke with my brother this morning, I assured him you would receive an adequate apology."

"Well, next time, could you just tell me that you're sorry instead of apologizing with your tongue." Unintentionally, I send my mind straight into the gutter, where I keep a file of all the stolen glances and undisclosed interactions we've shared thus far. Darc is fascinating, but he's also slightly terrifying. I've been trying to avoid him, but perhaps that was the wrong play. It seems my disregard has made me more appealing.

When he laughs in response to my request, I'm caught off guard. Darc isn't one to engage in lighthearted emotional exchanges. His intensity seems permanently set to an eleven, so it's strange to see him smile in such a genuine way.

"If that's what you want, I'll abide. Although, I do think my way is more fun... In addition, I would like to offer you full use of my office, since I heard you're working from home this week. I find it easier to be productive behind a desk. So, do you forgive me?" He takes the mug of coffee from my hands and pulls me into a one-sided hug.

"Depends on what all you're seeking my forgiveness for." I bring my arms up around his waist, completing the embrace.

"Well, there's no way I'm ever apologizing for this morning. So, I suggest you take what I'm offering and get to work." The richness of his voice hits differently than Kold's, as though Darc is speaking from a place buried deeper inside. Someplace previously undiscovered, even by him.

"Fine. I forgive you for last night. Now give me back my coffee, and let me grab my stuff." I finally take a sip from the mug, testing the flavor before exiting the kitchen. "Mmmm. This is perfection."

When I look up, he's smiling. "I pay attention."

The way he looks at me, with a gaze still soaked in desire, hints at something more. Darc is confusing. He flirts with me and then he's rude to me. He tells me he's there for me and then tells me I'm no one special. He turns me on only to stop before the follow-through. One minute, he likes me, and the next, he hates the sight of me. He's a tough nut to crack, but I'm no sugar plum fairy.

Darc takes my hand and motions for me to follow. "Your computer is set up and ready to go. I have your files stacked neatly in three piles. Your bag is next to the desk. And anything else you need can be found in the drawers. Right this way."

Leading me through his bedroom, Darc takes me to a room off the back of the house that I never noticed before. Or maybe I saw it and didn't bother to think about its purpose. Either way, here I am, standing in the most impressive home office I've ever seen, realizing Darc is much more than I initially picked up on.

"Well, I'll leave you to it." He stops at the door, turns to face me, and says one last thing before he goes. "Hey, Valentine."

I look at him and grin, feeling powerful and confident, positioned behind his desk. I rarely feel this way in my day-to-day life, but Darc speaks to a side of me that longs to break free. He calls to her by name, invoking fragments of her authority.

"Yes, Darc."

"Just so it doesn't go unsaid. I love you too."

Kold

After my workout, I went upstairs to shower, but Val was nowhere to be found. Her bag of clothes is on the chair, and Christmas is asleep on the couch in the living room, but my girlfriend is mysteriously absent. Darc isn't here either, and his car is missing from the garage, meaning they went somewhere together.

I'm trying not to overthink, but breathing through this one doesn't seem to be working. I've messaged them both at this point, with no reply. She didn't even pop her head into the gym to say good morning. And if she needed a ride somewhere, I would have taken her. How could she leave with him? Last night, she was talking about being friends after something happened in the kitchen that she refused to mention. And now the two of them sneak off together right under my nose.

I turn the water on and step into the shower without waiting for it to warm. Something is going on between them, and I need to find out what it is. Losing Val would be a death sentence, and Darc would fuck her just to prove he could.

> Evil Twin: What's your problem? Why are you blowing up my phone like some obsessed one-night stand? Go hang out with your girlfriend and leave me the fuck alone!

I respond immediately as the angle of my concern shifts.

> : Val isn't with you?

> Evil Twin: No. Why would she be with me? Because of you, she barely fucking looks at me. She's probably in the office, working. Did you try using your eyes and looking for her?

Admittedly, I did *not* think to look in there, though I did call her name repeatedly from various locations throughout the house. I even went so far as to ask the dogs if they had seen where she went, but they ignored me.

> : Why would she be in YOUR office?

> Evil Twin: Because you turned YOUR office into a gym.

I started rinsing off in the shower, but the rest will have to wait. Wrapping a towel around my waist, I head downstairs to check the office for signs of life. In the search for my missing girlfriend, it never crossed my mind to check Darc's bedroom, although maybe it should have.

Cracking open the door, I peek inside and find Val sitting behind her computer, listening to something on her headphones and inputting data. Her fingers move faster on the keys than I would have thought humanly possible, and I'm not sure how she can type that fast without making a million mistakes. I guess when something is your job, and you do it every day, you get pretty good at it.

When I first picked up a guitar, I had to think about each finger and each cord. And forget about singing while playing.

There was no way. Now, when I'm on stage, playing guitar and singing is little more than muscle memory. I find myself searching through the sea of faces, looking for some way to connect so that it won't all seem so pointless.

I walk over and sit on the edge of the desk, causing her to jump. She pulls her headphones off and eyes me suspiciously, leaving me to speak first.

"You look adorably studious while you're working. Do you mind if I join you after my shower?" Seeing Val on her computer reminds me that I have no less than a million things I need to be doing as well. People tend to get angry when their paychecks aren't deposited on time, and I need to schedule the club's liquor order before the upcoming show.

"I can take a break if you'd like some company." Her eyes suggest more than washing each other's backs, and I won't pretend to be disappointed.

To turn down an offer like that, I would have to be dead, and even then, my ghost would find a way to spiritedly address her needs. Every second naked with Val is time well spent. So, I stand and offer her my hand.

"Regarding your company, my love, I am fully invested. Consider me, all in." I take her hand and slide it under my towel.

"What's gotten into you this morning? Whatever it is, I like it." Val begins stroking my cock as I harden in her hand.

"I came in for an interview, but clumsy me, I spilled coffee all over myself and had to change into this towel. Can I still discuss the position with you, or do you need me to get dressed first?" I do my best CEO/secretary porn pitch and hope she plays along.

"Clumsiness is not something I value here at my company, so that's strike one. However, judging from the definition of your muscles, I can tell that you enjoy hard work and a vigorous routine. Because of that, I'm willing to allow you the opportunity to convince me. I will give you one chance to demonstrate that you're a worthy hire. I suggest you not disappoint me... This is a leadership position, though you may find yourself underneath me at times. No worries, there is plenty of opportunity for growth."

Goddamn, this woman is perfect.

She fell into character without hesitation, as though we had toiled over the details, discussing our roles and hard limits beforehand. I knew Val liked to get kinky and play around, but I keep learning new things, and I've yet to be dissatisfied.

"Is your expectation that I will come in and take control? Or will I be following your orders?" I stay in character, eager to see how this plays out.

"Hmmm. I will need you to fill in for me from time to time. So, for this interview, I want you to forget that I'm the boss and show me how you would manage a difficult employee." Val gets up from her chair and stands beside the desk, ready to be *managed*.

With my voice firm and my cock swelling, I reprimand her for this morning. "You failed to greet me when you arrived downstairs, disappeared without informing me of your location, and refused to respond to my messages. Each one of these offenses is unacceptable and grounds for immediate termination. Do you have anything you'd like to say on your behalf before I carry you out of here?"

Val drops to her knees in front of me, looks up with doe eyes, and begins to beg. "Please don't fire me. I'll do anything. When I came downstairs, I immediately said good morning to you, but it was someone pretending to be you. Only I didn't know until it was too late. The other man put me in here and took my phone away. He told me I would be punished if I told anyone what happened. So, you see, sir. I had no choice. It wasn't my fault."

What the fuck is she talking about? Is she making this up, or did this happen?

"Val, stop!" I lift her by the arms and hold her until she finds her feet. "Are you playing around right now, or did Darc do something again? I want you to tell me the truth!"

Her face hardens as any hint of the previous playfulness disappears. "You have failed your interview! Please see my secretary on the way out, and she will validate your parking."

"Oh, for Christ's sake! Avocado. Macintosh apple. Green

bean casserole. Cranberry Sauce. Whatever the goddamn safe word is, stop!"

Val sits on the edge of the desk, laughing before settling into a smile. "Why are all your safe words food?"

"Because guys who live in the gym are always hungry." I don't mean to sound cross with her, but it's infuriating when she dodges my questions. I want her to know she can tell me the truth, and I'll still love her.

She touches my collarbone with the tips of her fingers and runs her hand over my shoulder and down my arm, stopping to squeeze my bicep. "Well, whatever you're doing, it's working."

Coming up on her toes, she kisses me before leaning back against the edge of the desk. "Do you still want to shower together, or did I mess that up too?"

Leave it to me to overreact and kill the scene as things were heating up. I was two seconds away from bending her over the desk and having my way with her. But instead, we're here, dancing around the conversation, trying to pretend nothing happened.

"Come on, let's go. I'll make it up to you in the shower." I take Val's hand and lead her out of the office, through Darc's bedroom, and into the kitchen hallway.

"You can make it up to me on the bed after we shower." She squeezes my hand and falls half a step closer. "That way, I don't have to hold back."

When we reach the stairs, I let her move ahead of me. Mostly because I want to look at her ass but also because I worry about her getting lightheaded again on the way up. "I love the way your mind works."

Once inside the room, I close the door to avoid having an audience later. Val begins stripping off her clothes, and all I can do is stand in stunned silence and watch. She's perfect in a way that far surpasses the physical. I'm not sure what I could have possibly done over the course of my life to deserve her, but whatever it was, I'm glad I did it.

"Are you coming with me, or are you planning to watch?"

Her choice of words is always intentional. My girl knows how to flirt.

She bites her bottom lip as I remove my towel and follow her into the bathroom. There's no possible way I'll get through this shower without being inside her. Val might as well bend over the sink right now and take what's coming to her.

CHAPTER 27

Val

As the days pass, Kold and I fall into a natural rhythm, finding out where we fit in the other person's life. He has made it clear that I'm a top priority, and thus far, his actions have backed up the claim. I love his consistency and honesty, but I've been fooled too many times in the past, and I know better than to trust the declarations of men.

"Tonight, I want to take you on a date, so finish your files and let's call it a week. You've been hammering away at those keys nonstop since Tuesday, and I think it's time for a reward."

I look away from the computer long enough to absorb his smile. Then, it's right back into the light. Kold doesn't know this, but I've been working double time because I have off all next week. I hope to convince him to join me on a staycation, though I have no idea if that's even possible.

I had been nervous to ask about his work, but curiosity finally got the best of me. Apparently, Kold manages the accounting for a handful of local companies, including Club After Darc and two other bars he co-owns with his brother. And here I thought he was simply a pretty face, sexy voice, and impressive body. Who knew there was a remarkable brain in play as well?

I guess I did sort of know, if I'm being honest. Five minutes into our conversation that first night, I recognized his depth of character. Kold seemed to be brimming with untapped potential, but I was mistaken. He's doing more with his life than I initially gave him credit for, and I'm suddenly feeling insecure about my own meager accomplishments.

"Can you give me one hour? Then I'm all yours... I promise." I smile back without meeting his eyes. If I stop what I'm doing now, he'll start giving me that *Let's have Sex* look, and I'll have to slink back down here in the middle of the night to finish.

My fingers press the keys in succession with minimal effort as my mind wanders down a path that leads straight for a cliff.

I can only imagine what might await me if I snuck into Darc's bedroom in the middle of the night. Claiming I came down to work would only turn him on faster. Even if I were being honest, he would find a way to collect the toll before allowing me to pass. He never misses an opportunity to touch me, even with my personal guard close at hand.

Darc isn't afraid of anyone, including his brother. Though, I wonder if that isn't a potentially dangerous oversight on his part. Not that I want the two of them fighting over me. Kold knows if push comes to shove, I'll walk away rather than be the reason their relationship dissolves.

After a week together, morning, noon, and night, Kold has carved out a permanent settlement in my heart and maintains a second residence in my head. And don't even get me started on the frequent trips he takes to vacation between my thighs. At this point, I've resigned myself to the fact that my body is no longer my own. Severing ties with him, at this point, would be panic-inducing and potentially life-ending.

I keep thinking I'll get annoyed and need a second alone, but it doesn't happen. Given a choice, I'd never stop looking at him. The strength of his jaw and the grin that plays at his lips. Perfect lips that should be kissed with the utmost care. And eyes that rival the depth of any soul. He's more than I deserve and everything I desire.

Kold rolls his chair beside mine and places his chin on my shoulder. "What are you thinking about? You keep smiling, and I doubt it has anything to do with dear, sweet Jillian Humphry's medical records."

The proximity of his perfection is too much for me to ignore. I've held out as long as I can, and I give myself credit for making it this far. We've been in this room working for the last eight hours and haven't had sex once. That's a new personal best for us.

Yesterday, when Darc left to pick up lunch, he wasn't even out of the driveway, and Kold had me bent over the edge of the mahogany desk. And let's just say, this time around, he got the job. I did feel a twinge of guilt after having sex in Darc's office, but I figured what he doesn't know can't hurt him.

"I was thinking about how badly I want to kiss you." All I would have to do is turn my head. His lips are right there over my shoulder.

"Well, shit! I've been thinking about that since we woke up this morning. It's been torture, sitting three feet from you and being unable to touch you."

"I want to finish this file. Can I buy one more hour in here for the low price of a single kiss?" I continue to type while he considers my offer.

"You know you're supposed to cut out early when it's a holiday weekend, right?" Kold grips the arm of my chair and spins me ninety degrees so I'm facing him. "Come find me in the gym when you're done."

The kiss we share is sweet, but lingering. It's enough to satiate my need for him without throwing me into a chasm of desire. It's too easy for me to be distracted when he's around, looking as appetizing as he does. And I get it. I shouldn't complain. Every woman should be so lucky to have a man like Kold. I would make copies and hand them out to my friends if I had any. But as wonderful as he is, he's also intense and all-consuming. I'm not sure I remember how to exist without him anymore.

Now that I'm alone, I put on my headphones and type as fast as possible without my accuracy suffering. Kold and I haven't spoken about the upcoming holiday or the concert tomorrow night. We haven't talked about next week or plans for the new year. The feeling I get from Kold is that our being together is a given, and there is nothing further to discuss.

There's a comfort in feeling settled, but also a hesitation. Am

I letting my guard down and setting myself up for devastation? Is a week truly enough time to honestly know someone? Kold wants me to move in, but I'm not sold on the idea. Not that I want to be away from him. I don't. But I worry about finding a new place after he realizes I'm nothing special. Maybe I'm being stupid because I'm scared. It would be a shame to miss out on a lifetime with the love of my life because the mistakes of my past have left me emotionally damaged.

This is the kind of nonstop back-and-forth battle that's being waged in my mind from the time I wake up until I close my eyes at night. I'm nobody. Half the time, I feel like a non-player character in my own life, going through the motions, hoping no one will notice me.

With Kold's face, talent, and career, he's a viral video away from taking a one-way trip to the top, and I'm worried he might tear up the ticket if it doesn't include my name.

Overthinking everything and conveniently missing the most prominent pieces is sort of my thing. It's easy for me to want the best for others, cheerleading for their success, while my accomplishments go unnoticed. I prefer not to stand out. If life is a hunger game, my weapon of choice is camouflage.

Before I know it, my hour is up, my work is finished, and my mood is in the toilet. Life would be so much easier if I were pretty.

Kold

I catch sight of Val in my peripheral vision as she stands, watching me from the doorway. The crooked smile on her face could best be described as a suggestive smirk, and that's all it takes for me to stop what I'm doing mid-set. Val is gorgeous. She's the most beautiful woman I've ever seen, but that beauty is comprised of so much more than her looks.

"Can I please have you now, or did you come to renegotiate terms for more time?" The idea of waiting even one more second is excruciating.

"Let the weekend officially begin. I'm all yours." Before the words finish passing her lips, she's in my arms. Holding her is the best part of any day, and this hug has been a long time coming.

"You need a shower. You're kind of gross right now." Val pulls the sweat-soaked shirt away from my back, allowing the air to brush over my skin. There's no point in arguing the matter because she's right. I smell mildly disgusting, and my skin is tacky with sweat.

"So long as you love me, we can fix the other part." I back her into the wall and press my lips to hers before taking her hand and leading her upstairs.

I only have one week left to convince her to move in here. So, I'm pulling out all the stops for our date tonight. I've booked a table at the nicest restaurant downtown and a suite at the best hotel. I even considered getting a driver, but when I called to inquire about the service, I found out they use the same SUV I already drive, so that seemed pointless. Darc gave me the contact info for a stylist he sleeps with on occasion, and she'll be here in an hour to do hair and makeup, with possible clothing options.

Is it overkill? You're goddamn right it is! Do I care? Yes and No. I know Val. She'll be pissed at me for spending so much on her, but I refuse to believe she'll be mad enough to let it ruin the evening. My goal tonight is to make this the best first date she's ever been on, knocking her impromptu road trip to the casino out of the top spot.

It would be easy to stay home and watch a movie in bed, but we've done that every night this week. Val insists she's happy with free dates, and I believe her, but I want to show her what I have to offer. A life with me could be so much more than she's used to.

"Are you going to tell me where we're going tonight? I need to have some idea of what to wear, and you're being uncharacteristically quiet. Should I be worried?" She peppers me with questions as we undress, ready to shower.

The urge to spill my guts is so strong that the words taste like acid. "I've taken care of everything. All you have to do is shower and mentally prepare for our first date!" I pull her into the water, kissing her shoulder before allowing her to step away.

Since last Friday, we've showered together every day, and this afternoon is no exception. Thankfully, when Darc and I had the house built, we insisted on installing two shower heads in all of the bathrooms because you never know when you might want company.

I've become secretly obsessed with watching Val's hair-washing ritual. Something about it makes my heart pitter-pat against my ribs. The way she closes her eyes and breaths in the scent of the shampoo before massaging it into her hair. Then she stretches her neck from side to side, letting the hot water redden her delicate skin, before rinsing out the suds and moving on to the conditioner. She always smiles when she catches me staring and playfully calls me out on my creepy stalker behavior.

I can't imagine it's possible to love any one person more. She's my whole world, and I wonder if she knows.

She beckons me closer with the movement of one finger and a coy smile. Her simple gesture is a royal decree I would never dream of denying. When it comes to Val, if I have it in my power to give, I will, without question. Not that she asks for much.

"You know my wardrobe here is fairly limited, right? All I have is one work outfit and some relaxing clothes. Are you planning to stop by my place so I can grab something acceptable to wear? Or are we going out in sweats to see a movie?"

I can see the concern weighing on her as if she's worried about disappointing me. "My love, when I say 'I've taken care of everything,' I mean *everything*. I promise I've got you covered."

Her brows narrow as she eyes me suspiciously. "How much exactly did this 'date' cost you?"

"A lot less than I was willing to spend." I kiss her before she can argue, reaching around to turn off the water. "Come on. We need to get ready. Our reservation is at 6:30."

For a moment, I second-guess my decision to go overboard. It's not a first-class flight to Paris, although that thought did cross my mind. I wasn't sure if Val had a passport, and I didn't think we could make it back in time for the show tomorrow night, so I decided to keep things local.

As much as I love Val the way she is, her aversion to receiving gifts is something she needs to overcome. I want to spoil her rotten, but pleasure is the only tribute she will accept without complaint. And even then, she tries to make it about me.

It's too late to cancel the reservations. I need to be brave and hope she doesn't kill me.

CHAPTER 28

Val

The goddess-inspired brunette sitting on the edge of Kold's bed stands to face me as we walk out of the bathroom in only our towels. Maybe this is the on-again-off-again girlfriend from high school that I stupidly assumed Allen was lying about. Struck deaf by the sound of my breaking heart, I don't catch anything she says as she takes a second step in my direction. All I know is that this beautiful woman has come to drop a grenade in the middle of my fairytale, and I'm about to be sick.

"You need to breathe, my love." Strong arms wrap around me, pulling me back to the moment as Kold's voice brushes against my ear. "Whatever you're thinking, I assure you it's not that. She's here to help you get ready for our date."

"I am so sorry, you guys! I should have waited downstairs. Darc told me to come up here, so I did. But, yeah, that was stupid of me. When I heard the shower on, I should have gone back out in the hallway." The woman begins to collect her things, and I feel guilty about my initial reaction.

I reach out to touch her arm, hoping to start again. "No, please. You're perfectly fine. I wasn't expecting anyone to be here, and it surprised me. This perfectly crafted jerk didn't bother to give me a heads up because he's trying to give me a heart attack." I turn to bury my face in Kold's chest before playfully smacking his arm. "You're an asshole, and I hate you."

"No, you don't. You love me almost as much as I love you." He kisses the top of my head and then lifts my face to his. "I'm going downstairs to get ready, where I will be eagerly awaiting the big reveal. Try to enjoy yourself."

I shake my head and fight the urge to smile, eventually giving in. "Either tell me where we're going or how much you spent so I know how mad I need to be." My idle threat means nothing since I can't stop grinning up at him like some love-sick teenager.

"Two." That's all Kold says, not offering to elaborate.

"Hundred?" My guess is highly unlikely. Kold probably paid more than that for the woman standing behind me. So when he smiles and winks at me, I roll my eyes and revise my guess. "Thousand?"

"Not to interrupt, but I should probably get started if you two mean to get out of here on time. Kold, before you go, would you mind moving that chair over here so this beautiful lady of yours has a comfortable place to sit?"

Eventually, I resign myself to the reality that it's best to stop fighting and give in. There's no sense in wasting this woman's time when she's trying to do a job and get out of here. Even if Kold had dropped ten thousand dollars on our date, I couldn't be mad at him. One smile, and I'm putty in his hands.

"Don't overthink it. Believe me when I tell you you're worth it." Kold kisses me on the nose and grabs the chair from the corner of the room, still wearing a towel and nothing else.

In what I hope is my last flash of counterproductive over-thinking, I can't help but wonder if the woman currently standing with me is someone my boyfriend hooked up with in the past. The sight of him half-naked doesn't seem to be throwing her off in any way, and I can only assume that's because she's seen it before. Sort of like a *been there done that* kind of thing. Then again, would Kold be insensitive enough to throw an ex in my face or even a one-night stand? Seems unlikely, but not impossible.

After grabbing his predetermined set of clothes from the closet, he kisses me one last time before exiting the room and shutting the door behind him. I don't want him to leave, but I worry it might seem awkward if I ask him to stay.

"Let's get started so you two can get on to the fun part of your night, shall we?" She motions for me to sit in the chair, so I do.

"I'm so sorry. I'm embarrassed to admit this, but I didn't catch your name." I want to pump her for information, but first, I need to know what to call her, and then I have to work up the nerve to dig.

"Oh, sweetie, don't even worry about it. My name is Jamie. I'm friends with Darc. Or maybe not friends. More like sexual acquaintances. No. That sounds weird. Let me dry your hair, and then we can talk."

Once Jamie finishes with the blow-dryer, she pulls my hair away from my face and starts on my makeup. When it comes to being a girl, I've never been super great at it. I know enough to get by and catch the occasional guy's attention, but it doesn't take long for those same men to start griping about my cut-and-paste wardrobe and minimal makeup.

I guess it's okay to be in sweats and a t-shirt at the gym, but heaven forbid I change into that after work or on the weekend. Allen constantly hit me with passive-aggressive, backhanded compliments that thinly veiled his true feelings. Looking back, I'm not sure why he pursued me so heavily when he clearly wasn't interested.

"So, I'm dying to know. How did you melt the Ice King?" Jamie's question takes a moment to register. I get that his name is Kold, which is how he earned the nickname Jack Frost from me, but I wouldn't describe him as icy.

"I don't know what you mean, so it must have happened before my time. Kold has been consistently amazing since the beginning. We spent four hours laughing with each other the night we first met." When it comes to the two brothers, I've always thought Darc was the one with the frozen heart. Then again, Jamie did admit to having an intimate relationship with him, so perhaps that's skewed her opinion one way, while mine has been swayed in the opposite direction.

"I've known them *both* for a while, and neither has ever been the sappy type. They've always been closed off and slightly terrifying. Which is part of the appeal, I suppose." Her brush strokes stiffen the more she talks, and I'm thankful my eyes are closed. "I haven't heard from either of them in months. And then, when I finally do, Darc is all business, and Kold has turned into a goddamn maple tree. Seeing the two of you together is adorable. Don't get me wrong. But I'm wondering how you did it."

I want to be offended by what she's saying. It should piss me off, and I should defend them somehow. But all I can do is smile at the comparison of Kold and a Maple Tree. Next time he's gushing over how much he loves me, I'll remember this conversation and chuckle.

You're so sappy. I'm gonna tap ya the next time I need syrup for my pancakes is a line that will come out of my mouth at some point during the course of our relationship.

"I was hoping you could give me some tips. You know. Help a girl out." She finishes with my eye makeup and moves along in the process, but I keep my eyes closed for personal reasons.

"All I've ever gotten from Darc was the occasional late-night text telling me to stop by. When I'm here, we have the most mind-blowing sex. Then he hands me my clothes and walks me to the door without so much as a hug goodbye. I've never been allowed to spend the night. The man is sexy as fuck, but goddamn, is he infuriating."

There's a burning in my chest that feels a lot like jealousy when she mentions coming over late at night. Maybe because, in the back of my mind, I'm still wondering if she's hooked up with both of them. Thankfully, I have a good excuse to sit quietly as she continues applying layers of makeup.

"Kold is pulling out all the stops to impress you, and that bag of clothes suggests you've been staying here. So, how'd you do it?"

I give her a half smile and shrug my shoulders as if to say *sorry about your luck.* Even if I did know the secret, I wouldn't tell her.

Girls who look like Jamie don't need advice from people who look like me. Guys have been lining up around the block all her life, hoping to shoot their shot, and I guarantee she doles out rejection like Halloween candy to ninety-nine point-nine percent of them. Maybe that's why Darc isn't interested.

She would never dream of rejecting him, meaning she's too

easy to catch. The one thing I know for sure about Darc is that he enjoys a challenge. He likes to stalk his prey from the shadows until they submit and walk willingly into his den. Plus, he seems to have a thing for broken women, and Jamie is pristine.

"Sorry, I don't know him well enough to comment one way or the other. I'm not sure what Darc's looking for, but he'd have to be crazy not to like you." This is the lie I settle on since I can't bring myself to utter the truth. Either Jamie hasn't bothered to look past the surface, or Darc hasn't let her. He's complicated but not impossible to figure out. Both brothers are creatures of their routine, and if you watch them closely enough, for long enough, a pattern begins to emerge.

My thoughts race as I scroll through several mental checklists and cross reference those against what I've seen or heard. Both brothers are intense and passionate and nearly impossible to say *no* to. I try to avoid Darc as much as possible, but he always finds me, never letting me forget the kiss we shared and the words I spoke.

Jamie continues to talk while she curls my hair, but I've stopped listening. It isn't until she's finished and holds up a garment bag that I refocus my attention on her presence. "Are you ready to see the dress?"

The last time I wore a dress, it was a cheap knee-length ivory cotton blend with a black ribbon accent tied at the waist. It cost me $20 and came from the clearance rack of Kohl's teen department. That was the costume I wore as I stood next to John, in his wrinkled button-down and borrowed tie, during our courthouse wedding.

As for the dress Jamie's holding, there's nothing cheap about it. I might not know clothing labels and fashion designers, but I know quality when I see it. The black long-sleeved cocktail dress has a deep v-neck front that is revealing enough to be sexy and classy enough to look expensive. With a hem likely to fall two inches below my ass, I imagine I'll look like a high-end call girl with a little black book full of sugar daddies paying her way through med school.

"I love it."

<h1 style="text-align:center">Kold</h1>

Darc and I stand posed in the living room discussing tomorrow night when we hear the bedroom door open. Immediately, all conversation ceases as we turn our attention to the second floor. Coming down the stairs, carrying her shoes, is a version of Val I barely recognize. For a moment, I was worried she might hate being dolled up. But the smile on her face negates any concern. She looks genuinely happy, and I know we're about to have an incredible night together.

"Honesty is always welcome, gentlemen. But remember, I am sensitive." Upon reaching the ground floor, Val slips on the heeled shoes and gives us a spin. "What do you guys think? Is it too much?"

Before I can align my racing thoughts into a sentence, Darc walks over and cups Val's waist, whispering something into her ear. I can't hear what he's saying from where I'm standing, but Jamie obviously can. She looks like she's about to commit homicide. Taking two steps forward, I shoot her a look in case Val's the intended target of her rage.

Maybe I should let it play out. If Jamie kills Darc, it will save me the trouble of doing it myself. My initial reaction is always the same. Every time I see him touching her, I want to break the bones in his hand, one by one. I worry I've been too lenient the last two months, hoping he would back off on his own. But as I watch *my girl* smile and laugh, savoring his touch, I consider an alternative solution.

Once he's finished whispering sweet nothings in her ear, Darc cups the back of Val's neck and kisses her on the top of the head. He then retreats to his bedroom without so much as a glance in Jamie's direction, calling the dogs to follow. It's as if Val is the only person in the room, and I know the feeling all too well.

For months, my brother has been acting strangely. His usual even temperament has disappeared, and he's been in full-blown Jekyll and Hyde mode. Early on, I thought he was excited by the thrill of the hunt as we spent months looking every place she wasn't. And then, when we found her, I started to think he was jealous, knowing how annoyed he always gets when I have something he doesn't. But for the first time in my life, I don't know what my brother's thinking and the uncertainty leaves me apprehensive.

Tomorrow at the club, I'm making it a priority to finally sit down and talk. We need to discuss my plans for the future and the changes I hope to implement. If he isn't on board, I'm willing to walk away, but that conversation needs to wait until after tonight.

Finally, getting my chance to speak, I step forward and take Val's hand. "You have me stunned into silence, my love. How the fuck am I ever going to deserve you?"

Jamie stomps down the last few stairs and pushes past me on her way to the door. "Don't know him well enough, my ass. You fucking liar!" She exits through the front door, slamming it behind her.

"What the fuck was that? Was she acting like that upstairs?" I would love to ignore the childish temper tantrum being thrown by an irrelevant girl, but Val tends to downplay the details if time is permitted to pass, and I need to know what lines Jamie crossed.

"No, she was fine. It was the stereotypical girl talk. I promise. I think she's upset with your brother because he isn't interested in the same thing she is. When he walked away without an invite to his bedroom, I'm sure it set her off." Val is doing damage control, per usual, offering up excuses for the poor behavior of those around her. "Other than that, I don't know. To be honest, I was only half-listening. The way she was talking, I assumed you had hooked up with her as well. So..."

I'm shocked by the words coming out of her mouth and begin speaking quite loudly without refrain. "You still don't fucking get it, do you? I'm in love with you, Val! I'm infatuated to my core. My day begins and ends with you. And within each thought that crosses my mind, *you* are my primary consideration. I obsess over your happiness. And you think I'm such a thoughtless asshole that I would invite a woman I had sex with into *our* bedroom? You thought I would disrespect you in such an egregious way? Claiming to love you the way I do." My tone was more hostile than I intended, but my words reflected the sentiment I intended to convey.

"You're getting worked up over nothing, and you need to stop." Val touches my neck and looks at me with frustration set into the lines of her face. "If you're saying you never hooked up with her, I believe you. Honestly, I don't care if you did fuck her. I don't hold your past against you, and I appreciate that you extend me the same courtesy."

I push her hand off me, squaring up for a fight. There is no good reason to say what I'm about to say, but that doesn't stop the words from coming out. "What past is it that you're referring to, Val? The jerk you kept sleeping with after we met, the asshole you married, or the string of losers you allowed to disrespect you?"

Before the hurt registers in her eyes, I'm already disgusted by what I've said.

"You're right on all counts." She's calmer than she should be and wearing a smile. Her eyes are empty, as though she's already detached. "I have notoriously poor taste in men."

I take her hand and cord our fingers together before she can walk away. I'm such an idiot. I deserve to lose her, but I know I can't live without her. "No. I'm not. I was wrong to say that. It isn't your fault that men are assholes who disrespect women instead of acknowledging their insecurities. You're incredible, and they..."

"Can you please stop talking? I'm not interested in having this conversation, and I don't need you to convince me that I'm some helpless victim. If you say one more word, I'm taking your car and your credit card, and I'm going out in this dress without you. Do you understand?" She gives me the space to respond, but all I can do is nod my head.

"Silence is your punishment. It's also the only apology I'm willing to entertain. Do you accept my terms, or would you like to end our evening early?" Val lacks any hint of anger or playfulness as she awaits my retort.

I lock my lips with an invisible key and offer her my arm. At the door, we grab our coats, and Val yells our goodbyes to Darc and the dogs, to which none reply. Walking to the driveway in quiet discomfort, I squeeze her hand and pull her in for a kiss before opening the passenger side door. As badly as I want to speak to her, I'm glad the ban was placed on my words and not my touch. There are plenty of ways my hands can convey a sincere apology without the aid of my mouth.

Driving in the direction of downtown, I begin massaging the inside of Val's thigh, sliding my hand further under her dress. When she doesn't push me away, I press my luck further. I want to skip the restaurant and head straight to the hotel. To hell with dinner. We could order room service after I finish seeking forgiveness for the outburst that rendered me mute.

A moan escapes her lips as her legs part, inviting me in. This is the first sound she's made since leaving the house, and I need more. Fingering her while driving seventy-five on the freeway isn't ideal, but there's no place to pull over, and our destination is still ten minutes away. The second my fingers graze her panties. I'm done for. I bite my lip and focus on the road to keep from opening my mouth.

Val removes her seatbelt and reaches into my lap. "Goddamn! Is this for me?" She watches as I nod my head *yes* before kneeling in her seat.

I think I was eighteen the last time I received road head from a girl, but I remember how it works. Reclining my seat back the slightest bit, I try to focus on the road while Val unhooks my belt.

This isn't right. I should be pleasing her. But having her mouth on me feels too damn good to stop.

A cacophony of growls and praises are trapped behind my clenched teeth as she works me over. I set the cruise and keep one hand on the wheel. The rest of me belongs to her. Knotting my fingers into her curled locks, I push her head down while raising my hips until I feel her throat tighten.

Backing off long enough to inhale, Val's hand replaces her mouth, stroking near the base of my shaft. I don't want to know what she had to do to learn these skills, but I'm thankful for the techniques she's picked up along the way. She takes me deep again, this time all on her own, bringing me straight to the edge of an orgasm. I'm so close to cumming down her throat, but I can't let go. If I didn't have to focus so much on driving, I would've gotten off already.

Knowing exactly what it'll take to liberate my release, I slide my hand along Val's body and adjust her dress so the hem is around her waist. Again, she takes me down her throat as I reach between her legs and slip her panties to one side. Her pussy soaks my hand as I push two fingers inside, imagining her taking two cocks at once. As I slam my fingers deeper, she moans and chokes. The combination of sounds coming from my lap and the mental image of her getting railed from behind is enough to finish me off.

Val falls back into her seat, gasping for breath, before checking her makeup in the mirror. "Do you mind if I finish myself off before we reach our destination?"

The side-to-side movement of my head conveys my answer as I prepare to pull off at the next exit. I have a distance of five city blocks to plan my next move. The restaurant has valet parking, but that means waiting until we're at the hotel later to bury my dick inside her. My other option is to find a parking garage nearby and have my way with her, but knowing Val, she'll be polished off before I can find a place to park.

With the bottom of her dress still around her waist, Val reclines her seat and begins circling her clit as I tilt the rearview mirror. Not being able to properly watch as she pleases herself is torture. All I catch are flashes as we pass under streetlights, my eyes darting back and forth between the car in front of us and her circling fingers.

"I wish I had your mouth on me. I love the way you tease my clit with your tongue. You always make me cum so hard when you're between my thighs. I want you to be the one making my body tremble. I need to know that you still want me." Val's got me ready to slam on the breaks in the middle of the street before I die needing a taste of that pussy.

The faster she moves her hand, the more she moans until the sound cuts off. Brushing my hand along her thigh, I know she's holding her breath, forcing herself close to climax.

As the final light turns red, I shift the car into park and unhook my seatbelt, practically throwing myself into the passenger seat. I slam three fingers inside of her as hard as I can and push my tongue into her mouth. As her body convulses, her pussy tightens around my fingers, and a whimper of pleasure passes from her body to mine. Once Val finishes cumming on my hand, I lick her off my fingers and turn my attention toward the street in time to see the light turn green.

I ensure Val's dress is appropriately situated before pulling up to the valet and unlocking the doors. Her black lace panties are for my enjoyment only, and I intend to take them off later with my teeth.

When I get around to the other side, Val is already stepping out, having accepted another man's hand. I glare at him but say nothing. Any amusement I feel seeing her use her left hand instead of her right and knowing the reason why is overshadowed by my irritation at his audacity. How dare he touch what is so obviously mine.

"Thank you," she says, exchanging a smile for the valet's assistance before taking my offered hand.

I pull her into my arms and lift her hand, sliding her two fingers into my mouth before kissing the back of her hand. If I could speak, I would tell her the only man who's allowed to touch her looks like my mirror image. Instead, she reads my expression as *You're mine and only mine. Do you understand me?*

"Guess I can kiss all my threesome fantasies goodbye." She

smiles at me and presses her hand to the side of my neck. "You need to relax. You're far too tense for a guy who blew a four-course meal down his girlfriend's throat on the drive here. That kid is doing his job, and I have no interest in running off with the valet's assistant. Try not to kill anyone."

Once we're alone in the elevator, I press her to the wall and search her eyes. Why would she make that comment unless someone said something? How much does she know? Or think that she knows? Fuck! I need to talk to her, but I can't risk losing her. Not now or ever.

We should have stayed home. If I kill anyone, it will be Jamie, for whatever seed of doubt she planted about me in Val's head. Or my brother for his insistence on touching my girl every chance he gets. I've reached the end of my rope with everyone, and I won't be the one left swinging from the noose.

At the hostess stand, Val gives the name for the reservation. "*Our* last name is Jakobsson." Making it clear to the girl with the inflated lips currently trying to catch my eye that I am unquestionably off the market. Never to return.

I laugh under my breath as we're escorted to our table. My girl is feisty and territorial tonight. This is a side of Val I've never seen, and I like it. Our table is by the window, overlooking downtown, and I watch as she takes in the view. I love it here, but the lights of the city pale in comparison to the view I have across the table.

Turning her attention back to me, Val takes my hand, locking her eyes on mine. "I'm sorry for the misunderstanding earlier. I didn't mean for my comment to come across as an accusation, and I should have accepted your apology instead of souring the evening. While I am impressed that you could go this long without saying anything, I need you to talk to me. I miss you, and I can't endure one more second of your silence.

"I'm right here, love, missing you too. I never should have raised my voice or commented on your past. I love the woman you are. And I should thank each of those assholes for fucking up so I could have a chance with you." I press the back of her hand to my lips and leave a kiss there. "That car ride was hell. Even the good parts were torture."

"Well, I didn't mean for it to be torture. Perhaps I can make it up to you later."

Val goes back to looking out the window, but my eyes never leave her. I love that she's always willing to talk things out, but I hate that we even let it get to that point. Tomorrow night is the concert, and I worry she'll see something she doesn't like. And now, on top of that, I have to find out what she knows about the darker elements of my life. At what point does she stop being understanding and start running?

CHAPTER 29

Val

When the waitress comes by to ask about dessert, I'm stuffed to the gills. One more bite, and I'm going to burst. On the other hand, Kold has a reserve tank specifically designated for sweets, so he orders a slice of cheesecake.

The darker it gets outside, the more the city twinkles, and it's interesting to view a place I barely know from this perspective. I'm cheap, and I hate to pay for parking, so I usually avoid coming downtown. Allen and I went to a musical in the theater district, and I've been to some of the bars with people from work, but that all feels like ages ago. Before our week at home, Kold had been driving into the city nearly every day to work from his office in the club. Something I imagine he'll have to get back to after the holidays.

"Do you have any days off work next week, or is this a busy time of year for you guys?" I've gotten spoiled having him home with me all day. "Because of the way the holidays fall on the weekends this year, work gave us Monday and Tuesday off for Christmas and Thursday and Friday for New Year's, and then I used a vacation day for Wednesday."

"You're telling me this now with only two days' notice. I would have planned a trip for us had I known. My brother can cover for me if need be, and I can always sneak in some work while you're asleep, so long as there's an internet connection. Where do you want to go? I'll book us a flight and a hotel." Kold pulls out his phone as if my wish is his command.

"You're going to get so bored of me. I can already tell." I try to laugh, but it's not convincing anyone. "My plan for the week was to hang out at home under a blanket, reading a book, but I suppose I could be open to other suggestions."

"Hey, I like books." He tucks the phone back into his pocket as if the matter is settled.

When the waitress returns with Kold's dessert, my mouth begins to water, and I realize I messed up. There was crème brûlée on the menu, and I'm upset with myself for not ordering some when I had the opportunity. Now I get to sit here and watch Kold, blissful in his choices, while I chew on air.

I take the fork from his hand, steal a bite, and then two. "I knew you were gonna do that. The second you told the waitress you were 'fine,' I resigned myself to the fact that I would be losing half of my dessert." Kold laughs, sliding the plate to my side of the table. "Save me a bite."

"I only wanted a taste." I place the fork on the plate and push it back across the table. Cheesecake wouldn't be my first choice, and I am still stuffed from dinner.

"I know the feeling." He licks his lips and holds me in his gaze, no longer interested in the dessert on the table. "Let's get the check and go to the hotel so that I can eat something sweet before bed."

"What hotel? We're only twenty minutes from the house, and I didn't bring anything to change into." This is why I hate surprises. I'm someone who operates better in a controlled environment when preparations have been made, and boxes have been checked under my supervision. Giving up control in the bedroom is one thing, but when it comes to packing for an overnight trip, I'd like to know I'll be comfortable.

"You thought our first date would be dinner and then back home to cuddle in bed with the dogs? Come on, Val, you know me better than that."

"Don't go setting the bar too high. This is already a lot to live up to. Plus, I can't drop two grand on a date, so you might need to chill." I could afford this date and then some, but the money I have set aside is being saved for something bigger.

Thankfully, the majority of my inheritance was released after my marriage failed. Otherwise, I'm certain John would have forgone the divorce. Not that he would've stopped cheating. Heavens no. But he would've happily spent the cash while lying to my face.

As for Allen, I never mentioned the money because I knew I couldn't trust him, and he seemed to get off on the idea of *taking care of me*.

Sitting here across from Kold, I wonder if I should say anything. It's only been a week, but that week has felt like a lifetime. Being with him is the happiest I've ever been, even if I second-guess myself incessantly. I suppose the person I'm dating doesn't have to know all my secrets straight out of the gates. All truths are revealed in time. Thankfully for me, no one sticks around long enough to scratch past the surface.

"This is only the beginning, my love... And for the record, I'd never expect you to pay for a date. You don't even have to buy me ice cream. When it comes to the tab, I've got you covered." He says it in a way that should be comforting, without even a hint of cockiness.

I suppose that's nice. Isn't that what every woman wants? A man who works hard to support his household. My mom struggled for a long time after Conrad left, trying to juggle a work-life balance as a single mom. She never even bothered to date. It was too difficult for her to let go of the past in order to trust someone new. Sometimes, I worry I might be guilty of the same crime.

Staring out the window, watching the cars on the street below, I find myself running through the highlights and lowlights of the years spent before Mom's passing. We didn't have an abundance of money, but we did share a considerable amount of joy. My mom always found ways to make birthdays and holidays a special occasion. We took road trips and went camping instead of flying across the country and staying in a hotel. Sometimes, we'd set the tent up in the living room and toast marshmallows on the stove. She would read me books before bed, and we'd watch movies on the weekends. The quality of our time was never equivalent to dollars spent. Maybe that's why I like free dates more than elaborate ones.

"Watching you escape into your thoughts fascinates me. I'm jealous I can't go with you." Kold kisses my hand and holds it below his lips. "Are you ready for the next part of our date? I think you're going to enjoy it."

Why doesn't he understand? I don't care what we do. My enjoyment stems from being in his presence. The rest of it is fluff.

Kold

Holding tightly to Val's hand, I maintain contact until the valet pulls up with the car, and I have her safely tucked away in the passenger seat. If I have to watch one more guy touch my future wife, I will lose it. The scene from earlier keeps playing out in my head, and I would give anything to let it go.

"Hey babe, out of curiosity, what did my brother say to you before we left?" I know better than to ask, but I need to know.

"Um... I don't know. I think it was something along the lines of, 'You always look beautiful, and tonight is no exception. I'll be home with the kids, missing you. Try to have fun on your date.' or something like that. He was joking around, being funny." Val downplays the interaction, trying to convince me it was nothing. This is her go-to whenever Darc is brought up in conversation, and I'm starting to wonder if it's for his benefit or my own. Although I should be happy she told me anything. The last time I asked her to repeat what he said, she dove headfirst into evasive maneuvers and threatened to leave me.

"You know as well as I do that my brother doesn't do *funny*. The thing is, I see what he's after, and I understand the attraction. But honestly, what does he expect to happen? Does he want to have sex with you to prove he can? Or is he trying to take you away from me?"

"Babe, I don't know Darc the way you do. How do you

expect me to identify his motives if you, his twin-enemy-best friend, don't even know what he's up to? Whatever it is, I can assure you, he'll never be able to steal me away from you. And I don't think that's his intention." Val brushes her fingertips across my skin before linking our hands together.

My brother's not-so-secret infatuation isn't the best topic of conversation if I hope to make this Val's favorite first date. And honestly, what did I expect her to say?

"One of these days, you'll tell me I can't lose you, and I'll allow myself to believe it. But for now, let's find our room and relieve some stress." There is a couple's massage booked for eight o'clock in the suite. After that, she's all mine.

Pulling up to the front of the building, I stop and grab our bag from the backseat before handing off my keys and retrieving Val from the passenger side. Now that I'm allowed to speak, it was easier to warn away the second valet. "I will see to her door and anything else she needs. Thank you."

Dressed the way I am and driving what I do, I wonder if he thinks I'm security or the controlling husband. Either way, he's not wrong. Val's protection is my responsibility, and I take that seriously. When he backs away with his hands raised in front of him, I can see Val, through the window, shake her head.

"Don't take it personally. He's like that with everyone... Have a nice night."

Val's insistence on being friendly is going to be my doom. "You don't have to apologize for me." I lead her into the building and straight to the room. I checked in on my phone before we left and confirmed the add-ons. The door unlocks with a five-digit code, so we don't have to be bothered with the front desk.

Stepping into the elevator, Val squeezes my hand and continues the conversation where it left off. "Don't I? I don't know what's going on with you tonight. You're being more intense than usual, and that's saying something... It can be frightening to the passive observer."

"Are you afraid of me, Val?" I can feel my jaw tighten and my fist clench as if a part of me wants her to say *yes*. If I have to lose her again, it might as well be now. She should see me for who I am before agreeing to a lifetime by my side.

"I don't value my life enough to be afraid of you, dear. So, I guess, whatever happens, happens."

"You should know better than to say shit like that if you want me to be less overprotective." Those words will haunt me forever if anything ever happens to her.

"Nothing I say is going to fundamentally change who you are. And you could say the same thing about me. People can strive to be better, but at the core, they remain the same."

"A tiger can't change its stripes... Once a cheater, always a cheater... That sort of thing?"

"I think a person's priorities and motivations can shift, which can prompt a transformation of sorts. They might appear unrecognizable, even to themselves. Mothers are a great example of that. On a dime, a woman's life is expected to evolve from self-serving to an existence of self-sacrifice. That's why you'll find so many women in their 40s and 50s on a quest for self-discovery once their children leave the nest. But their true self never disappeared. It was merely neglected, as their identity became a reflection of their children, instead of themselves."

The doors open ahead of us, marking our arrival at the top floor.

For some reason, my brother's voice begins playing in my head. *She makes you weak. I don't even recognize you. You're a stranger, wearing my face, telling me to fuck off.*

"I understand why you might think that mothers are self-sacrificing and fathers are selfish fucks, but that won't be your experience with me if we have children together." I pause, set down our bag, and pull her into my arms. "Do you not want to have kids, Val?"

"It was only meant as an example. I didn't mean anything by it. I have no doubt that you'll be an incredible father when the time comes."

As we walk down the hallway, hand in hand, I try to focus on who I'm with and why we're here. Tonight is about convincing Val, once and for all, that I'm worth investing in. I didn't know what sort of life I wanted until I met her, and now there's no going back. I'm willing to give her everything, including my honesty, if she promises not to leave. All she has to agree to is a lifetime in a gilded cage.

Compared to a standard floor, the doors up here are spaced relatively far apart, giving me high hopes for the accommodations. When we arrive at the door, I type the designated code into the lock and step to the side. Since this entire night is about impressing Val, I want her to see it first.

"Wow. I thought hotel rooms like this only existed on movie sets. The dress, the dinner, the room. I feel like I've stepped into a remake of Pretty Woman." Val runs her hand along the crisp white cotton sheet covering one of two massage tables in the living room. "With the way you've been acting tonight, I'm surprised you're willing to allow someone else to touch me."

I wish the hotel staff had waited to set up the tables until after we arrived. Having them in the middle of the room like this does take away from the grandeur of the space and spoils the next surprise. However, the roses, candles, and chocolate-covered strawberries are exactly as requested. So perhaps this once, I can learn to be more agreeable.

"When I booked the service, I must not have been thinking clearly."

Immense care went into planning this evening, only to have the mood shift before we walked out the door. Between Darc's whispered pleasantries and his hand on her waist, Jamie's childish temper tantrum, and Val's offhanded remark about me killing people, this night went left before it could go right. I'm as bad as her date at the casino, losing all his chips in five minutes and spending the rest of the night punishing someone else for choices my ego made.

"It's hard for me to watch someone else take care of you. I don't enjoy seeing others succeed where I failed." Maybe my brother was right. Loving Val has made me weak.

"Are we still talking about car doors and massages? Because if that's how you perceive every situation, it's no wonder you're upset." Val embraces me and looks up. "Don't be so quick to admit defeat after lost yards on a play. This game can be one of considerable length so long as you continue to show up. We're on the same team, Kold. And I need your strength. But I also need your heart."

"You should've been a football coach. That was a good speech." I twist my fingers into the hair cascading down her back and lean in to kiss her.

Val always says life is a tradeoff. Maybe loving her is meant to make me weak so that being loved by her can be my strength.

CHAPTER 30

Val

You know how sometimes you aren't consciously aware of how badly you need something until you have it? Well, that's how I'm feeling about this massage right now.

I thought Kold might call the whole thing off when he opened the door and saw the two massage therapists standing in the hallway. The male and female pair looked so perfectly matched in age, style, and attractiveness that I wondered if they weren't a couple. Seeing that a man would be massaging one of us caused quite a bit of tension, though I was impressed with Kold's ability to hold it together until after we were behind closed doors. We privately debated in the bathroom while changing into our robes, eventually making our way to an agreement.

"Unless you ordered us a Nuru massage, I'm not sure what the problem is. Close your eyes, turn off your brain, and try to relax. I'll be waiting for you on the other side."

"Okay, wait. How do you know what a Nuru massage is?"

"Because I watch porn like a normal person."

"Oh, wonderful. That's exactly what I want to hear. I'm so happy to find out my girl is into massage porn minutes before I have to hand her off to some good-looking guy with tattoos and muscles and pants so tight, I could tell you how much change he had in his pocket... I thought you were supposed to be calming me down?"

"He didn't have anything in his pockets. But I agree that his pants were tight. I could see the outline of his dick."

"I don't care how much I love you. You're going to pay for that last comment after they leave."

"I'm counting on it. So, we agree. I'll take him, and you take her, right?"

Upon returning to the living room, ready to begin, Kold pushed the two tables together, and he's been holding my hand ever since.

"If you both want to turn over, we can get started on the other side. Take your time rolling over." Her words match the soft music playing on the TV in the background. "Are you celebrating an anniversary this evening?"

"No." I can't help but laugh, especially when I think about what I have to say next. "This is our first date."

Kold settles into the new position and finds my hand under the sheet. "The first of many."

I feel myself drifting on the edge of sleep during the second half of the massage as strong hands work to untie the knots in my shoulders. To his credit, the man kneading my flesh appears well-trained and experienced. Then, when you factor in the man stretched out beside me and the affectionate way he's maintained contact, this might be the best massage I've ever had.

The four of us remain silent until our time together ends, and Kold and I must continue our night without them. "All right. We hope that you enjoyed your massage. Please take your time getting up. If you'd like to head into your bedroom for a few minutes, we'll get everything cleared away and leave you to enjoy the rest of your night."

Sitting up, I can feel my head spinning before my feet hit the floor. Thankfully, Kold seems to anticipate the possibility and moves to my side before I have a chance to fall. Maybe Tracy was right when she told me to see a doctor. But with my luck, the hospital will inform me I have a brain tumor and six months to live. Isn't that how it happens in books and movies? You wait your whole life to find true love, only to get sick and die right after.

Does anyone get a happy ending anymore? Did they ever?

The overnight bag Kold packed for us is on the dresser, so I rummage through its contents and find that he's given me options. There's a t-shirt and jeans for the drive home tomorrow, sweats and a hoodie for lounging, and a sexy black lace set of undergarments that tie together with satin ribbons.

It isn't difficult to guess which set of clothes he packed for post-massage sexy time, so I choose the lingerie set and begin tying myself into the lace bra and panties. When I look up and see myself in the mirror, I'm mildly impressed by what I see in the reflection. Despite my self-doubt and insecurities, the scars and imperfections are reminders of the hell I walked through as I made my way here. I was never meant to be perfect, so I never tried to be. I covered myself in tattoos and wore them like armor, attempting to hide while simultaneously standing out.

Hey, I never claimed to be smart.

Since I enjoy playfully joking around with Kold when given the chance, and I know he'll be expecting me in underwear or nothing, I cover the sexy ensemble with the hoodies and sweats, then plop myself down on the bed. The pillow top mattress on the hotel bed feels surprisingly extravagant. I imagine the rooms on the top floor are outfitted with the best money can buy, while the other rooms have sheets, comforters, and towels ordered from the hotel bargain warehouse.

Kold is willing to spoil me rotten if given half a chance. After all, he and Darc were custom-made for life on the top floor, which suits them. But I feel slightly fraudulent lying here in the lap of luxury, knowing that I'm better suited for a broom cupboard in the basement.

Thankfully, before I get too far into my feelings, Kold walks out of the bathroom wearing boxer briefs, a hard-on, and a smile.

"Nope, not happening. Take it off. You can wear that outfit in the morning, while we have breakfast. But for now, I still owe you for that 'dick outline' comment you made when we got here." He rubs his hand over the length of his erection, stiffening his cock further. The sight makes my mouth water.

I stand next to the bed and begin removing my outer shell. The pants he packed for me are so big that they fall to the floor when I stop holding them on. Then I pull the hoodie over my head and open my eyes to find him prowling toward me, looking famished.

"Are you going to be rough with me?" I make it sound like a question, though I mean it to be a request.

If prior experience is any indication, Kold will take me in whatever manner he sees fit, which might involve me being restrained. We both enjoy our sex rough and kinky, so it wouldn't surprise me if he's got handcuffs or straps packed in his duffel bag. I appreciate his willingness to think outside the box, and I trust him to take care of me. Kold is always good about holding me until I fall asleep in his arms, especially on nights that get intensely passionate.

Taking my face in his hand, he rubs his thumb across my bottom lip and down my chin, prompting my head to fall back. "I want to try something else tonight if you're up for it."

When it comes to sex, I'm open to trying new things within reason. However, when it comes to having sex with Kold, I'm willing to endure pretty much anything he requires. Mostly because I trust him to stop before it goes too far, but also because I want him to be happy.

And if I'm being honest, the line of women standing over my shoulder, waiting for a chance to offer him what I can't, is a pretty good motivator.

"Do I get a clue, or am I agreeing to anything and everything?" My hands explore the ridges of his back, hips, and torso while I stare into his eyes, waiting for the green light. "Are there toys packed away in your bag that I missed?"

"Not tonight, my love. You've made it clear to me that words are easy and actions carry weight. So, I want to try something new. Something I've never done before." Cupping his hands to the sides of my neck, he draws my full attention. "I need to convince you that the depth of my love journeys leagues beyond my desire. Further than can be measured."

His thumbs play at the underside of my jaw, teasing against my throat. Each movement feels intentionally slowed down, and I wonder if he's seeking permission to choke me.

His hands move on before I can issue my consent, tracing the curves of my body.

"No matter how much time I spend inside you, I always want more." The warmth of his gentle touch lingers upon my exposed skin as he makes his way past my hips and along the crease of my thigh. "If you tell me you're mine forever, I'm prepared to worship at your feet."

A moan escapes my lungs as he cups my pussy in one hand in and grips my waist with the other. "You're my forever, and I am yours. But I don't want you at my feet when you belong by my side."

"I want to make love to you, but that's not something I have experience with, and I lack the necessary know-how. So, I'm asking for your help." His fingers caress the lace covering the lips of my pussy, as my knees threaten to give out on me.

"I'm not sure I know how to do what you're asking for." On the outside, I'm holding on by a thread, but inside, it's a five-alarm fire, and I'm seconds away from panic mode. Sex and Love are two things I've always kept separate from one another. I don't know how to do what he's asking for any more than he does. "Can't we stick with what we know?"

"You were married, Val. I'm sure you..." Kold's voice trails off as though he doesn't have the heart to finish as he brings his arms across my back and pulls me into his chest.

"Yeah, well. I hate to break it to you, but I was stupid and married a man who never loved me. Most days, he wouldn't even look at me. So, I don't have the expertise you assume I do." I've mentioned John in passing but avoided going into detail. My short-lived marriage makes me look like an epic failure, so I typically avoid the topic. When I look up to see if Kold is disappointed, I find he's anything but.

If Kold and I are in a space together, he rarely looks at anything other than me. The one exception is when we're in the car, and he's driving, then he holds my leg or hand the entire time. Since emerging from the bathroom, his eyes have been locked on me, and sometimes, I wonder if Kold is in love or obsessed.

Does it matter? Do I care? It's nice to have someone see me

for once.

"Say something." I wish he would speak so that the last words between us aren't in reference to the biggest mistake of my life. I feel exposed in a way I wasn't before, even though I'm standing here in panties and a bra I didn't pick out. When I reach below the waist of his boxer briefs, he catches my hand and brings it back up to his chest.

"I promise to love you for the rest of our lives... But I can't change the past." His lips brush against mine as I come up on tip-toes.

Finally, kissing him feels like a release and a trap. His touch is deliberate. Nothing is rushed, as reverence replaces his usual intensity.

Moving onto the bed, we spend more time than usual kissing and touching with our minimal clothing barriers intact. Having him touch me in this way is more emotional than I expected. I know they call it making love, but that's just stupid shit people say, right?

Each time I reach for a handful of what he's holding back, he stops me, and I feel my frustration grow in time with my yearning. "Please let me put my mouth on you. You're torturing me." I reach for him again, only this time, he pins my hands to the bed and refuses to release them.

"I'm not done playing with you. Stop being a brat." Kold sounds like I feel; horny and fighting the urge to indulge.

Using his teeth to untie the satin ribbon holding my panties together, he releases my hands while liberating me of what little clothing I have on. Then he pulls my thighs apart, snaking an arm around each, and locks me into place. By this point, I'm desperate to submit, but he continues to tease, alternating between light kisses and playful licks, until my clit throbs.

"You're killing me! Please, babe, I am begging you." I'm not cut out for this. My eyes squeeze shut, and my teeth clench as I continue to fight a losing battle. I have no control here, even if I beg.

He unlocks my legs and begins kissing his way up my stomach, making a pit stop at each breast before settling into my neck.

Without a word, he pushes himself inside me, causing my body to shudder and twitch.

"Goddamn! I might have to take you nice and slow more often. You feel so good." Kold pushes in gradually, taking his time until his full length is buried beneath my surface.

Trying to drive him deeper still, I attempt to thrust my hips up into him, but he's left me no space to move. All I want is for him to pound me into the bed and leave me a fragmented pile of bones, but he refuses to alter his intensity or give in to my pleas. In a last-ditch effort to get my way, I look into his eyes and tell him something I know he wants to hear.

"I stopped taking my birth control."

Short of agreeing to marry him tomorrow, I know this is the one confession that will lure the beast out to play. From the beginning, Kold has made it clear that he wants to start a family, and he speaks as though there is no time to waste. He won't pass up an opportunity if he thinks all options are on the table.

"Don't lie to me." He growls into my neck as he begins driving into me. "You know how badly I want that."

Normally, I'll say damn near anything during sex to get the other person off, but I am being honest this time. After repeated requests and my acceptance that Kold was probably right, my pills ended up in the trash. We're thirty-five years old. If we want to have a family, it's now or never.

"I'm not lying."

His strides ramp up in speed and pressure until I'm clutching at the sheets and screaming his name. If these walls lack soundproofing, the front desk might receive a few calls about a woman being murdered on the top floor. So be it. I have to hold back when we're at home so the downstairs resident won't overhear us and get jealous. A lesson I learned pretty quickly.

Images of Darc flash in my mind as I try to stuff them back into their boxes. My legs wrapped around his waist as he kissed me against the wall. His stiff cock pressed against me, pinning me to the counter in the kitchen. The grin on his face the first time he saw me. And the way his eyes lit up when he told me he loved me. No less than once a day, the wrong brother finds a way to come into contact with me. He enjoys cornering me when I'm on my own.

Even though I know it should be, Darc's touch isn't entirely unwelcome.

My mind swings back and forth between past and current events as shifting realities blend in transition. And for a moment, they're both with me. I feel my nails dig into Kold's back as my body begins to spasm, blissfully aware that he's finishing with me.

"Fuck that was good. Whatever you were thinking about to get off like that, keep doing it. You felt incredible." Kold kisses me and pulls me into his arms. "I hope I was there with you."

I tuck myself into his embrace as my body slips into shutdown mode. "You're always in my fantasies and on my mind. I'm not sure how I existed without you."

Give a girl the world, and she'll still want to sleep with your brother. What the hell is wrong with me? I suppose, worst case, I end up a single mother, which isn't ideal. Thankfully, I had a great example growing up.

Kold

Sleeping comfortably in my arms, Val is right where I left her, and I know better than to leave the bed without her by my side. A lesson I learned the hard way when she mistakenly kissed my brother one morning, thinking he was me. Darc told me the same day, practically gloating, but I never brought it up to her.

My brother and I grew up mimicking one another and spent thirty-five years perfecting our craft, easily misleading teachers, friends, girlfriends, enemies, and even our parents. I can't be mad at Val for what happened, although I do wish she would have told me. Then again, my girlfriend is the type of person who avoids conflict at all costs, and I get the feeling that her silence is more for my benefit than her own.

I don't care about a stolen kiss. My past holds real demons and a line of bodies tucked neatly under the trees. Unfortunately, love doesn't erase yesterday's mistakes, so I allow myself to imagine the possible futures that await. In a few hours, I need to have a serious conversation with my brother. But first, I need to know, with absolute certainty, where Val's heart is.

She turns over in my arms, twisting her legs into mine, before opening her eyes. "How long have you been watching me sleep?"

"Not long, maybe an hour or so. I've been organizing my thoughts before the day ahead." I brush a strand of hair from her face and kiss her forehead. "Should we order breakfast and shower?"

"If there's something I can help you with, feel free to let me know. I have no idea what goes into getting a venue set up before a show, but I'm happy to do whatever." She's sweet to offer.

"There is one thing you could do if it's not too much trouble. Could we stop at your place on the way home and pick up whatever clothes you need for tonight and next week? Darc and I will be at the club for most of the day, so if you get ready at the house, you can let the dogs out and feed them before you drive in for the show." As much as I want her by my side every second, I need to carve out time to have a private conversation with my darker half, and I don't want her around for that.

"I was already planning on doing that, so it's the perfect request for me to accommodate. Plus, I doubt my noodle arms would have been cooperative trying to carry in band equipment. Best to stick with what I'm good at so I don't embarrass you in front of your adoring fans."

"You're the only fan I adore, and don't you forget it." I kiss her on the nose and melt in the company of her smile. "The doors open at 6:00. When you get to the club, I want you to park in the side lot that says employees only. I'll give security your license plate number and name when I get in. Then text me from the lot, and I'll have someone come out the side door to get you."

"You know, I've been to concerts before. I'm pretty sure I know what to do." I can already tell from the look she's giving me that Val intends to pay to park, wait in line, and watch the show from the floor like a normal person.

As if she isn't the most important woman in my world.

"Forget it. I'll get my mom to come over and take care of the dogs. I want you to ride in with me at 1:00. Then you can see what I do for a living. We can check out my office, tour the backstage, and meet the bands when they come in, along with all the other boring shit I do. And if you're with me, I won't have to worry about you standing in the cold, surrounded by strangers." The reality of being apart hits like a baseball bat carved from my illogical, over-protective anxiety.

"It's gonna be fifty degrees tonight. I think I'll survive. But I get it. You're a super sexy rockstar club owner who wants to show off. That makes sense, but it's unnecessary. I'm already impressed." Val attempts to tickle me as if her defiance is adorable.

I want to scream and argue and order her to behave, but I respect her too much to do any of that, so I smile and kiss her and remind her that she's special to me.

For some reason, Val keeps thinking I'm the same as the guys in her past. She's acting like everything I have to offer is given in order to feed my own self-worth, but she's wrong. I don't give a fuck about any of that. I need to know she's safe. Otherwise, I'll be a nervous wreck all afternoon and evening.

"You asked me to prove myself through action, and that's what I'm trying to do. I would *like* you to park in the employee parking lot because it's close to the building, fenced-in, well-lit, and safe. I would *also like* for you to text me when you get there so I can have security meet you and escort you into the building because I don't want you walking around in the dark and standing in line alone. None of this is about my ego, Val. You're one of the few people in this world I care about, and I wish to keep you out of harm's way."

My frustration dissolves the second she touches my arm. "I never thought about it that way, so I'm sorry. Now that you've explained your side, I can appreciate where you're coming from, and I'll agree to park in the employee lot *if* you allow me to wait in line and go through the front door like a normal nobody. For tonight, let me be the supportive secret girlfriend and new fan."

If the strength of a relationship is measured by a couple's willingness to communicate and compromise, then this is pretty much the only real relationship I've ever had.

"Okay, I'll trade the parking for the line since it's important to you. As for the other part, you can be the supportive, *not* secret girlfriend at this show if you consider being my wife at the next one?" I could propose marriage right now, down on one knee, the whole bit. The ring is in my jacket, burning a hole in my pocket five feet away, tossed over the back of a chair.

"When is the next show?" Her question surprises me. I half

expected her to laugh off the suggestion, but now she seems to be considering it.

"There's a tour scheduled for this summer. I planned to talk to you about it next week, but I wanted to see how tonight went first." If I have to choose between Val and the band, I'm fully prepared to leave the group. I've already had this conversation with the guys, and they know when I'm being serious.

"So, pregnant by New Year's and married by summer, huh? You sure you don't want to think about all of that before diving in head first?" She pulls back the slightest bit and rests her hand against my chest. This is Val's version of a lie detector test.

"What do you think I do all day?" Now isn't the right time. I want my marriage proposal to be everything she deserves, not some post-first-date conversation in bed.

Taking her hand, I bring it to my lips and place a single kiss on her skin. "You know me. I'd marry you this morning, wrapped up in a bed sheet, if you would say *yes*. But we don't have to rush into anything. I'm not going anywhere."

"Whether it's today or six months from now, it doesn't matter, does it? You already know what my answer will be. You've ruined me for all other men. So, either it's you or no one."

I roll off the bed and grab last night's suit jacket from the chair.

"In that case, I have something I need to give you."

CHAPTER 31

Val

I haven't stopped looking at my hand since it happened. In the shower, during breakfast, waiting for the valet to retrieve the car, and on the ride back to my apartment. All of my attention is being absorbed into the diamond on my finger, rendering me stunned into stillness. When I said my answer would be the same today or six months from now, I wasn't expecting Kold to pull out a ring and get down on one knee.

I know from experience what can happen if marriage is rushed into. That mistake will haunt me from now until my last breath. Or maybe I'm wrong to give my ex that much power. Kold isn't John. The two relationships could not be more different, yet I find myself comparing rotten apples to perfectly ripened mangos more often than I should.

Marrying John was a mistake. I know that. Why should he get to move on with his life, and I don't? He doesn't have anything to do with my decisions moving forward. I'm allowed to be happy, aren't I? Don't I deserve that?

Recently divorced or not, is it smart to get engaged after a week? I hardly think so. And yet, when Kold asked me, I said *yes*. God help me if we have a daughter and she ever pulls some shit like this. I'll lock her in a tower for safe keeping and kill the guy who had the nerve to propose. Unless her dad and uncle beat me to the punch.

My thoughts are everywhere as I swing through a jungle of manic thinking, skimming above the bog of depression below. Why did I comment about saying yes, unless I was ready for him to ask me? I gave him the green light, knowing full well he was chomping at the bit, and now I'm over here questioning my sanity. Maybe it's not as crazy as I'm making it out to be. Engaged isn't the same as married. We still have time to figure each other out before signing anything binding. I should relax and enjoy the moment before I ruin everything with my nagging self-doubt and rampant insecurities.

"You seem deep in thought, my love. Are you planning a wedding or an escape?" Kold squeezes my thigh and glances over with a smile.

"I was thinking that I don't have family or friends to invite to a wedding, and I'm not a fan of attention. Couldn't we just get married on a beach in Tahiti and call it a day?" With so many rambling judgments and options, I'm sure the when and the where of tying the knot probably passed through my mind at some point.

"Whatever you want, I'll make it happen. I'm only doing this once, so the sky's the limit." Kold's words aren't meant to insult me. I know that. But I'm offended nonetheless. I wish this were my one and only time, but like he said, love can't change the past.

"Are you dropping me off at my apartment or hanging out?" I need to sneak away and stop by the leasing office next week. I'm still on the fence about moving in, but the days are passing, and I'm running low on time. If I don't renew my lease soon, they'll clear out my place and charge me for the dumpster.

"I'm coming up, if that's okay? We haven't been here in a few days, and I want to make sure everything's where we left it. And I can keep you company while you pack if you want me to load some of your stuff in my car and drop it off at the house before I leave for the club. I had planned to move everything on Monday, but we can start now if you want." He's speaking as though this is a done deal, but I can't remember agreeing to move in next week. That discussion was on hold the last I checked.

"Maybe we could hold off. I want to swing by the office and ask about a six-month lease."

Kold's breath is measured like he's trying to work his way back to the center before responding. And his hand moves from my leg to grip the steering wheel as if it was always meant to be there. He's not merely upset. He's angry. This isn't a side of him I get to see. Normally, his irritation exists in flashes when he thinks that I'm not looking. But right it's on full display, and it doesn't seem to be leaving.

Neither of us utters a word, and the last five minutes of our drive remain wrapped in tense silence until we pull into the parking lot of my apartment building.

"Do you still want me to come to the house to get ready? Or should I hang out here until you leave for work?" I want to avoid making things worse. If he needs some space to cool the fire, I'm willing to accommodate.

Kold and I are still learning how to fight with each other. Typically, his response to conflict mirrors mine, but it doesn't seem like his natural reaction. I can see and feel the effort he exerts trying to shut down and revisit the conversation from a productive angle. So far, we've been able to talk things out or ignore certain issues, but if he had a mind to, he could break me. I knew better than to mention the lease, conscious of the fact that it's a hot button for him.

"Let's go upstairs and have a discussion. You can pack some clothes for the week. Or were you not planning on coming back?" His question feels loaded with ball bearings.

"Real talk. Do you seriously want me to move in with you next week?" I agree that signing another full-year lease is ridiculous, and that option is off the table. However, I would consider something month to month, with a six-month max.

"I would like to build my life with you, and I would prefer not to wait. But it doesn't matter what I want. If you have something else in mind, I wish you would tell me." Whether he intends to or not, all I hear is, *you know what I want, now tell me what I want to hear.*

"I assumed it was a decision we would make together, but we haven't talked about it in any depth, and I thought it might be helpful to know what options are still on the table." I take off my seatbelt and turn to face him, leaning forward over the center console. "Are you mad at me?"

"I could never be mad at you." He mirrors my movement and meets me in the middle, lips hovering an inch from mine, teasing me. "I'm mad at myself because I thought I did enough to convince you. I want to wake up next to you. I want to come home to you. I want to fall asleep with you in my arms. I want to have conversations over home cooked meals and watch movies on the couch with your legs draped across me. But I need you to want it too."

"I do. I want all of that." My eyes fill with tears as I wait for him to kiss me. I need his forgiveness more than anything. More than air. Of course, he's mad at me. He simply doesn't want to admit it.

Pulling back slightly to look into my eyes, Kold searches for answers. "Then what's the problem? Is it the house or my brother? Or am I the one you don't want to live with?"

"It's me, Kold. I'm the problem. I'm scared you'll leave me, and I'll have to start over. And I'm afraid I won't know how to live without you."

"Babe, you need to let that shit go. I'm not going anywhere. That's why I proposed." He takes my face into his cupped hands and finally kisses me, breaking the last of the tension between us. "I'm sorry to be the one to tell you this, but... You're stuck with me."

Kold

I should've left for the club shortly after we got to the house, but the thought of leaving Val at home, even for a few hours, was enough to keep me from walking out the door. I never thought I would need someone as much as I've needed her. The last two months, I've considered every angle and forced myself to run through the list of things I'd be willing to sacrifice for a chance to call her mine. And now, here I am, engaged to the woman of my dreams, and she hasn't asked me to change a damn thing.

"Why are you staring at me with that grin on your face? Are you up to something? Is this some sort of fake concert, and really I'm about to attend a surprise wedding? I'm not sure I trust you when you look at me like that." Val sits cross-legged on the bed, playing with the dogs, looking more adorable than ever.

"That would have been amazing. Why didn't I have that idea?" I crawl across the bed toward her and join in the fight for her attention. "Come on, you two, move! Mommy and Daddy need a moment."

Val laughs and buries her face against Christmas as Midnight attempts a lick attack. "Mommy and Daddy, huh? Are we adding a new kink to the repertoire?"

I grab her around the waist and tickle her sides until she squeals and attempts to roll away from me. Seeing her happy in such a genuine way fills my heart to near bursting. I can't wait to

262

marry her. Let's hope she doesn't ask for a long engagement to counterbalance my quick proposal.

"Stop!" She shouts between fits of laughter before throwing herself off the edge of the bed. Both dogs follow after, jumping on top of her.

"Babe, are you okay? Do you need me to save you?" I reach over the side of the bed and pull her into my arms, but Val attempts to wiggle away from me, thinking I've come in for round two of the tickle fight.

"Truce! I promise I'll behave."

"My stomach muscles hurt so badly from laughing. Once a week, we should watch a comedy special in lieu of working out in the gym. Then I could look like an underwear model too." Val lifts my shirt, running her hands over the six-pack I've nearly killed myself to maintain.

"Happy wife, happy life," I grin, as my phone goes off again. I know it's Darc without looking. "Shit!"

Evil Twin: You leave me to do all this last-minute bullshit alone, and it's your fucking show. Seriously? I'm not filling in for you on stage. Get your ass here, and I'll go home and keep our girl company.

Evil Twin: And thanks for whatever you guys said to Jamie. She's been blowing up my phone like a lunatic since you left last night. You owe me, and I'm putting it on Valentine's tab.

: Sometimes I think you're suicidal, and you say all this dumb shit because you want me to kill you. Fuck the show! You say one more thing about my girl, and I'll drive there just to kick your teeth in.

Evil Twin: Hey, at this point, whatever gets you here. I gave you my word, and that should be enough. I won't do anything she doesn't ask for.

: Next time, make sure Val knows it's you BEFORE she asks. I'm still pissed about you kissing her. Why she lies to protect you, I'll never understand.

Evil Twin: You can be pissed all you want. I'm not sorry I did it. And maybe she lies because she doesn't want you to know how much she likes it... Are you coming in or not?

: I'll be there in 30 minutes. Keep your panties on.

Evil Twin: You might want to give that advice to your girlfriend before I take her in the office to watch the show.

: Make the most of your last half hour alive.

Looking up from my phone, I notice Val watching me and studying my reaction. "Did something happen at the club? You look pissed?"

"Nothing I can't handle, but I need to get going. I'll see you around six, right?" I press her hand to my lips before pulling her in for a kiss. "I hope you know how much I love you."

"As if you'd ever allow me the space to forget. Now go before Darc gives your time slot to another band." She tells me to leave but pulls me in for another kiss when I attempt to go. Nothing is worth walking away from her when she feels at home in my arms.

"Babe, you're gonna get my dick hard, and then I won't be able to leave until I fuck you. Is that what you want?" My words become a self-fulfilling prophecy the second she smirks at me and bites her bottom lip. "Goddamn, I love you."

My stamina increases each time I'm inside her, but there isn't time for a marathon. Thankfully, seeing Val's ringed hand pressed against my chest and hearing her call me *daddy* sends me crashing through the finish line with time to spare. Then it's her turn. I appreciate her offer to take the lead and am happy to assist. It's not that I can't get my fiancée off, but it's quicker when she does it.

The office Darc and I share at the club is a studio apartment complete with a kitchen and full bathroom, so I can shower and change after I've run through my checklist and the doors are open. My band headlines this show every year, so I know we'll be lucky to go on before ten o'clock. Plenty of time to hang out with my girl backstage and finally show her off to the guys.

I finish getting dressed and grab my bag from the closet, thankful I took the time to prepare in advance. "I'm sorry to run out on you right after having sex. I assure you that was not by design. I would stay home and hold you all night if you asked me to."

"Don't be silly. I've been looking forward to this show for months. And now that it's finally here, you wanna bail? I don't think so. I promise I'll find you as soon as I get there. Now go!" Her hands push and pull like ocean waves, threatening to drown me in heavenly oblivion.

"Why is it so hard to leave you?" The answer is one I know all too well. Val is my better half, and I cease to feel whole without her. I've left her side a handful of times since we found our way back to each other, but it's never been this difficult. In the back of my mind, I'm worried she might see or hear something tonight that's beyond my control, and she'll reevaluate the relationship and decide I'm not worth the trouble.

"Because our hearts remember how shitty it felt to be kept apart. And neither of us wants to go through that again." Val stands to meet me, wearing only our bed sheet and a smile. "Did I ever tell you about my concert fantasy? Well, I have two. The first is to have a guy stand behind me in the front row, with his arms on either side of my body, protecting me from the onslaught of fans behind us. And the second is to be the girl the lead singer walks up to and kisses after he steps off stage."

"Are you telling me I'm allowed to kiss you tonight in front of everyone? Because if that's the case, I'll pull your ass on stage and make sure everyone knows you're mine. As for your other request, that one might need to wait for a concert I'm not headlining, in a club that I don't own. Darc and I avoid being on the floor as much as possible." I want to be the only guy who makes Val's fantasies a reality, and if that means braving the chaos, I'm ready to prepare for the storm.

"You don't have to do either of those things tonight or ever. I only mentioned it because I wanted you to know that I'll be imagining you with me. I'm excited to see you guys perform live. After all, I am a huge fan. I've listened to the albums, stalked your groupie fan pages, and watched all the videos, but nothing beats a live show." Val is practically beaming as she speaks.

So much for staying home. There's no way I'll risk disappointing my girl when she's been counting down the days leading up to tonight. If I leave now, there's still time to ensure everything's perfect. Suddenly motivated to make this our best show ever, I kiss Val one last time and say my goodbyes before heading out the door.

I wonder if there's still time to book a minister and throw an impromptu wedding.

CHAPTER 32

Val

After Kold left, I crawled back into bed and snuggled with the dogs until I fell asleep. All three of us remained that way until my phone alarm went off an hour later, jarring me awake. In my bewildered state, I forgot where I was and accidentally threw my arm over a pile of dogs sleeping under the blanket next to me, setting off a secondary alarm.

"Okay. Shhhh! I'm sorry. It was an accident. Geez." I try to calm them down before getting out of bed to shower, but Christmas shoots out from under the blanket, still yelling at me. "Oh, and what do we have here? Big tough guy defending your girlfriend, huh? Let's see what you're made of, little man."

I begin play-fighting with the small white dog, remembering what it was like before moving here. Not so long ago, Christmas was the only one I could count on to be there for me. He was the reason I got out of bed in the morning or came home at night. I've missed our one-on-one time together. Only I didn't realize it until now.

As soon as we stepped foot in this house, my once best friend tethered himself to Midnight like she was his reason for existing. Seeing our dogs together, I know Kold is right. I could never sign an extension to my lease and split up the makeshift family we've become.

My only reason for concern is Darc and how he feels about

me staying here long-term. This is his home, after all, and I'm not trying to step on any toes. Maybe I should stop being scared and talk to him. Sounds easy enough in theory until he starts looking into my eyes and touching me and using that fucking voice that makes my insides melt. And don't even get me started on the kiss.

I've gone back and forth so many times, debating whether or not I should tell Kold what happened that morning when I accidentally kissed his brother. I sort of brought it up when we were mid-role pay in the office, but then I panicked and backtracked, and I've been lying ever since. Lies of omission are still lies, despite what ex-husbands will lead you to believe.

Since I picked out my concert outfit in advance, it doesn't take long to shower, do my hair and makeup, and get dressed. All that's left is to feed the dogs and let them out before I leave the house and make my way downtown. I have the address for Club After Darc saved in my phone and a driving playlist at the ready. As I wait for the dogs to finish eating, my phone begins to sing.

Kold: Are you leaving soon?

: Letting the dogs out. Then I'll get my shoes on and start driving. Was your brother pissed at you when you got there?

Kold: I let him live, and we came to an agreement, so we're square. He doesn't need me as much as he claims. This club is his second home, and he runs a tight ship. When I got in, most of my list was checked off. I'm triple-checking the sound and the lights. Then I'm good to shower and change.

Kold: Text me when you get here. I know we agreed that you'd wait in line, and I'm not backing out on our deal, but I need to know where you are and that you're safe.

: No worries. I understand how you feel. See you soon!

The dogs come sauntering in like they've walked through molasses, and I assume they're being stubborn because they know I'm leaving. "Come on! You two are killing me. Dad said I need to go, so that means now. Move it!" It's amazing how quickly excitement can turn to frustration when you're in a hurry.

At the front door, I do one last check. Clothes, hair, and makeup all look good enough, eTicket is saved on my phone, ready to go, directions are rolling, and I have enough cash for parking, drinks, and merch. This is going to be fun!

The drive downtown is about twenty minutes from the house, so I call Tracy, hoping to catch up. She spends the first five minutes inquiring about my health and hounding me about making an appointment to see the doctor. It's at this point that I begin to regret calling. Thankfully, she's ready to move to another topic as I pull onto the freeway.

"So, you're living in that big house with both of them? What's that like?"

"Pretty normal, for the most part. I was able to work from home all week, and Darc let me use his office, which was kind of cool. He's got this gorgeous mahogany desk that looks like it came out of a castle, shelves full of books, and a collection of unique trinkets. The whole room is a feast for the eyes."

"To hell with the books. Girl, those two guys are the damn feast for the eyes! Is the sex amazing? Tell me it's amazing. I already know it is."

"Yeah, I'm not even gonna try to downplay it. The sex is incredible, and Kold is a very *giving* lover. I appreciate his willingness *to take care of me* in all aspects of my daily life."

"You sound happy, Val. I think that's amazing. I take it you haven't heard from Allen?"

"No. Thankfully not. Why? Are you still talking to *Carter*?"

"He reached out last weekend, but he's been M.I.A ever since. Not that I want to talk to him. All his *baby, I miss you. Baby, I need to see you. Baby, you can trust me.* I'm not sure why I ever wasted my time."

"Because he looks good on paper. Until you look close

enough to realize it's one-ply gas station toilet paper, and he's a piece of shit!"

"Oh, my god. Stop! That's hilarious. Are we going to see you tomorrow at some point? Samuel has a gift for you. He made it himself and gift-wrapped at school, so I have no idea what it is."

"Well, you tell Samuel that Santa left a few special presents for him in my closet, so Aunt Val will make sure to stop by."

"Sounds good. Have fun tonight, and be careful. We'll see you tomorrow."

Hearing the sadness in Tracy's voice when she asked about Allen almost brought me to tears. That guy will never deserve her, but she clearly isn't closing the door on their relationship. Even though she tried to laugh it off a few minutes later, it was too late to mask her true feelings.

When I arrive at the venue, an attendant waves me into the lot away from the employee parking area. For a moment, I consider doing as I'm told and going with the flow until I remember my deal with Kold was a quid pro quo. My parking in the employee lot in exchange for my getting to wait in line.

"I'm sorry. I need to go over there." I point toward the fenced-in area lit up like a little league stadium and wait for him to ask my name, but no follow-up questions come. He steps aside and waves me through before directing the cars behind me to travel with the pack. Kold might want to have a team meeting with his parking lot security since they seem a bit lax.

> : Parked SUPER CLOSE to your brother's Lamborghini to piss him off. Don't say anything. It'll be funnier if he sees it on his own. About to get in line. I'm nervous and excited... Hope I don't run into any of your ex-girlfriends. I'd have to borrow a shopping cart from the homeless guy across the street.

I wait for a reply, but it doesn't come. He's probably busy or in the shower getting ready. I'm sure he's not with some groupie while I'm on my way to see him. He wouldn't be that stupid, would he? Plus, we had sex a couple of hours ago, so it's not like he's in dire need of getting laid. Then again, when is cheating ever actually about the sex?

Walking around the dark corner of the building, I feel lost amongst the crowd, and that's exactly how I like it. If I could have one superpower, it would be invisibility. Come to think of it, maybe I do. Lord knows the guys I've dated never seemed to notice me standing right in front of them, begging for their attention.

"Quit freaking out. You're going to get in. There are always sketchy people scalping tickets at shows like this, and if there's not, we can figure something else out."

I continue to eavesdrop on the conversation behind me as the line forms. Four of the girls have tickets, and one does not. I can't imagine how shitty that must feel, being the odd man out. What's the plan if they can't buy another ticket? Are the four girls going in without her and leaving their friend to sit in the car alone? In December? Thankfully, it's warm out, but that only addresses one of the issues. As a woman, I wouldn't feel comfortable being outside on my own, and the way this girl's voice is shaking, I can tell she isn't happy about the idea either.

"My friend, Sarah, said that the guys who own this club are hot as fuck and have a reputation for picking up girls from the crowd. So, if we can't buy a ticket, maybe one of us could get through the door *another* way."

"How would we even know who they are?"

"I don't want to have sex with some creepy club owner, even if the lead singer of Our Last Midnight is totally worth the price of admission."

"Look, that guy over there is selling tickets. I knew we could get you one. Hold my spot in line, and I'll see how much he wants."

During my twenties and early thirties, I went to over a hundred shows on my own, which fueled my depression while simultaneously acting as an escape. I would see people out with their friends having a good time, and I felt like I was missing out. But after hearing the conversation behind me, I think having friends might not be better than standing alone.

"Okay. The good news is he has tickets, but the bad news is he wants $500 a piece, and he's only got two left. So, we need to make a decision quickly."

"I can't afford $500."

I continue listening to the girls debate behind me while watching the sleazy-looking scalper slink over from the shadows. The closer he gets, the more uneasy I feel. Thankfully, security is three steps behind him, so this situation is about to resolve itself without my intervention.

"So, what's it gonna be, ladies? $500 or $400 and a trip to the backseat of my car?"

"I'm sorry, but no! You need to fuck off immediately!" The words come out of my mouth with such force that I can feel everyone around me stop mid-conversation.

"Bitch, nobody was talking to you!" His words spit in my direction, along with a heated look.

"Excuse me, ma'am. You need to come with me." The security guard joins the conversation, but not in the way I expected.

"I didn't do anything wrong. So, if you want to help, why don't you get this disgusting creep out of my face and away from these girls." As passive as I normally am, this situation has me heated. I don't know the girls behind me, and I'll probably never see them again, but they have the right to come out for a night without being sexually harassed by some pervert.

"She's a mouthy little bitch, isn't she? Well, I've got just the thing for that." I can hear the people around me gasp as the creep attempts to slap me, only to be grabbed from behind by two additional security guards and hauled off kicking and screaming.

"Like I was saying, I need you to come with me, and I'm not in the mood to ask again." The security here is for shit, and I have half a mind to bring this conversation to an abrupt end.

"Who's asking? You or *them*?" I don't need to elaborate.

"He sent me out here to get you, so will you *please* follow me inside?" His jaw tightens, and the word *please* is spoken through clenched teeth as though it pains him to be polite.

"Respectfully, *no*! Look, I'm not trying to make your job harder. But he and I had a deal, and I held up my end, so leave me alone! I will speak to him when I get inside." I can't believe Kold would do this to me after we both agreed to the terms and conditions. He knows how much I hate a scene, and now I'm standing in the dead center of one.

"Um, I think she'd rather hang out with her friends tonight, and we all came here together, so..." The voice coming from behind me belongs to the girl without a ticket. I recognize her tone and tenor as soon as she opens her mouth.

"I know for a fact that she came here alone, so stay out of this, child! The adults are talking." This security guard is officially on my last nerve, and I'm two seconds away from turning into a thirty-five-year-old Karen and asking to speak to a manager.

"Don't talk to her like that! And while you're at it, correct your tone when you speak to me. You're pissing me off and ruining my night!" I'm about to lose my shit when I notice a familiar face over his shoulder.

"Enough!" He steps past the show security like the guy's not even there and takes my hand. "Why do you have to be so difficult? Let me take care of you!"

My heart beats so loudly in my ears that I almost miss the whispers as they fan out around me. *It's him. Oh my god. It is him, you're right. Should we ask for an autograph?*

"You promised me!" My voice is nothing more than a harsh whisper belonging to a broken woman.

He cups my face and leans forward, his breath warm against my neck. This is the way he touches when he wants to win. Once I'm turned on, I lose my will to fight, and he knows that. As the rest of the characters disappear around us, his words brush through my hair and tickle my ear.

"Sweetheart, I'm not him."

Kold

I picked out the most stereotypical outfit I could, jeans and a t-shirt with a black hoodie and a solid black fitted baseball cap. Unfortunately, it's a hooded sweatshirt, not an invisibility cloak. If I'm lucky, I'll get ten minutes on the floor with Val before someone recognizes me. It's not that the band is some global sensation or anything. We're not. But my brother and I have always been big fish in a small pond.

A pond that's full of leeches.

When the office door opens, my heart leaps into my throat, expecting to see Val's face, but it's only my brother, empty-handed.

"I thought you were going to walk her up here after she came through the doors? How hard is that?" My disappointment over not seeing her is evident in my tone. "I knew I should have done it myself."

"There was a situation, and I pulled her out of line. She wasn't happy about it!"

"I told you specifically to wait until she got inside and used her ticket. It was important to her. Is she even here?" I swear, if Val is halfway home right now, I'm leaving.

"She gave her ticket to some random girl in line and walked in with me. But when I tried to bring her up here, she pulled away and evaporated into the crowd."

"So, she may or may not be here! And she's pissed at me! Thank you so very much." I pull my hood forward and head for the door. "I don't care if it's Christmas Eve. Call the lawyer and get the paperwork drawn up. You can forget about our deal. I'm fucking done with you!" Slamming the door behind me, I hope to solidify any lingering doubt. From this point forward, Val is the only partner I'm interested in having.

There's still a line of people wrapped around the building, so I locate Val without too much trouble. She looks adorably annoyed, tapping her credit card on the top of the bar while waiting for her drink. I sneak in behind her to hold up two fingers to the bartender making her cocktail. A minute later, the two drinks are dropped off in front of us, and her credit card remains unused.

"Wait, I only ordered one. And I need to pay for these." She calls after the bartender, who's already moved on to the next customer.

"Mind if I join you?" My hands come up on either side of her and momentarily linger on the top of the bar before collecting my drink.

"That depends. Are you, *you?* Or are you *him?*" The cute way she phrases her question makes me smile.

"I'm all yours, I promise. Now tell me what he did this time. He didn't kiss you again, did he?" I feel like I've witnessed Darc kissing Val on the top of her head half a dozen times with my own eyes, so I can't even imagine everything that's happened when I'm not standing next to her.

"No. Wait! What?"

"Nothing. I'd like to know what happened. I thought I was clear with him when I asked if he could find you and bring you to the office once you were inside, but I guess not. Nevertheless, you're here now." I press the front of my body into hers, backing her up to the bar. "Can you forgive me for breaking my promise?"

"I was never mad at you, so there's nothing to forgive. I was pissed about the disgusting creep in line who was trying to trade tickets for cash and sexual favors and the asshole security guard who was giving me a hard time and your brother showing up and everyone staring at us and... Okay, for a minute I thought he was you, and I suppose I was mad. But then I realized my mistake. I'm not going to let it ruin my night, so let's have a drink, and you can show me around."

"Did my brother handle the situation with the ticket-scalping sexual predator and the asshole security guard? If you tell me exactly what he looked like and what he said, I'll make sure it's taken care of. It's ridiculous! I can't even take a shower without everything going to hell. From now on, we go to shows together, deal?"

"Okay, deep breath. Now blow out all those feelings, and let's start again." She sets her drink on the bar and tucks her hands into the front of my hoodie pocket. "I know it was only a few hours, but I missed you."

"Let's go upstairs. I wanna bend you over my desk so I have something to think about the next time I'm forced to be here without you." This isn't a question or a command. My request can go unanswered if she chooses, but I know most likely she'll give me what I'm asking for. There was a time when imaging her naked, spread out in front of me, was the only thing that got me through the day. For six and a half agonizing weeks, all I had was the idea of her to keep me company, and it was torture.

"You're never satisfied, are you? I can't even imagine how many random women you've slept with to get the reputation you have." Val smiles at me as if she's unphased by the information within her statement.

This shit right here is exactly what I was afraid of. The life I led before finding my purpose was a filthy fucking mess, and now somehow, she knows. She's been here for less than an hour, and already I've been exposed.

"It's fine, forget it. We can do something else. Have any interest in seeing backstage?" I grab the drinks from the bar and lead her on a tour through the building, including some high-lights from my childhood.

My family has owned this building since it was constructed in 1945, and I grew up playing hide and seek with my brother and cousins during concerts in the 90s. This building, with its many corridors and hidden rooms, was our playground, and the bands were our personal entertainment.

When you're a kid, you don't know to be scared until after something bad happens. To this day, there's a room in this building that Darc and I refuse to enter. Even decades later, no amount of time will erase what we witnessed behind that door. As Val and I pass by it, I squeeze her hand and pull her close.

"I'll always protect you and defend you without hesitation. I should have done that the night we met, but I didn't know you were already mine. I thought I was doing the right thing by giving you the space to choose, and I'm sorry. If I would have known you needed me..."

"Please stop apologizing. I cherish my memories of that night. Whatever dumb shit Allen said or did, I don't care. He introduced me to you, and that's all that matters."

The music starts on the other side of the wall, and so it begins. "Should we go out and watch the show like some normal, nobody couple?"

"Absolutely. But if I'm not allowed to be a secret, neither are you." Val pushes my hood back and stretches to kiss me. "I want you to be every version of yourself. The man who cooks me break-fast and makes me smile is incredible, but I'd also like to meet the guy everyone else sees. I need to know who you are before we get married."

I can't argue with that logic, and even if I could, I wouldn't. Val's right. There are two sides to me: the one she fell in love with and the one she sees when she looks at my brother. Darc and I lived the same life for a long time because we never had a reason to be more than that until now.

CHAPTER 33

Val

When I asked Kold to be his most authentic self, I wasn't sure what to expect, but it wasn't this.

He takes my hand, and we walk right in front of the stage into the gated-off section reserved for security. The sea of people recognizes him immediately, hardly bothering to notice me. I'm sure he's had plenty of women on his arm, and probably not the same one twice.

At the center of the stage, Kold motions for a group of guys to clear a space, and they comply with quickened steps, pushing back the swarm of people at their backs. Once the bubble is clear of limbs, Kold steps on a black box and easily hops over the three-and-a-half foot railing.

"I can't jump over that." The panic must be written all over my face because he laughs and extends his arms to me. I take his hand and step onto the box. Being up twelve inches helps, but I'm still not convinced I can make it without falling flat to my face on the other side.

Of course, I never have to find out if I would have made it on my own because Kold isn't in the habit of taking chances. He lifts me over the railing and sets me on my feet directly in front of him. I can feel the eyes of every woman in the place suddenly locked on my position, silently passing judgment and wondering what I've got that they don't.

If they want to compare measurements and makeup, I'm sure plenty of them have got me beat. Even if we factor in education and economic status, I'm sure to fall short. There's nothing about me, on my own, that's special. The only thing I've got that they don't, is *him.*

"We've never played with these guys, but I like their sound. What do you think?" He leans forward, talking next to my ear. "They remind me of one of the bands on your playlist."

I spin in place, protected on all sides by flexed muscle, tattooed flesh, and bones strong enough to support the immense weight thrust upon him by others. Looking into his eyes, I forget about the people around us and kiss him with reckless abandon. Encased in this cage of flesh and bones, I feel untouchable.

"Babe, if you kiss me like that again, I'm going to need more of you. A lot more."

Spinning back toward the stage, I press my back to his chest and watch the show from the comfort of his arms. What is it about a hat that makes an attractive guy even sexier? This is the best seat in the house, no question. The only thing I find slightly annoying is when the guys around Kold start apologizing every time they bump into him.

Why are they apologizing? I hit him harder than that in the bedroom for fun. Then again, I suppose they wouldn't know that.

As soon as the first band plays their last note, Kold kisses my neck as I ask, "What's next?" I'm open to whatever he wants to do. Being with him is my only requirement, so he's welcome to choose the activity.

"I can have someone bring a round of drinks here, or we can check out all the merch tables in the back and find you a new hoodie to steal from me, or we can go to the office where it's quiet and have some time to ourselves. It's whatever you want to do."

"So long as you're beside me, I'm not picky about the rest. Can we get drinks and take them up to the office?" I have no idea what the rules are, but I suppose you can do anything you want when you own the place. Kold seems to find my naive thinking adorable because he smiles and kisses the top of my head.

"You're too cute. I have a bottle of cherry vodka and cans of

Red Bull already upstairs, so we can head that way whenever you're ready."

From where we're standing, I can see the front of the office above. It reminds me of club seating at a basketball arena with a wall of windows and open patio seating. I'm curious to see how much of the second floor is living space. Kold told me the office was a studio apartment they lived in at one point before buying the house, but I wonder if there are other rooms up there.

Getting a guided tour through such a large part of his past, I feel like I'm beginning to understand why both brothers invest so much of themselves into this place. The building itself is a family legacy passed down through the generations, adding to the pressure to succeed.

As we walk through the crowd, a few girls reach out to touch him before turning back to giggle with their friends. And I get it. Kold and Darc are definitely the hottest guys I've ever seen in real life, but that isn't a free pass to disrespect their personal space. I'm starting to understand why he didn't want to watch the show from the floor.

When we get to the stairs leading up to the office, security steps to the side. It's interesting watching the way various people respond to their presence. Kold and Darc command the attention of any room they enter. I've witnessed this each time we leave the house, but I wasn't expecting the seas to part for them the way they do here.

As we pass by security, I hear one of the men say, "That's an odd choice," and it takes a moment for his meaning to register.

Kold seems to process the comment faster than I do because the words halt him in his tracks halfway between two steps. I'm caught unprepared for the sudden stop and crash straight into his back, leaving me feeling like an idiot. As I shake off my embarrassment, I turn to face the man I assume made the comment. He looks like he's swallowed hot coals, clearly registering the caliber of his mistake.

"I suggest you apologize to my wife. Quickly!" I can feel Kold's anger as it passes through my body, spreading out in all directions.

"Um. I. Sorry." The man looks past me as he stumbles over a series of random words. "I wasn't aware. I'm sorry, sir."

I turn back around and catch Kold's arm. "Please don't do this. I don't need or want some half-ass apology. Let's go upstairs." I push against his chest, but he doesn't move. The downside of dating a guy twice my size is that I have zero control unless he gives it to me.

Seriously though, what the hell is wrong with the guys who work in this place? Do they have to complete a course on effectively disrespecting women before they can receive their official crew shirt? The light catches my ring, and I hear the guy stumble through his second attempt at an apology.

Kold takes a deep breath and releases it, and then another. With my hands snugly pressed into the front of his hoodie, I can feel the effort taking place below the surface.

"Babe, please. You can walk away. Let's go upstairs and have a drink." My voice is low enough that only he can hear me. I'm not trying to undermine his authority, but this night doesn't need to end with some guy bloodied up in the parking lot.

My flash of anger towards the idiot security guard dissolves the second my eyes meet Kold's, and I realize how deeply hurt he is by the accusation that I'm not his type.

"Go upstairs, and I'll be there in a moment. Darc should be in the office. If he's not, text him, and he'll come up." Kold guides me past him as we switch spots on the stairs. The movement is executed with such precision that it feels choreographed and well-rehearsed, as if he's moved me with his mind.

Part of me wants to insist on his joining, but I can tell from his tone that he's in no mood to be accommodating. So, I touch his shoulder and whisper into his ear, "Don't keep me waiting too long," before making my solo ascent.

I know I shouldn't, but walking to the office, I can't help but wonder how many women he's brought up here over the years. Based on the comment in line, I can assume it's been a lot. And the comment made at the bottom of the stairs is enough to tell me that the women who came before me were tens, compared to my best day at six and a half.

I pull the office door shut, blocking out the pressure behind me, instantly replacing it with a tension that clenches my central functions. Darc must have been on his way down because I walked straight into him, again feeling like the biggest idiot in the world. My spatial awareness has faltered twice in a minute, and I've only had one drink.

"Of all the gin joints in all the world, you come walking into mine as I was about to look for you. Now, what are the chances of that?"

Never missing an opportunity to flirt, Darc pulls me to his chest and locks me in place. His arms are a steel vice, and I know better than to fight. Until now, he's walked a fine line, except for our good-morning kiss that resulted in my mistakenly professing my love for the wrong brother. I've noticed he'll push me to a point but won't take it further without my consent.

Stop asking for permission and kiss me again.

"Why were you looking for me?" I don't mean for my voice to sound so pleading, but that's how it comes out. "And what do you plan to do with me now that you've found me?"

"I needed to talk to you. But right now, all I can think about is how badly I want to bend you over the arm of that couch and fuck you until you beg me to stop." He backs me into the door and holds me there, the cold metal drawing the heat from my core.

"I wouldn't..." My eyes already begging, I bite my bottom lip and fall deeper into his gaze.

"You wouldn't what, sweetheart... Beg? Or allow me to fuck you?" His lips hover dangerously close, waiting for an invitation.

"I wouldn't ask you to stop." Whatever part of my personality is in the driver's seat, it's not my better judgment. Not that I would be stupid enough to have sex with Darc while Kold is standing twenty feet away on the other side of the door defending my honor. Fuck. I need to dump some ice on this before I land in hot water.

"That's my girl. I wish you'd let *her* come out to play with me. I know plenty of games, and I'm certain we'd have fun together."

Kold

This night has been one thing after the next, and I haven't even gotten on stage yet. The last thing I need to see, walking through the back door of the office, is my brother about to kiss my fiancée again, yet here we are. I wish they would sleep together and get it over with.

Even as I cross the room, Darc keeps her wedged against the door, fully submerged in the thrill of the hunt. "I'll take it from here, brother." My hand squeezes his shoulder, pulling him back to reality. "Why don't you take a walk and get some air."

He falls back, retracing my steps across the room without a word, and locks the door behind him. My brother doesn't like to lose, but when it comes to Val, he's willing to play the long game. For reasons beyond my control, Darc is convinced she's meant for both of us, and sometimes I wonder if he isn't right. Maybe it would take the pair of us to fully satisfy the multiple versions of Val that seem to battle for control inside her head.

Even now, she's shaking, but not from fear. I know my girl and the way her body reacts. I can feel her desire snaking around me like vines, but it isn't my sudden presence that prompts their growth.

"Do you want me to do my best Darc impression while I give you what you need, sweetheart?" I take off my hat and throw it like a frisbee across the room, missing the top of my desk by a mile. This nickname for Val is not one that I use, but I've heard him call her that enough times to know she'll catch my meaning. I love this girl with everything I am, and I'm happy to play along and fulfill her fantasy the best I can.

"No." Her hands work on my belt while I pull off my hoodie and t-shirt in one motion. "I was pretending he was you. Babe, you're the one I want. I want it to be you inside me. Sometimes, my brain doesn't know how to separate the two of you, but I swear nothing happened."

Twisting my fingers into Val's hair, I lift her gaze to meet mine. Her pupils are enlarged in the dim lighting, turning her crystal blue eyes black. Her face is a mix of ravenous sweetness and innocent culpability. "Do you still love me?"

She doesn't speak, but the nodding of her head indicates her heart belongs to me, and that's all I need to know.

There's a couch in the office I've slept on a handful of times, dreaming of her mouth on me. Seems only fitting that I find out how good reality compares now that I finally have her here. Standing half-naked in front of her, my pants low enough to expose my cock, I'm already hard.

"I want you to show me how much you love me with that cute little mouth of yours."

Val begins to drop to her knees in front of me, but I catch her by the arms. Confused, she looks up. "What are you doing?"

"On the couch, my love. No wife of mine will *ever* kneel on a linoleum floor, even if it is at my feet." In my mind, Val and I are as good as married. I don't need a piece of paper to reassure me that this girl belongs by my side, and no one will convince me otherwise.

Wearing only a t-shirt, Val positions herself on the couch, ready to please me. As much as I want this, it feels wrong. She is my goddess, and I should be the one on my knees at her feet, primed and ready to cater to her wants and needs. She already gives me everything I could ever need by simply existing. The fact that she loves me, tolerates me, and fucks me on a daily basis is more than I deserve.

Sliding out of my pants, I drop them on the empty cushion as

I take a seat beside her. I attempt to pull her onto my lap, but Val has a one-track mind and the only path she intends to follow leads directly to her mouth on my dick. She takes me down like a pro, letting her tongue massage the length of my shaft while the head hits the back of her throat.

"God damn, sweetheart. You're so good at sucking my cock." I run my hand up the inside of her thigh and coat my fingers in her juices before circling her clit. Then I move to the entrance of her pussy and shove two fingers inside, forcing her lungs to empty. "I want to watch you swallow another guy's dick while I fuck this tight little pussy. Would you enjoy that?"

The way her body responds, clenching around my fingers while her mouth takes me deeper, I already know her answer. My girl wants to take on two guys at once, and I have a good feeling I know who she's imagining at the other end.

"Tell me whose cock you want, and it's yours." Curling my fingers inside her, I press against her G spot, causing her back to arch. "Tell me who you're thinking about."

Pulling her head up from my cock, she sucks in a gasped breath before answering my request. "I only want to be with two guys if they're both *you*." Her words are pleading, as if the fate of her continued existence depends on me giving her what she refuses to ask for.

As soon as her mouth is back on me, I retrieve the phone from my pocket, type a random letter into the text box, and hit send. The office lock clicks a minute later before the door swings open. I close my eyes and try not to react. We're about to find out if my suspicions about Val are correct, and I don't want to give anything away. However, if I've read this wrong and she ends up pissed at me, maybe I don't want her teeth sited to bite my dick off.

"Close your eyes and sit on my lap." She moves only where I guide her until she's hovering above me, about to slide down and begin the next scene. "Keep your eyes closed, and show me who that pussy belongs to."

I play the dominant from time to time, but Darc lives it. I'm not sure he knows how to be anything else, which is why he's always single. Girls think it's all fifty shades of fun and games until the real pain starts and never stops. He owns his monstrous impulses while I struggle to repress mine. Unwilling to give up the dream of a normal life, I need to be more than darkness.

Val works her body up and down the length of my cock, blissfully unaware of what lies ahead. With her eyes closed, she's so focused on the man filling her pussy, that she has yet to sense the identical copy standing in front of her.

Threading my forearm through her elbows, I pin her arms behind her back, slowing her to a near stop, then cover her eyes with my free hand. "I need you to trust me. You know I would never let anyone hurt you."

"I trust you," Val says, sitting back so that every inch of me is buried inside her.

Darc steps forward and coils his fingers into Val's hair, causing her body to clench.

"What the fuck? Kold, let go of my arms and move your goddamn hand!"

"Fuck. Your pussy gets even tighter when you fight me. I might need to piss you off more often." I keep her locked into place as she struggles to unhook her arms. "If you agree to play nice, I'll uncover your eyes."

She stops fighting and waits patiently for her reward. Once I remove my hand from her eyes, she gasps and falls back against my chest. "What the hell are you two playing at? This isn't funny."

"Nothing we do together will ever change how I feel about you. You're still my girl. But right now, I want you to open your mouth and show me how good you are at sucking cock."

She pauses a moment, no doubt contemplating her options. Sitting forward, she straightens her spine and tenses her shoulders.

"If you give me my arms back, I'll do anything you want." Her voice sounds distant, like she's watching all of this unfold from the other side of the room.

I nearly call off the game and wrap her up in a blanket, but it's too late to back out now. What if she ends up hating me after and never forgives me? Why the hell did I think this was a good idea?

"Valentine." Darc leans down to kiss her more gently than I

imagined. "If you tell me to stop, we'll stop." He kisses her again, only this time she falls forward into him, kissing back with such intensity that I can feel the prick of jealousy in my chest. I release her arms once I'm confident she isn't going to turn around and punch me.

She uses her new freedom to unhook his belt and unzip his pants. Soon she's back to riding my cock, only this time, she's giving me a show. Watching her from this angle, pleasing someone else while I fuck her, is turning me on more than I thought possible.

Initially, I thought giving them permission to fuck around without any guilt was a selfless act. Val has hinted, since the beginning, that this was something she wanted, and now she has the fantasy without the risk of losing her reality. And Darc made it clear that he intended to have Val one way or another. Establishing ground rules and being there to ensure it was what she wanted seemed like the best play. After tonight, there's no need for lies. No more awkward tension or keeping secrets. Everyone gets what they want, and we can move forward without the need for taking sides.

"You're so good at taking my cock." Darc doesn't hold back on anyone's account. "Eyes on me, Valentine. I want you to know it's me you're choking on."

"Let's bend her over the arm of the couch." I push her to the side and lift her into position, spreading her knees apart with my foot. "My girl enjoys a nice hard fuck."

"Then maybe we should switch sides and find out how rough *our* girl likes it."

"Next time." I thrust my cock back into her before I could complete my thought, and whatever I planned on saying disappeared with her breath. In this position, I doubt it will take me long to finish, so I reach around and begin rubbing her clit.

"Good girl. I love watching you swallow my cock. You look so pretty with tears in your eyes." He holds her head in place while she gags, unwilling to back off. "I've wanted to fuck you since the first time I saw you. But you already knew that, didn't you, babygirl?"

Val responds with a muffled whimper as her body tightens around me.

"You're gonna squeeze every last drop out of me if you keep clenching down like that." I smack her ass hard enough to leave a handprint. "I want you to cum with me, babe. Are you ready?" I increase my pace, slamming into her at a fever pitch. Treating her more like a back-alley whore than my soon-to-be wife.

It isn't long before I empty inside her. As soon as her body begins to convulse, I'm a goner, carrying her over the finish line with me.

The second I pull out, Darc is ready to take my place. What the fuck is he doing? That wasn't our deal.

"It's my turn, sweetheart." He pushes inside of her without warning, and her back arches in response. "How are you still so tight? I thought he would've broken you in by now. But I guess that's why you needed me."

I'm not sure why I waste my time worrying about his happiness.

I can't watch this. Grabbing my clothes off the floor, I kiss Val on the top of the head before making a beeline for the bathroom. Darc is a fucking asshole, but that's a conversation for another time. I'm not about to fight with him in front of Val and have her think she's the one who did something wrong.

However, if they're not finished before I get out of the shower, I'm going to look like a chump.

She'll leave me for Mr. Endurance, and I'll have no one to blame but myself.

CHAPTER 34

Val

Walking to the shower on baby giraffe legs, I worry I won't make it in time. Kold left me alone with Darc, and I need to make sure we're still okay. He assured me that nothing we did together would change his opinion of me, but people promise all kinds of things in the moment, only to hold it against you later on.

The door to the bathroom is unlocked, and I can still hear the water running as I slip inside. "Is it okay if I join you?"

We always shower together, but something feels different now. I feel dirty in a way I don't think a shower can wash clean. Maybe I should have asked them to stop before it started. There isn't a threesome in the world worth losing Kold over. Not even this one.

I pull off my soiled t-shirt and drop it beside the sink, ready to join him.

"I was about to get out." His voice rings hollow in a way I'm not used to, but he pulls back the curtain and smiles at me. "Don't overthink it, love. Everything's fine."

Thankfully, there's a robe hanging from a hook on the back of the door, though it does nothing to hide my shame. I grab the tube of toothpaste off the sink and use my finger to brush my teeth. Better than nothing, I suppose. Then I exit through the door I came in, sulk across the office, and curl myself into a ball on the couch, still needing a shower.

At this point, I might as well wait until Kold leaves. I need a hug and a kiss and his word that he still plans to love me forever. Is that too much to ask for?

Darc sits beside me, wearing only his boxer briefs, and pulls me into his arms. Somehow, even when I'm feeling invisible, he sees me. Darc has a knack for seeking me out, and I'm surprised he wasn't able to find me during the two months Kold and I spent apart. Not only is he well-connected, but he's also relentless.

Winding up in bed with him always felt like an inevitability despite my best efforts to resist. He was going to break me down eventually. Even Kold could see that. I only wish we had discussed the rules beforehand so that I might have known where the lines were drawn. Now that Darc and I have slept together, is that the end of it or the beginning? I don't want to do anything that puts my future at risk, but I also *really* enjoyed having them both.

"He isn't upset with you. Whatever he said or didn't say, everything's alright."

"Yeah, well. What's done is done. I wanted to talk to you about something, but maybe it's irrelevant now."

"I needed to talk to you as well, and now feels like as good a time as any. So, ladies first."

My head falls against Darc's chest, too heavy to be supported by my strained neck. His heart sounds identical to Kold's. When I close my eyes, I can feel myself forgetting that they aren't one and the same. As I'm about to ask his feelings on my moving in, Kold emerges from the bathroom, freshly showered and neatly dressed.

"Well, don't you two look cozy. I don't know what that idiot was talking about. From where I'm standing, you and I look perfect together, babe." He comes over and takes my arm, pulling me to my feet. "I'm sorry I didn't wait so we could shower together. I wasn't sure how long you'd be, and I need to get backstage. Can you forgive me?"

"Can I forgive you for taking a shower without me? I don't know. That's gonna be a tough one for me to get over. It might take some time and a fair bit of groveling on your part." I can feel my lips pull up on one side into a half smile. This is my involuntary facial expression when I'm trying to be cute. Kold mentioned to me once that it's one of the top ten things he loves about me.

"You know I'm willing to do *whatever* it takes. Maybe we should plan a six-day vacation and start the new year out right. Fly first class and book a honeymoon suite with ocean views and a private beach. Spend our week exploring an island paradise where it's seventy-two degrees and sunny. Someplace where we can cuddle together in a hammock between two palm trees, watching the sunset into the Northern Pacific Ocean."

"That sounds oddly specific. As if you've already booked the airfare and hotel." I study his expression, looking for cracks in the mask, but he never gives anything away unintentionally. "Is this trip a pre-honeymoon, or simply because you enjoy the pleasure of my company?"

"This particular hypothetical vacation is because I can't function without you by my side and because I want to watch you walk around in a bikini for a week." I already know he's being serious. Kold and I have great banter, but he isn't one to joke.

"You know I have a job, right? And we have dogs who need to eat and go outside and sleep in bed with us. We can't exactly take off without notice."

"Well then, consider yourself notified. We fly out on the 7th and come back on the 13th."

"The 7th of January?" If he weren't so goddamn cute, I would strangle him.

Even if I could burn through all of my vacation time at work, I'm not confident I'd have a job to return to. Why couldn't he have found me ten years ago when I was working one bullshit job after the next? I would have jumped at the chance to fly off to paradise with a mid-level Greek god.

"Don't make a decision right now. You have plenty of time to think about it. Take a shower, hang out with my dickhead brother, and come see me before I go on. There's another band after this one, and then the real fun begins." Kold always looks at me like I'm the most beautiful woman he's ever seen, and true to his word, that hasn't changed. "Stay and have your conversation with Darc. But don't replace me. Not yet."

There is no replacing you or what we have.

When he kisses my neck, I want to stop him from leaving, but I know I've already kept him longer than I should have. This is his job, after all, as odd as that concept is for me to wrap my mind around.

I watch as Kold walks out the door, locking it behind him. Is this security measure for my sake, or is there a mountain of cash hidden in the walls somewhere? I'm beginning to wonder after seeing both guys lock the door on their way out. Then again, I'm nearly naked and wearing a bathrobe, so maybe they don't want some bartender walking in and making assumptions about what happened.

"So, where were we?" Darc stretches his arms out and catches the belt of my borrowed robe, pulling me back into his lap. "You were about to ask me something."

I wedge myself between his legs, shifting back into a comfortable position. Being in the arms of another man when you're in love and newly engaged should feel wrong, but it doesn't. Maybe because they feel so much alike when I stop overthinking it.

"Your brother asked me to marry him and expects me to move in. Or rather, that's what he wanted this morning. Guess I shouldn't assume that's still the case, but I thought you should have a say in who you live with. Maybe I should hurry up and renew my lease. I don't want to step on your toes since it is your home." I feel lighter after getting this off my chest. It isn't pleasant, feeling like an uninvited house guest.

"Well, I can assure you, nothing with you and my brother has changed on his end. And you're free to step on my toes anytime you want." He pulls me tightly against his chest in a clear show of strength and playfulness. "I want you at the house. That's one of the things I wanted to talk to you about."

"Okay. So, you *don't* hate me? It can be difficult to tell sometimes." Even now, as he holds me in his arms, I can't help but wonder.

"No, Valentine, I don't hate you. Quite the opposite."

"So, you're okay with having a new upstairs neighbor and a second dog in the house?" I may have spent the last week questioning Darc's feelings for me, but I know without a doubt how he feels about Christmas. I've caught them cuddling on the couch more than once.

"I need you to understand something. When my brother told me that you would be moving in or he would be moving out, I freaked out. Not because I don't want you there. Coming home and seeing your face is the best part of my day, and I don't want to lose that. But Kold is fully prepared to throw away the life we've built to be with you. He wants to sell his half of the house, quit the band, split up the businesses, and start a new life with you. If he has his way, I'll lose both of you and the dogs. Leaving me in that big ass house all alone."

"Wait! What? I don't want him to do any of that. Kold doesn't need to throw his life away to be with me. That's stupid." My frustration spirals out in all directions in reaction to this new information. I try to pull away, but Darc's expecting that and pulls me in tighter.

"Can I ask you something that's been on my mind since the beginning?" He opens the front of my robe so his fingers can trace the questions into my skin, asking me in every language. The touch is soothing, and I feel myself relax into him. "My brother and I are one person, with one soul, split into two identical bodies. We're indistinguishable in every way that matters. So, I've been wondering... If he's your soulmate, which is what he believes, then wouldn't I be as well?"

I'm not sure if it's the tone of his voice, the depth of the question, or the touch of my fingers against my skin, but I shiver and break out in goosebumps.

"I'm going to have to think about that before answering. But it would certainly explain a few things I've been struggling with."

"Like what?" He grabs his shirt from the back of the couch and covers my feet and ankles. "You can talk to me, and it'll stay between us."

"I trust you. But I probably shouldn't tell you either." Things that are said can never be unsaid. So, whether Darc repeats it or not is irrelevant. He and I will both know, and that's already too many people.

"Tell me anyway."

I hesitate to open my mouth, knowing the truth will come tumbling out. It's impossible for me to lie to them. Not that I would even want to. Knowing Darc, he'll get the truth out of me one way or another, so there's no point in holding my tongue.

"When I'm alone with one of you, sometimes I get confused and forget you're two different people. Depending on who's running my brain, I find myself drawn to each of you in different ways. And I wonder if it's selfishness that makes me want to love you both or a force beyond my comprehension." My eyes well with tears that spill down my cheeks, dripping onto Darc's exposed flesh. "Please don't tell your brother I said that. I'm not ready for him to hate me."

Darc twists my hair around his hand, tightens his grip, and alters my gaze. As my eyes take in his expression, he leans in to kiss me. The intensity of his kiss threatens to swallow me whole. And I know I shouldn't want him as badly as I do, but I can't help it.

"You still don't get it, do you? We could never hate you. My brother and I are not the hearts and flowers type, but for you, I'd keep a florist on retainer."

I don't want to be the one to tell them, but both of them are far sappier than they realize. For guys who seem otherwise self-aware, it surprises me to hear them speak of tenderness and adoration as though they are foreign concepts. Kold and Darc seem to have fucked their way through plenty of women but never bothered with silly things like feelings.

"If I could offer a word of advice. You need to be careful when it comes to things like hearts and flowers. You wouldn't want someone to get the wrong idea and start thinking there's an option beyond being a one-night stand."

"If you told me I could have a piece of you, that would be enough."

I move to pull away, but he holds me in place. Tilting my head to align with his lips, Darc kisses me with a tenderness I didn't think possible. Maybe they truly are two parts of one soul, destined to complement the fractured halves of my own. It's certainly worth considering, I suppose.

"I think, for now, we should put this conversation on ice and have a drink. I still need to shower and get dressed. And your brother is expecting me downstairs."

"Fine. If I promise to behave, can I wash your back?" Breathing in deeply, he kisses me again. And then once more. "I swear, no sex stuff."

This man is going to get me into so much trouble, but maybe that's not all bad. Best to sort through my feelings before I get married so I'm not plagued by regret after the divorce. Who knows? Maybe everything will work out, and I'll get that small slice of happiness divvied up three ways.

Wouldn't that be a Christmas miracle?

Kold

I walk the same short path, back and forth, like a caged lion who still remembers what it felt like to be free. What the hell am I doing down here? I left my half-naked fiancée on the couch in the arms of my sex-obsessed twin brother, who's been infatuated with her since day one. And for what? So, I could stand here, obsessing over whether or not they had sex again after I left my office. As if the answer isn't obvious.

I served her up on a silver platter and then walked away.

Val wanted to get into the shower with me, and I blew off her request as if anything else could be more important. I'm acting like the jealous boyfriend, even though I'm not. Feeling her body respond to both of us at once was exquisite. She enjoyed the situation I put her in, and why shouldn't she? I knew it would happen eventually, and now it has.

It's not her fault that I walked away when I should have held her closer. For all I know, that was enough to make her feel rejected. Maybe she only went along with it because I asked her to, and now I'm the bad guy. Guess there's only one way to find out.

> : Are you coming to hang out with me backstage before I go on?

My Love: Yes! You know I'm not going to miss
that. Your brother was showing me the
cameras, and I've been watching you pace
around like a boxer before a big fight. LoL.
You seriously have no chill.

: Okay, stalker. Had I known you were
watching me, I would've tried to look cool.

My Love: Where do I need to go? What's the
best way for me to get to you?

: Tell Darc to get dressed and bring you the
back way. Then you won't have to deal with
the crowd.

My Love: Very funny! We're dressed and ready
to go. I was about to make a drink. Want me
to bring you one?

: I'm good. I'll steal yours when you get here.

My Love: Fair enough. I'll make myself two.
See you in a few minutes.

I read through the conversation again, to be sure, and breathe
a sigh of relief. I'm not sure why I keep worrying about Val being
upset with me. She sounds happy. Whatever my brother's been
doing to her in my absence appears to have put her in a good
mood.

Fucking asshole.

I thought the change in scenery and the loud music would
drown out the internal monologue berating me for my brash decision-making, but all it's doing is giving me a headache. I should be
the one holding her. Not him.

The first time Darc and I discussed the possibility of having a
threesome with Val was the night we first met her. After that, it
was a common topic of conversation. When she came to the
house with Allen, Darc was adamant that she belonged with us. A

sentiment I wholeheartedly agreed with at the time. At first, it seemed like a harmless fantasy since I wasn't sure she'd ever be mine.

Val's nonchalant comment in the car on the way to brunch about giving consideration to fucking us both turned happy delusions into inescapable realities. From that point forward, Darc was addicted. Once Val was finally mine, I wasn't sure I could share her, but the discussions with Darc persisted. I found myself getting angry, which seemed to fuel his pursuit, and every time I turned around, he had her cornered and blushing.

When I arrived at the club a few hours ago, threatening to cut ties, he suggested the idea of sharing her as if that would magically solve all our problems. He's always been good at planting the seed, but this time, he dug the hole with a backhoe and dropped in a fully grown tree. The more he explained himself, the more I bought into his logic.

I think my brother missed his calling as a cult leader.

Each time we would deliberate, I was firm about the rules, as ever-changing as they may be. Last week, he was allowed to sleep with Val if it was her decision, and she was fully aware of her choice. Meaning he couldn't trick her into sex pretending to be me.

The most recent agreement took sex off the table since I knew she went off her birth control. My brother had several thoughts and opinions to interject into the conversation, but I was unyielding. I offered him a choice between possibly sharing her a few times versus never seeing her again. He agreed to the terms and conditions to avoid losing everything and broke his word the first chance he got.

When sharing Val was a proposition, everything made sense. I was in complete control of the outcome, so long as I didn't stop to consider their feelings in the matter.

Hubris will be my fatal flaw.

Once Darc stepped into the room and Val opened her eyes, I realized my mistake. Honestly, I should have known better. I've seen how he looks at her and the way she has to force herself not to look back. It was never going to be only one time.

In the past, Darc and I never cared about the women we shared, so it didn't bother me when they ended up choosing him over me. I never wanted them to begin with. Most of the time, I was happy to see them go, and it was funny to watch my brother throw them out on the curb before sunrise. Darc got what he wanted, and I pretended to be bothered long enough to walk away, dumping the blame on whatever woman we recently finished fucking.

Well shit!

By walking away when I should have stayed, did I make Val feel like she did something wrong? Did I treat my future wife like some Tuesday night groupie without realizing it? The music is so loud I can't think, and my head is in a haze, thick with regret. I can't get my train of thought on one set of tracks long enough to think through a solution. I keep getting derailed at the first curve, praying I still have a lifetime to make it up to her.

When she taps me on the shoulder after approaching from behind, I nearly have a heart attack.

"I didn't mean to scare you. I said your name while I was walking over, but you must not have heard me." Val is freshly showered and changed into an old band shirt I cut the sleeves off of. I can see the sides of her lace bra and the tattoo on her ribs. Goddamn, she looks fucking hot.

I take the two drinks from her hands and set them on an equipment case before picking Val up and kissing her. Feeling her legs wrapped around my waist as my tongue slips past her bottom lip sets me ablaze. I love the feel of her hand as it brushes over the stubble on the back of my head and all the cute sounds she makes when we kiss, even though I can't hear them over the band.

"You know, only the guys in the band have that shirt, so you should feel pretty special right now. That's old school, from when we first started playing together." I stare into her eyes until I locate my future, wishing she could have been part of my past. "If only I could've found you sooner, I would have been a better man."

"I adore the man you are. So, if finding you sooner would've changed that, I'm glad we met when we did." She brushes her hands through my hair and squeezes her legs around my torso.

"Unless, maybe, your opinion of me has changed? Is that what has you down here wearing a rut into the backstage floorboards?"

"Not at all. I love you more than ever, and I should've told you that upstairs."

Before I walked away, leaving you to question the sincerity of my claims.

"Can we talk for a minute? Someplace slightly less loud. I don't want to leave things unsaid." There's a deepening pain in her eyes, and I already know what's coming.

Fuck! I pushed her too far into my world, and now she's ready to run in the other direction.

Val drops her legs, and I set her gently on her feet while keeping her within arm's reach. I consider grabbing the drinks and downing them both to numb the pain I know is coming. But honestly, I deserve whatever hurt extends my way. Karma for all the women I fucked over and kicked to the side.

I take Val's hand and lead her to a storage closet not far from the stage. It's not as quiet as I would like, but it's private. With most of the equipment being used for tonight's show, the space feels less claustrophobic and more like a room than a closet. I close the door behind us and turn to find Val's eyes glistening with tears.

Her voice cracks as the words rush out in a flood. "I'm sorry if I was being unappreciative. I'm not great at receiving gifts or processing large chunks of new information while someone's standing there, waiting for my reaction. And while I wish you would've talked to me before planning a trip, I know everything you do comes from a good place. You enjoy surprising me, and I need to be better about accepting what you offer. Being with you is the happiest I've ever been, and sometimes I worry that I don't deserve you."

I've heard more than I can stand and kiss her before she speaks another syllable. Val, undeserving of happiness? Give me a break. She's the best person I've ever met. If anyone deserves to be happy, it's her.

"The places your mind goes fascinates me. Only you could have an impromptu threesome with a guy and his brother and wind up concerned that you didn't appear excited enough when he sprung a surprise vacation on you ten minutes later."

"Trust me, I want to talk about the threesome as well, but one thing at a time."

"Babe, I've never thought of you as unappreciative. You've earned everything I have to offer simply by putting up with me. And I still want to be the one to give you the world." I press her against the door and lift her face to mine. "Unless my brother has convinced you to join the dark side."

"Not exactly, but I like what you did there." Val grabs hold of my belt and pulls so that we're pressed together from the waist down. "I'll be honest, I wasn't expecting that to happen, and I could use some time to process. How do you feel about the threesome you so kindly orchestrated?"

"I have mixed feelings about it, but not because of anything you did. You were amazing. And we all wanted it to happen for one reason or another, right?" I rake my tongue across her neck as her body shivers against mine. "Watching you suck his cock while I fucked you... Babygirl, I will dream of that for the rest of my life. I could feel you tighten around me each time you choked on him, and I never wanted it to end."

"Oh, so you liked watching me with him? That's good to know. When you walked away to shower without me, I was worried you might have been upset. But then you seemed fine when we talked about the trip, and less so when I watched you on the security camera. If I crossed a line and did something I shouldn't have, I want you to tell me."

"There are no lines separating you and me, my love. The real reason for my bad mood was far more embarrassing. I walked away because I can't last for shit when I'm inside you, and I didn't want to watch *him* please you the way I can't."

There is a flash of light in Val's eyes as she smiles and laughs. "Seriously? I don't know why you worry about that so much. You don't even finish that quickly. Maybe it took you longer in the past because you didn't give a damn about the women you were with, and it distorted your opinions on how long you think sex should last. But I assure you, when it comes to us, I am perfectly satisfied with your performance. I'm not someone who wants to spend twenty minutes getting pounded."

"I could probably last twenty minutes with you if it were the second go around, and I was drunk." The playful absurdity of our conversation is never lost on me. It's one of the things I love most.

"You always make sure I'm taken care of when we have sex, which is a *major* accomplishment. Most guys don't concern themselves with the orgasms of others. And not to be weird, but your brother finished soon after you walked away. He pulled out and came all over my shirt, which is why I had to borrow one of yours. Darc might know a few tricks when he's the one calling the shots, but he doesn't know how to touch me the way you do."

Her laughter is infectious. I can feel the warmth of it spreading in my chest before it ejects from my lungs. A laugh so strong and deep, after a minute, it makes my stomach hurt.

"Did he not get you off?" I can't believe I'm asking, but now I need to know.

"Not really, but please don't tell him I said that. I held my breath and dragged out the last of what you started. I mean, it wasn't bad or anything. But he's not you. He doesn't know me, and he certainly doesn't love me."

"What about after I left? You didn't have sex again?"

"No. Is that what you've been down here stressing about? A threesome isn't a free pass to have sex behind your back. We did shower together, but only because he insisted on making sure I was okay. Other than that, we had a nice conversation. He kissed me a few times, but..."

"Yeah. Well, that's nothing new. What was the conversation about?"

"I wanted to make sure he was okay with me moving in. I know it's your house, but I don't feel right bringing all my stuff there next week if he's gonna be pissed off about it. You know?"

"So, did you get his blessing? Will you be filling out a change of address form with the post office?" Darc knows my feelings on this. Either Val moves into the house with us, or I'm leaving and never coming back.

"I did, but I had to agree to sleep in his room every other Wednesday." She smiles up at me with doe eyes.

"I can never tell when you're joking about this shit and when you're serious. I suppose I could be persuaded to share you twice a month if that's what *you* want. But only until we get married. Which I will be scheduling for this Tuesday."

"Okay, slow down there. I was joking, but... If you're open to sharing, I could certainly discuss it with him."

"Yeah. That should be fun. You let my brother have a say in what happens, and he'll negotiate for three days a week and every other holiday. I think I'd rather it be a surprise. Lord knows he'd never kick you out of bed." I can picture Darc and I sitting on opposite sides of a long wooden table, flanked by teams of lawyers in expensive suits, arguing over who deserves more time with the only woman who makes life worth living.

"Oh my god, stop! Now I'm not sure if you're being serious or not, and I don't want to guess wrong."

"I tell you all the time, whatever makes you happy, my love. I can be accommodating to almost anything, so long as I don't lose you. That being said, please tell him to wear a condom next time. When we have kids, I want to know they're mine." The passing thought poses a series of questions I can't claim to know the answer to. Can a paternity test distinguish between identical twins? Would I even want to know if there was a possibility?

A banging at the door ripples through Val's chest, and someone tries to push it open, but I plant my feet and hold it closed.

"If our girl is getting fucked in the storage closet, I want a turn." The voice is muffled but unmistakable.

"God, I hate him," I say, holding the door shut behind her.

"No, you don't." Val looks at me and laughs, grinning in a way that tells me everything I need to know.

There are no limits to Val's devotion and no restrictions on my adoration. Nothing could change our feelings for one another. There's a certainty in the love we share. A love that might ultimately extend to my darker half.

CHAPTER 35

Val

The three of us hang out backstage until showtime, shaking hands and making small talk with the bands who have already finished playing. It's a unique experience, hiding out behind the action. One I never thought in a million years I would be a part of, having no real musical talent.

The entire time we're backstage, Kold and Darc stand on either side of me like armed guards. They're a personal security detail I'm not sure I require. No one cares who I am. Most people don't even bother to notice me. Or rather, they didn't. Not until my posted guards laid claim. Now, I'm a person of interest by default, simply because they know me.

Kissing Kold for luck, I say my goodbyes and head back upstairs. Since it's my first time at one of his shows, I insist on watching it properly. Darc and I make our way back to the office balcony, which they maintain is the most exclusive seat in the house and the most coveted. I would argue that the best seat in the house is one where I'm positioned between Kold's arms, but in this instance, that isn't a possibility.

"This is where you belong, Valentine." Darc hands me a new drink and joins me near the balcony railing. "These seats are reserved for family, which includes you." He brings my left hand to his lips and places a kiss above the joint of my ring finger. "We never let anyone else up here."

I'm not sure I believe him, but it sounds nice in theory. I move closer to the edge and lean slightly over the railing, enough to scan through the crowd below. When I spot the group of girls from earlier, we exchange a wave and a genuine smile. I'm glad they have each other, and they're all safely inside. It must be nice to have friends. I can't say I know what that feels like.

Tracy and I are friends of proximity, and there's nothing wrong with that. But I wonder if we'll continue to talk once I move out. We've never gone out for coffee or shared a meal outside the apartment building. Our friendship seems tethered to that place and contingent on our remaining neighbors. I suppose that's another thing I'm set to lose once I move into the house. My only friend, my stability, and my freedom.

Maybe that's a bit dramatic. It's not like they're a pair of beasts locking me away in a stone tower.

"Isn't that the girl you gave your ticket to?" Darc rests his chin on my shoulder and wraps an arm around my waist, following my gaze. "The way they were stationed behind you, ready for a fight, I thought maybe you were all friends."

"Hmmm... It's nice that it came off that way, but I met them tonight."

"And here I thought you were a peacekeeper, but it turns out you're a General. People can't help but follow you into battle." He kisses my neck and whispers against my ear. "Luckily for you, my brother and I are excellent soldiers."

"Oh, please." My words are carried forward, riding waves of laughter. "You two take orders from no one." I turn my face and find his lips waiting.

"Well, a Queen then, with battle-hardened Lieutenants who will die by her side." Brushing his thumb over my lips, his hand stretches back along my jawline. "Answer me one question so I know how to proceed. Was tonight a one-time thing, or can I look forward to being with you again?"

"I'm not sure." There hasn't been enough time to process what happened, let alone consider all the possible outcomes. "What do you want?"

"You know what I want. I want a piece of you to belong to me so that every part of me can belong to you. And I want you to look at me the way you do when you think I'm him."

"We both know I can't offer you enough to keep you satisfied, and there's a line of women behind me ready to give you what you need." Kold is willing to share me, but am I willing to share either of them? Is that part of the tradeoff that has yet to be discussed?

"I don't want them, and I'm not the kind of guy who would let you stand in a line. You're the only one. My full attention is on you, and I think you gravely underestimate what you have to offer."

By the time Darc kisses me, I'm so hungry for his touch that I damn near bite his bottom lip. I don't care who you are. No woman can resist a good-looking guy filling her head with whispered delusions of greatness. I want to act impulsively, but I shouldn't. There's so much at stake.

I pull away from his kiss the second I feel a shift in the energy below. The show's about to start, and I hope Kold wasn't watching the exhibition on the balcony. I'm going to need everyone to be crystal clear about the boundaries, but until then, it might be best to keep my hands and lips to myself.

When Kold walks out on stage, the club erupts into cheerful cries, accented by shifting stage lights. As he removes his hoodie, I see what he's been hiding from me all night. Turns out he's been wearing the slim-fit Dementors t-shirt I dropped off for Christmas, and it hugs his body in a way that makes me envious. I'm engaged to a rock star built like every woman's wet dream, and I'm over here debating the possible risks and rewards of cheating.

What the fuck is wrong with me?

I bought all six Our Last Midnight albums a few days after Halloween and have listened to each repeatedly. I know the words to the first track and nearly every chorus that follows. When he introduces a brand-new song, I finally realize what an idiot I've been. We danced to this in his bedroom one night, and I commented on how much it sounded like him, but I never realized it was him singing. I'd never heard the song before, and it isn't in the style his band usually plays, so I assumed it was selected for its heartfelt meaning, like the rest of the songs on the playlist.

Kold looks up as he belts out the chorus, finding me on the balcony, a Juliette to his Romeo. Only here, it's Mercutio with his arms encasing me, attempting to lay partial claim. What's a girl to do? My fractured heart has found a home, and I intend to live there until I'm legally evicted.

"I need to go downstairs and buy a few things before I leave. If Kold comes up here looking for me, can you tell him I'm in the back?" There is a shirt I have to get and probably a few other things. As unnecessary as it may be, spending money here is my attempt at being a supportive girlfriend, though I've been thwarted in my previous attempts.

"Don't be ridiculous. I'm coming with you."

I spin around in his arms and push my hand into his chest. "Darc, no. Please let me do this one thing on my own. You owe me that much after making a scene and pulling me out of line earlier."

"Making a scene? Are you fucking kidding me? I had to kill a guy because he took a swing at you, and this is the thanks I get."

"What?" I assume he means he got into another fight defending my honor, but this is news. "Explain what you mean."

"Nothing. Forget it." Darc pulls his wallet from his back pocket and drops it in my hand. "Buy whatever you want, then come straight back. He'll be pissed at me if you leave without saying goodbye."

I set the wallet on a chair as I pass by, heading for the office door leading to the main stairs. There's a way to get over to the merch tables using the back door, but I'm not confident I could find it alone, and I don't want Darc with me. When Kold took me on a tour earlier, I was distracted by the stories from his youth, and I wasn't paying attention to our path.

The band continues to play as I wind my way through the masses, wrapping up what turned out to be an amazing set. And I'm not only saying that as someone who's in love with the lead singer. I've been to a ton of shows over the years, and this was easily in my top ten. Top five once you factor in the threesome.

I skip past the tables for the other bands and head straight for a long-sleeve shirt decorated with a face I recognize. It's adorable that Kold's band is named after his dog. Or maybe his dog is named after the group. Either way, it's cute, and I wonder how many people get to see that playful side of him. I've seen hundreds of photos online of Kold, and he looks sexy in all of them, but he's never smiling. Then, when we're together, he's goofy and silly and grinning from ear to ear.

For some reason, I initially expected Our Last Midnight to be a heavy metal band, but they're more pop-punk-rock. The group has a sound heavily influenced by the 90s, and I wonder if that's due to him growing up here in the club. Sometimes, I wish I could go back and find him sooner so he'd always have a reason to smile.

"Can I please get that black hoodie in a large and those two t-shirts in a small?" I'm glad I got back here before the crowd, so I don't have to shout. My usual politeness loses sincerity when my voice is raised above its comfort level.

"And do you have a CD that includes the new song?" I could get all this stuff from Kold, but I want my actions and efforts to speak for themselves. If something is important to him, then it's important to me. Of course, that's the same mindset that landed me in a threesome with Darc, but I blame the love of my life for that one.

"If you scan that QR code, it'll take you to the song on iTunes, but I don't have it on a CD. Sorry about that. Is there anything else I can get you? Your shirt is amazing, by the way. Where the hell did you find that? I've known these guys since high school. Even I don't have that one."

"I stole it from my fiancé." Looking down at the faded shirt, I smile. "How much do I owe you?" I don't want to be a name-dropper. Plus, I get the feeling he might not believe me. I doubt I'd be the first woman to claim a relationship with the lead singer.

"Your dude must be a fan from way back. Is he the one who dragged you to the show?" He types everything into his iPad and looks up at me. "It's $95."

I hand him my card and smile as he swipes it through. Finally,

I get to be a normal, nobody fan-girl, buying shirts and obsessing over a guy who's out of my league. It feels good to be invisible again.

"I came to the show of my own free will, but he is around here somewhere." I slip the credit card back into my wallet and drape the new apparel over my crooked arm. The music ended seconds ago, and I can hear the audience shifting this way.

"Darc, what's up, bro? I haven't seen you in ages." The guy working the merch table addresses the man who's pressed himself into my back, bringing his arm around my waist.

"Hey, Tommy. I'll pay for whatever she's getting." His tone is friendly, and I'm guessing these two might have been friends at one point. Funny, I figured Darc to be a loner like me, but it makes sense that he would have been part of the crowd. I wonder which brother won the vote for Prom King. Knowing them, they probably insisted the rules be changed so they could both win.

"Oh shit! I didn't know she was *your* old lady. My bad, man. I already ran her card. But that does explain the shirt. Right on!" Tommy sounds like a California stoner. Not exactly the clique I would have pegged either of my guys to be in.

"Tommy, cancel the transaction. It's not that difficult." Darc takes a step forward, carrying me with him. The guys tower over me regardless, but right now, Darc feels larger than life.

"It's fine, honestly. Tommy, don't cancel anything." My voice feels lost to the clomping of boots as they crest the bar area and spill into the room I'm currently standing in.

"It's all good, man. I figured it out. Obviously, I wouldn't have charged her had I known she was with you." He keeps talking about me like I'm not standing directly in front of him, and it's starting to piss me off. Normally I enjoy being invisible, but this is bordering on disrespect, as if my wishes hold no weight because I lack a penis.

Turning to face Darc, I press my hand to his chest. "I want to pay for my own shirts. Why is that so hard? I specifically asked you not to come here and left your wallet on the chair. Was I not clear enough? God, I fucking hate you!"

His exhale comes out like a rumbling growl, and I'm

reminded that this isn't the brother one wants to argue with. When his hand comes up atop mine, I can feel myself wince under the immense pressure. "You're pissing me the fuck off, little girl! Now go upstairs."

"Fuck you! I'm not yours. And you don't tell me what to do. Everyone else might be afraid of you, but I'm not." I turn around, shove a hundred-dollar bill into the merch guy's hand, and take off for the door behind the table. "Merry Christmas, Tommy," I shout over my shoulder as I push through the metal door, disappearing into the hallway I recognize from earlier. Coming this way will get me away from the noise and the judgmental stares, but it might also get me lost.

I need to think, but there's no time. Darc will never allow my rudeness to go unpunished. He'll be close behind, but I'm not sure which direction to go. I need to hide so I can think. But first, I have to run.

There's a room near the end of the hall that Kold neglected to mention. It felt like he was going out of his way to avoid even looking at it. I'm sure it's nothing. Probably some broom closet, which might be perfect. I doubt Darc does much cleaning around here.

I'm still five steps from the door when strong arms catch me from behind. Even though I could hear the heavy footsteps trailing me, I remained unprepared to be knocked from my feet.

Darc swings me off the ground as we slam into the wall. Or rather, he slams into the wall, and the shockwave reverberates through him, into me.

Spinning us into the desired position, Darc pins my chest to the cinderblock wall and kicks my feet apart. He grabs my wrists, easily restraining them above my head as I struggle beneath him.

"Wherever you run, I will find you. You're mine now, and he isn't going to save you." Darc's words crawl across my skin like spiders as his grip tightens. There is no use in fighting him.

"I don't need him to save me because I don't care what you do to me." Darc might be able to overpower me, but at what cost?

Modifying his grip so that both of my wrists are locked by one hand, I should expect what's coming, but the sting takes me by surprise. The force of the first blow drives me into the wall as I struggle to free my hands. I've had men slap my ass before, but this isn't playful. The second strike steals the air from my lungs, and the third wells my eyes with tears.

"The first one was for talking back. The second was for saying you hate me. And the third was a long time coming. You let someone else fuck you on *my* desk, in *my* office, and you thought I wouldn't find out?"

"Darc, please! We can talk about this." So much for taking my power back. I want to stand up for myself, but if he's mad about something I actually did, I won't pretend to be innocent. "I'm sorry."

"You should be sorry. You should beg. Not that it'll help." Darc steps forwards, trapping me between his chest and the wall. "I'm going to fuck you so hard, babygirl. You're still going to feel me tomorrow."

"Stop," I say, attempting to sound strong as I tremble in his arms. A threesome isn't an open invitation to cheat. That's what I told Kold, and I meant it. If I let Darc have me, then I'm no better than those who deceived me in my past.

"And why is that, sweetheart?" He releases my hands and spins me like a top until we're standing face to face. Maybe it's the tears in my eyes that make him soften or the quiver in my bottom lip. Whatever it is, he loses his edge.

"I'm asking you to stop." The words cut like a knife, severing the sexual tension between us. At once, he releases me and steps back far enough to lean against the wall opposite me. "I'm not yours to do with as you please. If you're upset with me because I was rude, I apologize. I don't hate you, and I shouldn't have said that. As for having sex in your office, I'm not sure why Kold told you about that, but I am sorry."

"I don't want you to be sorry. I want you to make it up to me!"

This has all been more than I can handle, and I'm ready to call it a night. If I ever step foot in this club again, it will be too soon.

"When you see your brother, please tell him I went home."

Still unsure of the correct path through the labyrinth, I return the way I came and out through the crowd. I'm surprised when Darc stays behind, pinned to his spot on the wall.

Once I'm in the car, it's easy to get out. Since I'm parked in the employee lot, the boy directing traffic waves me ahead of the other vehicles, and I'm free to go on my merry way. However, my current mood is less than cheerful. In fact, I feel like shit. I left without saying goodbye, and it's too late to go back. This whole night has me questioning the steps ahead. I know I want to be with Kold, but I wonder how much distance I should keep between myself and his brother.

Normally, I'm not one to text and drive, but I have to say something.

> : You were amazing on stage. Your talent blew me away. Thank you for sharing the night with me.

> Kold: Where are you? I've been looking everywhere.

> : Headed to your house to let the dogs out. Then, I think Christmas and I might go to my place for the night. I have plans in the morning with Tracy and Sam.

> Kold: I'll be home in 20 minutes. Do NOT leave until I get there.

> : You don't have to follow me. I'm sure you have plenty to do at the club.

> Kold: I don't give a shit about anything going on here. You're my priority. I'm headed out the door now.

> : I'm sorry. I shouldn't have messaged you.

Before I can drop my phone into the cupholder, it begins ringing in my hand. What was I thinking? Of course, Kold would chase after me despite all the ways I've asked him not to. After sneaking away without a word, I'll be lucky if he takes his eyes off me. Sometimes, I feel like he's in love as much as he's obsessed, and I'm okay with it, but I need time to think before making any permanent choices.

I answer the phone, and we talk the entire drive home. He's only five minutes behind me when the conversation starts, which means he drives like a demon on crack and pulls into the driveway at the same time I do.

Now that it's quiet, I get a better sense of the ringing in my ears. Tinnitus is caused by exposure to loud sounds. This damage isn't permanent, merely mildly inconvenient. It will be gone by the morning after a couple of ibuprofen and a good night of sleep.

We walk, hand in hand, up the sidewalk and into the house, where we're greeted by a pair of overly excited mini monsters. Jumping and whining, wiggling and snorting, Christmas pitter pats while Midnight begs for Dad to hold her. Dogs are like furry toddlers, needy as fuck and annoyingly adorable. Thankfully, Kold offers to get them settled, and twenty minutes later, I'm in bed with my makeup removed, fighting off sleep.

"Do you have to leave in the morning? My Holiday breakfast is a family tradition, and I was looking forward to including you." Kold pulls me in closer, sinking into our nightly routine. "Can't we go to Tracy's together after we open presents here at home?"

"I'm not sure what their other plans are for the day, but I can certainly ask. Worst case, I'm gone for an hour and a half, at the most, and then I'm all yours." My words feel light as I begin to drift off.

"I wish you would tell me what happened. You didn't leave without saying goodbye for no reason. And if someone did or said something that upset you, I need to know."

"It's fine. He didn't do anything worth mentioning." My statement is punctuated with one final yawn. I'm physically and mentally exhausted. If he wants to have this conversation, it will have to wait.

My eyes close, and his voice is the last thing I hear. "Yep, that's what I thought."

Kold

When I got off stage last night, all I wanted was to find my girl and kiss her. Now, it's the next morning, and I still haven't felt her lips. Once we got home, I sent her upstairs to get ready for bed while I finished taking care of the dogs. After a quick shower, I joined her in bed, but Val was nearly asleep when I got there and drifted off mid-conversation.

"I thought I heard you in here." A gentle voice drifts in from the hallway, still coated in the grogginess of sleep. She crosses the kitchen and wraps her arms around my waist, embracing me from behind. "I was hoping you'd be in bed this morning. Have you been awake long?"

"No. Not long. You said you might not stay for breakfast, but I thought we could have coffee together. Then I'll get changed, and we can go."

In truth, I never slept. I couldn't stop thinking about our conversation and how she didn't sound like herself. So, I went back to the club to look for answers. Most people had cleared out, but there are always stragglers. Some girls will spread their legs for anyone wearing a black wristband.

"Not long, huh?" She pulls out her phone as the doorbell rings, and the house descends into chaos. Both dogs spring into action, growling and snapping at the glass, trying to get a look at our early morning intruder.

Val hurries to the door, grabs her coat from the closet, and slips into her shoes, still wearing the clothes she slept in.

She can't possibly be serious right now. Not only was Val planning to leave on Christmas morning, but she had someone come here to pick her up. What the hell is going on? "You're leaving without even talking to me?"

"Christmas, let's go." Val's dog knows better than to disobey, so he sits beside her leg.

"Babe, what are you doing?" I reach for the leash as she clips it into place. "You need to tell me what's going on. Who's out there!"

"I would love nothing more than to have an *honest* conversation with you, but I doubt you're capable of that." Her words come out in a bitter flurry. "When you sober up and you're ready to stop lying to me, please let me know." Val slips through the door, pulling the handle until it clicks into place, as I stand in stunned silence.

This is not happening.

Tripping over a barking Midnight, I'm out the door in time to see her pulling away. Val is in the passenger seat, but I can't make out the driver. I run back into the house and dig my phone out of a drawer in the kitchen.

: This is ridiculous! I'm not going to chase after you. Come home and talk to me.

My Love: No. You smell like booze, and you lied to my face. So, whatever you did and whoever you did it with, I don't fucking care anymore! I hope she was worth it.

: Don't you dare say that to me. I wasn't with anyone else last night, unlike you.

My Love: Merry Christmas, Kold. I'm sorry I'm such a horrible person.

: Goddamnit! That's not even what I meant. Who the fuck are you with? I want to know. Why would you have someone pick you up? Your car is in the driveway, and you're not even dressed. You need to start talking. What the hell is going on?

: I didn't fucking cheat on you! When I got out of the shower, you passed out in my arms, but I couldn't shut my brain off. I went back to the club because I had to make sure all the money was pulled, counted, and in the safe. I wasn't planning on being there all night. Then I started watching security camera playback. I did a shot each time my brother kissed you until I was so fucking drunk I couldn't see straight.

: Babe, please come home so we can talk.

My Love: I am home, and I need to shower. Maybe we can talk later.

: Where? Your apartment? That isn't home anymore.

Running toward the bedroom, I take the stairs two at a time. Val keeps her spare keys in a side pocket of her overnight bag, so I grab them and head back down to the car. When I said I wasn't going to chase her, I lied. Add it to the list, I guess.

I can't imagine Val's been at the apartment for more than ten minutes when I arrive. Walking up the stairs, I prepare myself for the worst-case scenario and work backward. I still don't know who picked her up, so I need to be ready for anything. If there's a guy in bed with her, things will get bloody for him. And if they're in the shower together, I will kill him slowly.

Christmas meets me at the door, but he doesn't bark. *Good boy.* Val's in the shower, so I sneak in and listen at the door. Instead of a man's voice, all I hear is my girl crying.

As I strip off my clothes, the only person I'm angry with is myself. I'm afraid I broke her heart because of my bruised ego, and instead of accepting what she told me, I jumped to conclusions.

Val handles things in her own way, and I need to allow her the space to do that. If she needed me to take care of something, she'd ask.

I thought she might be startled when I entered the shower behind her, but she turned and melted into my arms as though she'd been expecting me all her life.

"Shhhh. Everything's going to be okay. Don't cry over something that can be fixed with a conversation."

"You promise?" Her voice shakes with uncertainty.

"Nothing between us has changed." I lift her chin and fall into her eyes. "You are my forever. So, start packing. Unless you want me to move in here?"

"I'm not sure I have the closet space for a man of your fashion sense." Val's smile reaches her eyes, and I can't help but kiss her. I've been craving her lips for hours, and they're finally mine. Our mouths are well-versed in the love language spoken between our touch, but I use my hands to add emphasis.

"Whatever you want, we'll make it work. Okay? I don't care where we live, only that I come home to you. I'll give up everything, even my extensive wardrobe, if it means being with you."

All I could ever need, I have found within her. Why I ever allowed myself to question the depth of her love is beyond me. Val has made a concerted effort to reassure me. She insists that I'm her first choice and her top priority. Even on the phone driving home, she begged me to hold her. And I did, for about five minutes.

When I watched the numerous clips of her with Darc, stalking her every movement through the club, I expected to see more than kissing. With each shot, I convinced myself that the worst was yet to come, but it never did. I watched her sing along to every song I played until I got to the one I wrote for her. Even as she wiped away tears, she never stopped smiling at me.

"I'm fine with living at the house, but I need more information from you. You have to explain the boundaries and expectations. If you draw a line in the sand, I won't cross it, but it doesn't do me any good to find out after the fact. If you want me to play with you, I have to know the rules."

"That's fair. You and I should've spoken before anything happened with Darc. It was kind of a spur-of-the-moment decision on my part, but that's no excuse."

"I know. I'm not mad."

The heat of the water has turned her back a lovely shade of lobster red, so I reach past and turn off the water before taking her into my arms.

"You're allowed to get mad at me. In fact, you should be mad. I messed up. I put you in a situation you never agreed to, and I'm sorry." I kiss the top of her head, and then her lips, and then her neck. "That being said, when I do something stupid and you get upset, I need you to talk to me. I can't handle you walking away. That shit fucking kills me."

"I'm sorry." I can feel her heart breaking, shattering mine along with it. "Last night, I left because I felt overwhelmed and needed a minute. Your brother is intense. It felt like you opened a floodgate and then stood back while he crashed into me at full force. Then, when we got home, you left me in bed alone, snuck out, and never came home. I stayed awake for hours, waiting. I didn't want to assume the worst, but when you lied to me this morning, it confirmed my worst fears."

"I shouldn't have left you after we got home, and I shouldn't have lied to you. That will never happen again. At the time, I needed to know what made you leave, and I knew you would never tell me. When I watched the security cameras and saw you in his arms, it felt like you were choosing him over me. But I swear to you, I went downstairs to leave. I wanted to be home in bed with you. Tommy was at the bar with the guys when I was leaving, and he asked me what I thought of *Darc's old lady*. I was so pissed I grabbed the closest bottle to keep myself from choking him to death. Then I went back to the office to fuel my misplaced anger..." I continue talking while we dry off. "For some reason, I thought if you and Darc finally slept together, it would dissolve the obvious sexual tension and make it easier for us to live together. As arrogant as I am, I never considered losing you as a possibility."

"You didn't lose me, not even for a second, and you're never going to." Her whispered reassurance sets me at ease. "Like it or not, you're stuck with me."

Crawling under the blanket, I join Val in bed, taking her into my arms. This should always be the one place where she feels safe, tucked against my chest. "Is it okay if I close my eyes for a bit? I want to fall asleep holding you like I should have last night."

She wiggles her body, getting comfortable, then dissolves into me. I feel the exact moment she lets go of any lingering questions or hurt feelings. The small wall she constructed around her heart comes down, crumbling to dust. "That already sounds like the best Christmas present I've ever received."

Curled together in her bed, I trace invisible messages onto Val's skin until sleep overtakes me.

Val

It's Christmas morning, and the gifts in my closet still need to be delivered. I slip out of bed and craft a note, careful not to wake the man beside me. If Kold gets up while I'm gone, I want him to know where I am to avoid further misunderstandings. I've always known that in relationships, communication is key. And yet, I've allowed my reactions to be largely based on assumptions, nearly destroying my happiness as a result. That's something I'm going to need to work on in the new year. But for today, it is what it is.

I put matching sweaters on Christmas and I, and finish my look with a clean pair of jeans and some boots.

I need to take more clothes with me when I leave. Item by item, my things have been migrating to the house, but my clothing selection remains minimal. If I am moving in, I may need to take Kold up on the spare bedroom idea. Not that I want to turn his house into a storage unit, but I'm not prepared to part with my material possessions.

Grabbing the bag of presents, I tip-toe past the man sleeping in my bed.

Goddamn, he's sexy.

The blanket is pulled away enough to expose Kold's thick, tattooed arm and muscular chest, making me second-guess my desire to leave. He's the image of perfection, and for some reason, he keeps insisting that he's mine, even though I'm still not sure how that's possible. I'm still convinced that my life with Kold is a dream I never wish to wake from.

Christmas awaits me at the door, so I let him out without a leash. "Let's go find Sam."

We cross the ten steps separating apartment doors and knock on 200. I can hear Samuel's voice as he squeals with delight, running for the door at a sprint. "They're here! They're here! Mom! Hurry up and get the lock. Aunt Val and Christmas are finally here!"

"Okay, hold on a minute. Remember what I told you. We have to check before we open the door in case it's someone we aren't expecting." Tracy makes everything a learning opportunity, and I love it. Better safe than sorry. "I see Aunt Val out there, and she's got presents."

I hold up the bag in front of me, grinning wide like a grinch with a fully grown heart.

When the door swings open, Samuel drops to his knees and rapidly pats his legs. "Look at how cute you are in your tiny sweater. I've missed you so much." His eyes lock on Christmas as he fights back tears.

Not wasting any time, Christmas leaps across the threshold, straight into the boy's waiting arms. The two are a tangle of hands and paws as they roll around on the floor together. It isn't long before the scene playing out in front of me strikes me with a pang of guilt. Samuel was the first friend Christmas had as a baby, besides me, and it feels almost cruel for me to take him away.

"Come on, get in here," Tracy says, closing the door behind me. "I was beginning to worry you might have slipped in the shower. I was about to walk over to check on you."

"I had a visitor." My response is short and sweet, though I'm certain she knows who I mean without saying. "He's in bed, sleeping."

Tracy and I are used to speaking in shorthand when Sam is in the room. "Well, that worked itself out quickly. I take it you two 'made up,' and he's recharging."

"Oh my god, stop! You're making him sound like a sex robot."

"Shhh!" Tracy shoots me a look, but Sam is blissfully unaware, still rolling on the floor, pretending to hate puppy kisses.

"The last time I saw Kold, he planned to see your ex. Do those two still talk, or do they no longer have a friendship?" Tracy is fishing for information, but I've got nothing to share.

I'm fifty-seven percent certain that Darc is the reason for Allen's sudden disappearance, but I can't exactly ask him about it over breakfast, and this isn't a suspicion I plan to share with the present company or any other. I suppose I could be wrong. Allen could've cut ties with Tracy after realizing he'd been fully exposed as a liar. Or he could be out of town *on business* with some other woman.

When it comes to Kold and Darc, they seem to have the kind of secrets that one takes with them to the grave. And while I'm not entirely sure how I feel about my intuitions, I know I'm not one to spill the tea.

Last night, when Darc told me he killed the guy who took a swing at me in line, I knew he didn't kill him with kindness, but I also didn't automatically assume he meant murder. Now, the more I think about it, I'm not sure.

"Except for the concert and our date on Friday night, Kold and I spent the week together at home." I'm making a concerted effort not to think of Tracy as *the other woman,* but if she keeps asking about my ex, I will begin seeing her that way. "And we were too busy to talk to anyone, let alone hang out. I'm glad I was able to make it over here today."

"Speaking of the concert. I've seen that video of your man no less than a dozen times since waking up this morning. It's all over my news feed."

"What video?" My heart sinks as I imagine the worst. Please don't let it be a video of him with another girl. Not after he assured me his infidelity was an impossibility. "I don't know what you're talking about."

"Seriously? Your aversion to social media is ridiculous. Your boyfriend is going viral, and every gay man and straight woman in the country is claiming his new song is about them. Hell, even I posted a video using it." Tracy looks at me like two turtle doves are nesting in my hair. "You have no idea what I'm talking about, do you?"

I shake my head and pull my phone from my back pocket. "Where's the video posted? I'll look it up."

"Girl! You'd have a harder time finding where it's *not* posted."

Tracy's right. The video pops up straight away, and I recognize the song immediately. "That's my song. He played it last night at the show."

"*We* both know it's about you, but nobody online will think that. The rumor mill has you linked elsewhere after your recent engagement to Darc. So, unless Kold wrote a love song about his twin brother's future wife, no one is tying that song back to you."

"What the actual fudgesicles are you talking about? People are saying I'm engaged to Darc?" My head is spinning, and I feel like I might throw up. "Oh my god, stop talking." I cover my face with my hands, attempting to block out the world and every speck of light. When Kold wakes up and hears what people are saying, not only locals but the entire internet, he'll hate me. "If you're messing around with me right now, it's not funny."

Pulling up the original video, I begin reading through the comments. One after the next, women claim to be the girl referenced in the song, along with receipts in the form of photographs. Most of the pictures I've seen before, but a few of them appear to be from last night. Were these women still there when he went back, and did he entertain more than a photo request like they're claiming?

"This is ridiculous. I can't do this right now." I turn off my phone and bury it back in my pocket. "Who wants to open presents?" I can't waste my day being upset over false claims when I know these women are full of shit. The song was written about me during our time apart. I know this for a fact. The lines retell our story as if the words were pulled out of my chest and set to music.

Watching you leave with him
burns worse than cheap vodka.
A fire I'm willing to endure

> *if it means seeing you again.*
> *Anything for a second chance*
> *at bittersweet memories.*
> *Until you realize*
> *you were mine all along.*

Had I been paying attention the first time he played the song for me in the bedroom, I would have realized it was about us. No wonder he seemed so disappointed by my lackluster response. I was so focused on matching my steps to the melody, mirroring his touch, and drinking in the tenor of his voice that I blacked out on the lyrics. The song has my name in the title, and I still missed the obvious.

"We need some Christmas music to set the mood," Tracy says, choosing a preselected list from online. The first song to come on is Jingle Bells. Classic.

The three of us sing along while I pour coffee and hot chocolate and move the tray of cookies over to the coffee table in front of the couch. I intend to gorge myself on sweet, colorful goodness while enjoying the holiday with my found family. Especially if it's meant to be our first and last Christmas morning together.

Rudolph the Red-Nosed Reindeer seems to be a hit with the seven-year-old crawling around on the floor. "I learned this song at school," he bellows.

At the end of each line, I tack on the parts that truly make the song worth singing, and Samuel looks at me sideways.

"Aunt Val, that's not how it goes."

"Well, kiddo, when I was a kid, all the reindeer played Monopoly. I don't know what they play now, maybe Minecraft."

"That's silly. They don't even have thumbs." Kids these days know everything.

"Can't argue with that logic." Our conversation continues over the top of Its Beginning to Look a Lot Like Christmas but halts when Frosty the Snowman begins to play. I'm not sure why Tracy didn't select a kid's Christmas music station. Clearly, this boy has got favorites.

Surrounded by so much joy, I forget about the Christmas

mornings that came before and the hurt they left me with. Baby, it's Cold Outside starts to play, and I grumble under my breath, making Tracy laugh. "Oh my god, I hate this song. It's so cringy."

"Well, baby, you better learn to love it. If you and Kold get married on Christmas next year, this could be your wedding song."

I shudder at the thought.

"It's cute that you think he'll wait that long. If he had his way, we'd run off to Vegas with a marriage license this week." Part of me doesn't hate the idea, even if it did result in another epic failure. Calling Kold my husband appeals to my heart more than I was initially willing to admit.

"That would create quite the buzz online if he left town and married his twin's fiancée. Although, I am curious. Is *everything* identical?" Tracy laughs as if she's hilarious while I'm left reeling. "I'm sorry, it's only funny because I know you. It's not every day your best friend is tied to a famous rock star *and* his foxy, club-owner brother."

"Yeah. Well. There's a lot more to Darc than being a *foxy club owner*. If people bothered to look past the surface, they might be surprised by what they find." I feel myself getting defensive. Protective, even. Her words burrow into my flesh like alien parasites, and I want to dig them out with my nails.

"I'm sure he is, but weren't you the one who referred to him as *a philandering playboy wearing the devil's smile*, or have your feelings changed since last week?" Tracy is quick to use my words against me, as only a friend can. "I thought it was a drunken kiss or a case of mistaken identity, but maybe there's more to all those rumors than you're letting on. I mean, you two did look cozy together, watching the show from the owner's suit."

"Wait. What? There are photos of me online, with Darc?" There's no such thing as damage control when it involves the internet. Once something ends up online, the information spreads like wildfire, even if you're a nobody like me.

"Photos aren't even the half of it. You need to join the rest of the world and get your ass online."

CHAPTER 37

Kold

It takes me a minute to acclimate to the unfamiliar surroundings as I wake up in Val's apartment alone. I would have preferred to have her in my arms, but she left a note, which is more than I thought to do when I disappeared in the middle of the night.

Lesson learned. Mistakes happen. The trick is not to repeat them and to apologize when you're wrong. I wasn't planning on falling asleep, but it's probably for the best. This day is in serious need of a restart, and I owe my girl a heartfelt apology.

For some reason, I'm nervous walking over to knock on Tracy's door, and I'm never nervous. I can only assume she was the one who picked up Val from the house, which means they most likely talked about last night. And I doubt I was painted in a good light after the shit I pulled. Normally, I wouldn't care, but Tracy is Val's friend, and her opinion seems to matter.

I hear Christmas music and a child laughing as I approach the door, followed by a bark I've come to recognize. Trying to picture the scene playing out behind the door, I hesitate to knock. When Val wrote the note, did she mean for me to join her, or was it to keep me from freaking out?

I'll be the first to admit I tend to lose my cool when I can't find her. Another reason I should've known better than to leave without telling her. There's no good excuse. It would have taken five seconds to send a text letting her know I had left the house, but I couldn't be bothered because I was angry and acting like an asshole.

Rapping a friendly greeting against the door with my knuckle, I hear the people in the room go silent as Christmas sounds the alarm.

"Baby, it's Kold outside," a woman says. Her voice bubbles into a fit of laughter as the door swings open on its hinges.

I really hate that song.

I stand in the hallway, grinning as several things happen at once. Val hurries across the room, carefully avoiding the toys littering the carpet. Christmas pitter pats at my feet, begging to be picked up. And Tracy waves her hand, inviting me inside.

"I don't mean to impose, but..." It's Christmas morning, and I feel like the uninvited guest showing up as dinner comes out of the oven. "I was hoping *we* could spend some time together."

Val walks into my arms and buries her face in my chest as she gives my waist a squeeze. "I'm ready to go home whenever you are."

Elation stitches through the fibers of my being, hearing her say those words. I know she's chosen them intentionally, and I'm going to make damn sure she never regrets it.

"Home, as in apartment 202, or the house on Concord?" I already know the answer. But after the night we endured, I could use some reassurance.

"There was an envelope taped to my door and a letter informing me that I didn't renew my lease in time. So, the apartment isn't an option. That's part of the reason why I was crying in the shower."

"Ah, that's why you were so quick to forgive me. It all makes sense now." My response is playful, and she knows it.

"I could always move in downstairs if there's no room on the second floor," she says, matching my tone. Even though she's joking, I wonder if there isn't some truth to her claim. Darc would snatch her up in a heartbeat if I ever pushed her away. All the more reason to hold her close from here until the end of time.

"That comment is going to cost you, so be prepared for that when you get home." I want to squeeze Val's ass and lift her into my arms. But there's a child glaring at me, and his mother looks none too impressed.

"I'm not afraid of you," Val says, lifting up on her toes to kiss me before turning back to face the onlookers inside.

"We're gonna have to make a point to get together so that the two of you can meet New Year's Eve." Val's nickname for Midnight never fails to make me laugh.

"Aunt Val, do you have to go away? What if some mean old lady moves in next door? Or some big scary guy like Kold?" The boy looks up at me and then hides behind his mother.

I have to wonder what he means by that. Did Tracy say something about me that her son overheard, or is his opinion based on nothing more than my size? At 6'4, I'm not exactly huge, but to a seven-year-old, I'm practically Paul Bunyan. As for scary, maybe it's the tattoos. Or perhaps he sees the monster I struggle to keep at bay.

When Darc and I were around Sam's age, we learned about torture and torment. We saw and heard things no child should witness as we tucked ourselves away in small spaces. Hide and seek champions until the end. But the pain of men quickly fades from memory when you convince yourself that they deserve to be punished.

"That's not a nice thing to say, Sam." Val reaches back, lacing her fingers into mine. "That kind of hurt Aunt Val's feelings."

"He didn't mean anything by it, Kold. His dad's not a big guy. So…" Tracy fidgets at the doorknob, clearly uncomfortable with the situation. "You must seem like a giant by comparison."

The best thing for me to do is to remain quiet and let Val handle it. Anything I say will only draw further attention to everyone's general discomfort, and I tend to put my foot in my mouth when I'm annoyed. I tuck my free hand into Val's back pocket and apply the slightest pressure, pulling her back towards me.

"I suppose we should get going. Don't want to keep my fiancé waiting." Val laughs, stepping forward halfway and extending her arms out to Tracy. "I'm gonna miss you guys."

The ladies share a hug, and Sam offers a high five in the way of a goodbye. Seeing Val interact with Sam further solidifies my desire to start a family with her. She's the best person I've ever met, and with her as a mom, our children will be adorably quick-witted little angels, even if they are half mine.

Val waves goodbye as the door closes, and finally, we're alone. She picks up Christmas, but he wiggles out of her arms, trying to get to me. "I guess he missed you."

"Babe, I'm sorry I didn't stay in bed last night." The look on Val's face tells me my sudden recap of events has caught her off guard, but I have to get this out. "I'm sorry I walked away when I wanted to stay. I put you in the middle of a situation you never agreed to and then got jealous after I assured you I wouldn't. I can't live without you. I wouldn't even want to try. Since meeting you, I've reevaluated every choice I've ever made, and I would regret them all, except that somehow they brought me to you." The long-winded apology leaves me absent of breath.

"Fuck it!" Val says, throwing one arm over my shoulder. "Let's get married!" Her words hold a lit match to my gunpowder trail, setting off a series of explosions in my brain.

Somehow, my girl always knows exactly what to say.

I pull her into a hug, smashing the dog between us. I'm not sure why, but this moment feels more absolute than when I gave her the ring. Maybe because this time, she's saying yes to the act of getting married instead of simply entertaining an engagement.

Val

Seeing Tracy and Sam was nice, but I'm glad to have the visit over and done with. I will miss them. But the friendship we built and the apartment where it was constructed will always be a reminder of difficult times. A relationship bonded by heartache and struggle will always be stained by its glue.

As soon as I left the house this morning, I regretted it. I should've stayed and worked things out with Kold, especially since this is our first major holiday as a couple. I can be stubborn even on my best days, but walking out the way I did and disregarding his wishes was the wrong choice. The strength of his feelings, as it pertains to being disrespected, is well known. Even if he did lie, that's no excuse.

Deep down, I knew he would chase me, and I wanted him to follow, but I didn't have to leave the house. If a small test of his love and loyalty was truly required, he could've simply chased me upstairs to our bedroom. Even that seems juvenile. I wish I could give my trust the same way I offer love. Unconditionally. But I've been burned far too many times in the past.

One of the things I love most about Kold is that he seeks resolution through civil conversation. He chooses his words with intention, avoiding lies and half-truths, leaving little room to doubt his sincerity. He isn't someone who will serve you a word salad in an attempt at misdirection. What woman wouldn't love that?

Straightforward as he may be when speaking, there's also a lot that can be taken from his silence.

"I'm surprised you haven't said anything about the video." My anxiety is through the roof, waiting for him to bring it up first.

Kold hasn't even hinted at the song going viral or the rumors that I'm engaged to Darc. He seems as blissfully unaware as I was before Tracy pulled back the blinders.

"Babe, I don't even want to think about it. For the life of me, I don't know why I was stupid enough to watch it." He takes my hand and presses it to his lips, never taking his eyes from the road. The somber quality of his tone contrasts with the lightness of my question. If I were him, I would be floating to heaven on cloud nine, having died from the excitement of being suddenly famous.

Kold, on the other hand, sounds as though he's chastising himself for reveling in the uptick of acknowledgment, and I'm shocked by his knee-jerk reaction. "I thought you would've been excited."

"Excited? Seriously?" He looks at me and scowls. "I mean, I *was* excited when it was happening. But seeing it played back over and over again, scrutinizing the details, looking for flaws in my performance. The whole thing felt more like a punch in the gut."

"Well, for the record, I thought your performance was stellar. I can still feel you when I close my eyes and think about your voice." I would have thought every musician dreams of the moment when the world finally takes notice of their talent. Why has Kold spent the last two decades playing music if he doesn't want anyone to hear it?

"Maybe if we watch it together, I'll feel differently. Sounds like you're getting excited thinking about it." His hand runs up the inside of my thigh until his fingers brush along my inseam. "Do you like being shared?"

"I'm hardly the one who matters." The only reason I'm part of the conversation is because I got caught canoodling with Darc on the balcony like an idiot. Even then, it's Kold's song that everyone is talking about. He's the one in the spotlight. He's the one who matters. The rest of us are merely cast in his glow.

"Babe, you're the only one who matters. It is about you, after all."

"Well, I'm proud of you for knowing what you want and pursuing your passion. I'm impressed by you on a daily basis." I want to celebrate, and he's acting like this viral video is the worst thing in the world.

"Are we talking about the same thing?" He squeezes my leg before turning onto our street. "Because I feel like maybe we're not. The security camera footage I watched over and over while drinking and descending slowly into madness was not the good time you're making it out to be. Maybe I've misunderstood your initial question. What video are you asking me about?"

Well, that explains why we're on two different pages. As it turns out, we aren't even discussing the same book. Now, I have to replay the conversation in my head, plug new information into the answer key, and try to make sense of what was said.

Kold's reaction to the security footage of Darc and me together was less severe than I expected, no doubt blunted for my benefit. And now I'm questioning whether he knows about the video trending online.

He pulls into the driveway and shifts his SUV into park, leaving the engine running. There's a chill to the air this morning, and it's starting to snow, but I wonder if the ground is cold enough for anything to stick. Something about fresh snow on Christmas feels magical, adding to my concern that this may be a dream. I'll wake up in the hospital someday, with Allen in the chair beside me, phone glued to his hand, grumbling about work.

Wouldn't that be my luck?

"Love, are you still with me? I feel like maybe I've lost you." He squeezes my leg again, drawing my full attention back to him.

"I'm sorry, what? My mind wandered off." Getting caught daydreaming mid-conversation is embarrassing. It makes me look like I wasn't listening. "I swear, I heard everything you were saying until that last bit. I got distracted for a second, watching snowflakes."

"Well, if that isn't the cutest thing I've ever heard, I don't know what is. Are you ready to go in and have a Christmas morning redo?" There's excitement in his voice that makes my heart quicken.

I should have done more shopping and picked up a few more gifts. Now, the day is here, and it's too late. Kold and I weren't even dating when I bought his gifts, wrapped them up, and dropped them off. He's about to open presents from a girl who spent the vast majority of her day fantasizing about what it would be like to have him, and not one gift from the woman who's agreed to marry him.

"As ready as I'm going to be." It isn't Christmas morning with Kold that I'm running away from. It's the pressure of sitting in a room with Darc and smiling as if nothing happened.

Moving in this week is happening, whether I'm ready for it or not. I've lost my opportunity to entertain other options by dragging my feet and being indecisive. Of course, there are worse things than being forced to live in a big fancy house with the man I love and his flirtatious twin brother. Off the top of my head, I can think of a few dozen, but I've already endured all of those in my past and then some.

"I keep forgetting how much you hate this holiday, probably because I don't know why that is. If you want, we can spend the day in bed, watching movies." He's sweet to offer, and part of me considers saying yes and dragging him back to bed, but I want to see his reaction to the gifts I picked out. However, after that, naked cuddle time sounds like a must.

The first kiss Kold gives me fills me with courage, and the second makes me feel all tingly. "If you keep kissing me like that, I might opt for the day in bed."

"As tempting as that is, I'm ready to shower you with gifts that in no way represent the depth of my love for you. And I'm dying to see what the hell you bought me."

The third kiss reminds me that Kold isn't John, and this isn't last Christmas. I can't spend the rest of my life attempting to hide from ghosts.

CHAPTER 38

Kold

As my girl steps out of the car and into my waiting arms, a snowflake lands on the tip of my eyelashes and remains there, suspended in time. Although it will be fleeting in its perfection, I'm jealous of its proximity. Perhaps because I stand here, in sharp contrast, potentially damaged beyond repair. I've never been perfect, yet somehow, Val manages to see me that way.

I wish I knew all her secrets so I could do what's in my power to make things better, but she's as guarded as I am about the past. What was it she said to Conrad? 'Best to leave it buried.' I wonder if she'd say the same thing about the skeletons I'm hiding under the trees south of Route 32. Could she still love the man I am for her if she came face to face with the monster? Best not to test out any theories today. I don't want to give her another reason to hate the holidays.

Once inside the house, I unhook Christmas's leash and take Val's coat. "I'm going to unload the car before we get started. Do you want everything in the spare bedroom or our room?" Before we left the apartment, I convinced her to fill the bags and boxes she had, then loaded them into the back of my Range Rover. She only brought a handful of personal items and half of her clothes. Darc and I can move the rest out tomorrow.

"Oh, um. I'll come out and help." Her voice hitches, and she reaches for her coat with clumsy hands. "Otherwise, you'll have to make two trips."

"I think I can manage, and there's someone in the living room who wants to talk to you. Hear him out, okay?" I kiss the top of her head and pull her into a hug. "I'll never let anyone hurt you again."

I hope to god I'm doing the right thing. Val is only going to let me skate by on best intentions for so long before she tires of my antics. Driven by a reckless need to help, I put her into situations without her consent and then ask for forgiveness later when I should probably stop thinking I know what's best and let her make her own choices.

"Okay." Val issues her agreement and allows her arms to fall from around my waist, signaling her willingness to let me go temporarily.

I step past her and walk back through the door with my stomach in knots and my heart on the verge of breaking. So much for the most wonderful time of the year. Everyone's a bundle of raw emotions this morning, and I'm the one who's to blame.

Val only brought three bags and a box, barely enough for one trip, let alone two, and I know she doesn't underestimate my strength. She was telling me that she didn't want to be in the house alone with him, without having to say the words aloud. Am I asking too much of her? Will she bend past her breaking point to appease me? Of course, she will. The same way I would break for her.

Walking through the front door, I hear her raised voice, reading Darc the riot act.

"That's the most ridiculous thing I've ever heard! I can't believe you've had this here the entire time, and you're only telling me now. For people who claim to love me so much, you have a shitty way of showing it!" The exasperation in Val's tone is on full display, with a smidgen of something extra mixed in. "This shit ends today! We are NEVER doing this again."

I run upstairs, drop everything on the bed, and turn around as quickly as my legs allow, ready to officially restart our holiday. At the bottom of the stairs, I skid to a halt in time to see Darc lift a sprig of mistletoe over Val's head and kiss her. Because why wouldn't he?

"I take it all is forgiven?" Now that I've opened Pandora's box, I might have to get used to seeing them like this.

Val shakes off the mirrored version of me holding her and steps over to where I'm standing. "No, all is not forgiven. You, assholes, have had a Christmas tree and ornaments on a shelf in the garage this entire time, and you never thought to mention it to me? I could have been basking in the warm glow of mini, two-and-a-half-volt light bulbs all week, but I mistakenly assumed you two didn't own any decorations." It's cute seeing her so worked up, mostly because her outburst lacks any actual anger.

"We always put the tree up on Christmas morning. That's the tradition." Growing up, my mom had cats who would climb into the tree and break all the glass ornaments. So, as a solution, she would lock the cats in her bedroom on Christmas day, and Darc and I would be allowed to put up the tree and decorate before opening our gifts. Later that night, when we went off to bed, my mom would stay up until all the ornaments were neatly repackaged and the holiday decorations were stored away for the next year.

"I know. Your brother told me the story, and it's fucked up! We are *not* doing that to our children." The words part from her lips, free of doubt.

Our children.

I grab Val at the base of her ass and lift her into my arms as she wraps her legs around me. "You've already made this the best Christmas I've ever had. Now, let me return the favor."

Unlike my brother, I don't require cheap gimmicks or store-bought greenery. Val is my forever. She is the love I will search for in each lifetime that follows this one. She is my happiness, my redemption, and my certainty.

"Merry Christmas, love."

Val

It's an odd tradition, setting up the tree on Christmas morning simply to take it down later that evening, but I suppose that doesn't make it wrong. Darc and I decorate the flocked branches without conversation as holiday classics play softly in the background. With Kold in the kitchen working on breakfast, his brother never misses an opportunity to brush against me, constantly reminding me of his presence. As if I need the physical reminder.

The scent of his sandalwood body wash clings to the air around us, filling my lungs with every breath, while the deep richness of his voice wraps me in the holiday spirit. He sings along to familiar carols, well-versed in every chorus, as I catch sight of him glancing at me in the reflection of decorative baubles. The taste of his kiss lingers on my lips, and I wish I had a cup of coffee so that I could wash him away.

"I thought you accepted my apology?" The warmth of his breath kisses my neck as he pulls me back, pinning me to his chest like a second-place ribbon. "Do you intend to ignore me all day?"

"If I were ignoring you, I would be in the kitchen helping finish breakfast. And if your apology had been rejected, your kiss would have also been denied. I don't know what you want from me, but I doubt it's anything I can give you." When push comes to shove, I'll walk away from both rather than split them apart.

"I don't like it when you're mad at me, and I can't fix it. Stay downstairs with me tonight. It doesn't have to be about sex. Give me a chance to show you who I am."

The thin cotton fibers between us do nothing to mask the deep lines of his muscles. Now, I wish I had kept on my sweater, even as the heat rolling out of the fireplace threatens to set me ablaze. Or rather, that's what I keep trying to tell myself.

"I can't. The agreed-upon arrangement is for every other Wednesday." It isn't until I feel the shift in his demeanor that I begin to register my mistake. Darc and I never agreed to anything. That conversation was between me and Kold.

"Is that my brother's idea of a joke?" He releases my arms and takes off down the hallway leading to the kitchen. "Every other Wednesday!" His shouts echo into the room ahead. "That's only two days a month."

Kold looks up in time to see the pair of us spilling into the room, but he doesn't react. I reach for Darc, attempting to pull him back, but there's no stopping a moving train. "Who suggested every other Wednesday, and why wasn't I given a say?"

"Are we doing this right now?" Kold's calm disposition reminds me of my mother and how she could breathe through even the worst prognosis. I'll be honest, I expected a different response from my future husband, but I am pleasantly surprised to see him remain calm. "Can't we eat in peace and discuss it tomorrow?"

"No! We cannot eat in peace and discuss it tomorrow. Fuck you! We're talking about this now!" Darc snatches one of the three identical plates of food from the counter and grabs a fork. "Val and I work opposite shifts on Wednesday. I won't even get to see her. I want Sunday, Monday, and Tuesday. Every week!"

"I'm not splitting my fiancée fifty-fifty with you, so rethink it and be reasonable. For the record, Val was the one willing to give you two days a month, not me. Had it been my decision, you would have gotten nothing." His words sharpen to a point like daggers. "It's Val's choice, not yours! Maybe you should shut the fuck up, thank her, and be glad she's willing to give you that much."

I pick up a fork and remain at the counter, tucking myself into Kold's side. How is this my life? Sometimes, I wish the two of them would hammer out the details of my future without me and email a list of their growing expectations. Then, I could avoid the tense negotiations. It's all starting to be too much, and I feel myself preparing to run. Sex is easy. If Darc wants to throw me into the rotation and Kold doesn't care, I'm fine with it, but he's acting like my name is the only one on the roster.

"Right, because you had nothing to do with it? How is she supposed to make a choice with you standing over her, watching her every move? She can't even talk to me without you freaking out and threatening to kill me. Do you think you hold a claim because you put a ring on her finger? That's fucking bullshit. Deny it all you want, but you knew how I felt about her. That's why you've kept her hidden in your room this entire time." Darc sets his plate on the table and sits, fork in hand, awaiting our retort.

Kold's strong arm runs the length of my back, hand gripping my pocket as though he's preparing to move me out of the way in a hurry. "If Val wants to spend time with you, she knows where to find you. I'm not in the habit of taking her choices away. But make no mistake about it, brother, she is mine. The only reason I'm even entertaining this fucking ridiculous back and forth with you is because Val asked for the two days. Otherwise, I would have stabbed you in the fucking throat when you walked in here and been done with it."

"I'm happy to settle things that way, anytime you are. If that's what it'll take, let's find out who's man enough to keep her."

The kitchen air is thick and heavy, polluted with male aggression. I'm finding it difficult to breathe as the panic twists my vocal cords into a tangle of knots, like strings of Christmas lights thrown haphazardly into a box.

"Enough!" I shout, looking at Darc with pleading eyes, begging him to stop. "We're not doing this today." Placing the fork down on the lip of the plate, I push my breakfast away, no longer interested in food, or conversation, or men who look like gods and fuck like devils. "If it's going to start a fight, then forget it. I'll sleep in the spare bedroom, alone. Hell, I would rather sleep in my car in the Walmart parking lot than endure this unbelievably misogynistic conversation. I'm not the property of either one of you, so if you want to have sex with me, I suggest you direct your comments and concerns this way instead of arguing with each other."

Both men are temporarily paralyzed, recalculating their next move and the odds of success. Ultimately, it's Kold who speaks first. "Okay, let's *all* relax and take a minute." He centers himself behind me, pinning me between the granite counter and his chiseled torso.

Attempting to smooth over the situation, Kold keeps his voice level and his tone soft. "You and I need to have a conversation if this is something you want to do. As for you sleeping alone, that's not happening. The spare bedroom is for storage purposes only, and you're *never* sleeping in your car."

I close my eyes and retrace my steps, trying to find the right voice amongst the bellowing chaos within me. I'm not a fan of conflict, and these guys fight like it's their favorite childhood hobby. Darc takes everything from zero to sixty, and I'm not sure my heart can handle it.

"I have my apartment until the thirty-first. I can stay there if it keeps you two from killing each other. And there's an entire house in Indiana, full of my stuff, that I could move back to."

How did I think getting involved with both of them was a good idea? These guys are lightyears beyond my league and competitive beyond measure. When it comes to dating, I should probably retire from the sport altogether. I've never been good at relationships. What made me think this time would be any different?

"You aren't moving to Indiana, and that's final! Stop being ridiculous. I don't care if you're joking or not. You're not going anywhere." Darc begins digging into his breakfast, letting the intensity of the moment burn itself out. "Brothers fight with each other, Valentine. It's what they do."

Maybe that's true, but I wouldn't know. I've never had siblings to argue with. It's always been my mom and I, or rather it was. These days, I'm running low on people to fight with or lean on. My mom is gone, my father never existed, and my only friend is hung up on my ex-boyfriend, who seems to have disappeared. All I have is myself, my dog, and an identical set of greedy guardians. Although, maybe that's what fate intended. The guys certainly know how to fill a void.

"Well, I won't be the reason you hate each other. The only time I want to come between you is in the bedroom."

Kold lets out an amused laugh under his breath and pulls me in tighter, kissing the side of my neck. "It's probably not the best time for jokes like that unless you want us to break you in half."

My intention was to lighten the mood and distract them with humor, releasing any remaining pressure, but it appears I may have gone too far. If I'm not careful, they'll make me pay up. Thankfully, silent seconds turn into minutes as Kold and I remain locked in an endless embrace.

In truth, we all deserve more than what we've received in the past. Even Darc. And while it might take two of me to satisfy one of them, I have a feeling we'll find a way to make do. Thankfully, I've always been good with my mouth.

"I guess we should probably eat this impressive breakfast, or is the tradition simply to look at it?" I smile, still trying to smooth any lingering tension.

Pressed snugly against Kold, I can feel him swelling with measured intensity. "To hell with the food. I'm ready to eat something else. Let's go upstairs. I still owe you for that comment earlier." He keeps his voice low, whispering his offer so only we can hear. "Unless you want to use the bedroom down here?"

"You think you're being cute and playing around, assuming I won't go in there. But I'm curious. Is it still gonna be cute when he's saying my name and finishing down my throat?" My words are hushed but intentional. I'm looking for a reaction. However, quiet isn't the same as silent, and sound travels. When Darc's fork drops onto the plate, I can only assume he's overheard my question.

There's a shift in the atmosphere around me as Kold lifts me from my feet and sits me on the island in front of him.

"So long as you're still mine." He doesn't phrase it as a question, although I suspect he might appreciate an answer.

My thoughts race, acknowledging multiple realities in rapid succession. If I do this now, fully aware of Darc's feelings beyond the physical, then I'm signing my name to a contract I haven't even taken the time to read. The idea of which scares and excites me. Some small part of me will belong to him indefinitely.

"From now until the end."

CHAPTER 39

Kold

Sitting on the couch in the living room and staring at the tree Val decorated an hour ago, I watch as she carries in the box of previously delivered gifts and carefully places them beneath the bottom branches. I already ran upstairs and grabbed the gifts I'd been hiding under the bed, so now we're waiting on Darc. He's in his room, crying about blue balls and likely jerking off.

The way Val denied us both at breakfast, after toying with the idea of another threesome, was an act of exquisite cruelty, and I loved it. Watching her call the shots and own her power was incredibly sexy. And since I get the pleasure of taking her to bed once we finish opening gifts, I'm relatively unfazed by the rejection.

"What's taking him so long? You'd think a guy his age would know how to get himself off." Val drops onto the cushion beside me, allowing her head to fall against my arm.

"He's probably thinking about all the ways he wants to torture you before hate fucking you." Darc is not one to shy away from playing rough. However, if he tries that shit with my girl, it'll be the last thing he ever does.

"And you're okay with that? With him taking me in such a forceful way?" Val lifts her head and turns to wrap her arms around my bicep. "That doesn't do much to alleviate my concerns about moving in here."

"Thinking about and acting upon are two vastly different things. So long as everything remains safely filed away in his head, I'm not going to dictate my brother's masturbatory material. I'm confident he knows better than to cross that line with you, but if you need me to talk to him, I will." That's probably a conversation worth revisiting, regardless of what Val decides. "I didn't realize you still had concerns about moving in. Is that something you'd like to discuss while we wait for Ebenezer Scrooge to emerge from his bedchamber?"

The words spring from her lips without pausing a beat.

"I don't want to lose you! I know that you and your brother are a package deal, and I would never dream of splitting you apart. But I'm in love with you, Kold. I hope you know that. If this thing with Darc becomes an issue between us, I'll never forgive myself. Having casual sex, I'm fine with, but I'm pretty sure your brother is looking for a full-on girlfriend experience." There's a heaviness in her rapid delivery that drops on me like a steel plate. "If you wanted it to be the three of us, I wish you would've told me that from the beginning. Honestly, I'm not sure there's enough of me to go around, and I'm afraid you'll find someone else when I fall short. Someone better. You'll move on without me, and I'll disappear."

If Darc turns out to be the reason I lose Val, he's a dead man. I'll put a bullet between his eyes and follow him into hell.

"I'm going to keep saying this until you believe me, and then I'll say it again for good measure. I will *never* break up with you. So, stop trying to convince yourself that's even a possibility because it's not. If you decide that you don't want to date my brother, Hallelujah! I never wanted to share you with him, certainly not to this extent. It's taken every ounce of willpower not to kill him every time he touches you."

Val looks at me with a pained expression, her brows pinched, trying to make sense of my intentions. "If that's true, I don't understand what you want. Darc didn't wander into the office accidentally and catch us in the act. I saw you text him. Why would you invite him to join us if you hate him touching me so much?"

"This is going to sound horrible, but I wanted to watch you take on two guys at once, and he's the only person I trust. I thought it was what you wanted. I was so certain that I convinced myself having a threesome would make life easy for everyone." For some reason, I assumed Val might be like the other women who came before her, but she's not. "I figured you wouldn't have to keep secrets if things were out in the open, and I didn't like that he was the reason you had to lie to me. Sharing you felt like the lesser of two evils when the other option was losing you."

"I wasn't lying. Or rather, I wasn't trying to. I didn't want you to be upset with him, and I thought I could handle the situation on my own. I should've gone back to my apartment instead of coming here and never leaving. Then I could've signed the lease renewal, and none of this would've happened." She looks down at her hands, unable to meet my eyes.

"Okay, pause. I should've phrased that better." I want to clear the air, not break her heart, and send her running. "You didn't lie to me. You merely left things unspoken for his benefit, and I used the empty space to jump to conclusions. But I was never mad at you, and I never lost faith in us. You maintain my full trust."

"Okay, but I thought *we* were good after our discussion at the apartment. Then we got here, and you sent me straight into his arms again like that was where you wanted me to be. Or am I mistaken?" Val's gentle touch sends a warm, pulsing energy radiating up my arm, and the longer we talk, the more I see things from her side.

"That wasn't my intention, and honestly, I never thought of it that way. On my way out the door, Darc said he wanted to talk and that he needed you to forgive him. I knew he did something to upset you at the club, and I wanted you to get whatever apology he owed you." I turn to face her straight on, catching her eyes, before continuing. "All I care about is you and your happiness." Now that we're having an honest conversation and laying it all out on the table, I can understand why she's been slightly detached the last twelve hours.

"Okay, that makes sense, but I'm still confused. You don't necessarily want me hooking up with your brother, but I'm free to do as I please, so long as it makes me happy. Am I hearing this right? Does that same rule apply to you? Because I'm not okay with you sleeping with other women."

"No. We are *not* in an open relationship, and I will never cheat on you. Your connection with Darc is an exception because I like to watch and because you enjoy being with him. But make no mistake, he is the *only* exception. If you ever have sex with another man, I will kill him. I'm happy to keep you all to myself if you prefer."

"Well, that escalated quickly. You do realize I've already agreed to give Darc every other Wednesday, and you signed off on it? So..." She trails off before asking the question, but her eyes voice everything her mouth neglects to say.

"If you don't want to be with him, I'll talk to him. I'll tell him I changed my mind and can't handle the thought of you with anyone else. He won't be mad at you." This conversation with my brother will *not* go over well, but I don't want Val to sweat the details.

"Can we hold off on that conversation? I need time to think."

"Say what's on your mind, babe. Tell me what you want, and don't hold back attempting to spare my feelings. No more misunderstandings or truths unspoken, and no more filling in the blanks with assumptions. So long as you and I stay together, I don't care what you do with him. But you have to start being brutally honest with me."

"Alright, well... Does it make me a bad fiancée if I admit that I might want to have sex with your brother again?" Val hides her face behind her hands, trying to block the rest. "Because if I'm being *brutally honest*, I should probably acknowledge that I'm a tiny bit more than somewhat interested."

I laugh at the adorable way she beats around the bush before admitting to what we both already know. "Oddly enough, my love, I think that makes you an incredible fiancée. Does it make me a terrible future husband if I admit that I want you to keep having sex with him?"

I didn't even have to drag Val into my fucked-up life. She

walked straight into it with open eyes and a crooked smile, asking what more she could do to make me happy.

"What I don't understand is the *why*. You get mad every time he kisses me, but you're encouraging me to have sex with him. It doesn't make sense. Is there something you're not telling me? Is this a loyalty test that I'm failing miserably? If this is solely about making me happy, I don't want to do it. Not if it upsets you."

"I knew my brother wanted to find you, but I thought it was because of my feelings for you. And I knew he wanted to sleep with you because he's Darc, and that's kind of his thing. I was okay with the threesome because it was something we all wanted. And I was fine until I saw the way you two were together. That's when I knew I fucked up and panicked because I realized that I could lose you."

"You're not going to lose me."

"Till death do us part?"

"It doesn't matter how many times you ask me. The answer will always be *yes*. Although, now that I think about it, I might be too boring to be married to a famous rockstar. What are we going to do about that?" She smiles at me, and I want to kiss her more than anything.

"I don't know what you're talking about. It was a good crowd, but it's the same local show we play every year on Christmas Eve. I promise you, very few people outside of this area give a shit. You know I'll quit the band for you. Last night was a bit of a disaster, and we haven't gotten the chance to talk about it. If the idea of me going on tour this summer makes you question our relationship, I'll tell the guys I'm done." Everyone in my life knows I intend to put Val before all others from now until the end. I made that clear from day one, long before she was mine. Or rather, before I knew she was mine.

"You're sitting here acting like you have no idea what's going on, and I don't understand how that could be possible. Why are you pretending to be clueless? Where's your phone? How is it not blowing up with a million notifications?" Val's voice gets faster when she's excited or frustrated. It's adorable to listen to.

"I'm not pretending to be anything. I don't know what's

happening, and whenever I ask you, we talk about something else. Darc and I adhere to a strict No Cell Phone policy on Christmas. It's another rule carried over from our childhood. A rule I was willing to break when you walked out the door earlier. My phone is on silent in the junk drawer. After you left, I grabbed it to text you, but I didn't stop to go through it. Once I knew where you were headed, I put it back in the drawer and haven't thought about it since." This time, we're staying on topic until I find out what's happening. As for my holiday traditions, I'm throwing them in a dumpster and lighting it on fire.

"No tree! No cell phone! Is there anything else? Why not celebrate the holiday on a deserted island?" My girl is back to sounding like her usual self, playfully exasperated.

Funny how something feels normal because you've always done it a certain way. Then you see it through someone else's eyes, and it sounds ridiculous.

"We have plenty of time to create new traditions as a family, and I'm ready to get married sooner rather than later. After all, I can't live the life we dreamt without you." I'm on pins and needles, and my heart hurts from being in my stomach. "So, what do you say we make this a short engagement?"

"I have no interest in being reminded of what it felt like to exist without you." She bites her bottom lips and runs her hand along my jawline.

"So, is that a *yes*?" Her answer is as clear as mud, so I follow the Santa Clause rule and check twice. After tying and untying the strings of conflict we could have avoided with a conversation, I need to ensure Val and I are back on the same page. I still don't know what's on my phone that's got her worked up, but we can circle back to that in a minute.

Between us, we have all the pieces required for a lifetime of happiness, but it turns out someone forgot to include the instructions.

Val

Since seeing the video this morning, the views and comments have jumped exponentially, leaving me a bit in shock. I hand Kold my phone and sit back, taking in his expression. There's a smile playing at the corner of his lips, but he's making what seems to be a considerable effort to suppress it. I don't get it. This gorgeous man should be jumping up and down screaming, but he's sitting here doing his best impression of a potato.

"How are you not freaking out right now?!?" My excitement is turned to eleven, as though I'm feeling the emotion for both of us. Maybe I've drained him of sensation like an emotional succubus, leaving him nothing more than the attractive husk of the man he once was.

"I'm processing instead of getting lost in the moment." He finishes the video and returns my phone, a smile finally gracing his presence. "It's cool. I'm sure the other guys are losing their minds."

"Ha!" I don't mean to laugh, but I can't hold it in. "Where was all that controlled processing when you carried me to your car to have sex in a parking lot? Or when you told me you loved me after being together for only a few hours? Or when you sat outside my job because you were afraid that I would disappear? Or when you pulled this ring from your pocket after a week of sleeping next to each other?" I hold out my hand and wiggle my fingers, letting the light from the tree catch in every impressive cut before dropping my hand onto his leg.

"The processing for all of that happened during the two months prior. And the control was me waiting as long as I did. Funny, I didn't hear you complaining at the time when you were taking off your pants and sliding down my cock. In fact, I recall you being the first one to say *I love you*. And since the beginning, you've known that I intend for you to be my wife."

Images of our first time play out in my head like a highlight reel from last week's game.

"I know, I was just messing with you. Didn't mean for you to start talking dirty and get me all worked up." One look, and I'm on the edge of my seat. Add to that a passing comment about his dick, and I'm horny beyond reason. "Would you be interested in recreating that scene from the car while we're on the couch?"

He quirks an eyebrow and smirks at me, but before he can answer, I pounce. Planting my lips on his, I rub my hand over his cock. Thankfully, he's as ready to go as I am. Lifting me onto his lap, we continue to kiss while grinding against each other through our clothes.

"Should we go upstairs? Your new boyfriend might hear us and come out here." Kold makes the suggestion, but his corresponding action lacks follow-through. He could stand and walk upstairs, carrying me like a baby koala if he wanted to. However, I get the feeling this is exactly where he wants to be, and the suggestion of an alternate venue is for my benefit.

"He can watch, or he can join in. I don't care. So long as you're inside me."

Kold yanks me to the side, returning me to the couch so he can remove my pants. The way he throws me around in the heat of the moment hits like a shot of adrenalin. Knowing that he could break me is sexy because I trust that he never will.

Naked from the waist down, Kold pulls his shirt off before removing mine. "Get on top of me, and fuck me like you did that first time. And don't you dare stop until I'm cumming inside of you. I want to feel that tight little pussy squeezing every drop out of me."

"Yes, sir," I say, moving into position. When Kold plays at being more dominant, I do as I'm told, eager to please him in whatever manner he requests. I appreciate his readiness to satisfy my various temperaments, even if I'm not always sure what they want.

Unwilling to waste time adjusting to his size, I take him in and allow myself to bathe in the pain. The sensation is bittersweet. Even though I'm wet, taking him deep on the first drop sends a stinging pleasure up my arched spine and into my orbitofrontal cortex. It feels amazing now, but I'll be paying for it once the endorphins begin to dwindle.

"You feel so fucking good, babygirl. Stop biting that lip so I can hear how much you enjoy my cock." One hand clutches my hip, driving my movements, while his other hand rests against the base of my throat. "You either moan for me, or you don't breathe. Those are your options."

Freeing my bottom lip from the grip of my clenched jaw, I let go of every sound I've been biting back. The release is so powerful that it feels like a mini orgasm. My body begins to shake, and I close my eyes, willing the sensation to overtake me. Before I can count to ten, I feel Darc standing behind me.

Kold digs his fingers into my hips, using both hands to control my rhythm. Thrusting his hips as he pulls me down. Darc wraps his hand around my throat and forces my head back.

"Open your eyes and look at me, sweetheart." His words are an order, so I comply without hesitation. "Do you want me to fuck you after he's finished with you?"

Kold is nearing the edge. I can feel the shift in his body as he pushes himself closer to release. Even though I can't see him, I know his body, and I'm certain he's about to explode.

"Tell me what you need, and it's yours." Darc leans forward and kisses me. His tongue pressing past my teeth. Then pulling back long enough for me to exhale an answer before taking my lips again.

"That's it. That's a good girl. Take it all." Kold drives in hard one last time, filling me with everything he's got. His body convulses once, twice, three times, and his cock twitches as the last of his orgasm escapes.

I fall forward, hoping to share a kiss, but without so much as a second to regain my bearings, Darc wraps his arm around my waist and lifts me straight into the air, hoisting me onto his shoulder. Carrying me down the hallway, he gives my bare ass a hard slap, and there's pain, I'm sure of it. Only I'm too blissed out to register anything beyond the lock of his bedroom door clicking into place.

He takes me into the bathroom and sets me gently on the counter before wrapping me in a thick cotton robe he retrieved from the back of the door. The cold marble countertop draws out the stinging pain from within, soothing my tender flesh. Knotting his fingers into the hair at the back of my head, Darc moves my face slowly to one side before whispering into my neck. "I don't want to hurt you. But I *need* to be inside you."

I wrap my arms around his shoulders, locking him into place. "I know you do." The realization feels like a wooden stake to the heart.

Not ready to consent to his departure, I hold firm. Tightening my grip until he stands and takes me with him. Sometimes, I forget how strong they are and how small I feel by comparison.

"Sweetheart, you can let go. I'll never truly leave you." His words ring in my ears like church bells as I allow my legs to descend toward the floor. Reaching with my toes, he lowers me in increments until I'm standing flat-footed on the tile. "Take your time. I'll be on the bed when you're ready."

He exits the room and closes the door behind him, leaving me to my thoughts. I'm thankful for the nightlight, casting its soft glow so I don't have to blind myself with the harsh overhead lighting. As I get into the shower, attempting to clean what's left of Kold off of me, I question the logic that landed me here.

Two days in a row, huh? I don't remember that being the deal.

"I didn't plan for any of this to happen. I love Kold."

You can't lie to me, remember?

"I'm not lying. I do love him."

Oh, I know you love Kold. The lie is tangled inside what you don't say.

"You don't know that, because I don't know that."

Keep deceiving yourself. It should make for an interesting downfall.

"Fuck you!"

I'll be sure to take a number.

I finish rinsing off and step out onto the mat. Wearing a wet towel doesn't appeal to me, so I thoroughly dry myself before tucking my damaged body back into the oversized bathrobe. Opening the door, I see Darc exactly where he said he would be, sitting on the edge of the bed waiting for me.

He opens his arms, drawing me into his trap, and I go voluntarily. I make myself at home between his thighs, awaiting his command. Without a clock in the room, the concept of time beyond us has stopped, granting us a reprieve from any need to rush. He slides his hands gradually under the robe, being deliberate with his touch. As though he's reading the history stored in my skin, I remain still as he caresses the outside of my legs, causing the flesh to pimple with goosebumps. He rests his forehead against my chest as his hands explore my curves. Squeezing my ass, he pulls at the loose knot with his teeth, opening the front of the robe.

"My brother loves you because you're perfect, and he believes you are his redemption," Darc's words absorb into my chest as he cups my breast in one hand and lightly kisses the other. "I love you because you're broken, and you accept us, knowing we can never be redeemed."

I don't know how to respond, so I remain silent, desperately needing more of his touch. There is an ache pulsing within me, a craving only he can satisfy. If he doesn't take me soon, I may fall to pieces like ash in the shape of what it once was.

"Darc! Please!" I run my fingers through his hair and over the back of his neck, wanting him to feel something. "Tell me what you want."

When he stands, he towers over me, casting me in shadow. I shrug the robe from my shoulders and begin peeling off his clothes. Thankfully, he's feeling cooperative, and within seconds we're equally naked.

"I want you to get in bed as if we're going to sleep, and you've been waiting for me to join you."

He doesn't have to explain further. I already know what he's asking for. Darc doesn't want to punish me. He wants me to belong to him. This sort of role-play isn't typically my go-to, but I know how to play the part.

I get in bed, sliding over to the side I know he leaves vacant, and pull the sheet up to my stomach. Then I roll onto my side and rub my hand over the empty spot beside me. "Will you please come to bed with me? I've been missing you all day, and the only gift I want this year for Christmas is your attention." My voice is so full of longing that I almost believe what I'm saying. "You've been working more than usual, and I feel like I never get to see you."

He remains planted at the end of the bed, with his eyes locked on my location. The look on his face is difficult to describe, as if he's capturing the memory and saving it for later. When he moves, it's with purpose, never releasing me from his gaze. He gets under the sheet beside me and pulls me into his chest. "I've missed you too, sweetheart. You have no idea how badly I've wanted to come home to you."

The way he says it twists the stake, piercing my heart with splinters. I brush my hand along his jawline, wanting to ease his suffering but worry that I might only be making it worse. "You know where to find me if you ever need me."

Darc rolls me onto my back, pinning me beneath him.

Shifting his weight from one arm to the other, he repositions our legs so that mine fall outside of his, leaving me splayed open and ready to accept him. Then, he rubs the head of his cock along my swollen clit, as my hips rock against him. With his face an inch from mine, I require his kiss more than anything else.

"I always need you," he says, pushing himself inside me while granting me the kiss I impatiently seek. There's nothing forced or rushed. Darc takes his time, backing off when I cry out and driving forward when I moan. I'm nearly lost completely when he looks into my soul and tells me, "I love you."

Is this still role-play? Was it ever? A person can say anything during sex. They don't have to mean it.

"Oh my god! Darc. Don't stop!" Our bodies move together, taken over by ecstasy. "Tell me again. I want to hear you say it. Please!"

The length of his stride increases, hitting every nerve ending on the way out and again on the way back in. The head of his cock teases at the opening without ever leaving.

"I love you." Now, in the home stretch, he forgets to be gentle and pounds into me, careening towards release. "I love you so fucking much. I think it might kill me."

It's almost cruel how good he feels, and I'm so close. One last declaration, and we'll topple over the edge together. Placing one hand on his shoulder and the other over his heart, I look up at him through tear-filled eyes. "You're not allowed to leave me. I need you too much."

CHAPTER 40

Kold

I went upstairs to shower, hoping to block out the sound, but as luck would have it, I turned off the water in time to hear the finale. Val is in the room below my feet, giggling as I'm standing here naked, wondering if I'm the other man. This is the most fucked up Christmas Darc and I have ever had, and we haven't even exchanged gifts.

Considering my brother is with my wife for the second time in less than twenty-four hours, I'd say he's already gotten his present from me this year. Then again, can I blame them? Wasn't I the one who stripped Val naked in the living room, hoping for this exact outcome? I wanted to share her, to watch her tremble under another man's touch.

Granted, I wasn't expecting my brother to pull her off me at the tail end of my orgasm, carry her to his bedroom, and lock the door. I suppose that's what I deserve for underestimating their feelings. I know I can trust him to keep her safe, but can I trust that she'll always choose me when both options are on the table?

Getting dressed in something comfortable, I grab an extra set of clothes and head downstairs. I call the dogs and make my way to the kitchen, only half listening to the conversation taking place behind closed doors. Val sounds happy. And oddly enough, so does my brother.

If I'm the reason these two end up together, I'm throwing myself in the lake wearing cement boots.

Watching the dogs chase each other around the backyard, I'm so deep in thought that my heart jumps into my throat when the doorbell rings. "Shit!" My mom told me they were stopping over, but I didn't think they were coming until later.

"You guys better get dressed. And quickly!" I shout from outside the bedroom door, still locked from the inside. "Babe, unless you're jumping ship, I need you out of that room before I answer the door."

"Wait! Give me one second. I'm coming!" As always, Val crashes through the door on the heels of her words, the image of perfection. Except this time, she's wearing Darc's clothes instead of mine. "Why didn't you tell me we were expecting company?"

She takes a black hairband from around her wrist and pulls her hair up into a messy bun as we walk side by side down the hall. When she's finished, I take her hand and pull her to my side, pausing a step before the door. "Are you still my girl?"

She lets out a quick laugh before turning to wrap her arms around my neck. "Are you planning on asking me that every time? You should know it's unnecessary. I'll love you for the rest of my life. Best accept that you're stuck with me unless you choose to leave. In which case, I would cease to exist."

At the mere mention of us parting ways, Val's eyes twinkle with oncoming tears. If her words weren't enough for me, her physical reaction tells me everything I need to hear. This is the last time I seek validation from a woman who's given me no reason to question her feelings. Her relationship with Darc exists separately from ours, and while that may seem crazy to everyone else, it makes sense to me.

"I have a sneaking suspicion you might be stuck with two guys, so you don't need to worry about ending up alone. If something happens to one of us, you have a spare at the ready."

She rolls her eyes and smiles at me.

"Are you ready to meet the rest of the family?" I give her one quick kiss before moving to answer the door, but when it swings open, there's no one there. On the welcome mat is a flower arrangement with a card stuck in the top.

I pick up the arrangement and see Val's name written on the front of the card with a message on the back that reads: *You're the only woman in the world who could make me the hearts and flowers type of guy.*

"These are for you," I say, handing Val the vase and taking in her expression.

I watch her features shift as her usual one-sided smile pulls up at both ends. She closes her eyes and lifts the vase to her nose, filling her lungs with the scent. "Oh my god, babe, these are gorgeous. How did you know that chrysanthemums are my favorite? This cranberry red is so elegant against the snow-white roses. A bouquet like this must have cost you a pretty penny, but I promise it was worth every cent. I'm obsessed. I love them, and I love you. If this is the only thing you got me for Christmas, you've already made this my new favorite holiday!"

Holding her extravagant collection of flowers in one hand, she stretches on tiptoes to grace my lips with her appreciation. "You don't have to be a hearts and flowers guy for me to feel loved. But, if you want to send me arrangements like this on occasion, I won't be mad."

I can't help but laugh to myself at the absurdity of this current situation. Val is standing here gushing over an expensive bouquet of her favorite blooms, singing my praises, and I never thought to order her flowers. Part of me is pissed at Darc for one-upping me, and another part is concerned they might not be from him either. If there's a guy after Val's heart who doesn't share my face, he's about to have a violent set of twins paying him a visit.

From here on out, everything she needs, she gets from us.

Before I have a chance to confess, Val takes her flowers into the living room and displays them proudly on a side table as Darc retrieves the dogs from the backyard. I'm starting to feel like a Christmas ghost, looking in on the life that could've been had I not spent the last two decades being such a cold-hearted brute. Let's hope I awake to find time still left on the clock.

Val

Removing the last present from under the tree, I separate the gifts into four piles: one for Kold, one for Darc, one for myself, and one for the dogs. The furry creatures curled in front of the fireplace have a large pile of gifts to open, though I shouldn't be surprised. All three of us bought them presents, even though they didn't think to get us a damn thing in return.

"Alexa, playlist holiday instrumental." Kold's request, directed at the speaker across the room, is received and abided. He reaches up to touch me as I pass, pulling me into his lap. "I'm looking forward to a lifetime of holidays spent together."

I smile in response as memories of the past come flooding in. There was a running *joke* in my house regarding holidays and my dating life. My mom always said, "No sense in me learning his name. He'll be gone before the next major holiday." Every time she said those words, I took it as a personal attack. I would get so irritated, but I never gave that anger a voice. I would swallow the feelings with a spoonful of sugar and a dozen shots of vodka.

In the end, she wasn't wrong in her observation. No one ever lasted a full calendar year. Not even the man who agreed to *from death do us part.* So, what's the likelihood that this time will be any different? Have I changed in the ways I needed to? Probably not.

I rest my head on Kold's shoulder and relax in his arms, trying not to overthink the inevitable. If my life with these guys is stamped with an expiration date, let me make the most of it while I'm here.

"How do we determine who goes first? I was an only child, so I grew up the winner by default." I look up in time to catch Darc's expression as he eyes my current location with obvious displeasure. "I suppose we could let the kids go first."

I move from where I'm seated on Kold's lap and relocate to the floor in front of the fireplace. One by one, I open the gifts tagged for NYE or Xmas. When I was wrapping the gifts, I decided to steer clear of using their real names in case an undisclosed wife or girlfriend happened across the box of packages. With nicknames, they had plausible deniability if they should need it. For that same reason, I included a card with the box but left my name off the individual gifts.

Hard to believe it was only a week and a half ago when I dropped the box of presents off on the front porch before retreating like a coward. How has so much happened in such a short period of time? In Kold's world, we've always belonged together, drawn to one another like the moon holding sway over the tides. He feels strongly that we've walked through time, hand in hand, bound for an eternity.

Only now, in this timeline, he's split in two, and I have to sort out whether I'm meant to love one of them or both.

Christmas appears to be smack dab in the middle of his own moral dilemma, having to choose between a squeaky gingerbread man and a chicken-flavored nyla bone in the shape of a pine tree. However, as soon as Midnight takes a bone for herself, the decision is quickly made. I scoop up the unchosen remains and pitch them into the toy basket before finding my seat on the couch.

"I'd like to apologize in advance before you guys open your gifts from me."

Have you ever done something in the moment that felt perfect, and then later, when you look back at it through a different lens, you wonder what the hell you were thinking? Well, that's how I'm feeling. If I'm being honest, I never anticipated spending the holiday with them. When I ordered the gifts, I assumed their reactions would remain a mystery to me, and now that I'm here, I'm freaking out.

"Okay. So, I'm a big fan of one-of-a-kind, personalized presents, and I realize it's a bit weird, given the timeframe, but I hope you like them. And I'm sorry I didn't go out shopping again after we started dating."

Kold leans over to kiss me before picking up the flatter, rectangle-shaped box labeled Jack Frost from his end of the coffee table. "You worry too much, babe." He holds the box to his ear and gives it a shake, then places it flat in one hand as though he's trying to measure the weight. "I have no idea what's in here, but I already know I'm going to love it."

Darc selects the matching box from his pile and turns it over in his hands, attempting to conjure an image in his mind that might explain the dimensions of the box and the heft of its contents. "I have a couple of ideas, but nothing concrete."

As the two guys shake and flip the boxes over in their hands, the anticipation grows inside me like a weed, taking root in my overactive subconscious. "Oh my god, will you finally open them and put me out of my misery?"

Gift-giving is my love language, but there's so much opportunity to be disappointed, and I hate being on the receiving end of any gifting holiday. "Before your birthday, I need you both to send me your Amazon Wishlist so we can avoid any future disappointment. I don't think you realize how badly I'm cracking under the pressure of my choices."

This time, it's Darc who gets up, squeezing onto the couch beside me. There's plenty of space available to my left, so I attempt to move over, but he wraps an arm around my waist and pulls me snugly against him. His words, whispered into my ear, are slowly becoming my new favorite lullaby. "Stop being perfect."

I turn my face towards him, leaving my lips primed for a kiss. "Perfectly broken," I say, keeping my voice low. Of course, Kold is only on the other side of me, and I'm sure he's got his listening ears on. Whatever game this is, it wasn't designed for the faint of heart, and I wonder if I have the strength of character to see it through to the end.

"Fuck you both, I'm opening mine." Kold declares, laughing under his breath. On the surface, his words could suggest annoyance, but there's no hint of anger in his tone concealed underneath. Despite that, I slide over, splitting the distance between them.

"Alright, you goddamn crybaby, let's open them together." Darc begins to tear the paper from the back, following the peel around to the front as Kold mirrors his effort. They pause to scrutinize the plain cardboard boxes. Thrown off by the lack of clues. "My best guess is a magnifying glass, but I have a feeling I'm way off."

Kold smirks and shakes his head. "Why would Val buy you a magnifying glass? That's such a random guess." His fingers play at the edge of the packing tape, prepared to unveil his prize.

"I don't know. Maybe as a fucking reminder that we should've been looking harder." Darc goes with a more aggressive approach and wedges two fingers under the flap, ripping the box in half.

Thankfully, the knife I bought him came with a sheath. Otherwise, we might have been headed to the ER. The kunai drops on his leg with a thud before I can reach to stop it. Kold frees his ax from its box, and both men exchange a look.

"You bought us weapons for Christmas?" Kold says, examining the marking engraved into the blade. "And here I thought you couldn't get any cooler."

The walls close in around me as both guys lean in. Kold delivers a string of kisses against the side of my neck while Darc bites into my shoulder. They linger long enough to get me hot and bothered before returning to the blades at hand.

"I thought I asked you to stop!" Darc's tone matches his serious expression as his eyes burn into mine. "Do you need me to say *please*?"

Confusion freckles my cheeks as I challenge myself to sort out his meaning. He's accusing me of perfection, and I couldn't be further from it. What does he want from me? I'm sitting on a couch behaving myself, and somehow, I'm pissing him off. "I'm not doing anything."

Darc mouths the words, *Yes You Are,* attracting the attention of his brother.

CHAPTER 41

Kold

I eye the pair of them as curiosity gives birth to concern. Before I can lend my voice to the conversation, the entire situation is resolved. Val places her hand on Darc's leg, and on contact, his mood shifts, his demeanor softens, and he smiles. He actually smiles.

Sometimes, I think Val's enchanted, possessing the ability to manipulate the emotions of people around her. Her intent seems selfless, and maybe that's why it works. She isn't after personal gain. She simply wants the people around her to have the happiness she refuses to accept for herself.

Give a girl the world, and she'll gift it away to those who need it more.

Of course, my brother is also well-versed in the art of manipulating the emotions of others, but his intent has always been purely for selfish gain. Even now, I wonder if he's pretending to be upset because he knows she'll stop what she's doing to offer comfort and her full attention. It's not the most subtle tactic, but effective, nonetheless.

"So, babe..." Sitting here, watching them interact, I realize how much I need her notice. I miss her eyes and the way she chooses to see me. I love her smirky little smile and the way she laughs along with me, even when she insists I'm not funny. Val hears all the things I don't say and says all the things I need to hear. I want to touch her and kiss her and feel the delicate weight of her hand on *my* leg. I need to be the one making her heart beat faster and be the reason she's left gasping for breath. I want her twitching and shaking and calling out my name. There's a lifetime of happiness in my future that only exists because she never gave up hope.

It's no wonder he's in love with her.

As Val turns to face me, Darc laces his fingers into hers, unwilling to break their connection. The action reminds me more of myself than him. My brother's interest in displays of affection has previously remained behind closed doors, but it would seem Val might have turned him into a hearts and flowers guy after all. Maybe it's not the performance I thought it was.

"I'm curious about the ax you bought me, and I was hoping you could tell me something about it. Besides the fact that it's the best Christmas present I've ever received. Also, I love you." Telling her I love her is a cheap trick, but it makes her smile. And I do love her. Deeply. So, maybe the trick isn't in the words so much as in the timing.

Val bites back the smile teasing both corners of her lips, but her eyes give it away. "I love you too. As for the ax, it's for cutting pizza. The Norse runes reminded me of the tattoo on your arm. And what guy doesn't like pizza? Well, I mean, normal guys who eat carbs. I suppose you could use it to cut up baked chicken and broccoli."

When she laughs at her own cleverness, a wave of exuberance washes over me, and even Darc smiles. Inside my body, there's a fuzzy feeling, like my organs are growing fur, and holding back is no longer a viable option. She can have whatever relationship she wants with my brother, up to and including love, but she also needs to know I'm still here.

Leaning in, I close the distance between us, leaving my lips an inch from hers as my hand slides up the inside of her thigh. "From now on, we're making pizza once a week."

Her laugh fills my lungs as I inhale her peppermint-scented breath. "Finally, a tradition I can get behind," she says, coming forward to meet my lips with her smile.

One by one, the surroundings fall away as I consume her with my kiss. Dogs chewing, music playing, warm lighting coming from the tree. Even Darc fades away once he releases her hand. Val wraps her arms across my shoulders, locking us together in a lover's embrace.

Without words, I empty my feelings into her as she pours into me. The mutual transfer makes me ping-pong between feeling drained and energized as I hold nothing back. Let her take me, soul and all. It belongs to her anyway.

I could spend the rest of my life kissing this woman and never want it to end. My every happiness is tied to her, tethered by heartstrings and vocal cords. Whenever we speak of the future, it plays like a movie in my mind, and I'm excited to see how the story shakes out, but I'm also terrified of the ending. In spite of how much we worship each other, we can't stop time. Love is cruel that way. I could spend the next sixty years at her side and still beg Death for one more day.

Her cheeks are wet with a river of tears that fall onto her chest as I pull away. Gently, I wipe away the stains, regarding her pain with mirrored sadness.

"If you tell me what's upsetting you, I'll fix it. I'll do anything." Seeing the tears swell and spill from her eyes breaks me. I'm unable to hold back as Thirty-five years' worth of suppressed emotions spills out of me, and I shrivel into her lap, kneeling on the floor at her feet, hopelessly seeking a stay of execution. "I swear to you, I'm worth the trouble. And if I'm not, I can change."

"Why would I want you to change? You're perfect!" Val runs her fingers through my hair, over my shoulders, and down my back, as I crumble like a toddler with his first skinned knee. "I can't imagine my life without you, but I don't want to be the reason you hold yourself back. I wouldn't forgive myself."

I understand the individual words coming out of her mouth, but nothing makes sense when I string them together. "What are you talking about? If you're upset about the comments on that video, say that. We can break the No Phones on Christmas rule and post pictures and videos of us together. We can tell everyone we're engaged. I would love nothing more than to show you off. Fuck! I only played that song at the show because you were there. The women online claiming it's about them are full of shit. That song is yours, and so am I."

"Babe, I know."

"Then why does it sound like you're giving up on me?" I bring my arms around her waist, still lying across her legs. This time, I'm not letting go. "Protecting you and what we have is the only thing that matters to me."

If Val leaves me, the flash of absolute certainty, the months dreaming of her face, the pleasure of her company, and the fantasy of a future well spent all evaporate back into the ethos, leaving only pain and emptiness. Returning me to the person I was before.

"I'm not breaking up with you. Don't you know how much I love you? They were happy tears. I was thinking about the life we plan on building and picturing what we might look like as a family. Why is it that every time I imagine our future kids, it's always twins?" Her words are so light I'm convinced they're a figment of my desperate imagination. "For some reason, the matter feels settled, as though it's written in stone instead of sand... Don't take this the wrong way, but sometimes it feels like the two of you are experiencing emotions for the first time."

"Because we are. I was a confident and angry kid who grew into an emotionally stifled adult with big dick energy. Before you, my sensitivity range moved in one direction. Unbothered being the baseline, en route to blinding rage. And my brother is infinitely worse than I ever was."

Speaking of my brother, where is he? I was so engrossed in my conversation with Val that I hadn't even realized he'd left. It'll be interesting to see her reaction once she registers his absence. Will she follow after him to make sure he's okay? I'm certain that's what he's expecting her to do.

Her unwavering focus remains on me. "That *big dick energy* was one of the first things I fell in love with. In fact, it's left me a bit tender at the moment." She tugs on my arms, conveying her wish for me to rejoin her on the couch. With renewed confidence,

I oblige. Then she picks up another box from the table and hands it to me. "Can you open this one on your own, or do we need the evil twin in here?"

I laugh, accepting her generous offering. "You should start calling him that. He hates it!"

Val

Darc is a grown man. He doesn't need me to chase after him. That's what I tell myself as I carry his final gift into the kitchen and find him standing by the coffee maker. He's got one mug filled and a second in the process of brewing.

"Is that for me or your other half?" I ask, brushing against his arm as I lean on the counter.

He takes the present from my hand and replaces it with the first mug of coffee. "This one's yours."

I pretend to examine the contents before taking a sip and setting it back on the counter. I desperately want to hug him, but first, he's going to have to acknowledge me with a degree of eye contact.

"Did you spit in it?" I ask, clearly joking. He laughs but doesn't look at me. "I'd still drink it, even if you did. But it would be nice to know if you're mad at me or not."

Still refusing to glance in my direction, he stares down his cup of coffee like it's trying to pick a fight with him. "Why would I be mad, Valentine? You're not mine, and you're never going to be. So, enjoy the holiday with your fiancé and forget I'm here." His words are sharp and cut like razors.

"If that's what you want." I attempt to reclaim my coffee, but he catches my wrist.

"What do you want me to say? I'm happy for you. I'm

fucking thrilled that my brother found his person. I kind of thought we'd both be single forever since we're such a pack of assholes, but somehow, he managed to find the one woman who could see past all of that. And I know how much he loves you. Listening to him gush about you for two months is half the reason I fell in love with you. But therein lies the problem, doesn't it? I'm in love with you, and I can't have you. I get a front-row seat to the life I'll never have. I get a taste. A fucking sample. Enough to make me crave you morning, noon, and night, and then I'm expected to go off and starve."

"I think you've gotten a little more than a taste," I say, trying to be playful. He doesn't need to know how much I'm hurting. Hearing the pain in his voice is killing me, and I want to make it stop. I want to give him everything he needs to be happy, but I can't split myself in two.

"Stop being so fucking cute. You're turning me on, and I'm trying not to kiss you right now." He turns away as if holding me in his peripheral vision is too much temptation to bear.

"What if I want you to kiss me?"

Still holding my wrist, he faces me, licking his lips. "And then what? You walk away and go back to him."

"I'm standing right here. No one's asking you to starve." I want him to kiss me. He's the only one who can lift the heaviness that's weighing down my soul, but I can't bring myself to ask him. If I'm meant to suffer along with him, I will, but I'll do so in silence.

He doesn't kiss me. Instead, he cups my face in his hand and rubs his thumb across my lips. With his eyes locked on mine, Darc steadies his breathing and presses my hand against the front of his pants. His cock stiffens under my touch. "This is yours, and only yours, anytime you want it."

I lace my free hand around his arm and pull his hand over my heart. "And this is yours. But you have to share it." My heart beats steady under his palm, and I wonder if I'm strong enough to love them both until the end. If the three of us have any chance at making it, we have to find a way to work through the jealousy.

"Can you two kiss and be done with it? I want *our* girl to

open her presents sometime before the clock strikes midnight."
The unexpected voice coming from the hallway makes me jump,
even though it shouldn't. How long did I expect him to sit out
there and wait for me?

"We're coming," I say, realizing too late how sexual that
sounds, given the current mood of the room.

Kold laughs and carries on with the conversation. "That's
going to have to wait, babygirl, but I promise we'll take care of
you later. For now, you need to mentally prepare yourself and
pretend you still love me. Our parents will be here in five minutes,
and Conrad is coming with them."

CHAPTER 42

Kold

For a moment, I thought this day might never wind down, but now that we're at the tail end of the evening, lying in bed together, I wish we could pause here indefinitely. There was no mention of viral videos or awkward sexual tension. Darc even let me take credit for the flowers when Mom questioned how Val was able to turn me into such a sweetheart.

The three of us exchanged a subtle glance and an under-the-breath snicker at Mom's use of the term *sweetheart*. Having Darc and Val both in on the joke offered a new sensation. All my life, I thought it would be Darc by my side until the end. Then I met Val, and I was convinced it was the two of us against the world. No matter what direction I went, it became clear that I would have to sacrifice part of who I was, which felt wrong.

"Babe, I have to tell you something, and I don't want you to be upset."

I could have phrased that better, but here we are. Val flips onto her other side to face me and studies my expression.

"I haven't been entirely honest with you about something, and it's been eating away at me all evening." Every time I open my mouth, I make it worse, but I can't get my brain and my lips on the same page. "I should have told you straight away, but..."

Val cuts in, on the verge of tears. "Please stop talking. I don't want you to tell me. If you had sex with someone at the club after the show, when you were drunk and mad at me, I don't want to know."

"No. That's not it." I hold her tightly in my arms so that she has no choice but to stay and hear me out. Anytime Val thinks there's a possibility of me with someone else, I can feel her ready to run. "Babe, I'm sorry Allen was an asshole. And I'm sorry your ex-husband was even worse. They were fucking idiots for cheating on you. I promise you won't ever have to worry about that with me. No one could convince me to be unfaithful to you."

"Okay, then what is it? Did you not like your pizza ax and your personalized candle? I'll do better for the next holiday, I swear." Hearing Val grasp around in the dark, searching for straws, I realize I need to spit out what was on my mind instead of dancing around the truth.

"I didn't order the flowers!" And with that, I'm released from the pressure of my kept secret, and Val goes from devastated to dazed. "They're from Darc."

"Seriously! You couldn't have told me that when they got delivered?" She slaps my arm, then rubs away the sting. "Now I look like an asshole because I never thanked him, and you made me lie to your mom."

"I know, I'm a prick. You looked so unbelievably happy when you saw those flowers, and I wanted to be the reason for your smile. I thought Darc would say something, and when he didn't, I started to worry they might be from someone else. I didn't want to ask in a way that made it seem like I was accusing you of something. So, I let it go. Once Mom got here and the two of you started talking, it was too late to own up to the truth."

This entire situation is so stupid. Lesson learned. Next year for Christmas, I'm filling the house with all her favorite flowers.

"That's all fine and well, but why did you make it sound so much worse? You gave me heart palpitations for no reason, and now I have to go down and apologize to Darc for being an ungrateful moron." She tries to wiggle out of my arms, but I'm not ready to let her go.

"You can fuck my brother again tomorrow. He'll forgive you."

I reach down, grab her ass, pull her against me, and grind my cock into her. "Right now, you're mine."

She rolls her eyes and stops pulling away. "I'm always yours. Even when I'm with him. And for the record, I intended to thank him with my words, like a normal person."

I can see the sleep behind her eyes and know that whatever I have planned can wait. It's been a long day. Val already gave me everything I needed earlier, so taking her again would be selfish. But goddamn, if I don't want to be self-seeking.

I grab her phone from the nightstand and use it to turn off the light before rolling onto my back so she can curl into my chest. My girl sleeps like a flamingo, with one leg straight and the other bent at the knee. Always the same, whether she's facing me or turned away. Regardless of the position, our bodies fit together like puzzle pieces, conforming to the curves and locking into place.

"I plan on waking up early and leaving for work before sunrise. That way, I can be out by noon. I'll meet you at the apartment and carry down whatever you have packed, okay? Don't go proving how independent you are by moving it all yourself. I'm serious. I love you, but I know how stubborn you can be. This is important to me, Val. Please let me help you."

Her response consists of a yawn and an "Mmhmm."

So that I don't forget, I type a note into her phone, set the alarm for four thirty, and set it back on the side table. I thought there might be messages from co-workers, friends, maybe even an ex or two, but not one person thought to text or call her today. Tracy responded to a message from Val this morning and drove here to pick her up, so I guess that's something. But I expected more.

The thought of Val spending a holiday alone makes my chest tighten. It's no wonder she dove into this life with such reckless-ness. Val always said she had nothing to lose, but I thought she was downplaying it for my benefit. Surely, there would be a slew of people wrapping her in love and well wishes for the holiday, but there wasn't. It was only us, and somehow, that was enough for her.

Val's steady, rhythmic breathing makes my eyelids heavy. I have only enough time to kiss the top of her head before I join her in the land of slumber, with every intention of finding her in my dreams. This girl is my everything. Awake or asleep, my heart knows not the difference.

CHAPTER 43
Val

Taking a deep breath, my lungs fill with the scent of men's body wash as I register the weight of his arm draped across my stomach. I'm awake, but my eyes refuse to flutter open even though I know the sun has already risen. Feeling a yawn coming, I turn my head and cover my mouth.

"I thought you were going to work early? Couldn't bring yourself to leave me, huh?" A smile crosses my lips as I roll against his chest. "You smell good. Did you shower already?"

He kisses my forehead and plays with my hair. "You're adorable when you're asleep but even cuter when you're half awake. He left the house around five-thirty."

My brain forces my eyes to open as I shift away from the man holding me. "You're not allowed to do that! You can't pretend to be your brother to get into bed with me. I know for a fact that's one of the rules."

He allows me to roll onto my back only to follow, positioning himself over me. "For the record, Valentine, that rule applies to sex, not cuddling. It's not my fault you still can't tell us apart."

I release an exasperated huff, forgetting all about my possible morning breath. "My eyes were still closed! And you're in his spot." The small part of my brain telling me not to be turned on is losing handily to the battalion of horny impulses overtaking my senses. "You shouldn't even be in here."

In what feels like one continuous motion, Darc rolls off of me, stands next to the bed, and snatches off the comforter before grabbing me by the ankle and yanking me to the edge of the bed. "Fine! If you don't want me in here, I'll leave." Lifting me off the bed, he pitches me over his shoulder and walks to the door as two barking dogs trail behind us.

I swear, he missed his calling as a firefighter. The ease with which he carries me around like I weigh nothing is both sexy and infuriating. "Darc, you're going to drop me on the stairs, and I'm gonna die."

It doesn't matter what I say. He's going to do what he wants because he knows he can. "If you quit squirming around, I'll be less likely to drop you."

Traversing the stairs on his shoulder is a smoother ride than expected but still slightly terrifying. It isn't until we get inside his room that he finally sets me down on my feet.

"Brush your teeth, go to the bathroom, shower, and let's get this day started, shall we? I'll let the dogs out and make coffee." He registers my confusion and smiles. "All of your Christmas presents from me are down here. Body wash, shampoo, conditioner, deodorant, and lotion are all in the bathroom with a toothbrush. And your clothes are in the right-side drawers of my dresser. Except for the dress. That's in the closet."

I'll be honest, Darc's gifts did throw me for a loop last night, but they make a lot more sense in the light of day. The heaviest box was full of toiletries, all in a matching scent. I would have never considered myself a mint and rosemary girl, but I was forever changed once I popped the cap open on the body wash and held it under my nose. The scent was divine, leaving me looking forward to the shower ahead.

The rest of my gifts were clothes in varying degrees of comfort and style. Sweats, t-shirts, jeans, socks, underwear, a sexy new bra, and a dress. Darc bought me everything a girl might need if she was heading off to her freshman year in college. I couldn't figure out if he hated how I smelled and dressed or if he thought that the personal items I brought to the house were all I had. But apparently, it was his way of moving me downstairs, like a part-time parent with limited visitation.

"You know, I could've gotten ready upstairs, right?" Of course, he knows. Nothing important ever seems lost on him. Darc lives a calculated existence, or he did until I came along. "This feels more like a Thursday morning activity."

He steps forward and knots his fingers into my hair. "We can have as many Wednesday date nights and Thursday morning kisses as you want. Trust and believe I will be taking full advantage of my allotted schedule. But, on the six other days that don't begin with W, I plan to steal as much time as possible. Unless you ask me to stop."

My certainty waivers if I think with my head instead of my heart. "Maybe we should stop. You know I don't want to lose him." This isn't what Darc wants to hear, but that doesn't make it any less true.

"You're never going to lose him because I won't let that happen." Backing me towards the bed, he pauses before lifting me off my feet again and dropping me where he sleeps. "You made your feelings abundantly clear with the quotes on our candles."

The second and final gift the guys received from me was a personalized candle with a quote I came up with. Lame, I know, but it seemed unique at the time.

"I ordered those before..."

"Before what, Valentine? Before flirting with me? Before ignoring me? Before fucking me? Because it certainly wasn't *before* you fell in love with him. I get the *twin* candle, and he gets the *I can't live without you* candle!"

I sit up, tossing my legs over the side of the bed, one on either side of him, as his chest heaves. "I'm sorry that my gift upset you. Obviously, I should've gone shopping again. Had I more time, I could have bought you something that accurately reflected my feelings, but I didn't get the opportunity. I ordered your gifts before I spent time with you. Before I got to know you. Before I realized that loving you was an option. Why can't you forgive me?"

"Because I don't want you to be sorry," he says, finally kissing me.

Falling back, I guide him down on top of me.

"Then let me make it up to you." I run my hands over his shoulders and down his arms, appreciating the tone of my muscles. "The last thing I want is for you to be upset with me over a stupid candle. Throw it away, and I'll order you a new one as soon as we're done."

Darc looks at me, shaking his head. "I'll be in the kitchen when you're ready." The defeat is evident in his voice, but I'm not sure how it got there. He leaves me on the bed, alone and confused, while he escapes to the kitchen. Calling the dogs to go outside, he carries on as if the last few minutes never happened, and I have too many feelings to sort through.

Fuck this!

I sit up, grab the unwanted candle from the nightstand, and stomp into the bathroom, slamming the door behind me.

"Fucking asshole! What do you want from me?" I drop the candle into the trash and locate my reflection in the mirror. Only it isn't me looking back.

He wants you to choose him.

"Even when I do that, he gets mad. I was practically begging for it, and he walked away like I meant nothing. He doesn't want me!"

Of course, he does. He's obsessed with you.

"I don't want him to be obsessed. I want him to be happy."

Then stop trying to be perfect. Darc doesn't want the lie. He wants to protect the broken piece you conceal within the pretty packaging. He's not Kold.

"I know that. But I don't know how to be you anymore."

Bullshit! You think you have to spread your legs to find me. As if that's our only value. Stop selling us short. We're not cheap!

She's right, of course. She usually is. I probably should have let her out while I was married to John, but we both would have ended up in jail. Instead, I made her small, trying to be invisible so his anger would hit the wall behind me. Valentine doesn't always know how to play nice, unlike Val.

One of me for each of them.

Darc has seen her from the beginning. He speaks her name, calling her to the front of the class.

"I don't want to lose control."

Even though the rapping at the door is soft, its sudden presence startles me. Darc opens the door and steps behind me, finding us together in the mirror. He doesn't waste time admiring the shell when he looks at me. I love and hate him for that. I want to lie and say everything is okay, but he already knows it's not.

This time, my tears come without their usual apology, and I can't be bothered to stop them from falling.

Kold

Every step forward I take this morning, there's a phone call on its heels, knocking me back a minimum of two paces. I've counted the same bottles and bills a dozen times, needing a break from payroll, only to accomplish nothing. The video of Val's song is spreading like wildfire online, along with the rumors about her and Darc. I shouldn't care since I know the truth, but the rumors have come with receipts, and the guys are begging me to leave it alone.

In this age of the internet, it wasn't exactly difficult for Darc and I to find ways of making extra cash. I accumulated my following mostly by playing the part of an attractive lead singer with a nice car and a cute dog. As for Darc, he built his following with shower selfies and workout videos. The online presence helped sell tickets and drinks, making our bars a success, while others failed.

The attention served a purpose. Playing it up for likes amounted to vacations, gifts, money, and more pussy than a guy could need. By leaning into the narrative of our choosing, people stopped looking past the surface. No one bothered to see who we were beyond the muscles, tattoos, and money. Now, all I want is for it to go away, but it's impossible to disappear when you're standing in the spotlight.

Sitting in the office at my desk, I input the remaining

timesheet data into the computer, hoping to be out the door before noon. When my phone goes off, I consider ignoring it, but the name on the text catches my attention.

Evil Twin: I need you to do me a favor, but I don't want you to overreact. Send your fiancée a text and tell her that you miss her.

What the fuck does that mean? He says not to overreact. Then tells me, out of nowhere and with zero context, that Val needs reassurance that I'm thinking of her. Is that a joke? I started missing her when I got out of bed this morning, and she's been on my mind every second of every day since I met her.

: You mean your fiancée??? You and I need to have a talk about that, and if I find out you started the rumor, I'm going to stab you in the leg. First, tell me what you did to upset my girl so I know if I need to come home or not. Then fuck off and fix your own problems. If you messed up again and she hates you, I'm fine with that. Every time I ask her what's happening between the two of you, she lies to me. And I'm not in the fucking mood right now.

Evil Twin: You know what, forget it. You're a piece of shit. You don't even deserve her.

: You're probably right. But if you want me to fix it, I have to know what's going on. Did something happen? Does she need me to come home?

I watch impatiently as the three gray dots chase each other on the screen, indicating that a response is incoming. It takes Darc forever to respond, and I wonder if it's because he keeps erasing and restarting his message or if he's typing out a novel.

Evil Twin: I wasn't asking you to fix it for my sake, so stop being an asshole. I made a stupid comment about the quote on my candle, and in typical fashion, she apologized. Me being the dickhead that I am, got pissed and walked out, so she got upset and threw it away. That's what happened, but I don't think that is what's actually bothering her, you know? When I went back to apologize, she was shut down. I got her to stop crying, but she's not in any condition to pack and move.

I'm halfway through reading his text when I try calling, but it goes straight to voicemail.

: Call me back! Why would you send me all of that over text?

Evil Twin: Because I don't want her to hear me talking to you.

Do I leave now, take care of Val, and come back? Or do I see what can be accomplished with a text? My responsibilities here are important, but certainly not more important than my girl's well-being. One quick text to gauge her response, and then I'll decide.

: I'm counting and typing as fast as I can to get out of here, but my phone is blowing up, and it's distracting. I should've worked from home. I miss you like crazy and can't wait to see you. I could really use a personal assistant, if you'd be interested in applying for the job. There's a lot we need to talk about. Am I still meeting you at the apartment?

My Love: I miss you too. I was going to head over to my place after breakfast, but I can go now… Personal assistant, huh? I think I'd like to sit in on those interviews so I know how jealous I need to be.

Val sounds fine. No surprise there. With a crack, the pencil I've been fidgeting with snaps in half between my fingers. My brother is making me feel like a third wheel in my relationship, and my girl is too damn nice for her own good. Or maybe I'm the one being too nice, and Val is following my lead.

> : You're the only candidate for the job, my love. It's either you or no one. Take your time and enjoy your morning while I finish here. Text me if you go to the apartment and I'll drive straight there.

> My Love: Sounds good. I'll pack quickly since I know you're busy. Love you.

One of them is lying to me, and I'm irritated. This shit with Darc is turning my restless morning into a potential nightmare. Or maybe I want it to be his fault because that's easier. I need to have a face-to-face conversation with Val, and thinking about her likely reaction is making me anxious.

CHAPTER 44

Val

Standing at the stove in new panties and one of Darc's shirts, I'm about to flip the last pancake when he comes up behind me wearing a thin pair of pajama pants and nothing else. Darc wraps his arms across my chest and kisses my shoulder. He's been hovering more than usual since finding me in the bathroom mid-breakdown, barely taking his eyes off me.

His embrace consumes me as he presses himself along my back, leaving the bubbling batter to brown in the pan a second longer than I had planned.

"I told you, I'm fine." A claim I've made more than once in the last half an hour. Sliding the spatula under the cake and giving it a flip, I'm disappointed to see I've burned one. "Look what you made me do. Now I've gone and burned the breakfast." The last sentence is spoken quite overdramatically, reminding me of Petunia Dursley on the morning of Duddy's special day.

"Stop trying to make jokes. I've got you." His muscles flex and tighten around me, wrapping me in security. Releasing one arm, Darc reaches into the cupboard beside us, grabs a second plate, and places it on the counter. "Let me have that one. I'll eat it."

He can't see my expression, but I crinkle my face, stifling a laugh. "When was the last time *you* ate a pancake? I was about to make you eggs."

Moving one beat faster than slow motion, his hand slides

down my stomach and cups between my thighs. And whether Darc realizes it or not, he takes full control of my senses, leaving me on autopilot. "I'm willing to eat anything you have to offer me."

Those words, in combination with his touch, cause my core muscles to tighten and my breath to stutter. I forget all about the spatula in my hand as it falls onto the counter and the burnt pancake drops to the floor, attracting the attention of two hungry gremlins.

Turning off the stove, I have only enough time to push the empty pan off the burner before Darc pulls me out of the way. Both dogs lunge at the dropped cake, tearing it in half and retreating to the living room with the morning's fresh kill.

"Do you still have all your toes?" He jokes, swinging me up and setting me down on the island counter. "I should probably count them to make sure."

I lie back as he pretends to examine my feet, kissing the top of each. He places my feet on the counter, shoulder-width apart, leaving me vulnerable. In this position, I'm spread out in front of him like a buffet, hoping he brought his appetite.

Kissing up my calf and down my thigh, he pulls me towards the edge of the counter, resting my legs over his shoulders. "I'm still mad at you for throwing my Christmas present in the trash."

I sit up enough to watch my fingers disappear into his blonde hair. "Well, I'm mad at you for walking away and acting like you didn't want me."

Pausing where he's at, Darc looks up from between my thighs. "You thought I didn't *want* you?" He holds me in his gaze, refusing to break the connection as my desire replicates. "That's ridiculous. I always want you."

"Well, it didn't feel like that when you were rejecting me!" Caught up in the moment, I forget to hold back, and slightly too much truth slips out. Darc doesn't owe me anything. He can walk away at any point and never look back. He doesn't have to want me. He shouldn't want me. But I need him to.

His arms uncoil from around my thighs as he drops his shoulders, allowing my legs to fall aside. Then, strong hands grip my forearms, pulling me into a seated position. We linger there, inches apart, suspended in time, until the warmth of our shared breath thaws the frozen seconds. "Tell me everything you want, and let me be the one to give it to you."

What I want is the fantasy. But how can I say that to him? Stop loving me, and fuck me like I'm nobody. Use me. Degrade me. Break me. Throw me away with tomorrow's trash and forget you ever knew me. "Stop treating me like your girlfriend. I want to know what it feels like to be some girl you brought home from the club."

I can see him thinking through the list of rules, weighing the odds of forgiveness. Having sex with me on a day other than Wednesday is a slap on the wrist at best. But I'm certain that's not the rule concerning him now. Kold made it abundantly clear that Darc is not allowed to deceive me, and under no circumstance is he allowed to *hurt* me.

"If I do this for you, and I lose you. I'm going to be pissed." His tone conveys the depth of his emotion, which goes far beyond anger. I lean in to kiss him, but he stops me, stepping back with a disregarding look. "You get nothing from me unless I give it to you. Do you understand?"

"Yes." My voice is small but steady.

"For the next twenty minutes, I do *not* love you, and I do *not* respect you. You will do as you are told, and I will not stop until I am done with you or your time is up. Do you understand?" He sets the timer on his phone for twenty minutes and awaits my response.

"Yes. I understand." And with that, we have begun. He presses start, the phone beeps, and the timer begins counting backward.

Darc yanks me off the counter and drags me into the bedroom, shutting the door behind us. Wasting little time, he pulls off my shirt and pushes me onto the bed. Starting with my wrists, he ties me down at the corners with straps I hadn't noticed before. Then he repeats the process at my ankles.

I'm in a pair of small black lace panties and nothing else, tied to the bed of my fiancé's brother when I'm supposed to be at my apartment packing. In thirty-five years, this is the stupidest thing I've ever done, but also the most exciting. Darc wakes *her* up and makes me feel alive. I don't want this to cost me everything, but goddamn, he's worth every cent.

The timer on the nightstand continues to race, though I can't make out the numbers. It can't have been long because he takes the time to light a candle before joining me on the bed. Not just any candle, the one I threw away in the bathroom trash an hour ago. He must have taken it out and returned it to the side table before joining me in the kitchen.

Distracted by thoughts of candles and quotes and kisses and pancakes, I'm jolted back to reality by a wave of pleasure as he shoves half his hand inside of me and begins finger fucking me as if my impending orgasm determines the fate of the universe. His free hand starts rapidly vibrating over my clit, and I'm sent hurling over the edge in what feels like a world-record-setting time.

I make a feeble attempt to close my legs, but they don't budge, nor can I move my arms. He's tied me down tight, with no key to escape, and there's still plenty of time on the clock. Darc never offered me a safe word because there is no stopping what has to happen. I asked for this, and now I'll see who he is when he's not holding back.

With barely enough time to regain my focus, he repositions his body and slides his tongue in clockwise circles over my sensitive clit. Flooding my body with blinding gratification, I struggle against the restraints as he refuses to relent.

How could I ever deny my need for him? Even now, I want to beg and plead for his cock. My mouth waters, painfully jealous of the attention my pussy is receiving. I lick my lips, and the sensation conjures vivid memories of taking him down my throat. The combination of physical and mental sensations makes my body convulse for a second time.

Still holding my panties to the side, he sits up and begins rubbing himself over my clit, then down to tease my pussy.

When I was younger and first discovered masturbation, I would see how many times I could push myself over the edge while watching bootleg porn. Back then, alone in my bedroom, I think the record was six. But it's a lot easier to get off when you're hopped up on teenage hormones and novel desires. After a few minutes with a massaging shower head and a shared kiss with the back of my hand, I was rendered weak in the knees.

I should be expecting it, but I'm not. When he shoves his cock inside me for the first time, my body tightens, and I cry out. "Fuck. Darc. Please stop. I can't take anymore." I huff out the words with a staggered breath, but he shows no signs of stopping.

I try to bend my knees, to shift my hips, anything to regain control, but I'm lost. I'm trapped beneath the weight of my request. Darc slams into me once, twice, three times before pulling out and replacing his cock with a few curling fingers.

"Tell me. Why should I stop?" His fingers twist inside me, pressing against my constricting walls.

"Because I love you," I call out, but my plea only seems to fuel his desire. And then it stops. I open my eyes as I struggle to catch my breath, only to see him kneeling on the bed beside my head.

"I'll make you a deal. Tell me you love me, and only me. Convince me that you're my girl, and I'll stop. Otherwise, open your mouth and stick your tongue out. You've made a mess of me, and you're going to clean it off." Again, not willing to waste precious seconds, my lips have barely begun to part when he pushes his cock down my throat. I choke and gag as tears pool in my eyes and fall to my cheeks. "Fuck. That's a good girl. You do love me, don't you? Mmhmm. Look at me. I wanna watch you cry."

I try to do as I'm told, but before I can look up, he pushes his cock deeper into my throat and slams his fingers back into my pussy. My muscles seize as my body begins to shake.

"Do you like the way you taste?" He asks, without giving me the ability to answer. "Mmhmm. I bet you do. You're such a good little whore."

I cum again as he pulls out, leaving my mouth and pussy painfully empty. I want to scream at him to untie me. The command is on the tip of my tongue, painted in our combined juices, but I can't bring myself to say it. I agreed to the rules. The same rules I asked him to break. Back between my legs, he drives himself inside me as a door-rattling moan expels from my chest.

The dogs begin to bark in the living room as they make their way to the hallway. No doubt they think I'm being killed behind the bedroom door.

That's my initial thought until I see the door open.

Kold

I should be angry or annoyed, but I half expected this to be what I'd walk into. Val hasn't responded to my calls or texts, and according to the doorbell camera, she never left the house. I leave her at home one time, and Darc already has her tied to the bed.

Paralyzed by the embarrassment of being caught, Val is frozen beneath my brother as I walk over to the nightstand and pick up the phone, noting the time. "You're halfway there, babygirl. Don't let me stop you."

Grabbing the chair from the corner, I carry it closer to the bed and sit where I know she can see me. If I'm going to watch my girl get fucked by a monster, I might as well have a good seat.

"I fucked up. I'm sorry. Darc, untie me. Please don't make things worse." Whatever part of Val enjoyed being restrained to the bed has retreated, leaving her logical side to negotiate for her release.

Darc loosens the knot at each ankle, allowing the straps to fall away, but he's only playing with her. She's got another nine minutes to endure before he's finished, and I know as well as he does that no amount of begging will change that.

I watch as he pushes her legs together and drops them to one side, twisting her at the waist. My girl is so close to the edge. I can hear it every time he thrusts into her, but she tries to deny him. I can only assume this is for my benefit.

Darc wraps his hand around Val's throat, pushing her to the brink as her eyes plead for my forgiveness. "Eyes on me, Valentine!" He applies as much pressure as it takes to get her attention and no more. "*You* asked for this. *You* wanted this. Come back to me and finish what *you* started."

Val likes to play games. To tease. To give up power. To bend to the will of others. And bend she shall.

When Darc first untied her legs, she attempted to fight him off. They always do. But I was surprised by the speed at which she fully resubmitted once he told her to finish what she started. Even with me sitting in the room, she deemed her situation hopeless, realizing time would be her only savior.

With only a few minutes left on the clock, Darc propels her to orgasm, not once, but twice, leaving her a twitching, boneless pile of sweat and cum.

At the sound of the alarm, Darc presses his forehead to Val's, seeking absolution. "Valentine. Please don't hate me. I can't lose you."

I reset the timer and push the phone into Darc's hand, ready to continue the game. But when he looks at me with fire in his eyes, I know we've finished playing.

"She's had enough. You're not going to touch her! Not right now. She never agreed to both of us."

I'm curious how far my brother is willing to take this, but I get the feeling that once I cross that line with him, it won't end until one of us is dead.

"Kold, I know you're angry. I deserve that. Yell at me. Kick me out. Tell me you hate me. But please untie me." Val looks at me and then to Darc, her face streaked with exhaustion. "I can't take anymore."

Her eyes search only his expression, rendering me invisible. "You promised."

Taking her face into his hands, Darc wipes her tears and begins untying her wrists. "Shhh. Sweetheart, I'm not leaving you. No one's going to yell at you. No one's going to kick you out. And no one's going to make you do anything you don't want to do."

My brother's right. She's had enough, and the agreement Val made was with him, not me. I retrieve a pair of sweatpants and a t-shirt from the dresser, hoping to dissolve her concerns. When I turn around, she's sitting on the edge of the bed, wrapped in a sheet, barely holding her head up. Thankfully, Darc located his pants before standing guard by her side.

"I want my time with her," I say, holding up the clothes. Eventually, Val will meet the monster inside of me, but not today. "We need to talk alone."

Over the years, I've seen my brother be protective of buildings, businesses, cars, reputations and occasionally his only brother. When we were kids, he would stand in my place, accepting punishments he never earned. But I've never seen him shield a woman, especially from me. Does he honestly think I would hurt her? Perhaps I've stepped too far back, leaving them room to doubt my feelings.

Darc starts for the bathroom behind me, pausing for a moment at my side. "I would never treat her like the others, even if she asked me to."

My response is honest and to the point. "I appreciate that."

There's no need for me to question his claim since I witnessed the interaction myself. Pushing a girl to orgasm repeatedly is hardly the form of sexual torture Darc normally engages in, but it was fun to watch. When I made the rules, it was always with Val's safety in mind. But I've seen them together enough times to know there is no further need to worry. This is the worst she'll get from him, even if she begs for more.

I step away from Darc and any further discussion he wishes to have. My brother and his newly found romantic feelings for my girl will have to wait. Right now, there's only one person in this room I care to talk to, and she's waiting for me on the edge of the bed.

Gently removing the sheet from her shoulder, I massage my thumb across her muscle and allow my fingers to graze her tender flesh. Her back arches in response to my touch, and her eyes close. When she licks her bottom lip, it takes everything in me to remain composed. I still want her in all the ways I've promised, but I need to get better at proving it.

I take my time, moving with intention. This act of dressing her needs to be every bit as seductive as undressing her will be later. My love for her has never wavered, and my desire will never dwindle. If Val could read my mind, she would find that my every thought regards her and our happiness.

Kneeling at her feet, I slide off the single lace undergarment while kissing her thighs before surrounding her legs in the warmth of cotton. Seeing her in Darc's clothing irks me, but she can change after we've talked.

"Can we have this conversation upstairs? I don't want to be in here when you break up with me," she asks, with grief woven into her every word. "Your fight should be with me. I know you like to think that everything is *his* fault, but I asked him to do it. He didn't want to break the rules. He didn't even want me."

I don't mean to laugh, but her assertion is ludicrous. "I'm not sure what reality you woke up in, Val, but if you honestly believe there's a timeline that exists where my brother doesn't *want* to sleep with you, you're wrong. I'm happy to go upstairs so we can talk, but not because you want me to avoid a conflict with my brother. The only person I'm fighting right now is myself. So, stop thinking the worst. I'm not mad at you or him. I need to talk to you about something important, and I want you to remember that I love you."

I'm starting to understand why it's been so difficult to get Val to move in here. She seems to live in a constant state of fear, expecting whomever she's with to give up on her at the drop of a hat. With one foot out the door, I wouldn't be surprised if she left her bags and boxes packed.

Taking her hand, we tread the well-worn path to our bedroom in silence. Actions are all I'm left with as words escape me, but interlocked fingers do little to convey the depth of my feelings. Once inside, I take a seat on the bed and usher her to join me with open arms. My phone rings loudly in my pocket, halting Val's forward progress. I remove the phone with a groan and silence the ringer before reaching over to place it on the side table.

"They can leave a voicemail. Right now, it's only you and me." I've been fielding calls all morning without so much as a moment to think. This time, when I open my arms, Val walks straight into them and takes a seat on my leg, making herself at home. "For the sake of saving time and avoiding any unnecessary hurt feelings, I want you to know I'm not upset about the whole you and Darc sex thing I walked in on. In fact, I wish I had left the office ten minutes earlier. I like watching you with him, but that doesn't mean I want to lose you."

She nestles in before responding, resting her face on my shoulder. "I appreciate your kindness and your kink, but I think I might avoid your brother for a while. Unless you think that's a bad idea?"

In truth, I think it's a horrible idea. If Val avoids him now, there's no telling what Darc's reaction could be, but I'm certain it's nothing either of us wants to be around for. He'll blame me the same way I would blame him. Neither of us is prepared to acknowledge Val's true feelings should they change.

"I think, ultimately, you call the shots when it comes to that relationship, much the same as this one. So, if you want to spend time with him, you should. And if you want to take a break, you can. He'll be disappointed if you pull back. Especially if you leave without cause, but he's a grown man. He'll learn to deal with it." Knowing my brother, he'll deal with it by kicking the shit out of the next person who looks at him sideways.

"You're a bit too calm about this entire situation. It makes me feel like you don't care."

"Well, I assure you I care a *lot*. My feelings for you have never changed, and they never will. We can get married, buy a house, start a family, and live happily ever after. I'm here. I'm in. The sooner, the better. But we need to talk about something else first."

"Spit it out already. I don't understand what could be so important."

CHAPTER 45

Val

Two weeks of TV and radio appearances, then straight into a three-month tour, all set to begin this Wednesday. Kold wants me to quit my job and join him on the road as his wife and personal assistant. All I have to say is yes. This stupid viral video is going to make his career and destroy every one of our plans.

"What about the summer tour? Is that still happening? This is crazy." I'm going to require every detail imaginable if he anticipates an answer. Of all the things he could've said, after finding me in bed with his brother, *quit your job, let's get married, and go on a world tour* was not within the scope of my expectations. "I don't think I can go with you."

"You're right. It is crazy. It's too much too soon, and if you're not going, then I'm not going. It's that simple." Always quick to throw everything away to be with me, Kold isn't thinking about the once-in-a-lifetime opportunity being presented to him and his bandmates.

"I didn't mean that you shouldn't do it. I meant that the situation is crazy, which it is. But you have to think about your friends and what this could mean for their families. You guys have been playing music together since high school." I have to slow things down and think about this logically, which is not exactly my strong suit when I'm within ten feet of either one of them. "Why don't we wait and revisit the marriage topic after the summer tour? Can you cancel our trip and get your money back?"

Up until now, we've been having a somewhat calm discussion while lying in bed together. At the mere mention of postponing our hypothetical wedding, Kold bolts upright, sitting cross-legged at my side. "I'm not willing to risk *our* future on a tour and some album sales. If we can't get married at the start of the year, before this first tour, then I'm done. I'm out of the band!" His all-or-nothing mentality is starting to feel like an ultimatum.

"Can you please chill the fuck out and give me one second to think. Maybe there's a compromise in there somewhere, and we don't have to throw the baby out with the bathwater." I sit up, position myself in front of him, and take his hands. Something about being able to look into his eyes as we speak makes the idea of him leaving less heavy.

"You said the tour starts on the 8th, right? Before that, it's mostly interviews and TV appearances, and some of that can be done over the phone or prerecorded. So, would it be possible to jump into the tour on the 14th after we get back, or is that a deal breaker?"

Kold squeezes my hands and smiles. "At this point, they'd agree to anything. See, this is exactly why I need your help. You're better at planning things out and thinking things through. I'm more of a brash decision-maker."

It says a lot about a person's character when they can admit to their flaws. Most people disregard their shortcomings, but Kold seems to embrace them, leaning on others to fill in the gaps. Of course, he's still perfect compared to normal human males.

"There's something on your mind that you don't want to say. I can see it written all over your face. You know you can say anything to me. What's worrying you?"

I'd prefer to keep my personal concerns private, but since he's asking, I might as well spit it out. "Is it possible you could meet someone or change your mind about us while you're away? I want to marry you. I do. More than anything. But not if there's a chance you might divorce me for someone else."

"Babe, there's no divorce in our future, and there's no woman who could momentarily make me forget my feelings for you. I want you to come with me, but I understand we have responsibilities here in Ohio that you aren't comfortable dumping on my brother. I get it. I understand why you feel like you need to stay home. But whenever you want to see me, I'll book you a flight. We'll video chat every day. And if it gets to be too much, I'll drop everything and come home to you. If you tell me that you can't do this, then we won't do it. Honestly, if things keep trending the way they are, your song will bring in enough money to keep the guys happy with or without the tour." He makes it all sound so easy.

"I know you're going to miss me. And I'm going to be miserable without you. I couldn't handle you leaving me for eight hours to go to work. How am I supposed to do three months without you? But you don't have to be lonely." He pulls me onto his lap, wrapping my legs around his waist. "You don't ever have to feel guilty if the person you're with looks like this." With his pointer finger, Kold draws an invisible circle around his face and winks at me.

"We're really doing this, huh? So be it. Can you reach your phone?" I ask, nodding my head in the direction of the side table.

Kold lays back and stretches his arm over his head, retrieving the phone with his fingertips. When he sits up, he hands it to me without hesitation. Any question of his loyalty could easily be put to rest with this one simple action if any such reservations existed.

I set the timer for twenty minutes and show him the phone. "You get nothing from me unless I give it to you. For the next twenty minutes, I do not love you, and I do not respect you. You will do as you are told, and I will not stop until I am done with you or your time is up. Do you understand?" I repeat the rules like a mantra.

If my future husband truly intends to leave for the next few months, I need to give him something good to think about while he's gone. I want him to need me, to miss me, to realize he can't live without me. I want him to come home more in love than he left and know that distance doesn't affect my priorities.

Kold looks at the time on the phone and then back to me, biting his lip to stifle a smile. "I understand."

CHAPTER 46

Kold

Today has certainly been more productive than yesterday, and it's not even noon. Val and I switched phones before I left the house this morning after she agreed to field my calls and set up interviews. We spent the evening pouring over the details, discussing hard limits, and agreeing to a plan. Our safe word is *Divorce*, even though she refuses to marry me before I leave. If either of us so much as thinks about breaking up, I'll drop everything and come home.

Val keeps trying to convince me that this is a once-in-a-lifetime opportunity. But a viral video, a trending song, and being asked to join a national tour isn't my once-in-a-lifetime. She is. That song wouldn't even exist without her.

I shouldn't even consider leaving without her, but I'm holding out hope.

There's so much to do between now and the tour, and never as many hours in the day as one needs. I feel bad dropping my daily workload onto my brother's shoulders, but I'm leaving him my future wife, so hopefully, that'll help soften the blow. They're supposed to be at her place packing, but if yesterday was any indication, her box is the only one getting filled.

I pull out Val's phone and scroll through the contacts, stopping when I get to J. And there we are, Darc Jakobsson and Kold Jakobsson, labeled with our regular names like any old nobodies. I edit Darc's name to reflect his true nature, changing his contact to Evil Twin. Then, I amend mine to indicate my inevitable change in status. Digging around in Val's phone is all fun and games until my phone number pops up under a contact already labeled Hubby, and I quickly go from playful to unreasonably annoyed.

It's strange calling my own phone, but Val answers on the second ring.

"Hey, what's up? I promise I'm being good, and haven't carried any boxes to the car." The cheerful tone in her voice disarms me instantly. "If Darc didn't have that ridiculous sports car, we might've had this place empty before you got here."

Listening to how happy she sounds renders me temporarily mute.

"Babe, are you there? I'm going to hang up and call you back, okay? I can't hear anything." Val disconnects the call before the phone begins ringing in my hand.

"Hello! Is everything all right?" Her playful sweetness begins to teeter on the edge of concern. "Say something, please!"

"Darc, do you have your keys to the club on you? We have to go up there... I don't know... He called me, but I couldn't hear him, so I called back. And someone answered my phone, but no one's saying anything."

Snapping out of my trance, I get the words out in time to catch her at the door. "Hey, I'm here. Everything's fine."

"Babe, you scared me. I was about to send in the cavalry." Her relief floods the phone, washing over me.

"The fact that you think of my brother as the *cavalry* is concerning." I laugh to keep from being offended. Since the concert, I can't help but notice how highly she thinks of him. And I wonder if my star still shines as bright by comparison. "There isn't anything he's capable of that I'm not."

"Well," she huffs in faux exasperation, "I was referring to myself. Your brother was meant to be my ride and means of access, but I had every intention of saving you all on my own."

"Well, in that case, I take back everything I said. It might be fun seeing you come to my rescue. Maybe we could play hostage and hero before I leave. Darc could reprise his role as the bad guy, and you could kick the shit out of him." This is one of my favorite things about Val. I love when we can banter back and forth, building a story as we go. Reminds me of the night we first met.

She must have me on speaker because I hear Darc say, "Or the hero and villain could run off together and live happily ever after, leaving the pathetic hostage to fend for himself."

"Will you stop! You're gonna make him think we're over here doing something we're not. Why don't you put your muscles to good use and carry something to the car? Sorry about that. Did you need something, hun, or were you calling because you missed my voice?"

Hearing the way they talk to each other when I'm not in the room, I wonder what the odds are of Val forgetting I exist and choosing the brother who stayed. Leaving without her feels like a mistake, but she refuses to entertain my suggestions. If I offer to quit, she tells me to go. If I beg her to follow, she tells me she can't. I'm damned if I do and damned if I don't. Neither of us wants to be apart, but she won't allow for other options.

"Well, I do miss you, but I was calling to let you know I'll be heading out of here in the next hour or so. I was able to get a lot more accomplished this morning, thanks to you. How have things been on your end? Did you have fun going through my phone?" If Val jokingly admits to digging through my phone, looking for dirt, then I don't have to feel guilty about looking in hers.

"There's been a handful of calls, but I have everything written down, so we can talk about it later. Other than that, I've been packing and entertaining your brother with stories about my past. He keeps wandering off and coming back with random items, insisting on context and a full backstory. It might have been quicker to pack without him, to be honest."

"I'm glad you two are having fun."

"Yeah. Unfortunately, being around him isn't the same as having you, and I want to spend every second with you while I can. If missing you hurts this bad already, what's it going to feel like when you can't come home at night?"

"You know I don't have to go." I pack a stack of files into my computer bag and grab my coat from the back of the chair. The rest of my work can be done at home on the computer while Val is resting comfortably beside me. No reason to stay away longer than necessary.

"I keep telling myself everything is going to be fine because the alternative is too painful to consider. But what if it's not fine? What if we lose each other? I would never recover."

"We aren't going to let that happen. I can't survive without you either."

"Jesus, you two are depressing. You know he isn't going to make it one day on tour with you at home, crying about how much you can't live without him." Darc's observation seems to strike a nerve, prompting a change in Val's attitude.

"Darc's right. I need to *buck up, buttercup* if we're going to make it through the next few months. I'm gonna finish packing, and I'll see you when you get here. Love you."

Of all the possible word combinations that exist in the English language, *Darc's right* has got to be in my top five least favorites of all time.

Val

Seeing a small pile of boxes in the living room makes me emotional. I have to keep reminding myself that I've already taken things to the house, and Darc loaded both of our cars to the roof. Not that his stupid, panty-dropper sports car holds much. How the hell are you going to offer to help someone move, then show up in your Lamborghini? You'd think he could've borrowed the neighbor's truck or something.

Most likely reading the sadness written on my face, Darc sits on the couch and opens his arm, signaling his desire for me to join him. "Come on. This is the only time I get to spend with you here in your element. Indulge me with a cuddle while we wait for Mr. I Drive a Fancy SUV."

Darc has clearly taken offense to my light-hearted jabs about his ostentatious choice of vehicle. So, as a way of offering my amends, I sit as close as I can without being on top of him. Resting my head against his chest while his arms encase me in quiet fondness.

"I wanted to thank you for helping me today and for indulging me yesterday. I feel bad I never got a chance to tell you how much I loved the flowers I received on Christmas. I should've known straight away they were from you."

He pulls me in tighter and kisses the top of my head. "You don't have to thank me, Valentine. Spending time with you and seeing you smile is all I ever needed. The seconds I steal with you have to hold me over for a lifetime, so let me enjoy them while I can."

I look up at him, brushing my fingertips over the curve of his jaw. "It makes me sad when you say shit like that." My lips pucker as I close my eyes and propel my body forward to where I find him waiting.

It's not surprising when he meets me halfway. I expect that. What surprises me is the feeling I get in my chest when he kisses me. The tightness feels like ratchet straps and zip ties and rubber bands, threatening to compress me down to dust.

"I never want to be the reason you're sad." His voice is a whisper, as though he's sharing a secret. "If you let me, I could make you happy."

I don't want to lose control, but it's hard to know what the right decision is when they're around me. My heart and my head never seem to agree from one minute to the next, constantly turning over in midair like a coin flip. It must be exhausting, living inside my head, always fighting to be heard and constantly compromising.

"Once your brother leaves, it'll be me and you, alone, twenty-four-seven." I make an exaggerated face to express my horror. "You'll be sick of looking at me after a week."

It hasn't hit me yet that Kold will be leaving, and I'll be alone. I keep secretly hoping that it's a joke they're both playing, trying to get a rise out of me. If I let myself believe what he's been saying, I'd fall to pieces, and he'd stay with me so that I wouldn't have to be sad.

"My brother's an idiot. If you were mine, nothing could pull me away. In fact, I'm looking forward to tomorrow. Twenty-four hours with my fake girlfriend. Zero sharing."

Something about the way he says, *fake girlfriend*, digs under my skin and drives like nails into my soul. It hurts, even though I know he doesn't mean anything by it. Sadly, feelings and logic rarely run in the same circles, and I'm upset before I can convince myself not to be. I pull away, get up from the couch, and grab a box as I head for the door.

"I'm going to the house to start unloading my car. I'll come back and help when my *real boyfriend* gets here." My hand closes around the handle of the door, steadying the tremble in my fingers. Walking away has always been my go-to nonverbal cue, signaling to anyone who might care that I'm on the verge of breaking down.

"Valentine, stop!" The commanding nature of his voice causes me to freeze in my tracks as alarm bells ring, warning me of his proximity. The door is open, but I have yet to cross its threshold when he steps beside me and removes the box from my hands, setting it on the ground at our feet. "Don't you dare walk away from me!"

"Why? What does it matter? You don't care, and neither do I." The force of my lie convinces no one within earshot. "I'm nothing to you, and you're not anything to me."

Darc grabs me by the arms, halting my forward progress. "Well, now you're being mean."

"Let go of me!" I shout, unconscious of my current surroundings. My voice echoes down the hall in both directions, louder than I intend. Luckily, it's a Tuesday afternoon, so the majority of the people living on this floor will most likely be at work.

"No. I'll let go of you when you stop pretending to be mad at me." Darc pulls me to the side and tacks me to the wall, pinning me with his body. An hour ago, there was a coat rack standing here, but it has since been packed away, leaving room for this moment. "I sat on that couch, holding you in my arms, telling you how much I want to be the one giving you the world. I told you again, for the hundredth time, that I want to make you happy. That I would never leave you. Then, I make one stupid comment, in jest, and somehow, that negates our entire morning. You know I don't think of you as my *fake girlfriend*. You're the only real thing I have."

I drop my eyes, too ashamed to meet his gaze and watch as the cotton of his t-shirt stretches tight against his chest every time his lungs expand. My mind wanders past the fibers, pulling up images of the inked skin below. Darc's tattoos are the mirror opposite of his brother's, covering the left side of his chest and half that arm, filling in every square inch of his back, and wrapping around his right arm down to the wrist. His right leg is also sleeved to the ankle, which makes my mouth water thinking about it. Identical twins through and through, the guys were committed enough to cloak their bodies in matching tattoos but individual enough to put them on opposite sides.

"Look at me," Darc says, placing his hand under my chin. "If I could make you mine, I would. I would hold on and never let go. But I don't get the option of spending forever with you. I'm lucky I get anything at all."

Reflexively, I wrap my arms around Darc's waist, wanting to erase the pain I hear buried in his assertion. "I know. I'm sorry. I shouldn't have said what I said." My misplaced anger was never meant for him, but he was the only one around. "I've been feeling unimportant. Like I'm a fake fiancée and fake girlfriend in a fake life that I don't even recognize. Your brother is leaving me, and I want to scream at him, but I can't. I have to smile and lie and encourage him to go because that's what he should do. But I want him to love me enough to choose me, and he doesn't. If I tell him how I feel, maybe he'll stay, but then everyone will blame me when he throws this chance away. When the time comes, he's going to leave, and he's going to forget all about me because I never mattered as much as he thought I did. Why am I moving in if he isn't going to be there? Nothing makes sense anymore."

"Have you tried having this conversation with him, or is this the first time you're saying any of this out loud?" Darc closes the door and takes my hand, walking me back over to the couch. "I get it. There's a lot changing all at once, and you feel a little off-balance. That makes perfect sense, but I can assure you that none of what you said is true. I hate seeing you disappointed. If you need him that badly, you should tell him. I can go on the tour in his place, and then you won't have to be upset."

I sink back into him, making myself at home in his arms. "What makes you think I'd be any happier losing you?"

Darc sees himself as a temporary fixture in my life, but I'm not sure I believe in that sentiment anymore. Initially, I would have thought it impossible to carry on a relationship with either one of them, let alone both. When it comes to self-confidence, I'm running on a quarter tank at best. These guys deserve tens across the board, and most of the time, I feel like a four-point-two. Or rather, I did before they started feeding my ego and investing in my stock.

Now, I can't imagine my life without them.

CHAPTER 47
Kold

When I arrived at Val's apartment, I noticed the boxes had already been packed and loaded into the car, except for a small pile of things near the door. I walked in, not entirely sure what to expect, and found myself painfully under-prepared for the sight awaiting me. Sex I can handle, but finding them asleep on the couch together was a harder pill to swallow.

Once she woke up and realized I was there, Val made me the center of her attention, but even that couldn't dislodge the seeds that were already planted. There's not a single doubt remaining in my mind that I'm in love with Val, and she's in love with me, but if I leave her for any amount of time, I'm going to lose her. Why would she waste her hours missing me when there's an identical copy waiting for her downstairs?

I need to find a way to convince her that joining me on tour is the only reasonable option. Otherwise, I'm tearing up the contract and staying home.

As Darc and I carry her couch into the garage, I play the conversation over in my head. Once the script is sufficiently revised and copied to memory, I find Val inside and make a suggestion. "Will you take the dogs for a walk with me?"

A smile brightens her face as she lifts onto the balls of her feet to kiss me. "I would love to."

Val told me from the beginning that the key to her heart was free. Effort made would consistently amount to more than money spent, despite the quality of the gift. She wasn't interested in affection that had been bought and paid for. Her time didn't come with an hourly rate. And while I tried to impress her with upscale reservations, hotel suites, in-room massages, VIP concert packages, and a diamond big enough to be taken seriously in every social circle, asking her to join me for a walk has meant more than any of it.

So, when a woman tells you point blank what makes her happy, don't waste time questioning her intentions. Believe her.

Walking down the street, hand in hand, led by dogs in little coats, Val and I are the picture of happiness. It's hard to believe that either of us would be willing to gamble on the outcome of our future, and yet here we are.

"I printed out a copy of the tour schedule and a contract that I'd like for you to read over." I need Val to choose me again and again, especially when she has every option available to her.

"You know I'm more than happy to help you in any way that I can, but I wouldn't know the first thing about tour contracts and legalese. It would be better if you took the paperwork to a lawyer."

"That's fantastic advice, and you'll be happy to know that I sent the tour agreement to our attorney as soon as I received it, and it was pretty standard. The contract I need you to read over is for you." I match her pace as we coast to a stop, and the dogs await an indication that it's time to return home.

"Yeah. I mean, that makes sense. I guess I hadn't given much thought to getting a prenup, but you have significantly more assets than I do. I can understand why you feel you'd need something like that." Val sounds like someone who's pretending to be okay while slowly dying inside.

"Babe, it's not a prenup. You already know I'd give you everything." Come to think of it, maybe Val's on to something. If I sign a prenup, giving her the balance of my savings in the event of my infidelity or abandonment, maybe that would be enough to ease her mind. Since I know that I'll never cheat and I'll never leave, I'd have no problem backing up my claims with every cent I've got.

"It's a contract of employment, and I would like for you to consider my offer before saying no."

Thankfully, the sun is shining, and the wind is lacking its usual end-of-the-year bite. Otherwise, we might all freeze to death waiting for Val's reaction. I give her hand a squeeze to check that she's still with me and find relief in the responding pressure she returns.

"Should we finish the loop and continue our conversation, or would you rather head back to the house?" I'd like to talk while we're free from distractions. "I wish you'd say something."

"I'm sorry, I was still thinking about prenups and... It doesn't matter. Yes. Let's continue the loop, and you can give me your best elevator pitch." Val flashes me a smile, laces her fingers into mine, and takes a step in her desired direction.

The contract for employment that I had drawn up offers her the financial security she requires to feel safe and enough independence to avoid feeling trapped. It's a legitimate offer based upon her education and skill set, with a perks package reflective of my love for her. I have an entire speech at the ready, but maybe this isn't the right time.

I cup the side of Val's neck in my hand and dip down to kiss her. "Let's talk about something else, shall we? After all, there are more pressing matters to discuss."

She lifts up to kiss me again, and I'm eager to meet her halfway. Val's kiss is one of many things I have come to require. "I have no idea what you're talking about, but I'm certain you will enlighten me. Might I request that said enlightenment take place as we walk? I'm beginning to chill in my bones, and the children are shivering."

"Alright, let's go, you bunch of freeze-babies. Let's get moving and get the blood flowing." I take Val's hand and set a healthy pace, eager to get home under a blanket after our conversation has been completed. "Now that you're officially moved in, I need to clear out half of my closet and sacrifice another drawer of my dresser."

Val laughs over quickened steps as our boots thump in measured time along the sidewalk. "You're the one who *begged* me to move in, and now you're talking about making sacrifices. Ha! Darc didn't have an issue giving me half of his dresser. Maybe I should ask if he can spare any room in his closet?" Her tone is playful, and I'm tempted to give her a solid crack on the ass for making jokes, but secretly I love the way she teases me.

"Oh, hardy har har. Aren't you hilarious? Is this what I have to look forward to, you pitting us against each other in order to get your way? Because I can tell you right now, it'll work like a charm every time." I'm fully prepared to give her anything, including half of my closet.

"You know I was only joking." Val reaches down to lift a panting Christmas from his feet. "Maybe we should go on a date tonight since the rest of your week is booked solid."

At the mere mention of a date, I scoop midnight from the ground, ready to get home and into a hot shower. Val rarely allows me to spoil her, but I have an idea she might enjoy. If there's even a chance that we'll be spending time apart in the near future, I want her to have several reasons to think about me.

"I know the perfect place, and we can get dinner after."

Val and I are both fond of reading, though our preferred genres are vastly different. My bookshelves are loaded with horror novels and science fiction series, while Val loves all things romance. I had an idea that maybe we could go to the bookstore and each pick out a couple of books that we'd like to read. Then I'd buy two copies of each, and we could start our own two-person reading club.

Being on the road can get boring, especially when you have a good reason to behave. I thought reading something together could be a nice distraction, since we'll both need something to keep us from counting down the days and constantly missing one another. Plus, reading the same book would give us something to talk about.

I know that Val gets scared easily, so my plan was to forgo the horror section altogether and choose books with alien love scenes. Maybe something with tentacles or ice giants. I need her horny enough to have phone sex with me but not so horny that she skips my calls and spends the day in bed with my brother.

"Any idea where the darkling is taking you tomorrow on your date?" I've been trying not to think about it, but Wednesday is nearly upon us.

"I'm not sure where we're going. All your brother said was that I should be ready for the best first date I've ever been on. Whatever that means." With a smirky little smile that I adore beyond measure, Val winks at me and places Christmas back on the ground. "Unless Darc intends to propose, I think he's got some stiff competition."

I hadn't considered that a possibility, but now that she's mentioned it in passing as though it's no big deal, I can't help but wonder if I should be concerned. Knowing my brother, he's already bought a ring, and I doubt he'd feel guilty about asking her to choose.

As much as she claims to hate our sibling rivalry, Val certainly knows how to make a guy feel like he's got to fight for her attention. I guess I'd better step up my game while she's still mine to lose.

Returning Midnight to the sidewalk, I take Val's hand and fold our fingers together. Her skin is cold, and I wish I had thought to grab a pair of gloves. Thankfully, I run hot, and now that the dogs are back to walking on their own, she's able to slip the leash around her wrist and stuff her other hand into a jacket pocket.

"Do I even want to ask what your answer might be if he were brash enough to pop the question?"

"Well, you know how much I love diamonds, as evident by my massive jewelry collection." Val never wears jewelry. Besides her engagement ring, I'm not certain she owns any.

"Be serious for one second." I assume there's a degree of honesty in every playful response, but I need to know to what extent she sees him as an option.

"Okay. Well, my serious answer is that in the highly unlikely event of your brother randomly proposing marriage, I'm not sure what my answer would be. I can only be married to one person at a time, and I want that person to be you."

"You have an exceptional talent for leaving the door open."

"I'm not entirely sure you mean that as a compliment." Val pauses our walk to meet my eyes. "If you don't want me going out with Darc tomorrow, you can say that. I'll blow off whatever he has planned and spend the day in bed with a book. Honestly, I'm still struggling to figure out what you both want, and I'm striving to keep everyone happy, but all of that is secondary. At the beginning, middle, and end of my day, *you* are my priority."

"I know. That's why I want you to go out and have fun." My feelings on the topic remain mixed. "I'm sure he's looking forward to it, and I know he'll go out of his way to make you feel special."

"Alright, new topic. I'm done talking about your brother. Tell me what the plan is for the rest of this week."

We make our way towards the house, hand in hand, reviewing the detailed timeline for the days ahead. As I list off the hours and obligations that foreshadow our impending separation, Val wears her usual encouraging smile and continues to remind me that this tour is a once-in-a-lifetime opportunity.

I want to disagree. I want to argue my points and discuss the details until she lets me stay home. If she refuses to cave, I want to stomp my feet and insist that she join me on the road. I want to stop being reasonable and start fighting for the future we planned. But why would I waste our time bickering when we have so few moments remaining?

"I wish we could spend more time together." Val steals the words from my mouth, rendering me temporarily speechless. "I miss you when you're not around."

Bringing her left hand to my lips, I leave a kiss on her ring finger and revise my standard promise. "After this tour, we'll spend the rest of our lives together."

"You promise?" Her eyes pool with the verity her smile attempts to hide.

Pulling her into my arms, I allow the strength of my embrace time to fully register, and for a moment, there's no viral video, national tour, cheating ex, flirtatious twin brother, cold breeze, or panting dogs at our feet. There's only Val and I and the love we share for one another.

"You have my word."

CHAPTER 48

Val

This morning, when I awoke, I was anticipating a limo parked in front of the house or a helicopter in the backyard, primed and ready to whisk us away to some mountainside chalet. At the very least, I thought I would feel Darc in bed next to me, but when I opened my eyes, I was alone. No massive bouquets of my favorite flowers, no pristinely wrapped packages holding new clothes or expensive jewelry, not even a cup of coffee on the nightstand.

After I got dressed and went downstairs, I discovered more of the same. Nothing had changed from the day before. I started to wonder if I had slept through Wednesday altogether and woken up at some point later in the week.

I checked the kitchen, letting the dogs out the backdoor to run a lap around the yard while I poked my head into the office. Kold left me a note on the kitchen island, so I knew he was already at work, but Darc was nowhere to be found.

Running low on places to search, I checked the garage and found his shiny black sports car parked in its usual spot. That's when I heard a faint clanging coming from down the hallway and located Darc working out in the gym. I watched from the doorway for a few minutes before he noticed, stopping mid-set to join me where I stood.

"Had to make sure I was looking good for you, this being our first date and all. My nerves had me awake half the night." I might have assumed he was joking, except that his voice lacked its usual cockiness.

"You're nervous about going out with me? That's funny." I pulled up from my heels and steadied myself by pressing both hands to his firm chest so that my words could be whispered in his ear. "Don't go getting too sappy on me. I kinda like it when you're an asshole."

Unsurprisingly, my flirtatious comment led me into his shower and then landed me in his bed. We've had sex every day since the threesome, even though the agreement was for twice a month. I kept expecting Kold to care, but he didn't. In fact, he seemed more upset about Darc and me sleeping fully dressed on the couch together than he'd ever been about us having sex.

After a second round of showers, Darc suggested I keep my attire casual before tossing me jeans and a t-shirt from the dresser in his bedroom. Nothing about Darc is ever casual. The guy lives and breathes high-end. The clothing he wears, his collection of watches, his office, his car, his job, his online presence, everything screams, *I have money, and I'm not afraid to spend it.*

When he told me we were going to an adult arcade and throwing axes on our date, I had to double-check his tattoos to make sure I had the right brother at home with me. Then, I pressed the back of my hand to his forehead to make sure he was feeling okay.

Once we were dressed and ready to go, he left me staggering and stuttering when he tossed me his keys and told me I was driving.

"I... I... I can... I can't... Darc, I can't drive your car." My words continued to stumble through my brain as I watched him laugh and get into the passenger seat.

If you've never driven a sports car that costs as much as a house, let me tell you, it's an experience. The sound of the engine was enough to make me squirm in my seat. Then factor in the man seated beside me and I'm surprised we made it out of the driveway without having sex.

And now, here we are, playing video games before indulging in an afternoon of ax hurling.

"Anytime I think I have you figured out, you do something unexpected." Watching Darc crush my score on a gigantic Pac-Man arcade cabinet is both interesting and infuriating. Why do they have to be so good at everything?

"Kold and I love this place. A friend of ours from high school owns it, and we like to sneak up here once in a while when it's quiet. I'm glad he never thought to bring you here so I could do it first."

These two find a way to turn even the simplest act into a competition. Is this what I have to look forward to, a lifetime of each brother trying to one-up the other? I imagine myself dangling precariously in the center, patiently waiting to be collateral damage.

"Jakobsson party to the ax pit." A voice comes over the loudspeaker. "Darc, get that sweet ass over here."

If the voice overhead had been female, I might have experienced a twinge of jealousy. Instead, I find myself laughing as Darc takes my hand. He seems to know exactly where he's going, winding a path through the flashing lights and digital sounds. I follow a step behind, with our arms outstretched between us.

Waiting for us at the ax throwing station is a nice-looking man with medium brown hair and a grin that stretches clear across his face. "Now, hold on a minute. This isn't the future Mrs. Jakobsson, is it?" The man extends his hand, meeting me with his eyes. "I've heard a thing or two about you from my brother, but his description didn't do you justice. Probably because he's smart enough to be terrified of your boyfriends."

All I can do is smile and hope that Darc takes over the conversation. Thankfully, he doesn't leave me hanging for long. "Valentine, this is Casey. Corey's brother."

It takes me a second to put two and two together, but eventually, the pieces fall into place. "Corey from the band? Nice. Is he freaking out about everything that's going on, or is he like Kold and can't be bothered with normal human emotions?"

The smile on Casey's face remains, but it's more strained than it was initially. "I think everyone's reserving their excitement, for the time being, waiting to see if Kold backs out at the last second."

He seems to be exerting quite a bit of effort, trying to convince me everything's fine. "Maybe you'd be willing to part with this one for a few months."

I give Darc's hand a squeeze and lean against his arm. "Probably not, if I have any say in the matter." I mirror Casey's forced smile as he attempts to sort out which part of his statement I responded to, studying my face for clues. "Kold can make his own choices. He doesn't need my permission."

This tour seems to have everyone on edge, and Casey's reaction to meeting me has confirmed my suspicions. Despite my fiancé's claims to the contrary, if he backs out at any point, everyone is going to blame *me*.

"Normally, I would believe that, having known the guy for over twenty years, but he doesn't seem like himself lately." Casey's smile fades, and his eyes narrow. "It would be a real shame if..."

"It would be a real shame if you finished that sentence in a way I deemed disrespectful to my girl." Darc cuts in, stepping forward enough to make his intentions clear. Anyone who wishes to get to me will have to go through him first. "You're standing on a line I suggest you not cross. Why don't you send someone to take our order? While I explain the mechanics of ax throwing to my date."

Casey swallows the lump in his throat and walks away without further exchange, allowing space for any tension to evaporate.

"Are you good? If you don't want to stay here, we can go somewhere else. I'm fine with whatever, so it's up to you. I never want you to feel uncomfortable." Darc is getting to be as bad as Kold. Both guys automatically defer to my needs, and I wish they wouldn't.

"You know, I don't always want or need the final say, although I do appreciate the offer. If you're good to stay, then we should stay." So long as Casey's willing to drop it, I'm nearly certain conflict can be avoided. "This is the date you chose for us, and I'd like to continue with whatever you have planned."

Darc hangs our coats on the back of a tall chair at the high-top bar attached to the throwing area, then pulls me in for a hug.

"Should we keep score? The winner gets a prize of their choice from the loser?"

I consider my options for a moment and agree. Worst case, depending on what he asks for, I can parle the bet on a round of bowling. I've been knocking down pins since I was a kid and captained my school league in both high school and college. I'm what you might call a ringer, but it's a skill I rarely admit to. You never know when you might need to hustle a guy out of some money, and no one ever expects a girl like me to be good at bowling, of all things.

If Darc wins at ax throwing, he'll most likely ask for sex, which is a complete and total waste of a prize because he's already going to get that. Whereas I intend to ask for something he's previously refused to give me. Looks like it's time to stop being cute and get competitive.

As the waitress walks over to take our order, Kold's phone begins vibrating in my pocket. I think it's endearing that he has me listed as *My Love* since it holds true even when we switch phones.

My Love: That asshole took you to Headliners on your date?!? Without me? Unbelievable! The nerve of some people! Also, don't play him in Pac-Man. It's his favorite.

: Hahaha. I'll let him know that he is OFFICIALLY dead to you. How'd you know where we were? And how's the interview going? Tell Corey I met his brother.

"Do you want your usual?" Darc brushes my arm to make sure he has my attention. "I ordered a bunch of random stuff. Do you want anything else?"

"I'm always willing to accept anything you offer. You know what I like." Flirting with him is all too easy.

"I do indeed. And I'll be giving you that as soon as we get home." Darc takes pleasure in making me blush, and I enjoy letting him.

My love: I downloaded the tracking app we use and added you to our family plan. When it pinned the location of my phone, I messaged you. Now, if I leave, you'll always know what city I'm in.

My Love: Corey said hello. He also wanted me to tell you that his brother is an asshole and that you should ignore him… I'm not even going to ask what happened because I know you won't tell me.

My Love: We finished with the building tour, and now we're sitting around while they set up for the next shot. They want to film us on stage, and then we're headed over to the practice spot. They also want shots of us walking around the city and sitting at some bars, but I only agreed to film at a bar if they used ours. This shit is going to take all night.

My Love: Have fun on your date, and remember I love you more. I'll be home at some point tonight, but I'm not sure what time. Have Darc show you the app, and you can follow my movements through the city. Get a bullseye for me! I love you.

My Love: One last thing. Don't worry about answering any calls. You have us pretty well booked, so anyone who calls can leave a message, and you and I can sort it out tomorrow.

Kold's messages come in rapid fire, one right after the next, leaving me enough time to read what he's typed without an opportunity to respond.

: Try to remember that everything happening is supposed to be fun. Enjoy it! I'm not sure what the plan is for tonight, but once you get home, I'm looking forward to hearing about your day. Love you for a lifetime and well into the next.

I slip the phone into my coat pocket, not wanting to be preoccupied while I have a deadly weapon in my hand. The last thing I need is to get distracted by an incoming text and slice off my own ear. Darc is meticulous while explaining the dos and don'ts, giving me plenty of time to practice before we begin keeping track of our points. For fun, he brought his Christmas present with him to throw at the target while I worked on perfecting my technique.

Surprisingly, hurling axes at wood targets is easier than I expected and a lot more fun. When the waitress delivers our food and a second round of drinks, the score is tied at thirty. I'm feeling pretty good about my chances until Darc hits a bullseye dead center, followed by another.

Walking together to retrieve our hatchets, I pause in front of the wooden wall at the end of the throwing box and wait for Darc to look at me. "Can I ask you something?" I ask, waiting long enough to get a response and not a second longer. "Have you ever killed anyone with an ax?"

Darc's eyebrows pinch together as he cocks his head to one side. "If you thought I was capable of something like that, would you still be on a date with me?"

I turn my head to look at him while yanking my ax from the four-point circle. "Is that a serious question? Because if it's a serious question, I'm willing to give you an honest answer."

When he doesn't respond, I continue. "I think you're fully capable of such a thing, and I'm here. So, I guess if a guy is sexy and rich and fucks as hard as he loves, a woman is willing to overlook damn near anything."

I end on what seems like a light-hearted joke, even though I answered his question truthfully. Maybe the guys aren't exactly what I think they are, but they certainly aren't saints. There are skeletons piled floor to ceiling in each of their closets, and whether they killed them or not is irrelevant. Maybe I should be scared. Perhaps I should walk away while I still can. But where would I go, and who would I be when I got there?

"You never cease to amaze me, Valentine. And just when I was about to ask you something important." He strolls back to the throwing line and drops his ax into the box.

"Well, come on then," I say, taking my place by his side after depositing my ax back into the holder. "Don't leave a girl in suspense."

We exit the throwing area and take a seat at the bar, reacquainting ourselves with the boatload of food Darc ordered and a fresh round of drinks. I take the seat holding our coats, but resist the temptation to check Kold's phone for a new text or any missed calls. Darc sits next to me, sliding his hand between my thighs.

"Since you're engaged to my brother, it would be rude of me to ask you to be my wife, but what would you say to being my girlfriend?" He asks as though it's a normal request and not the strangest situation in history. "Meaning, I would only be with you."

I set my jaw, locking my teeth together to keep from screaming *yes* at the top of my lungs. Being in this position with Darc, while exciting, sounds like I'm doubling my chance at heartbreak. There's no way I can keep a guy like this satisfied, let alone two of them. Kold is going on the road, and Darc will be back in the club until the wee hours of the morning. A tracking app isn't going to help me sleep at night when their dots are both away from home.

Kold

My fingers tap along to the beat of a new song as I avoid checking Val's current location. I'm not sure why I expect anything to change from one minute to the next, but my curiosity remains thoroughly disinterested in making the acquaintance of logic. By three o'clock, they were at home and have remained there all evening. So, they either had the worst date imaginable and spent the entire day fighting, or they couldn't keep their hands off each other, and it's been a sexual free-for-all.

Changing the station to something heavier, I look for a distraction in the growled screams and vibrating drum beats of death metal. There was a moment during the early history of the band when we toyed with the idea of playing this kind of music, but the guys said I was too pretty, and the whole point of being in a band was to get women. So, we settled on pop-punk-rock and hoped for the best.

I never had a problem getting laid, so for me, the band was never about meeting girls. It was an escape from the preplanned existence my parents had laid out since I was a kid. Being a rock star was never the goal. In fact, none of us expected it to last this long, but when you have a packed venue at your fingertips, it isn't difficult to grow a following. Now, in our mid-thirties, we all have a laundry list of priorities that stand front and center, making the band nothing more than a *hobby*.

I speed down the highway, well over the posted limit, still trying to distract my thoughts. As I reflect on the day, I can't help but wish Val had been with me.

Fuck!

The second I think about her, I'm undone. This fake dating relationship she's got going on with Darc is driving me to the threshold of my sanity. I'm so afraid of losing her, even though she assures me that it's impossible. Their sexual connection was supposed to last one night before turning into twice a month and becoming a daily occurrence.

Usually, I despise the twenty-minute drive from the club and how it steals my time. If I could spend every second with Val, I would. Tonight, however, my feelings have shifted. Knowing they're together for twenty-four hours on what could be their first date in a lifetime of many has me struggling to find where I fit in.

Coming down our street, I spot Val's car parked in the driveway and comment to myself, "One of these days, she's going to let me spoil her."

Is it terrible that every time I see her car, I want to take it to the dealership and trade it in for something new? I refrain because I'm smart enough to know she'd be pissed at me for a week. It might have been a risk I'd be willing to take if I wasn't staring down the barrel of a three-month separation.

My legs feel abnormally heavy as I drag myself up the walkway to the front door. Waiting for me behind the glass, I can see and hear the pair of monochrome monsters I have come to love. I'm only one foot in the door when Midnight stands up on my legs, begging for a hug, while Christmas attempts to gain my attention from behind her.

"Okay, I see you. Give Dad one second to get his coat off, and then you'll get your hugs." The words spoken out of habit conjure a clear image in my head. For a moment, I picture a pair of children in human form, both with their father's light blonde hair and their mother's crystal blue eyes.

For the time being, our children are shaped like furry loaves of bread, with bug eyes black as night, and I wouldn't have it any other way. Once they have each received a hug, the dogs retreat back to the living room, claiming their usual spot by the fire.

Val and Darc are mid-conversation as I walk into the room, a movie playing softly in the background. Sitting on either end of the couch, Darc is massaging her feet while she digs into the muscle of his calf. "Does that hurt or help?" she asks, as her hands knead the tattooed flesh.

"It feels amazing, in a painful way. If that makes sense. I don't know why, but I keep getting a charley horse in that leg when I'm sleeping."

Again, I feel like a spirit hovering invisibly in the corner, forced to witness the life I could've had. Only I'm not invisible. Val smiled at me the second I walked into the room. My bruised ego keeps trying to convince me that I'm in second place, even though my girl constantly assures me that my top spot is a lock.

"Next time I go to the grocery store, I'm buying you bananas." She says, giving his leg a teasing smack. "So, come on, rock star, tell us about your day."

There's a playfulness to Val's request that I find endearing, but her use of the word *us*, as innocent as it may be, sets my teeth on edge. Since when are my brother and my fiancée an *us*?

I should be the one sitting on the couch with her feet in my lap, worshiping every inch of her from the base of her toes to the top of her head. Caressing her delicate skin with the tips of my fingers and the palms of my hands. He doesn't deserve to touch her. He might wear my face, but that doesn't mean we have the same heart, and even if he does share my soul, it changes nothing. Val is my other half, my better half, the best thing about me, and I can't lose her.

"Most of the day felt like a game of hurry up and wait. They wanted to get footage of us on stage at the club, at the bars around town where we've played, at local landmarks, and even at the old high school. You know, back where it all began, or some bullshit. The best was when we stopped at Served Kold, and they did some interviews with the local drunks. Elliot was there, and boy, did he have a story to tell." I look at Darc with a knowing expression, and we both laugh.

"Wait a minute. Do you guys own Served Kold? I mean, I guess it's pretty obvious now that I say the name out loud and think about the spelling. How did I never realize that before?"

I love the way Val flusters when she realizes something she now perceives as obvious. As if the entire room is looking at her through the lens of judgment and silently questioning her intelligence.

"Have you been there?" I ask, eyeing her suspiciously as Darc mirrors my expression. Unlike Darc's club, the bar that displays my name is not a place I would want the love of my life to visit unless under my protection. It draws a notoriously rough crowd of bikers and ex-cons. The beers are cheap, and the bartenders are a group of tattooed vixens who were looking to go straight after doing some time behind bars. I also employ two barbacks who were looking for something full-time outside of the local MMA octagon. Turns out it's more fun to crack skulls behind the bar than inside the ring, and the pay is better.

"I've been there a handful of times over the summer. A girl from work wanted to go, and I was the only person in the office with tattoos. She probably figured that having me there might help her blend in. The first time we went, there was a band playing. I loved the whole *stage behind a chain link fence* vibe. After that, I was hooked." Val pauses, taking in my expression. "It's a cool place. It's too bad we didn't run into each other while I was there. Could've skipped past the whole *me and Allen* thing."

Whoever's running the ship at the moment, recalling memories of wild nights and laughing off the danger as if it never existed, is not my girl, but I am intrigued by her. The Val I know is calculated. She's willing to step full face into danger, but only in defense of another.

"Valentine! You're not to step one foot inside that bar unless one of us is with you, do you understand?" Darc's sudden appearance in the conversation catches me by surprise, even though he's stolen the words from my mouth.

"Let us not forget who won today's ax-throwing competition." A tone of condescension rings in her voice, one I'm not accustomed to hearing. "I'm more than capable of taking care of myself, and I will go anywhere I choose. I don't answer to you, and Kold is leaving." Her words hit like a shot of rock salt to the chest, stinging long past the initial blow.

The pair of them seemed so happy when I walked in, and now it appears a fight may be brewing on the horizon. Am I the reason for the sudden tension? Is my presence unwanted? Or is it the realization I'm leaving that's set her teetering atop a knife's edge?

"Perhaps we could swing by tomorrow and have a liquid lunch. You're still going to the office with me in the morning, right?" I attempt to quell the tension by honoring her request. If Val wants to throw caution to the wind while I'm away, I'll make damn sure everyone knows who's standing beside her. Present or not, our name means something in this city, and all the wrong people know enough to be scared.

"Tomorrow morning, I'm at your service. As for the liquid lunch, it's a date." Val smiles at me, accepting my words as an acknowledgment of her victory. Something about her is different, and I'm not entirely confident this change is for the better. Hopefully, my girl will be back by morning because I have a series of questions I want to ask, and I'm not sure Little Miss Tough Girl is going to give me the answers I need to hear.

My stomach growls, and I stand, needing to locate food before I succumb to my hunger and die. "Have you guys eaten? I'm starved."

"We made pizza," Val says with a wink. "There's still quite a bit left in the kitchen if you're willing to indulge in a few carbs."

"At this point, I would eat a loaf of bread and a stick of butter if someone left it out on the counter for me."

I sneak a look back over my shoulder as I make my way down the hallway to the kitchen, two small dogs prancing at my feet, looking to inhale any crumbs I should care to drop. Val and Darc remain quiet behind me, but I catch sight of him leaning forward to kiss her, assuming the coast is clear. Perhaps it was my presence that altered the mood, after all.

In the kitchen, I find what appears to be two partially eaten, homemade pizzas. So, this is what they've been doing at home all evening. Having a free date and cuddling on the couch with a movie they can't be bothered to watch because it would mean tearing their eyes off of one another for more than five seconds. How does he seem to know her better than I do?

No. Not better. I refuse to believe that. He knows what I know because I was stupid enough to tell him.

Reaching into the cupboard to grab a plate, something in the sink catches my eye. Lying there, with sauce crusted along its edge, is *my* pizza ax. They used my goddamn Christmas present on their fucking date!

"I Hate You Both!" I shout from where I'm standing at the sink, certain the sound will travel. Then I shake my head, certain I couldn't mean the words I'm saying even if I wanted to, and mumble them again to myself, "I hate you both."

CHAPTER 49

Val

Retrieving my apartment keys from his pocket, Kold sets them on the counter without letting me go. The realization of what's happening pulls sharply into focus as I attempt to hide in the fading comfort of his embrace. We both know this hug will be our last and when it ends, the possibility of our future together becomes a memory, fading away to nothing. I can already feel myself disappearing. Once I pack everything back into my car, it'll be like I was never here, and his life will be no worse for the wear. I've only held Kold back temporarily. Not long enough to stifle his immense potential. He's on the cusp of being famous, and he's taking his friends with him, but there's no place for me in that life.

My mind plays out worse-case scenarios while Kold drives into work, his hand casually resting on my thigh. He's been quiet most of the morning, even though our night ended on a high note. I insisted that Darc accept a raincheck for our Wednesday night sleepover and made my way upstairs, where I found my future husband waiting with open arms.

Even though I assured him I was staying, Kold was hell-bent on stealing away any possible regret I might have about my decision. He spent nearly half an hour worshiping my body before making love to me. Even now, when I close my eyes, I can feel him releasing inside me as he professed his unwavering devotion.

Unfortunately, the morning brought with it a painful

reminder that we're living on borrowed time, counting down the seconds until we're forced to say goodbye. Kold's phone was already lighting up with messages and notifications as we stood naked in front of the bathroom sink, waiting for the water in the shower to rise in temperature.

Barely enough time for a kiss, we hurried through our usual routine, throwing on casual clothes and meeting at the front door. I could smell coffee brewing in the kitchen, so I sent Kold out with the dogs and assured him I wouldn't be more than a few steps behind.

I found Darc standing at the kitchen counter, making coffee, but he refused to look at me. I wrapped my arms around his waist and pressed my face against his back, needing his forgiveness. "I promise I'll make it up to you." There wasn't enough time to beg, but I didn't have to. He turned, handed me a to-go mug, and kissed the top of my head. And with that, I knew everything was already forgiven.

When I got to the driveway and into the running car, the dogs were asleep in the back, and the heat was beginning to kick in. Kold scoffed at my single tumbler of coffee, removed it from my hand, and took a sip. "Just how you like it," he said with a scowl as he set the beverage in the cupholder and backed out of the driveway.

It's been quiet since then, even though I can feel Kold vibrating with words unspoken.

"Do you love him more than you love me?" His hand squeezes the upper part of my leg as he hurls his question at me from two feet away.

"No," I respond without hesitation. Not needing time to think. "I've never loved anyone the way I love you. I'm sorry that I've given you a reason to question my feelings. That was never my intention."

He shakes his head and pulls back his hand, leaving me chilled without the weight of his warmth. "Stop being diplomatic, and give me a real fucking answer."

My insides wretch as I fight the urge to scream at him. *You were the mastermind of this entire situation, and now you're mad at me for going along with your plan. I'm sorry you didn't reason it through to the end. Your lack of forward-thinking is not a short-coming on my part. If you didn't want me to fall in love with your brother, why did you hand me away so carelessly?*

"The answer to your question is NO. I do not love Darc more than I love you." If my relationship with Kold survives this ride into work, I'm cutting things off with Darc, and that will be that. I knew from the beginning that this was a recipe for disaster. And maybe the damage is already done.

"Do you want to renegotiate the terms of your relationship with him, or does my approval not matter anymore?" He clenches the steering wheel with both hands and stares dead ahead, not bothering to glance my way.

"We can renegotiate if you're willing." My voice remains level, giving away nothing, as my insides twist into knotted coils from which I will later hang. "Beginning immediately, I'll break things off and cease all interactions and communication with Darc, extending on through the foreseeable future. I will also find other accommodations before the day is out, leaving no further room for you to question my loyalty. Do you accept the terms of my offer?"

Leaning against the door, I press my cheek to the chilled window and will myself not to cry. Kold is leaving in a matter of days, and he's stripping me of everything on his way out the door. Of course, he is.

Cutting over three lanes of traffic, he pulls onto the shoulder and slams the SUV into park. "Your offer is shit, and I do not accept! Do you hear me?" He reaches over and grips my arms, pulling me towards the center. "I don't want you living alone while I'm on the road! Stop talking like everything's over! You've spent every day with him since the concert, and I need to know if the next three months are going to be more of the same! I want to feel like I have some sort of fucking say in the matter!"

One by one, I can feel the voices slipping away, retreating back into the darkness, leaving only the weakest of us to smooth over the wrinkles. "I stayed at the house this week with the intention of spending time with you, not your brother. I'm sorry that things happened beyond our control, and our time together was cut short. I can acknowledge that I stepped back, and that was a mistake. You were being pulled in so many directions at once that I didn't want to add additional stress to your agenda. On Monday, I'll be back to my usual eight-to-four schedule. By the time I *would have* returned to your house after work, your brother would've already left for the night. But that's no longer relevant."

Kold squeezes my wrists so tightly that I wonder if he's aware of how much he's hurting me. "You're Not Moving Out, And That's Final! I can't even look at you when you're like this. I want my fucking girlfriend back!"

One side of my face turns up in a smile, and I sigh. "I'm sorry. I'm the only one here right now."

"Fuck!"

He releases my arms and straightens in his seat, attempting to look past the glaze of my eyes. After a minute, he gives up, resigning himself to the fact that the girl he's searching for is currently unavailable. Taking the wheel in one hand and my thigh in the other, he pulls onto the freeway headed toward downtown. There are no more words exchanged, only silence, as the previous conversation lingers within the space, sucking the oxygen out of the air.

Still feeling brash from our first real argument, I remove my phone from Kold's coat pocket and replace it with his own. Then I send a text I instantly regret.

> : I'm afraid I lied to you last night and again this morning. I will not be able to make good on that raincheck or any other debts between us. I'm sorry I couldn't be what you deserve. There's a good chance you'll never see me again, and this is the last you'll hear from me. I'm sorry to have wasted your time.

My hands tremble, and my eyes well with tears as I keep my attention locked on the face of my phone, grossly unprepared for any response that's set to come.

> Evil Twin: Kold, if you're fucking around, it's
> not funny. I know you have her phone. She
> chooses you time and time again. Isn't that
> enough? You don't have to rub my nose in it.

Naturally, he would think the message was from Kold. The two of them take jabs at each other all the time, ever prepared to dual at dawn over the slightest thing. I could stop now, and he'd never believe the text came from me or reflected my wishes. Not being in the right mind when I stupidly sent the first text, I never stopped to consider the follow-up. The plan was to send one message and disappear. As if he was going to let that happen.

> : No. I have my phone. It's me.

> Evil Twin: Valentine? Are you hurt? Can you
> tell me what's going on? If I call you, will you
> be able to answer?

Even as I endure this self-inflicted heartbreak, my lips pull into a strained smile, and I let slip a breathy laugh. The places Darc's mind is willing to go in order to avoid the most obvious truth makes me love him all the more.

> : I'm not kidnapped. I'm breaking up with you.

I watch my phone, waiting for a response, but nothing comes. Did I genuinely expect him to fight or beg? Why would he? My tearful smile fades, and I accept that whatever we have is over. A guy like Darc doesn't need to waste time on a fake girlfriend he never wanted. Girls like me are a penny a dozen, and he can well afford to do better.

Looking out the window at nothing in particular, I try to imagine my life without them as though we had never met. Christmas and I would be signed on to another year at the apartment, and my on-again-off-again boyfriend would've continued to sneak around with my neighbor. Tracy hasn't bothered to reach out since Christmas, and neither have I. Another friend I lost, who I never truly had.

Kold pulls into the fenced-off section to park and walks around to open my door. Taking his hand, I step out into the cold December morning and think about how quickly things change. Ohio is funny like that. Two days ago, it was fifty degrees and sunny, warm enough to walk hand in hand, planning for a future we both still wanted. Now, there's a bite to the air as the cold needles its way through my jeans and into my bones, punctuated by continued silence.

Grabbing the dogs from the back, we carve out time for a quick walk on the patch of grass reserved for furry children, then head inside. Kold unhooks their leashes, and Midnight takes off towards the bar, with Christmas trotting close behind. This place is brimming with new smells, all needing to be investigated.

"Can you forgive me?" Kold says, gently pulling me to his chest.

"I'm sure whatever it is you're apologizing for is already forgiven."

There's no version of me that is willing to stay mad at him. He could lie and cheat and do terrible things, and I would forgive him. I would love him no matter what because my soul is as cold and dark as theirs is.

Kold

The taste of her honey and almond chapstick lingers on my lips, conjuring vivid memories of our first kiss. "I love you," I say, fighting back the urge to fall to pieces in her arms. Since Halloween, I've thought of Val damn near every second of every day, and the idea of leaving her is shredding my insides to ribbons.

Leaning in to continue our kiss, I come up short when the back door flies open on its hinges and smashes into the wall. Seemingly out of nowhere, Darc sprints over to Val and yanks her from her feet. Instinctively, I want to grab her, to pull her back, but I remember that we brought the dogs with us and hurry to close the door before they register the commotion and come bolting over.

"Valentine, look at me! Tell me what happened, and I'll fix it!" Darc takes her hands and presses them to his lips as the sleeves of her oversized hoodie slip down to her elbows.

And that's when I see the imprint of my fingers tattooed red and purple around each of her wrists. I know what's coming, but the sight of her bruised body leaves me paralyzed. The first punch connects with my jaw, and I stagger backward. Years of training and muscle memory keep me upright, but only barely. The next shot is to my stomach. Followed quickly by a jab to my ribs that leaves me hunched over and steadying myself against the wall. I spit a mouthful of blood, ready for my own brother to finish me off, but the final blow never comes.

Val grabs him from behind, screaming for him to stop, and I watch as the monster wilts under her touch, bending to her every request.

"Look at me! If you agree to walk away, I'll go with you," she says, and I find myself soothed by the words meant for someone else. He takes her hand and exits the room, leaving me to tend to my wounds.

Over the years, I've been in numerous fights with my brother, but nothing like this. Even when he's pissed at me, I know he holds back and pulls his punches, reserving the real pain for our enemies. But there was no holding back this time.

Thankfully, he didn't hit me anywhere vital, and I don't think anything's broken.

This isn't a game to him, nor is it to me. I've come to realize there is nothing higher than Val on the list of Darc's priorities. It was stupid of me to make her feel like she had to choose. I put her at risk, and for what? My ego. He'll never let her go. Not anymore. Not if he feels anything close to what I do.

Dragging myself off the wall, I make my way over to the bar, where I find the dogs playing tug-of-war with a white towel. There's a bottle of top-shelf whiskey with my name on it, and I'm eager to make its acquaintance. I pour myself a double to start and allow the liquid to burn away the taste of my own blood.

The construct of time passes differently as I make my way down to the bottom of a bottle. When Val joins me at the bar, I couldn't tell you if it's been twenty minutes or two hours. But I can say with absolute certainty that she's the most beautiful woman I've ever seen.

"Is he taking you away from me?" I ask, catching sight of Darc lurking protectively from ten yards back, no doubt a distance insisted on by the goddess in front of me.

"I promised him tonight in exchange for staying with you right now." Val's hand reaches toward mine, bringing an end to my descent into caramel-colored darkness. "Unless you prefer the company of this poison over me?"

She quirks her lips into half a smile, meeting my eyes for the first time. This is what I've come to expect from her. When faced with discomfort of any kind, Val will smile through it and act like everything's okay in order to quell any remaining tension.

The idea of marking her body in a way she never consented to is making my insides churn with disgust. Leaving a handprint in the bedroom is one thing, but I lost control during a heated conversation, and she didn't even react. Had I remembered my own strength, I would have stopped immediately.

"I'm curious, my love. What other promises did you have to make in order to spare my life? My brother isn't known to be forgiving." He would never agree to the deal she's suggesting, especially for a night that was already owed. She's bartered away more than what she's saying, and I can only hope that I'm worth it.

"We can discuss it later, over lunch, if you'd like. For now, why don't you show me what it is you do all day, and maybe I can help." She brushes the tips of her fingers over the back of my hand, gently tracing over the knuckles and down to each nail before moving to the next finger. Her light touch sends electrical pulses through my arm as I lose myself in the thought of her.

"Are you still mine?" I ask, more afraid of the answer than ever. There's an apology I need to make and a list of questions in my head that I need answers to, but none more pressing than this one.

The smile on her face reaches both sides of her lips and extends clear up to her eyes as she nods her head and whispers, "Nothing will ever change that."

I come around the edge of the bar and lift her into my arms, pressing a long overdue kiss to her lips. Whatever deal she made with Darc, I can renegotiate later. For now, she's mine, and there's nothing else that matters more. Our kiss continues as I set her back on her feet, never wanting to let her go.

"Valentine." The voice of my brother rings in my ears as he crosses the room and places a hand on her shoulder. "I'll be back at three o'clock sharp unless you need me sooner."

My body pulsates with the urge to kill him, but I have a good feeling he's armed, and I can't risk Val being caught in the cross-fire. Despite what our previous interaction might suggest, Darc and I are evenly matched on our best and worst days. Of that, I have no doubts. But I also know that Val would throw herself between us without hesitation and float away without a backward glance. She's made it clear that she'll leave us both rather than watch us fight.

Val spins on her heels, facing our uninvited guest, and lifts her hand to rest on his chest. "I'll be ready to go at three when you get here, and then we can do anything you want." Her voice is sickeningly sweet as she trades her body for my life.

"Perhaps not *anything*," I say, no longer willing to remain quiet. "There are still rules in place."

Darc laughs before leaning forward to kiss her. His embrace lingers longer than it should, undoubtedly for my benefit. "Three o'clock sharp." He repeats, this time directing his statement toward me. Then he releases her, crosses the room, and exits through the door leading out to the parking lot.

"Should we get on with our morning now that all that's settled?" Val turns back to me with a smile as if the last hour never occurred. "I'm looking forward to spending this time with you while I still can. Let's not waste it." Her hand moves to the side of my neck, and her thumb rubs over the line of my jaw. "I hate that you're leaving me, but I understand why you have to go."

I sway on my feet, forgetting for a moment that I'm halfway to being drunk, and correct my footing before I fall. "You need to start being honest with me, and I need to be more forthcoming with you. If you type everything into the computer with those lightning-fast fingers of yours, we can take an extra-long lunch break."

"Okay. First, we work, and then we lay it all out on the table. No more holding back for the other person's benefit."

I've been dragging my feet and biding my time, trying to sort through my own feelings and the expectations of others, not wanting to be the reason everything goes left. If Val asked me to stay, I would. I have until 11:59 pm on New Year's Eve to sign and submit the tour contract, but I can't commit to three months without her unless I know for certain that I'm coming home to a lifetime with her.

"Deal!" I say, shaking my head in agreement, ready and willing to spill my guts.

CHAPTER 50
Val

"Absolutely, fucking not!" Kold shouts, waking the dogs from their afternoon nap. "Why the hell would you ever agree to that? Those rules were in place to keep you safe. I don't think you fully understand what he's capable of." He paces back and forth across the office as I sit watching from the couch. "He's not who you think he is, Val. Neither of us are."

"How can you say that to me? You think I don't know you?" I sit forward on the couch, bringing my hands to my knees, but make no effort to stand. "I've seen who you are, who you both are, from the beginning."

"I'll make him a better deal. I'll renegotiate the terms and get him to agree. There's still one thing that I know he wants more." Kold alters his path and drops to his knees at my feet. "He'll take my rules and turn them into a checklist, hurting you because he can."

He wraps his arms around my waist and lays across my legs, sinking with me into the cushion. "Val, I know you think you can control him. He seems so tame around you, but he's a fucking monster. Honestly, I'm not much better. If I told you the truth, you would understand. You should run and never look back."

I'm silent for a moment, considering the weight of his words before responding. We've been talking, open and honest for most of the day, and now he's telling me to run. After pouring my heart out and listing every concern, large and small, he's sending me away.

"Where could I go that he wouldn't find me?" I brush my fingers through Kold's hair, trying to remain tethered to the moment. "And what makes you think I could endure a life without you?"

The alarm I set earlier begins sounding from the depth of my back pocket, and I remove the phone to silence it as a text comes through.

> Evil Twin: Tick tock, my love. Say your
> goodbyes and meet me downstairs.

"I can't let you go. I'm not ready." Kold says, climbing on top of me and straddling my legs. He takes my face in his hands and lifts my gaze, falling forward to hover an inch above me. "You're the one person I can't live without."

Our lips meet, and our tongues move together as the tingling between my thighs builds. I pull my head back, gasping for breath. "If you don't let me go, he'll come in here."

Kold places one last kiss against my lips before standing and offering me his hand. My knees are weak from the passion of his affection, so when he pulls me to my feet, I stumble forward into his arms. Thankfully, he catches me with ease. "Come on. I'll walk you out and help you get the dogs in the car."

The short trip from the office to the parking lot passes quicker than I had hoped, and I'm left wanting so much more. We haven't had enough time together this week, and before I know it, he'll be gone.

Standing beside his black Lamborghini, Darc pretends to be the perfect gentleman as he opens the passenger door and offers to help me in. And in typical evil twin fashion, his mouth is quick to spoil the illusion. "Happy to see you're still in one piece for the time being."

Kold pushes past his brother without a word and helps each dog onto my lap one at a time after I snap my seatbelt into place. "I'll see you tonight when I get home." He says, leaning in for one last kiss before closing the door. Almost instantly, the lock engages.

I watch, unsure of what to do, as the two men walk back towards the building, engaged in what looks to be an intense exchange of words. I can't hear the conversation, but their body language is coming through loud and clear.

For a moment, I feel like I'm on the verge of losing them both, and then it's over. They shake hands, and Darc walks to the car, wearing a smug expression. He gets in and revs the engine as Kold stands frozen in place, not bothering to wave goodbye.

"Rough day at the office, my love?" Darc asks as he pulls onto the highway headed home. "I was hoping I might hear from you."

Reaching over, he gives Midnight a scratch behind the ears before turning his attention to Christmas. I want to be mad at him, but hearing the playfulness in his voice and watching him give attention to the dogs melts my heart faster than a solar flare.

"I was trying to learn Kold's job in case you need help at the office. It's quite an extensive list of items that he's in charge of, which meant that I was pretty busy. But I should've made time to send a text. How was your quiet day at home without the wife and kids?"

"Don't be cruel, Valentine. You know I'd give anything to have that future with you."

I take his hand and press it to my lips, kissing along his knuckles before sliding my tongue across two of his fingers. Letting out a soft moan, I guide him past the creatures on my lap and tuck his hand between my thighs. "I'm sorry. I misunderstood. I thought we were going home to play mommy and daddy. Perhaps you have a different game in mind."

His fingers curl, pressing firmly against the seam of my jeans. "We can play any game you want, babygirl. I still owe you a reward of your choosing from yesterday. What's it gonna be? Do you want to be tied up and eaten alive or bent over and broken in half?"

"First, tell me why you're so happy. Did you get something you wanted? Shouldn't I know what it is if it involves me?" My back arches as he rubs circles through my pants, trying to distract me. "Please tell me. Are the rules in place, or are they not?"

"The rules remain unchanged." He weaves in and out of traffic, increasing his speed as we race towards home. "Although, it would've been nice to have one night without them."

"Please slow down before you kill us!" I wrap my arms around the dogs and pull them against my chest. "If you want to be careless with my life, that's fine, but leave the kids out of it."

He slows to match the flow of traffic and gets stuck behind a minivan. The last half of the drive is quiet, and I spend most of my time looking out the window, wondering if we'll see any real snow this winter. As we pull into the garage, I'm fully lost in a memory, skiing down a bunny hill and dreaming of hot chocolate.

"Should we take a shower, order takeout, and binge the next season of our show?" Darc asks as I make my way around the front of the car. Both dogs bolt through the open door ahead of him, no longer concerned about Mom when there are toys inside and beds to snuggle on. "I want to spend the entire night holding you in my arms until I forget that you tried to break up with me this morning."

I pause before the entryway, bringing him to a stop. "A quiet night together, like a normal couple. I like the sound of that." I lift onto my toes and wrap my arms around his neck. "I want to be your girlfriend. But in order to do that, I need to know what deal you made with your brother."

He wraps his arms around my waist and steps into the warmth of the house, closing the door behind us. "He offered me Wednesday through Saturday morning, so long as the previous rules remained in place. And I'm not allowed to touch you during his half of the week."

Seriously?

Kold gave his brother fifty-fifty time without even discussing it with me first. As if I'm some trophy whore who can be passed back and forth.

I'm seconds away from taking the phone out of my pocket and calling to scream at my so-called fiancé when Darc kisses me. He backs me against the wall and lifts me off my feet, all while penetrating my mouth with his tongue. I wrap my legs around him as he pins me to the wall with his hips, retreating from my lips so that he can begin teasing my neck.

"So, you two think you can shuffle me around, and I don't even get a say in the matter? Even you have to see how fucked up that is. I agreed to be your girlfriend, not your shared property or your insignificant sex slave. If you wanted three days a week, why didn't you make that deal with me this morning?" I grab him by the hair and yank his head back.

"Ow, babe!" He looks me in the eyes and smiles. "Keep going. I like it when you're rough."

"Fuck off. I'm mad at you." I do my best to look angry, but eventually, I have to look away before the sight of his stupidly handsome face turns me into a dewy-eyed fangirl.

"No, you aren't, but it's cute that you're trying." He rubs the end of his nose against mine, then presses our foreheads together. "I needed *him* to agree to it on his own, and he did. But that deal is between brothers, not us. You're under no obligation to spend those days with me unless you want to."

He kisses me again, causing my thighs to clench around him. "I like you being my girlfriend, and I enjoy pleasing you, so I hope that means I get to see you." Carrying me down the hallway to the bedroom, he kicks the door shut behind him and lays me on the bed.

"I'm still mad at both of you, but I know what I want my prize to be." I bite my bottom lip.

He climbs onto the bed, pressing his body over mine, applying enough pressure to trap me in place without crushing me. "Please tell me it involves us getting naked and me burying myself balls deep inside you. I've wanted to fuck you all day."

I look at him with a grin and chuckle under my breath. "No, baby, that's not it. We both know you're going to give me that whether I ask for it or not." I lift my head off the bed and kiss him. "What I want from you is five honest answers."

Kold insists that I don't know them as well as I think I do, but he's wrong. I don't need Darc to tell me shit, but I want to see if he'll honor our wager, even when it's in his best interest to lie.

"Okay. Well, I don't lie to you. So, let's hear what you've got." He rolls off of me and begins undressing, starting with his jacket and then his shirt. Before I get out the first question, he's naked and turns his full attention to removing what clothing I have on.

Sitting up, he removes my hoodie and seems surprised to find I'm wearing nothing underneath.

"Do you love me, or is this a game to you?" I ask, hoping to throw him off. Initially, I considered this as a softball question, something to ease him into things, but now that I take a second to remember who I'm in bed with, maybe it's not the easy answer I thought it might be. Easy or not, it doesn't matter because he agreed to give me honest answers. And surprisingly, I find myself genuinely needing to know.

"I love you with everything I am, which is more than I ever thought myself capable of. But you don't have to win a bet to ask me that. I'll tell you as many times as you can stand to hear it for as long as you'll have me." He begins kissing down my neck and over my breasts as his fingers make quick work of the button and zipper of my jeans. "I know we have a tendency to play around, but our relationship isn't a game to me. But now I'm curious. Do *you* love me, or is this a game to *you*?"

Every sentence out of his mouth adds a lump to the back of my throat until I feel like I'm choking on a bag of marbles. Is he being insincere? Maybe. I've been lied to by every man I ever bothered to care about, but it's never felt like this.

Sucking in a breath, I respond and ask my next question. "I love you as much as I can allow. But if you want answers from me, you'll have to take me out on another date and challenge me to a rematch. Winners ask the questions, and losers answer. So, next question. Have you had sex with anyone besides me since I started staying at the house?"

I arch my hips, lifting my ass off the bed, while he removes my pants and underwear. So much for ordering takeout and cuddling in front of the TV. Or maybe that's the plan for after.

Kissing the inside of my thigh, he pauses to respond. "I haven't been with anyone else since meeting you on Halloween."

His answer surprises me, and I have to stifle the urge to waste another one of my questions on a follow-up. The way he answered made it sound like he hadn't been with anyone because he'd met me, but that can't be true. Can it? It doesn't matter. I can't let myself get distracted. The important questions still need to be asked and answered.

I'm not an idiot. It's possible that Darc is messing with me and lying through his pearly white teeth, but I don't think that's the case.

He pulls off my socks one at a time, kissing each foot, and brings them to rest on his chest. Then he leans forward, pushing my knees towards my breasts, leaving me split open down the center.

I cry out in a moan, though the pain is nothing more than a minor irritation. I get the feeling I'm not as flexible as Darc seems to think I am.

"Excluding your sexual exploits, have you ever physically hurt a woman?" I'm well aware of his reputation in the bedroom, though I've yet to experience anything unfavorable. I'm more interested in his standard temperament and back-alley dealings. They're both trying to hide something, but a person's true nature can only be buried so deep. Eventually, everything comes to light when there's no place else to dig. I'm not entirely sure to what depth their depravity sinks, but I'm smart enough to acknowledge the obvious.

Rocking back on his heels, Darc wrinkles his nose and sucks on his teeth, clearly unhappy with my accusation. "No," he says firmly, putting my feet over his shoulders. The new position instantly quenches the burn in the back of my thighs, no longer stretched past their limits. "With or without my brother's stupid fucking rules, I would never hurt you. I might tease you until you beg for death, but only because you ask me to."

Coming forward, he rubs the head of his stiff cock over my clit, causing my body to jump. "You've got two questions left, babygirl. What is it you truly need to know before you let me fuck that tight little pussy?"

I allow my knees to fall to either side, granting him ready access as he slides two fingers into my mouth. He works them in and out, applying pressure to my tongue with every stroke. I moan again, wanting it to be his cock in my mouth.

Removing his hand, he leans forward again to kiss me, forcing my thighs apart with his torso. His muscles bulge and tighten as he presses his hands into the bed on either side of me. "If you don't finish asking me questions in the next minute, I'll assume you're being a tease, and I'll make you pay for it by stretching out this hole right here."

Rubbing the head of his cock, over my clit, down past the entrance of my pussy, and stopping at my ass, he applies slow, steady pressure.

"Okay, stop!" I shout, making a half-hearted attempt to pull away from him. Secretly, I would love for him to put his dick in there, but not without a *lot* of lube. "Do you and your brother make money some other way outside of the clubs and the bars that you own?"

With the head of his cock still pressed against the opening of my ass, Darc shoves two fingers into my pussy, as deep as he can go. "Yes. We both have other sources of income, some of which you may not approve of, but you'll never want for anything so long as we're in your life."

I realize now that I wasn't specific enough with my question, leaving him space to answer it honestly without incriminating himself. "To be clear, I don't want or need your money. I can take care of myself." Thankfully, my last and final question is as straightforward as they come. A simple yes or no is all I'm looking for.

"Last question, and then you're mine," he says, bringing his hand to his mouth. Running his tongue over the two fingers currently soaked in my juices, he coats them both in spit before moving his cock and pressing his fingers into the sensitive opening of my ass.

I dig my teeth into my lip to keep from crying out and circle my hips, pressing my body further down his hand. "Oh fuck!" I gasp. "Put your cock in me while you finger my ass."

He slides in the head but denies me the rest. "Ask your last question, and I'll have you squirting cum all over both of us."

There's only ever been one question I've wanted to ask. The rest were only ever meant to loosen his tongue. I buck my body, trying to get more, but the only thing he offers more of is in the next hole down. His fingers slam into me as deep as they can go, and it makes my eyes roll back in my skull as my back arches from the pleasure.

"Valentine, ask the goddamn question so that I can release us both from this fucking torture." He presses his free hand into my stomach to keep me from getting to his cock, while his other hand continues to stretch me out.

My body begins to tremble beneath him, anxious for his release. I've never needed anyone more than I need him now, and I'm terrified of losing him. "I can't. Babe, please. I need you." Tears bead along my lashes and fall from the far corner of my eyes as I repeatedly try to push my hips into his cock.

Maybe I should abandon the mission and ask for something else. What difference does it make to me if he's a monster, so long as he's mine? I've already promised to love him, and I have no intention of going back on my word. These guys are a package deal, and Kold is guilty as well, even if he wasn't there.

Darc pulls his fingers out of me and grabs onto my hips with both hands, unable to deny his own pleasure. He thrusts into me, filling me with the swollen length of his impressive cock, making my moan rise in a crescendo. Pumping into me hard and fast, he slams our bodies together at the core.

"Hurry and ask me," he chokes out, before sucking in a staggered breath. His hand wraps around my neck as he splits me in half. "Ask me before I cum for you."

My mind goes blank as he begins to squeeze, and the euphoria overtaking me steals the words from my lips. I claw at his forearm as the veins rope beneath his skin, struggling for a breath. He's so close, and if he goes, I won't be far behind.

Loosening his hold on my throat, he moves his hand to the back of my neck and pulls me into a kiss. His tongue pressed into mine, driving me straight to the edge. When he pulls his lips away, I dig my nails into his back and release a cry, "Did you kill Allen?"

The second the words part ways with my lips, the walls of my pussy constrict around his cock, and my stomach muscles convulse, milking every drop from his shaft as he explodes inside me, filling me beyond capacity.

"Yes," he says. Though I'm unsure if he's responding to my question or merely crying out as the orgasm passes back and forth between us. "You already know I did."

Kold

It's late when I get home, well after midnight, and the house is eerily quiet. I take a quick shower and let my mind wander, trying to imagine what life on the road is going to feel like this go around. It's the first time I have to say goodbye to someone I can't live without, and I'm still not convinced I'll be able to do it.

Except for my brother, the people who come in and out of my life are always meant to be temporary. We hold everyone at arm's length and deceive them into believing the lie because we can't trust anyone with our truth.

Going downstairs to let the dogs out, I try to distract myself by pacing around the kitchen, but it's no use. Once Midnight and Christmas are safely back inside and the door is locked and bolted, I peek into the bedroom to check on my girl, needing to know she's okay.

They're both passed out, tangled together on Darc's side of the bed, and for some reason, seeing them like this makes me smile. While I'm gone, Val will still be satisfied and comfortable, and my brother will have a reason to be happy for the first time in his life, even if it is limited to three days a week.

Oh, who am I kidding?

Once I leave town, they'll throw the rules straight into Monday's trash and carry it out to the curb. I thought I needed to protect her, but seeing them like this, I know Darc will never hurt her. Val has always been free to make her own choices. My rules were never meant for her. They were put in place to slow him down, but I always knew nothing would stop him.

It's been a long day, and I'm tired, but I miss my girl and the peace she brings me. I can't sleep without her, not unless I want to toss and turn for a few hours before giving up and going in the gym.

I watch silently from the doorway before stepping inside the room, hesitant to disturb the serene exhibition. I've never seen the two of us asleep together, but I can imagine this is what it looks like. Val passed out, content in her slumber, blanketed in the protection of one of her fiercest defenders. While the man at her back sleeps blissfully aware that the dream he's living is far greater than any that will come in his sleep.

Walking with muted steps to the empty side of the bed, I crawl in next to her as gingerly as my steel frame will allow. I'm there less than a second when Val lets out an adorable moan, rolls forward, and brings her arm across my chest.

"I'm sorry. Did I wake you?" I keep my voice as low as possible, not wanting to intrude further. Perhaps her body moved on its own as an involuntary reaction to the shift in the mattress. Covering her hand with mine, I pull the blanket over us with my free hand and allow the comfort of her nearness to soak into my skin.

She inches her body closer, flattening herself against the length of my arm and pressing her face to my bare skin. "I'm glad you're home," she says. Her voice is nothing more than a hushed sigh. The sensual whisper that states her claim is enough to make my cock twitch, but I didn't come in here for that.

"There's no place in the world I'd rather be than home with you." The hard truth of my admission tightens in my chest like Celtic knots, seeming to exist without beginning or end. I don't know how to leave her. My love for Val transcends standard human emotion, and she has matched me in words and actions every step of the way, but is that enough to keep us together?

Sitting atop the side table next to our bed is a candle Val gave me for Christmas. The scent is bourbon, vanilla, and oak, and the inscription on the side feels like it was torn from my heart every time I read it.

I thought waiting for you was the worst part,

until I realized that someday I would lose you.

My girl is a big fan of sentiment, which I wasn't sure I would be able to give her, but I've come to realize the immense importance of romance and the value of a free date. Of course, I still want to eat at the best restaurants, shower her with expensive gifts, and take her on luxury vacations. But for the first time, I have found comfort in silence and a home in her embrace, two things money could never buy me.

It was never my intention for Darc to become a main character in our story, yet here he is, embezzling my spotlight while I ready myself to step away from this stage. If I didn't care for him like a brother, I might consider it rude, but it makes sense that she would love him. Val sees the best in people, even more so when they're broken. She isn't interested in hanging out on the surface, not when everything worth knowing lives buried underground.

This afternoon at the club, I was seconds away from slicing open my belly and spilling my guts. The full confession was on the tip of my tongue when her alarm went off, and the text came in from my brother. She deserves the truth about who we are, not merely a version of it.

Kissing my arm, Val moves her hand back and forth across my chest before walking down the path leading to the waistband of my shorts. Everywhere her fingers graze over my skin, the individual muscles clench and tighten. "I want to give you every reason to come home to me."

Again, my hand goes to hers, drawn together by magnetic forces. "You already have," I say, halting her forward progress.

Val is the positive to my negative. She made me someone I didn't think I could be. For her, I'm a good man. And for me, she's a bad girl. But for now, I want to hold her.

I guide her hand back to my chest and press her palm over my rapidly beating heart. "Look what you do to me." I groan, lacing our fingers together.

She releases a silent gasp, fighting back tears, and bites into my arm. All week, Val's been smiling through it, offering to help, and playing the part of the supportive girlfriend. But despite her best efforts, I can feel all the emotions sunk below the surface and the sadness she refuses to give a voice to.

Ask me to stay, and I'll never leave your side.

"You've been making my heart race since the beginning and every day after." Our fingers move in tandem, tapping out the rhythm. "I'm trying so hard not to be selfish, but I don't want to let you go."

I roll onto my side and pull her into my arms, waking Darc in the process. He lifts his head to assess the situation, sees that it's me, and rolls onto his other side.

"Do you two need a minute alone, or are you staying?" Darc's question is vague, and I'm not entirely sure if it's directed at me or the girl currently crying in my arms. Either way, it doesn't seem to matter. He tosses back the comforter and swings his legs over the side of the bed, escaping to the kitchen and closing the door behind him.

For a moment, Val goes rigid in my arms as if unsure of where she belongs.

"If he's not back in two minutes, I'll get him. Although, I'd imagine he likes it more when you're the one chasing after him." The realization makes me laugh. My brother has always hated when women pursue him, making it one of his top five deal breakers. That's why he stopped hooking up with Jamie long before her tense interaction with Val. Darc has never been interested in anything easy. He has no tolerance for clinginess. And until recently, he didn't bother with emotions.

"I wasn't going to chase after him. Why would I when I have you?" She finds my lips in the dark, and we share a kiss that feels long overdue, and before I know it, she's straddling my waist as I grip her ass. The palms of her hands press firm into my chest as she rubs herself against me. "I know it's unfair and maybe a bit unreasonable, but I don't want you to hook up with anyone else while you're on the road. And I want you to call and text and video chat with me all the time because I'm going to miss your face and your voice and the way I feel at home in your arms."

As she flattens against my chest, I wrap my arms around her and squeeze as tightly as I can without crushing her. Then I roll onto my side, taking her with me, and give us both a moment to reposition. Val flips over and molds the length of her body to mine, pressing ourselves together like spoons.

"I know you think I'll be fine because your brother is here to hold me over, but you're my best friend and the love of my life. The hole you leave can never be filled. Although I suppose, knowing Darc, if there's a hole, he'll try to stick his dick in it." She giggles at her own joke, and the waves of her laughter ripple out in all directions, vibrating against my ribs.

"Facts," I spit out, as I laugh along with her before dialing it down to continue the conversation. "But seriously, back to what you were saying before you started fantasizing about my brother's dick and all the places you're going to let him stick it."

All jokes aside, when it comes to Val, if he ends up in a hole I've yet to be in, I might reconsider killing him. I may need to amend the rules before I leave, although I'd hate to give them ideas.

"I'm going to call and text so much while I'm gone that you'll get sick of hearing from me. And I'll send you videos and pictures constantly, so you'll know exactly what I'm doing. As for me being with anyone else, it will never happen. But I'll assure you repeatedly because I know you need to hear it, and I'll reinforce that promise with my actions because I know you need to see it. You're *my* best friend and the love of my life. I would never disrespect you."

Holding her in my arms, we remain motionless as the significance of our terms sink in. I could promise her the world, and given enough time, I could deliver. But Val isn't asking for the world. She's simply requesting loyalty, and I intend to give it to her in spades.

My future wife will want for nothing. Once this tour is over,

I'm making every one of her dreams come true, and I'm going to be standing by her side when I do it.

My eyes grow heavier the longer I hold her, and I know that soon sleep will overtake me. Thankfully, Darc comes through the door as I'm debating whether or not I should get out of bed to find him or simply yell his name and hope he hears me.

Filling the empty side of the bed, Darc lays on his back as Val shifts over to split herself evenly between us. It's an ideal setup for another threesome, but I'm exhausted, and sleep overtakes me as her fingers thread into mine.

CHAPTER 51

Val

Peering over the edge of my morning mug of coffee, I can still feel the warmth of their presence soaked into my skin. The remnants of last night's sleepover. Or maybe it's their lingering presence. They're practically glued to my side as we sit tucked away in the corner at our usual table. Kold and I had plans for breakfast before heading into the office, and Darc decided to join us. For some reason, he's going in early this morning, but he's being cagey about the details.

"I'll be at The Jakobsson until late afternoon, but I'll make sure I'm done in time to pick you up from the club at 3:00. Are you good to ride in with this guy?" He uses his fork to point in Kold's direction and grins.

"Yeah. I think I'll survive." I smile back as I touch Darc's leg under the table, fully aware that he intends to leave after he finishes inhaling his breakfast.

Shoveling the last forkful of eggs into his mouth, Darc lacks his usual polish, and I enjoy the change. He's always so buttoned up, especially before work, but being proper takes time and this morning, he's in a hurry. Although, clearly not in enough of a hurry to pass up breakfast at Valentine's with his two favorite people.

"Send a text if you need me. I might not be able to answer my phone if you call." He wipes his mouth with the cloth napkin from his lap and stands to leave before coming around the corner of the table to kiss me goodbye. "Make sure you pay attention today. I'm in the market for a new partner, and I have my eye on you for the promotion."

"I'll be sure to take good notes." I smile at him from my seat, secretly hoping for one more kiss before he walks away.

"I'll see you this afternoon." He presses his lips to mine as his thumb strokes my cheek. "I love you."

With a wink, Darc turns on his heels and walks away, not waiting for a response, as Kold's dropped fork clatters against his plate. The sound momentarily draws my attention as I turn to look at him, registering the shock inscribed in bold print across his face. By the time my attention returns to Darc, the front door of the restaurant is swinging shut behind him.

"I am deeply concerned by this development and yet pleasantly surprised." Kold is quick to release his official statement. "I didn't think I'd live long enough to hear my brother say those words to anyone, let alone my soon-to-be wife. Unless there's something you need to tell me?" His eyebrows raise, adding a playful emphasis to his half-serious questioning.

"It's not like he says it *all* the time, but he has mentioned it before..." My words trail off a bit at the end, but I come back strong for the important bit. "And no, he has not proposed or convinced me to leave you. As of now, you and I are still engaged. Unless your feet are feeling chilled?"

"It's not the temperature of *my* feet that has me worried, love." He takes both of my hands into his and presses them to his lips, releasing a warm, steady breath into our cupped hands.

"Well, my tootsies are toasty warm, so you have nothing to worry about." I hold his gaze, wishing we could stay like this forever. "Not the change the subject, but the other day you mentioned a *contract*, and you've yet to produce the document. Care to explain? If it has something to do with your fantasy of us getting married before you leave, I suggest we find the time to discuss it sooner rather than later. Unless you're okay with me getting married to you in sweatpants and a tank top, I'm going to need enough warning to find a dress."

When it comes to my current feelings on marriage, the jury is still deliberating. If Kold is going to cheat and leave me, a piece of paper certainly isn't going to do a whole heck of a lot to stop him. In theory, he's got as much to lose as I do, but relationships always seem that way when you think you're in love. A marriage without a husband feels pretty pointless to me, but if it gives him peace of mind, I'm willing to say *I do*. Mostly, I want to make him happy, so my feelings on the matter are irrelevant.

I used to think that I would get married once and it would last a lifetime, but I wasted my chance on a person who never loved me, and now my views on the institution have been tarnished. I think the entire outdated ritual is a sham meant to make women prisoners or property. Not equals. But I can't tell Kold any of that. The idea of marriage still means something to him, and who am I to spoil it?

"The contract is on my desk at the office. We can discuss it when we get there if you'd like."

"Or you can give me your best elevator pitch now, and I can look over the details at lunch." I'm not sure what made me think about the contract in the first place. I had pretty much forgotten soon after he said it. But now that it's on my mind, my curiosity is getting the best of me.

Kold clears the table between us, moving the plates, cups, and silverware to the empty side, smooths a wrinkle from the linen tablecloth, cracks his neck, and takes a deep breath. "I'm offering you a salary position requiring one week on the road per calendar month during active tour schedules. Weeks to be chosen at your discretion can be taken consecutively so long as each consists of no less than seven days. While on the road, you will be acting as my personal assistant, requiring you to be within a half-mile radius at all times unless duties dictate a need for greater distance. Permission can be sought and granted on a case-by-case basis but should never be assumed. A full list of duties has been outlined in the contract, along with corresponding descriptions, that should elevate any risk of misunderstanding. Travel, lodging, meals, and entertainment will be covered by your employer, and a company credit card will be issued in your name. Your salary during tour weeks is based upon a twenty-four-hour-a-day rate since you will remain on call and at the ready at all times. Duties for non-travel weeks have also been meticulously detailed. You are required to be on-site or in the office no less than three days a week, with an option to work from home on the other two. Salary is based upon an eight-hour day, though hours and times may vary. Overtime must be approved and will be paid out on the last day of the following month. You will receive four weeks of paid vacation time, which must be used in one-week increments and scheduled no less than two weeks in advance. You will also receive two weeks of paid personal leave to be used as needed. Paid time off will not be approved during travel weeks unless emergency circumstances arise, adequate proof of emergency is provided, and permission is granted. Failure to adhere to the job's requirements can result in reduced wages, physical punishment, and a temporary loss of first-class flight status. To be determined at the time of the incident. On-the-job training is to commence immediately following the approval of the aforementioned contract. The position requires an indefinite commitment lasting no less than five years. Contract to be renegotiated annually on the anniversary date of the original signing. All questions pertaining to the contract should be submitted in writing, and you will receive a response in a time-frame no greater than twenty-four hours. The attached non-disclosure agreement must be signed, notarized, and submitted with the contract in order for your employment to be approved. You are the *only* candidate being considered for this position. If you have not responded by 11:59 pm on December 31st, your rejection will be assumed, and the position will cease to exist."

"Jesus Christ! I said elevator pitch. Where did you think we were going, to the moon?" My lighthearted response evokes a shared smile as I take his hand across the table. "I'm starting to think you get a kick out of seeing me overwhelmed."

"I don't want you overwhelmed, my love. And I think once you review the offer, you'll find my terms to be far more generous than perhaps I let on."

"So, I have until tomorrow night to make a decision, and if I refuse..."

"You know I can't do this tour without you."

"I know you think that." I feel myself pleading with my eyes, begging him to see reason. "Okay, I'm willing to consider your generous yet massively intimidating offer once I've had a chance to read through the details. But regardless of what I decide, you have to keep telling yourself, *this is a once-in-a-lifetime opportunity.*"

Kold reaches around the leg of the table, gripping the front of my chair, and with one swift pull, he repositions me in front of him. His hands come up to rest on my shoulders as he leans in closer, stopping when our foreheads meet. "*This* is my once-in-a-lifetime opportunity, you and me and the life we're building together."

"I agree with you, but both can be true at the same time. We can still build a life together even if you're out of town on business." If I want Kold to go on this tour, I either have to agree to his terms and sign the contract or make one hell of a counteroffer. Or I could let him stay home and have everyone hate me.

I catch sight of Conrad as he exits the kitchen carrying three to-go coffees and a folded paper bag. Kold hurries to help, handing me a coffee and the freshly baked lemon poppyseed scone before taking the other two cups for himself.

"I'll take both of these. I'm dragging this morning. Thanks, Dad. You're a lifesaver."

Conrad and I freeze in place and exchange a look before eyeing Kold with similar expressions. I've always been proud to look like my mother, but when the other contributor to my DNA is standing less than a few feet away, it isn't difficult to spot the resemblance.

"I'm trying it on for size, seeing how it fits." Kold chuckles, mostly to himself.

"Well, I appreciate that, son." Conrad pats him warmly on the shoulder before nodding his head toward me. "Now, if you could get my daughter to start calling me that, we'd be all set."

I offer a half-hearted smile and a slight wave goodbye from the hand holding my coffee, but that's all he'll get from me. If he wanted to hold a position in my life, perhaps he shouldn't have waited so long. Now, he's nothing more than the man who delivers my meal.

"Thanks for breakfast. Please pass on my compliments to the chef." I have nothing else to say.

Conrad has been trying to use his personal relationship with the guys as some sort of free pass back into my life, but any ticket he held on to expired three decades ago, around the time I learned to live without him. He even went so far as to show up, uninvited, on Mr. and Mrs. Jakobsson's doorstep on Christmas day as they were heading out to see us, claiming it was all some sort of happy accident. Kold's mom sent a text on their way to the house, informing her sons of their surprise guest, but there was nothing much that could be done about it by that point.

Having my long-absent father arrive at the door with my future in-laws for my first major holiday with the man I'm recently engaged to and his twin brother, who I'm secretly dating, was awkward. Honestly, the entire situation was more than my nerves could handle.

We all played our parts and got through it. At one point, Darc tried to kiss me under the mistletoe in front of everyone, and I slapped him, which garnered a chuckle from the on-looking crowd. I felt bad about it at the time and even worse later on when I found out that the flowers I'd been gushing over all night were from him.

My brain continues to sift through the details of our previous holiday throughout the drive to work. However, as soon as we pull into the employee parking lot behind the club, flashbacks of yesterday flair into the forefront like fire burning behind my eyes. I clutch at the hand I know will be resting atop my leg and tighten my grip.

"I should have moved faster. When Darc took a swing at you, I should have grabbed his arm. I'm sorry that I hesitated."

"Babe, the fact that you stopped him at all was impressive. That wasn't the first time my brother punched me in the face, and I assure you it most likely won't be the last. If it makes you feel any better, I gave him a black eye during a sparring session a few weeks before we met you, and a couple of years back, I cracked two of his ribs while training."

"Jesus. What the hell is wrong with you two?" I knew they were competitive, but bruised faces and broken bones are worlds beyond what I had envisioned. Sure, I know they're capable of far worse things, but I didn't think they would ever direct that anger at each other. I always took them as the *Us Against the World* type, but maybe that changed when I stepped into the picture.

"My brother and I are immeasurably flawed. You know that better than anyone, and yet you still love us. So, the real question might be, what the hell is wrong with *you*?" He smiles and leans forward to kiss me.

"Well, if I told you, *she'd* have to kill you."

"You know I was joking. To me, you'll always be perfect."

I roll my eyes as the words float past his lips, already knowing what he's about to say. The idea of me being *perfect* is laughable, but I like hearing that he still thinks of me that way.

We spend the rest of the morning going over checklists, making schedules, entering end-of-year payroll data, double-checking the backstock, and making sure that everything is prepared for tomorrow's New Year's Eve event. As promised, I take detailed notes, and as a reward for all my hard work, Kold orders Thai food for lunch and has it delivered to the bar three blocks over.

Served Kold is a piece of shit, hole in the wall, but that's what I like about it. It's not the kind of place that pretends to be something it isn't, which makes it hard to hide if you're trying to convince someone you belong when you don't. Being here, sitting at the bar next to Kold, feels normal. Even though it's only noon, and this place lacks a menu, there are people at the bar having drinks and sharing a laugh. Give me tattooed and misunderstood any day of the week. Despite what the guys think, I feel safe here, amongst my people.

"You know I'm serious about the job offer, and I sincerely think you should consider it. Once I get back, you could make your own schedule, work from home whenever you want, delegate whatever you don't feel like doing, drink for half the day, and ask for a raise. That's what I do." Kold lays it all out between fork-fuls of coconut chicken and white rice, making it all sound so simple.

"No, you don't," I say, my mouth half full of pad thai. I pause a second to chew and swallow so that I can avoid choking to death. "I see how hard you work. And there's no way I'd be able to do your job and mine. But I'm happy to help as much as possible."

I know they mean for me to quit my job and work for them full-time, but it's a risk I'm struggling to consider at the moment. I already gave up my apartment to be with Kold, and he's talking about leaving me for three months. That's going to have to be enough sacrifice for the time being. If I tie every aspect of my life to them, and things go badly, that's a whole lot of broken pieces for me to fix and no ground in place to rebuild on.

Since college, I've bounced from one relationship to the next, packing and moving across the city, the state, or even the country in my ignorant pursuit of a love I never truly understood. Every six months to a year, I would have to start fresh with a new job, never staying anywhere long enough to make friends or climb the corporate ladder.

I don't mind my current job, though it's not going to lead to a career. But what it lacks in prestige, it makes up for in simplicity. I like the anonymity of cubical-based employment. I get to listen to music while I type, and my duties require minimal thought. My boss is friendly enough, and my co-workers are quiet. I've made a couple of connections with people I would never think to call, and I've carved out a place for myself in the cookie-cutter office where no one knows my real name.

Okay, so I don't like my job all that much, but it's better than nothing. When I'm on my own again, my mind-numbingly boring position will be a much-needed distraction until I can retreat to Indiana.

"Next week is going to be busy for both of us, and I feel like I'm barely going to see you." I wash down my disappointment with the last of my beer and push the glass forward. "You've been burning the candle at both ends, and I know you're exhausted. I appreciate you making time for me today."

Kold puts his arm across the back of my chair and pulls me to his chest. "You know I would spend every second with you if I could." He squeezes my shoulder and kisses the top of my head. "I should be the one thanking you for spending your holiday break fielding my phone calls and sorting out my schedule. I couldn't have survived this week without you. Now all I have to do is wife you up, Mrs. Jakobsson, so that I can survive the rest of my days."

I haven't given much thought to changing my last name, especially after the hassle of swapping everything back to my maiden name only a few short months ago after my divorce from John was finalized. But I suppose Valentine Jakobsson does have a nice ring to it. Not that anyone besides Darc calls me by my given name. Honestly, I'm not entirely sure why he calls me that or how he knew. Maybe he saw *her* from the beginning.

Kold and I stay at the bar for a few more rounds, and it's nearly 3:00 when he looks at his phone. "Guess we'd better get you back before the warden tracks us down," he says with a laugh before standing and offering me a hand. "Are you two planning on listening to the radio interview tonight, or do you have other plans?"

"I'll make sure we listen to it." I can't help but notice the shift in Kold's demeanor once he notes the time and realizes our day is coming to an end. Walking hand in hand to his designated parking spot in the lot, I wish I knew a trick for making time stop.

"Tomorrow's Saturday," Kold says, opening the passenger side door. "Glad the holiday falls on one of my days." His smug, short-lived expression rises and falls like the tide as he takes in my response.

"Yeah. I've been meaning to talk to you about that."

CHAPTER 52

Kold

Today, I'm making the most of every second. I'm stealing every glance, finding every reason to touch her, and making every effort to remind my girl that she is loved, even if she's sick of hearing me gush about how beautiful she is. Val is gorgeous, intelligent, and funny, but goddamn, is she terrible at accepting a compliment.

Somehow, she keeps me guessing while offering me every certainty, keeps me grounded while encouraging me to strive for more, and remains my focus when the pressure from the outside world has become an overwhelming distraction. From day one, she has invested herself fully in my stock, not because I was a sure thing, but because she believed I was worth the risk.

Whenever I think about the woman who's agreed to marry me, I see the expanding outline of our future laid out before me. I would move Heaven and Earth for her happiness. However, I'd imagine Heaven would turn me away at the gates. And if I were moving earth, it would be to bury a body. I suppose I could walk through Hell for her, but if she ended up there, it would probably be because of something I did. In which case, she might not want to see me. For now, my efforts are reduced to free dates and the occasional grand gesture. And soon, I may be limited to phone calls and plane tickets.

On the drive yesterday from my bar to the club, Val laid into me over my decision to split time without discussing it first. I agreed that my actions were inconsiderate, though not without reason. There are too many unknown variables within the weeks ahead, and much of it feels outside my control.

I want to stay, but I know she'll never allow it. And in order to leave, I need to know beyond a shadow of a doubt that Val is protected and moderately happy. If I can't convince her to join me on the road, I need to ensure she'll still be around when I return.

After an extended shower that got steamy in more ways than one, I left Val upstairs to get dressed. New Year's Eve at the club is black tie. So, as I stand here in Darc's room looking at myself, I feel a bit like James Bond. Of course, who needs a reflective piece of glass when I could look at my mirror image standing to the right of me, currently checking his hair and straightening his tie for what feels like the hundredth time?

"Will you calm down? What the hell is wrong with you?" His nerves seep into the air and soak into my skin like acid rain. My brother has been acting weird all afternoon, but he won't let slip what's on his mind. In an effort to break him, I'm being an annoying shit and asking him the same questions repeatedly, but he keeps saying that it's not my business anymore and refuses to speak on it further. "Is this about your *meeting* yesterday? Val cannot find out about any of that."

"Obviously, I'm not a fucking idiot! But neither is she."

"Have another drink and relax. I'm the one who has to live without her for three months. I don't know what the hell you're so stressed about."

"I'm stressed because I have a kingdom to rule, *alone*, while you're off singing with birds in the forest and dreaming of fairy-tale futures."

"Oh, please! I'm leaving you our queen. What more do you want?"

Despite my employment offer and its generous compensation, I get the feeling Val intends to stay behind. She expects me to believe it's her job keeping her here, but it's not. When I remain unconvinced, she adds our dogs to the list as if we couldn't take them with us. I feel like the real reason she's staying is standing right in front of me, and some days, I'm better at facing that fact than others. I pretend to be okay with her decision because that's what she needs me to do, but the thought of leaving her is eating me alive.

"You know I could make her happy." Darc takes one last look in the mirror before heading for the living room to wait. "But I suppose a shared queen is better than a lifetime alone."

I'm ready to begin pacing the floor when I hear Val call down from behind the bedroom door. "Are you guys ready for my grand entrance?"

"Waiting on you, babe." I do my best to project my response without sounding like I'm shouting. Watching Val descend the stairs to a chorus of barking dogs isn't nearly as endearing, and thankfully, they remain quiet.

There's something charming about seeing her all dolled up, descending the oak staircase like the best friend turned love interest in one of the rom-coms she's forced me to endure. They aren't actually that bad, though I still pretend to hate them because it makes her laugh. Unlike the guys in those movies, I wasn't stupid enough to miss the obvious when my soulmate was standing right in front of me wearing a t-shirt and a pair of jeans.

In an effort to avoid being spoiled or going shopping, Val decided to wear something from her current wardrobe. Besides the dress I bought her, I can't imagine what her other options are. I was beside her when she unpacked, and we share a closet, so unless she's hiding a super-secret garment bag full of evening gowns under the bed, I fully expect to see her walk down the stairs in her outfit from our date last weekend.

The bedroom door opens, and Val steps out in a black floor-length dress slit to the top of her thigh. My eyes are drawn to her exposed leg as she takes each step with calculated apprehension. At the base of the stairs, she slips on her shoes, completing the look, and gives us a spin.

Darc is dying to say something. I can see it etched into his shifting stance, but we agreed to wait. Neither of us is allowed to speak until Val has properly identified us. Since the online rumor mill is churning out conflicting stories regarding who Val is with, Darc and I decided to play our favorite game.

"Why aren't you guys saying anything? And why do you look the exact same?" Val takes a step closer and cocks her head to the side, trying to spot the difference that doesn't exist.

"I've been living here for two weeks, and I still can't tell you apart." Her eyes shift back and forth between us, and she smiles. "Never mind, I see it now."

Crossing the short distance between us, Val wraps her arms around my waist and rests her cheek against my chest. "You ready to go, rock star?"

"How the hell did you know it was me? What gave it away?" Darc and I have spent thirty-five years perfecting this act, and somehow, she sorted through our well-rehearsed charade in under a minute.

"Darc's mouth twitched on one like he was trying to stifle a smile when I said I couldn't tell you apart. I knew you'd be annoyed that my heart couldn't tell the difference, whereas he would find it amusing."

I kiss the top of her head and rock her gently in my arms. "Nothing about you annoys me, my love, least of all your heart."

Val turns her face and finds my lips before moving on to the man beside me. Thankfully, there's a knock at the front door, calling me away. I don't need to begin the night by watching my fiancée make out with my brother. It's bad enough she's wearing the dress he gave her for Christmas.

Val

Darc's hand brushes along the slit of my dress until he's tickling the top of my thigh. If I had my way, the three of us would be ringing in the new year at home, where I'm allowed to love them both. I don't require an explanation to understand why they're dressed like identical copies of one another.

People online are weirdly invested in this story, and the buzz around Kold's love life is driving his song up the charts. Tonight, it won't matter who I'm filmed kissing if people can't tell them apart. So, the mystery will continue, and I'll remain socially tied to the evil twin. The problems with this awkward situation are many, but the most significant has been Kold's constant denial of our engagement. His lie strengthens the tie Darc has to me, on and off of the internet, and social media gossip has begun to feel like an inevitability. The more I hear about Darc and I being together, the more I question whether or not it's true.

Had I not kissed Darc while Kold was on stage, none of this would've ever happened. But Kold had an opportunity to clarify the misunderstanding, and he opted not to, bringing us to where we are now. My love life is further proof that the internet is a collection of lies, and I'm happier to remain in the real world.

Distracted by the intensity of his kiss, the confusion of my thoughts, and the playfulness of his touch, Darc has me wishing we could run off to the bedroom. I'm lost to the moment until his mother's voice breaks through our cone of silence and shatters my false reality.

Attempting to back away, Darc pulls me in closer.

"You two look stunning this evening. I love seeing you together. It's every mother's dream that her child finds their soulmate. And Val, I know your mom would have felt the same. The way you two look at each other, I know you're going to give me the most adorable grandbabies sooner rather than later. I wish you'd hurry and get married already." Turning back to the son she mistakenly assumes is Darc, she continues with her unsolicited parental critique. "Maybe now that Kold is finally settled down, you'll find a nice girl and do the same."

"I suppose I'll have to live vicariously through these two for the time being. If only Valentine had a twin sister, I'd be all set." Hearing my real fiancé call me by the name that only Darc uses is jarring to my senses.

The two brothers fall into character as though it's their second identity. And I suppose, in a way, it is. They've perfected their craft with such precision that even their own mother can't tell them apart.

I smile and play along with the gag, certain she'll sort it out eventually. But with no need to question what's right in front of her, why would she bother to look past the surface?

"Speaking of grandbabies..." The dogs enter from stage left, whining and wiggling, eager for their portion of the attention. "I suppose you two will have to hold me over for the time being until Mom and Dad are ready to add to the family."

"Come on. Grandma brought you special treats for our New Year's Eve party." She carries her reusable shopping bags full of goodies into the kitchen with the dogs tailing behind. "You three had better get going. Your ride is parked out front. Have fun tonight!"

I'd almost forgotten what it felt like to have a mom come crashing through the door like a tidal wave, heaping unsolicited advice and gracious praise on everyone in her wake. My mother would have enjoyed Mrs. Jakobsson and her unfiltered commentary. My mom also would have enjoyed seeing me happy and in love, sitting on the edge of infinite possibilities. She always wanted grandkids to spoil and a son-in-law to dislike. I wonder what she would have thought of having identical son-in-laws and furry grandkids. Would she have been disappointed with my choices or pleased to see that I finally found everything I'd always wanted?

The black SUV limousine the guys rented is overkill, to say the least, but it fits the image they work so hard to maintain. Kold records a quick video and then hands me his phone. "Can you take some pictures of the two of us? After all, you aren't the only one with a twin kink."

He's right, of course. Individually, the guys are impressive, but together they're extraordinary. I still remember what it was like to see them side by side that first night. I was fully convinced they were too good to be true. Little did I know, they were already mine.

"I'll make sure you look extra sexy. Wouldn't want to disappoint all your fans and your mystery lover."

"Yeah. Well, it turns out she's a mystery to me as well." Kold steps forward to take the phone from my hand. "Forget it. Let's go."

"Babe, wait." I reach out to grab him before he's able to step beyond arm's reach. "I'm sorry. Can I please take the video? You guys look fantastic, and you're right. The women online will eat this up."

I may not be well-versed in the art of influencing social media, but I have shot enough dog videos to understand the concept of proper lighting and the importance of good angles. Not that the men in my life require any help looking phenomenal.

Inside the limo, Darc slides over beside me and tucks his face into my neck, breathing in my perfume. "You are absolute perfection, per usual. Will you take a picture with me? The way I see it, this night is either going to be the start or the end of everything, and I want to remember what it felt like to be in this moment with you."

"I don't know how to do what you guys do. You're way better at the whole *sexy model* thing than I am. I'm not entirely sure that

I even know how to look sexy without a filter. Maybe I should stay behind the camera so you don't start losing followers."

"All the women in the world, and not one of them holds a candle to you. Let them leave if they want. I don't need them." Darc pulls in closer and whispers against my neck. "I need you."

His phone lights up as a notification comes through. It's a text from the *Good Twin* containing a series of candid photos taken as I protested and questioned my ability to present as appealing, and a message that says, *You were right.* I'm not sure what Kold means by the comment, but the images attached are more impressive than I thought myself capable of.

Thankfully, the dress I chose for tonight offers me a full range of motion, making it possible for me to traverse the short distance between the seats with little difficulty. Even as we encounter a bump in the road, I manage to maintain my footing. As I aim for the seat beside him, Kold catches me in his arms and pulls me onto his lap.

"Should we talk now or save it for the office?" Since Monday, whenever Kold talks to me, it sounds like the beginning of a business transaction. "Choices need to be made before the clock strikes midnight. Otherwise, our indecision will be granted the final say."

"You make it all sound so romantic." In case my sarcasm isn't enough to highlight my mood, I move from his lap and slide into the seat beside him, further driving the point home. "Can you remind me what the options are so I can waste my night dwelling on it instead of enjoying the party?"

"You sign your contract, and I'll sign mine agreeing to the tour. Or neither of us sign, and things go back to normal." Kold reissues the ultimatum, presenting the option in black-and-white terms.

"So, either I give up everything to be with you, or you're going to give up everything to be with me. How do you still refuse to acknowledge how stupid that sounds? I don't want to quit my job, and I'm not interested in being your contractually obligated tour whore. I don't care what *personal assistant* bullshit title you give it. We both know what your expectations will be."

"That's not what this is! I need you with me because I'm in love with you." Kold maintains my focus as he registers Darc, shifting in his seat. "But it seems like now that you've replaced me, you can't get rid of me fast enough."

"I never replaced you, you fucking asshole! You gave me away!" *Valentine's* influence spits from *my* throat, rendering all others voiceless. Time freezes as the enormity of *her* claim fills the interior of the limousine before collapsing around us.

"You said that Darc was the one who loved the chase. You insisted he would hunt me down for the thrill and then walk away once he caught me. But I think you've been pretending to be one another for so long that you confused *him* with *you*. You're the one who loves the chase, Kold. You spent two months trying to hunt me down, and then once you had me, you pushed until I agreed to everything. Then, as soon as I accepted your proposal, you passed me along because you thought he would do your dirty work and get rid of me. I don't fucking want you to leave, but I can't even look at you. You made me buy into your fucking fantasy, only to take a sledgehammer to my dreams on your way out the door. So, no, I will not be signing your employment contract. But I do wish you well." Drying my cheeks with gentle pats so as not to ruin my makeup, I suck in a breath before removing my ring and placing it in his hand. "I can find my own way home. Even if I don't know where that is anymore."

"Are you fucking kidding me right now? I love you more than anything, but what you just said to me is bullshit! I never wanted to walk away. I hate it when we're apart. You know that. I feel like I have no control over my life, and I thought that you, of all people, could see past the fake smile and forced acceptance. Everyone's happiness is hinged on my choices, and I don't get a say in anything. I've told you over and over again that I want to be with you, and you keep telling me that I'm selfish if I ruin this opportunity for my friends. But I can't help that I don't give a fuck about a tour if it means losing you. If you don't want either of us to give up who we are for the other, fine, let's find a compromise. We don't have to throw the whole thing away. I hated chasing you. I was miserable the entire two months we were apart.

And for some reason, you think I could walk away and give up, but I can't. I never will. I would give anything to be at home with you. This week has been a nightmare, and I'm holding on by a thread. I'm trying to get everything in order at work because I know I'm leaving my brother a mess. I'm trying to do all this PR bullshit for the band because if I don't, the invite to the tour will be revoked. I'm doing my best to come home and spend time with you, but every time I walk into the house, you're in *his* arms. And I know that's my fault. I fucked up letting you two sleep together. But it was going to happen one way or another. We all know that, and I didn't want you to leave me because you felt guilty, and I never wanted you to have to choose between us. Your home is with us. We're a family, Val, albeit a fucked up one. But a family nonetheless. We're all you've got, and you're the only woman we will ever need. I want to marry you. I want to buy a house. I want to have kids. I want to grow old together. And I'm sorry that I didn't post about us online. I'm sorry I didn't set the record straight. I shouldn't have allowed the other guys to convince me to leave well enough alone because it helped to drive sales. Fuck the sales. Fuck the tour. And fuck anything and everything that keeps us apart. I'm done with it. I cannot live without you."

"Then tell me what the reasonable compromise is. Make a deal with *me*. Stop going behind my back and negotiating my time with your brother. If you want me to be your wife, you need to start treating me like an equal partner. You keep saying it's my choice, but I haven't felt like I had a say in my life this entire week. You both keep deciding for me like I'm a possession instead of a person. And I'm sick of it!"

"That was never the intent. You've always been free to make your own choices. I needed certain assurances from him so that I'd know you were taken care of, but that was never about dictating your boundaries or actions. I can't leave unless I know I'm going to see you at some point. You don't have to agree to one week a month, but I can't go three months straight without having you in my arms. I need you to promise me that you'll still be here when I get back."

"Now, all of a sudden, my word is enough for you?"

"Well, you're pissed off and yelling at me. So, I'm afraid to ask for more."

I laugh and shake off the last of my anger. "You need to toughen up, my love. What happened to the badass with the big dick energy that I fell in love with?"

"He's right here," Kold grabs my hand and presses it against his cock. "Still very much in love with you."

CHAPTER 53

Kold

The lingering tension from the car ride softened as we ate dinner in the office. There was a private candle-lit meal served upon our arrival that was meant to set the tone of the evening. I painstakingly planned every detail, wanting to prove that despite the distance, Val was never absent from my mind.

There was a moment in the limo before voices began to rise, where I considered the possibility of Val being happier without me. Darc will always protect her. He will meet her every need, grant her every request, and fulfill her every desire. I see how much he loves her and how she returns that love without hesitation. But she loves me as much, if not more, and I could never walk away.

After dinner, Val calmly asked for thirty minutes to blow off steam before agreeing to revisit the contract and compromise. That was twenty-five minutes ago, and she's been on the dance floor with Darc ever since.

Projected on stage behind the DJ is a countdown to midnight. The twenty-foot-tall numbers seemed to mock my wishes as they ticked closer to zero, foreshadowing my imminent demise. No longer able to watch the seconds being stolen from us, I retired to the couch in the office, stretched out, and closed my eyes.

"Did you fall asleep at your own party, or are you pretending to sleep so that I go away?" Val joins me on the couch, tucking her knees against my legs and lying flat against my chest. "I wish you could feel how much I miss you when you're not around. I don't know how we let it get to this point, but I'm willing to do anything to fix it."

"Anything, huh? I like the sound of that." I know that sex isn't going to resolve our predicament, but I doubt it would make the situation any worse. "Should we discuss our future plans with my dick inside you?"

"You can't mention your dick and expect me not to want it. Why are you being a flirt? I thought you were mad at me, and we were meant to be having a serious conversation?" Val sits up, still straddling my cock, with her dress bunched slightly at her waist.

My brother knew exactly what he was doing when he bought her this dress for Christmas. Val looks elegant and expensive, effortlessly pairing with the esthetic Darc and I strive to present. But the high slit is suggestive enough to be erotic and allows for easy access.

"Stand up and take this off. I want you naked for this discussion." My eyes trace her every movement as she obeys my command. "Neither of us walks away until we've reached a resolution. Agreed?"

"Agreed." The airy fabric tickles over her skin as it falls to the floor.

"Panties on or off?" She steps toward me as I right myself on the sofa, sitting at eye level with the undergarment in question. "Do you trust me not to run into a crowd of people wearing only a lace thong?"

I scoot to the edge of the cushion, fixated on the intricate lace pattern between me and my unquenchable desire. Whatever we were meant to be talking about can wait. I dig my fingers into the meat of her outer thighs, locking her in place as I press the bridge of my nose along the slit of her pussy.

"I need to taste you." With a single deep breath, I'm stiff with desire.

"You and your incredible tongue are impossible to say *no* to. But maybe we should talk first, and you can eat your dessert after." Val's fingers brush through my hair as I kiss and tease.

"We're running out of time, and you need to make a final decision."

"Why don't you ask me yes or no questions while I play? And then you can try to translate my mumbled responses like they do at the dentist's office."

"Babe, I don't know what kind of dentist you're seeing, but that's *not* how they should clean your teeth." Val shifts her weight as I tap her ankle and re-position her foot beside me on the edge of the couch.

"Very funny!" With her thighs spread open, I slide my tongue over her panties, soaking her from both sides of the thin fabric. "If you don't stop telling jokes, you're going to be the one mumbling responses, and I'll be the one asking the questions."

"Oh, really! Well, in that case. Have you heard the one about the chicken crossing the road?"

I run my hand along the inside of Val's thigh, over the curve of her ass, and up her spine, stopping when her wet pussy sits comfortably on my bicep. Then I stand. A gasp escapes her lungs as I lift her from the ground before laying her on the couch. I push her knees apart and wedge myself between her thighs.

"I'm done playing games with you, little girl." I pull off my tie and drop my shirt on the floor before removing my belt. "I have been far too lenient, and my patience for your disrespect has run out."

"Babe, wait. Pause." Val props herself up on her elbows. "Are you playing around, or are you actually mad?"

I grin at her and wink, and her body relaxes beneath me. "I don't wish to leave you, and I don't want to lose you."

Val unzips my pants and bites her bottom lip. "I don't want to lose you either. And I don't want you to leave. But I still think you should sign the contract and join the tour."

"You know I won't last two days without you." I unbutton my pants and free my cock from behind my boxer briefs. "Why won't you let me stay? I want to start our life together."

"What if I like the idea of being engaged to a famous rockstar, and you're going on tour is part of my fantasy?" Val encircles my stiff cock with her fingers and begins stroking the length from base to tip.

I grab her wrist and remove her hand momentarily, long enough to stand beside the couch and strip from the waist down. Fucking black tie bullshit makes it a lot harder to fuck on a whim. Once I'm naked, I slip off her lace panties and make myself at home between her thighs.

"If that's the reason you want me to go, I'll sign the contract. But I need something from you. I need a commitment that you'll still be mine when I return home. And I need you to fly out to see me, even if it's only one weekend a month." I push myself inside her, getting us both nice and wet. Then pull out and rub the head of my cock over her sensitive clit.

"Oh god, that feels so good. I love it when you do that." Val begins to wiggle and whine as I continue to tease. "I'll agree to one weekend a month because I hate being away from you, but you still have to call me every day, and we're reading one of my books first."

"Deal. You pick the first book. What else? Come on, babe. You know what I want." I rub against her clit as beads of precum mix with the fluids of her arousal. "There's only one thing you can give me to make me sign that contract. I can't walk away from you without it."

"Okay. Fine. I'll do it." Reaching for my hand, Val redirects my efforts and guides my attention to a location of her choosing. "Now stop being a tease and fuck me."

"First, you have to tell me what you're agreeing to." I thrust inside her and pull all the way out. "Then you have to tell me what you want in exchange. We're not lying to get each other off, Val. We're negotiating our future."

"I know. I'm willing to give you what you want."

I push inside her again, groaning as her walls tighten around me. "Fuck, babygirl, stop holding back. Tell me what you want, or we're going to continue this conversation from opposite ends of the couch."

"I don't want anything." Val tries to reach for me, but I push her hands away and pull out. She sits with her back propped against the arm of the couch while I fall away to the opposite side. "I'm consenting to a legal marriage after two weeks of dating. How is that not enough to prove my loyalty to you?"

"It's more than enough. That's the problem. You're too willing to give me what I want, and your one-sided sacrifices are unwelcome here. I'm not like the men in your past looking to take everything from you and offer nothing in return." To hell with Val and her threats. I'll join her in the fire if I have to. If we can't come to an agreement, I'm deleting the tour contract and fighting for the woman I love and the future we deserve. "Tell me five things that you truly *want* in order to be happily married to me."

"Oh my god, you're making me nuts. Fine. I want a kiss from the man who loves me more than anything else in the world." Val leans forward and puckers her lips.

"You get all of my kisses. That's a given." Shifting to the middle cushion, I pull Val to my side and kiss her. "Come on. Tell me five things, and then I'll make you cum and let you go back downstairs to the party."

"You're ridiculous—ly cute. But I don't know what you want me to say, and five things is a lot. I know that I want to keep my current job. I'd be willing to volunteer at the club and help as much as I can, but I need something in my life that isn't controlled by you."

"Okay, that's one." Wrapping my arms around her naked frame, I hold her closely. "My employment offer was never about controlling you. I thought if I made it a legal document, that would grant you a level of personal security beyond what my words could guarantee. I know you worry about the rug being pulled out from under you, and I wanted to alleviate your concerns."

"I know. Once I read it, I understood what you were going for. And I appreciate your incredibly generous offer, but I can't accept it. Not right now. Perhaps we could set it aside and revisit the topic later."

"So long as my name remains on the businesses, your job offer will be in my center desk drawer, signed and ready to go."

"Alright then. Moving on. For my second request, I want

your word that you won't cheat on me. But if you do cheat, I want you to be honest and forthcoming. I don't need you to lie to me in order to save a relationship that doesn't fulfill you."

I intend to do more than offer Val my word, but for now, that's what she's asking for.

"I have loved you always, and tomorrow will be no different." I kiss her forehead as she snuggles into my chest. "There's no way I would ever cheat on you. *But* if a line should get crossed, I'll be honest about what happened."

"Okay. I'm pretty sure this next one is going to make you happy. So, for my number three, I'd like a new car."

"Done." I require no further explanation. I already planned to leave Val the keys to my Range Rover, and I added her to the insurance a few days ago. But if she's willing to let me spoil her, I'll snatch the opportunity and run with it.

"Seriously? You hate my car so much that you don't even want to hear my reasons? Fine. But I'm making the payments. I'm only asking for your help with the buying process."

"Yep. Moving on. What's your number four?"

Let her work a job of her choosing, don't cheat, and buy her a new car. So far, this list is a cakewalk. Val either greatly underestimates the depth of my love or the balance of my checking account. Either way, I'm going to have fun proving myself and spoiling her rotten.

"When it comes time for the summer tour, I don't want to rehash this bullshit. You gave your word. You committed to the dates. And we're both willing to do whatever it takes to make this relationship work. We don't have to talk it to death. I need you to trust that my love for you is unwavering and eternal. End of story. No further negotiations are needed."

I have to survive this winter before I can worry about the summer.

"Robot mode. Got it. When the time comes, I'll swallow my feelings and do my best Darc impression." I didn't intend it as a joke, but it makes Val laugh, which in turn, makes me smile. "Speaking of my brother, I'm surprised he isn't here stealing you from me. I assume he's your number five. I kind of figured you'd save that request for last."

Val shakes her head from side to side, but we both know that lie won't part from her lips.

"Sweetheart, look at me." The words are his, but I skimp on the authority, leaving her wiggle room to disobey.

"Valentine! Eyes on me!" This time, she follows my order without hesitation. "Tell me your number five, and I'll reward you. Or silently lie to me again, and spend the next ten minutes choking on my cock. It's your choice."

"I'll tell you my number five. But for future reference, if you're trying to make me choose one thing over another, you can't make your punishment sound like a reward. And your brother doesn't offer choices." Val straddles my legs and grips the back of the couch. "Although, I am curious. What sort of reward are you offering in exchange for my candor?"

Licking two fingers, I brush my hand up her thigh and begin circling her clit. "I want to eat that sweet little pussy until you cum for me."

"Oh, that sounds nice." Val arches back as I continue to circle and then falls forward. With her head on my shoulder, she whispers, "I don't want to make you mad."

"Tick-tock, babygirl. What's it going to be?" I lick my lips, preparing to reward her.

"I want Darc to end the relationship when he's ready for it to be over. I want him to leave me because he doesn't need me anymore."

"If that's the case, you might as well say *till death do you part*."

CHAPTER 54

Val

I make sure to double-check the mirror before leaving the office. Kold practically licked the soul from my body and then filled up the hollow space with wood glue. I wasn't entirely certain I'd be able to walk after he was finished with me. It's almost unfair how good they are in bed, on the couch, in the shower, and in the car. I'm annoyed that I wasted my 20s and half of my 30s having mediocre sexual encounters with guys who ate pussy like it was a tootsie pop. Three licks in, and they were ready to bite into the center and move on. Funny how those same men always expected me to get lockjaw from sucking off their whiskey dick.

What's worse is that I always gave in, even after they had given up.

Taking the stairs from the office to the main level, I scan the dance floor before heading toward the bar. The guys told me they ordered a limo for the night so they could enjoy themselves, so I'm moderately certain I'll find Darc on a bar stool with a drink in his hand.

The music pouring through the speakers vibrates in my chest as I make my way through groups of sharply dressed men and stylish ladies. I've never been to a New Year's Eve party like this one, and the atmosphere in the room feels charged with sexual energy. The beautiful people have all come out to play, and the prize is a midnight kiss and a Sunday morning walk of shame back to the car.

Excusing myself as I pass through the center of a large group, I emerge on the other side, eager to locate my dance partner, but my enthusiasm quickly dissolves when I spot him at the bar, otherwise engaged. Seeing the goddess-inspired blonde giggling at his side stops me dead in my tracks. Engine failure, no doubt caused by a shattered heart.

I always knew that Darc would need more, and eventually, he'd find what he was looking for. Still, I hadn't expected him to stop loving me so soon after I negotiated my hand in exchange for our continued relationship. Shame on me for neglecting to acknowledge that feelings rarely run in both directions.

"Hey! I recognize you. Long time no see." The abrupt greeting is accompanied by a hand on my arm, drawing my attention away from the handsome man at the bar and his dazzling conquest. "I was talking to Kold about the tour, and he asked me if I'd seen you. Then poof, here you are."

"You know me, Tommy. I'm a regular ol' David Copperfield."

"Yeah, totally." He clearly has no idea who I'm talking about.

"I'm loving this whole fancy casual vibe. I've always said that a man can't go wrong with a tuxedo t-shirt and a pair of linen trousers." I make sure to hide my broken heart behind a perfectly crafted smile. "How long ago was Kold looking for me?"

"I don't know. Maybe, like, a minute ago." He motions in the direction I'm making an effort to avoid. "Before that groupie walked up and started asking about Darc..."

Tommy's eyes go wide like he's swallowed hot coals. "Not that your old man would ever give someone else the time of day. No way. I've known that dude forever. He's as loyal as they come. They both are."

I'm not sure if I'm simply mishearing him over the music or if I had sex with the wrong Kold in the office a moment ago. No. I know that's not it. Kold's left arm and leg are solid with tattoos, and the right side of his chest. The played-back memory makes my left hand tingle as I vividly recall the heat of his tattooed skin beneath my palm and fingertips. I left Kold naked and panting in the office, so I know that's Darc at the bar. But then, why is he pretending to be his brother?

"I'm not worried." I lie to myself to keep from crying. "Darc is allowed to do whatever makes him happy. Let's try to get a drink and toast to the exciting year ahead." Linking my arm to Tommy's, I move to the end of the bar, wanting Darc to see us.

"Are you anxious to get on the road with the guys? Or do you have things in your life that keep you close to home?" Making conversation with the stoner beside me seems like a better choice when staring a hole through Darc and murdering Jamie is the only other option available. Then again, I suppose I could go back to the office and spend the remaining hours of the evening with my real boyfriend.

One quick drink, and then I'll find Kold and never leave his side.

"The tour is still hypothetical unless you know something I don't. Did Darc say something to you about it? I'm always the last to know, and Kold wasn't offering any hints."

As the bartender approaches, I glance in Darc's direction, needing a new dose of some old pain, but there's someone else occupying the seat. Darc is nowhere to be found, and Jamie has disappeared with him. I shouldn't be surprised. Of course, he would fuck her.

No, wait. Hold on a minute. Jamie walked over and asked about Darc because she saw him talking to Tommy and assumed he was Kold. So, as far as she was concerned, she was flirting with my actual fucking fiancé. The man who claimed he'd never slept with her.

As the anger grows in my chest, replacing the pain of the previous moment, strong arms wrap around me from behind, taking me from my feet. I swing in the air like a rag doll, unable to identify my assailant.

"What the fuck?" The question expels from my lungs as I reach for Tommy, but he makes no attempt to reach back. Apparently, I'm on my own.

Popping my elbow back sharply, I make contact with flesh and bone and incite a verbal response from the man hidden behind me. "Fuck, babe. Try not to kick the shit out of me in my own club." He sets me down and spins me on my heels. "You keep me waiting for an hour, and then you come to the bar and have drinks with another man? Tell me why I shouldn't be mad."

My eyes jump from his face to the girl on his right, offering the only answer I care to provide.

"Fair enough." Darc grins at me and turns his head slightly. "Kold is in the office working, and I'm not wasting the rest of my evening pretending to be him. Go away! I came here to spend time with my girl, and that's exactly what I'm going to do."

Jamie begins shouting something about Darc being an asshole and how she'll never sleep with him again, but it all gets lost in the sauce once he pulls me in close and kisses me. His lips taste like brown liquor, and his tongue hints at an unquenchable thirst. "It's bad enough sharing you with my brother. I'm not willing to add anyone else to the list. Say goodnight to your new friend, and let's get lost in the crowd."

"Have a good night, you two." Tommy takes the hint and makes his exit without further persuasion.

"You're coming with me." Darc leads me through the crowd at the bar, past the tables of New Year's Eve trinkets, and into the back hallway that is strictly off-limits. "I want you to run!"

"In high heels? Are you crazy? I'll break an ankle." I'm not even sure what he's telling me. What are we running from? There's no one else here.

"I'm giving you to the count of five to run, and you'd better be quick about it." Darc looks at his watch as though he's noting the time. "Tick tock."

"I don't understand what you want."

"Five." His tone lacks any hint of playfulness, and I know better than to deny him.

I take off running down the narrow hallway in the direction of backstage and the alternate entrance to the second floor. I'm still not sure why I'm running or where I'm going, but I assume Darc has his reasons.

The building's width is a quarter of its length, and I feel light-headed the farther I go. I was a bowling phenom, not a local track star. I have half a mind to give up on this game of cat and mouse, but my options are stolen when I'm hit from behind and thrown from my feet. Darc and I slam into the wall with such force that the remaining air is knocked from my lungs, and my vision flashes black.

Now I'm beginning to understand what he's going for. Darc pins my chest to the wall and my wrists above my head. I know what's coming this time, but I don't know why.

CRACK!

With only a thin dress between my ass and his hand, the first slap stings my flesh. "That's for making me wait for over an hour while you fucked my brother."

CRACK!

The second slap fills my eyes with tears. "That's for having a drink with another man when you saw me sitting ten feet away."

"Flirting with another woman," I whisper into the painted block wall against my cheek.

CRACK!

The third slap steals my breath. "And that's for questioning my loyalty."

"You believed that I would entertain the advances of another woman when you, of all people, should know better." Darc releases my wrist and turns me on a dime to face him. His fingers locate the slit of my dress, and within seconds I'm exposed. Ripping my outfit in half from thigh to tit, the soft fabric tickles as it falls away and the thrill of being naked in public freckles my skin with goosebumps.

I press myself against the cool cinder block wall and allow the chill to calm the reddened handprint painted on my right ass cheek. "When you're finished being mad at me, I'd like you to kiss me."

Darc's chest rises and falls as his eyes narrow. "If you want my forgiveness, I suggest you get on your knees and earn it."

Kold would never allow me to kneel on a concrete floor at his feet. And he wouldn't shred my clothing in public and risk having another man see me naked. Kold would never fuck me or punish me out of real anger. He would only do those things if I asked him to, and out of love for me. But Darc isn't Kold, and he's never going to be.

Isn't that why I love him?

Unable to bear the weight of his disapproval, I do as I'm told and drop to my knees. There's something cliché about a woman in lace thong panties and high heels blowing a guy wearing a tuxedo, but this is where fate has brought me. And who am I to argue?

Darc's cock is stiff before it touches my tongue, as though he's been ready for me all night. He kicks off his shoes and drops his pants, leaving me to free him from his boxer briefs. My hands and mouth work in tandem as he heaps praise on my talents.

"Oh, fuck. You are too good at taking that cock, and so pretty. If this is how you plan to ask for forgiveness, I'll never be able to stay mad at you."

I suck him down deeper as he drops articles of clothing around me. I register each item as it falls to the floor but remain focused on the task at hand. My pussy has no doubt soaked the crotch of my panties for a second time tonight.

"As much as I love fucking your cute little mouth, you won't be swallowing my cum tonight. Get up!"

Pulling him into my throat as deeply as I can, I permit the tears to spill from my eyes as I choke. I know what my man likes, and I'm happy to accommodate. Looking up at him, I fall back against the wall and dry my chin with the back of my hand.

My legs tremble as I stand uneasy on stilted black heels, adapting to our new position. I use the wall behind me as a crutch as he pushes his fingers inside, soaking his hand in my unapologetic yearning.

"It's hard for me to stay mad at you when your pussy gets this wet from sucking my cock. Do you think I should forgive you?" His fingers twist and curl, making the muscles in my stomach tighten.

"I was in the office making a deal with your brother so that I could stay with you. And I had a drink with Tommy because I didn't want to say something I couldn't take back. I was hurt that you were with her, but not because I don't trust you. Someday,

I'm going to lose you, and I'll have to pretend to be happy for you even though my fucking heart is breaking." The hurt cracks my voice along the edges.

"You're not going to lose me, but I understand how you feel." His lips connect with mine, signaling the end of his anger.

Our kiss continues as I step out of my shoes and kick them aside, adding them to the pile of clothing littering the ground around us. Then I slip my panties past the thickest part of my thigh, allowing them to drop on their own. Darc and I are naked in the hallway of a packed club, and I don't think I could get more turned on.

Last week, when he had me pinned against this wall, he'd already been inside me earlier that night, and still, my body wanted more. Why did I ask him to stop? Kold has given me a free pass to love and fuck them both as I choose, and Darc has fought his own brother tooth and nail for equal time.

Pulling back from my lips, Darc hooks my leg with his arm and stands, spreading me apart. He shoves inside, pushing his cock past my comfort level on the first thrust, not bothering to take it slow.

I link my hands behind his neck, squeezing my fingers together and balance on one leg as he pounds into me. The sounds of pleasure expel from my lungs. Moaning and gasping and calling out his name, I beg for his release.

"Please, Darc. Please. Please. Please, cum inside me. Show me that you're still mine, and I promise I'll be yours forever."

"Oh yes. Fuck!" Darc feeds off of my encouragement. "Tell me you're mine, babygirl, and beg for me like the little whore I know you are."

"Let go of my leg so I can make it tight for you." I find my footing, lean forward, and face the wall. Once he's inside me, I cross my feet and squeeze. "Babe, please. I need to feel you cum for me."

Darc's hand wraps around my throat, tipping my head back as he takes me from behind. He slams into me with fierce determination as his grip on my body tightens. With my arms braced against the solid surface, I hold us both upright as he blows his load inside me and collapses against my back with a growl. "Don't ever let him take you from me."

Stuck together from head to toe, I try to catch my breath as Darc twitches inside me. My dress is shredded, and I desperately need a shower, but I have to resolve the situation beside me before I address issues two through ten. For whatever reason, Darc requires my reassurance, and because of my deal with Kold, I can meet his request.

"I'm yours for as long as you want me."

Peeling himself off of me, Darc retrieves his pants and shirt from where they lie discarded on the floor. I accept the white button-down from his extended hand and allow his scent to envelop my battered frame. He didn't even attempt to get me off, the selfish prick. I laugh, amused at the prospect of giving him shit about that later.

Darc zips his pants and kneels to collect the rest of our clothes, pausing to search for something in the pocket of his jacket. "Tell me again, Valentine. How long do I get to keep you?"

"What is going on with you?" I smile and lean forward to kiss him, refusing to acknowledge the tension knotting his shoulders. "I'm yours until you get sick of looking at me or until you move on to someone better."

"Well, if that's the case. I think I'll keep you forever."

CHAPTER 55

Kold

I'm sitting at my desk, reading through the tour contract for what feels like the hundredth time this week, when the back door to the office swings open. Val's laughter draws my attention from the screen, and I look up, excited that she's returned to me. However, she has not come back in the same condition she left.

Stepping through the doorway wearing a long-sleeved, white button-down shirt and a pair of high heels, Val's black dress is nothing more than a ball of wrinkled fabric being clutched with disregard. She kicks her shoes towards the wall and skips across the room with bare feet, holding the dress out and giving it a shake.

"Do I even want to know?" I smirk at my love as she fastens a playfully annoyed look on her face. Darc drops the clothes and shoes he's walked in carrying and plops down on the couch. Seeing them disheveled and half-naked doesn't surprise me, but I am disappointed that I missed the show.

"Your brother ripped my dress in half!" Val unfurls the shredded material, highlighting the tear that runs from slit to neck.

This entire week, I've been stressed and overthinking to the point of madness. My phone has been nonstop alerts and phone calls and messages. Everyone who's ever met me wants to reconnect, and the only person I care to spend my time with has backed away from the picture, like a first date plus one at a family reunion. Val has been acting as though she's insignificant, when in reality, she's the only one who matters. Now she's standing here, dress torn to shreds after another round of sex with my brother, and all I can do is laugh.

"It's not funny!" Val slaps my arm as she pretends to be offended. "I really liked the way it fit, and it was a Christmas present. Who gives someone a gift and then destroys it a week later? Is that another one of your stupid fucked-up holiday traditions?"

"Babe, it's fine. He'll buy you a new one tomorrow. But I suppose that's not much help tonight, is it?" I glance over my shoulder and note the numbers being projected on stage. "We've got one hour and twenty-seven minutes remaining until the ball drops, and you are officially without a dress. Looks like we're headed home early tonight."

"No way! I'm taking a shower, throwing on whatever clothes you have here, and then all three of us are having drinks and making the most of every one of those eighty-seven minutes. I'm done with the back-and-forth and the split time. To hell with what people on the internet have to say. I love both of you."

She joins me in my office chair, careful to avoid knocking over the stack of papers on my desk and curls up in my lap. "I'm sorry I lost my temper in the limo, and I'm sorry that I haven't spent more time with you. I don't know what's wrong with me. I've been living in my head all week trying to avoid acknowledging how I feel about you leaving. I wanted to make the most of tonight in case this is *our last midnight*."

I squeeze her body to mine, pulling her in tighter.

"We have a deal, remember? And a lifetime of midnights." I remove Val's engagement ring from my pocket and take her left hand into mine. "Or maybe not."

My heart catches in my throat when I see the platinum band on her ring finger. There's no diamond, but there's also no mistaking its significance. Darc has officially tossed his hat in the ring and proposed to my fiancée.

"Our deal stands," Val whispers against my neck and seals her promise with a kiss. She takes the ring from my fingers and adds it to the band already in place. Holding her hand out in front of her, she smiles. "But for now, that's our secret."

I kiss her, or maybe she kisses me. Sometimes, when we're tangled together, it can be difficult to discern where she ends and I begin. I haven't been able to figure out how I'm going to survive without her. And I can't wrap my head around the thought of parting ways, even if it is temporary. Val is my everything. She makes me a better man because she loves all of me. Not once has she asked me to change, but her presence in my life has inspired a transformation nonetheless.

"I'm gonna take a shower. If you'd care to join me, I'd love the company. And when I get out, I plan on ringing in this New Year with my two favorite people." Val shifts and attempts to stand, but I hold her in place. "What's wrong?"

"I wasn't finished holding you, and I'm never going to be ready to let you go." I loosen my embrace to allow her release, but Val drops her head to my shoulder and melts into my chest.

"You cuddling me is one of the things I'm going to miss the most while you're away. As cheesy as it sounds, your arms are my safe haven, and I'm not entirely sure I'll be able to let you leave, even though I know I have to." Hearing Val say I'm her sanctuary fills my heart with purpose.

"You know, we could stay together and avoid this unnecessary turmoil. I haven't signed the contract." I can't bring myself to fill out the bottom of the paperwork. For the life of me, I'm not sure why I've even considered it. My answer should have been a resounding *no* from the beginning, and I should have immediately squashed the rumors about Val and Darc.

Pulling out my phone and opening the camera, I stretch my arm at an angle that flatters us both and take a photo. Then I position her left hand so that her ring is showing, kiss her shoulder, and take another.

"Come on, let's get in the shower." I slip the phone back into my pocket and stand, taking Val with me. Once we're in the bathroom, I set her on her feet and unbutton the dress shirt she's wearing, kissing her as my fingers work their way down.

As the shirt falls to the floor, I pull back to examine the goddess in my arms. Her hair falls in chestnut waves, highlighted in gold and long enough to sweep against her hardened nipples. I tip her chin upwards and brush my thumb across her lips before replacing the touch with my kiss.

"I don't want to spend three months apart. I can't." I search her eyes for the answers I lack and the strength to do what she's asking.

Val's gentle touch reaches my neck and brushes along my jaw before dropping to settle on my chest. "This isn't going to be like last time. You know where to find me, and I'll fly out to see you as often as possible. You never lost me, and you're never going to lose me. I've been yours all along, and regardless of the physical distance between us, I'll always be yours."

Darc steps into the bathroom and slips between me and the sink, brushing past Val to turn on the shower. I hear his pants hit the floor behind her and see the curtain pull to the side as he steps in before the water can rise in temperature. "Fuck, that's cold!"

Val and I laugh and smile at each other as the sadness of our longing fades into memory. I have three months to miss her. Until then, I'm making the most of our time together.

I strip out of my clothes while Val joins Darc in the shower. She lets out a sound that tells me the water still isn't as warm as she likes, and I smile, amused by how damn cute she is. They're kissing when I pull the curtain aside and step in, but Val reaches for me. I guide her outstretched arm and open hand to where my stiff cock awaits her touch and groan as her fingers encircle me.

I'm not sure how our girl has a round left in her after I devoured her like an all-you-can-eat buffet and Darc fucked her hard enough to rip her dress in half, but I appreciate her willingness to end the year with a bang.

Her hand strokes my length without pause as I step forward to bite into her shoulder. Pulling back from the kiss she's engaged in, Val turns in my direction and finds my lips. Soft, delicate moans escape from her mouth, turning me to stone.

The smell of body wash mixes with steam as the heated water rains over our skin. Darc runs the lathered loofah over Val's shoulders and across her back before kneeling to wash her legs. Reaching for the bottle of soap, I squeeze some into my palm and continue to process around front. I make sure to pay extra attention to the parts of her body that respond to my touch, watching as her head tilts back and her eyes close.

Darc's arm comes across her chest, cupping Val's breast as her back arches and her eyes widen. Growling into the back of her head, he offers her a choice. "Should we be nice and get you off first?"

Nice enough to offer her a choice but not nice enough to wait for her response, Darc begins fingering her ass without warning.

"Oh, fuck. Darc stop. I can't." Her pleas fill the space around us as I reach between her thighs. My fingers circle her clit, making her legs shake as indiscernible requests turn into breathy groans.

"Yes, you can. Now be a good girl and cum for us, or I'll use my cock instead of my fingers." Darc continues to slam into her from behind as I circle her clit faster, knowing she's close to the edge. "I'm not going to let you fall. Stop holding back and give me what I want."

On command, Val's body convulses. She presses herself tightly to Darc as he supports her weight, keeping her upright. Her hand slaps at mine as I draw out her orgasm with slow movements while the muscles in her body spasm and twitch.

"You both need to stop joking about fucking me in the ass. It's not funny." Val finds her footing and steps forward, throwing her arms over my shoulders and kissing me. "Now I need a shower to wash off my shower... Unless you need something from me."

I lick my lips, and her mouth is on me before I can exhale a response. Rinsing any remaining soap from my hands, I turn off the water to avoid drowning the goddess swallowing my dick and twist my fingers into her hair.

"Do you want him to fuck you while you choke on me? You're such a good little cock sucker. I bet that pussy is nice and wet, ready for him to fill you up." I thrust deeper, locking her head in place as Darc clutches her hips and pushes inside.

"I bet you're still sensitive, aren't you? We might need to give your pussy a break." Darc works her over slowly, pushing two fingers into her ass while filling her pussy with his cock. "I wonder if we could use shampoo as lube?"

Val smacks at his hand as she attempts to dislodge herself, but I hold her head in place and thrust deeper. When she drops her teeth without applying pressure, I release my grip rather than risk getting my dick bit off.

"Are you trying to give me cancer?" Val spits out the words as she pulls away from both of us. "Shampoo is not lube, you fucking animals, and you're not getting that thing in my ass. Stop trying to use my own kinks against me."

It's cute when she tries to be defiant, but her voice hints more toward desire than disobedience, and she lacks the resolve to keep us at bay.

Pulling the curtain aside, I step on the mat with one foot and reach into the cabinet beneath the sink where I know the lube is located. I fist the bottle and return to the shower, smirking as Val's eyes widen.

"Has he been in there before?" I direct my question to the woman I'm set to marry, even though I know she'll perjure herself for his benefit. Val has certain tells that are easy to read, making it impossible for her to lie convincingly. Perhaps that's why her deceptions are frequently lies of omission.

"We haven't done that," Darc responds without meeting my eyes, and his lips twist into a grin. His gaze remains locked on the woman between us. "Not yet."

Val shoots him a look, but I pull her into my arms with her back pressed tightly to my chest before she has the opportunity to retort. The water on Darc's side of the shower has remained on, filling the room with steam, and the look in his eyes tells me that he's boiling.

"I get her first. Then you're free to stick your cock in any hole you want while I'm gone."

"Um, don't I get a say in this?" Val wiggles against me, trying to pull away or spin around. I'm unsure of her intention, but I am certain she's mistaken if she thinks I'm letting her slip away. "Babe, you're too thick. It's never getting in there."

"Come on, babygirl. Do this one thing for me. I need to take this memory with me."

Val relaxes under my restraining embrace, indicating a willingness to comply. "You know I'd give you anything, but does it have to be this? You understand it's going to hurt, right?"

"Shhh." Darc steps forward, stealing her away. "I'll never let anyone hurt you."

I want to amend his statement to include myself. *We'll never let anyone hurt you.* That's what he should have said, but he didn't. His words were chosen with intention, and he meant to imply that his protection knows no limits, and he will not hesitate to choose her over me.

Kissing the top of Val's head as she sinks into his chest, Darc holds up two fingers. "You've already taken this much, and I know you can do this. Breathe through the pain and focus on me until the pleasure comes. I will *always* protect you."

Shock stuns me into silence as I watch her nod in agreement. I say nothing, but I know better than to let the moment pass. Coating two fingers with the lube, I move behind her and push inside. My fingers slide in slowly, giving her body time to accept what I'm offering. I need her primed and ready, pre-stretched but still insanely tight. I want to hurt her, but in a good way.

"I'm only doing this because I love you." Her heartfelt admission gives way to cries of pleasure as I attempt to add a third finger.

"I love you too." The mirrored statement plays in stereo as Darc and I respond simultaneously.

Leaning in to kiss her neck, I whisper my promise against Val's neck. "I'll go slow until you're ready for me, and then I'll give you as much as you can take. I want this to feel good for you. And after I'm finished, I want to watch you fuck him."

"Okay." Val buries her face in Darc's chest as I add a generous amount of lube to my swollen cock and press against her clenched opening.

"You need to relax, sweetheart. I know you can take him. You're such a good girl." Darc's soothing encouragement and praise showers over her, and I feel her body ready to accept me. "That's it. Just like that. You're doing so good. Look at how well you take his cock. Are you going to be my good girl and let me have you like that when he's finished?"

The more he talks, the deeper I go as she accepts me inch by inch. Once I've buried the full length of my cock in her, I pull out to the head and push back inside, controlling my strokes as I gauge her response. As my speed increases, so does the power of my strokes. Val reaches back, attempting to control my pace, but I'm too far gone to stop now.

"I'm almost there. Fuck, you feel so good. I knew you would be tight, but goddamn, your ass is amazing."

Darc spools the tendrils of Val's wet hair around his hand and adjusts the position of her face. "Everything about you is amazing, Valentine." He kisses her, causing her to tighten around me as she orgasms.

"Fuck."

There's more I want to say, but words fail me as my balls constrict, and I release inside her. Panting and shaky, I hold her in my arms until I'm certain she's taken every drop. Then I pull out slowly and turn her toward me, taking her face in my hands.

"Thank you."

CHAPTER 56
Val

Stepping out of the bathroom, wrapped in a towel, I check the time as I approach the balcony window. There's less than an hour remaining on the clock, and for some reason, these decreasing minutes still feel like a countdown to the close. Why does tonight seem like the end of everything? Aren't we still at the beginning?

The muscles in my legs continue to spasm as I lean against the glass, exhausted from hours of fucking and cumming over and over again. The pulsing in my thighs and the sting in my ass serve as a reminder that I have one twin left to satisfy.

Strong arms wrap around my waist as Darc appears behind me, and I'm proud of myself for finally being able to tell them apart without looking. "We don't have to do anything, but I want you to know how much I need you. I'm not a voyeur like my brother. I don't get off on watching you with another man. In fact, I fucking hate it."

"I've always pegged you as more of an exhibitionist. Would it make you feel better if I let you take your turn?" My breath fogs the window as I press my cheek to the glass. "You can fuck me right here, where someone could see us."

"Is that what you want? You want everyone to know that you're mine? Because if that's the case, I'll take you on the balcony where I can guarantee they'll see us." Darc kisses and nips at my shoulder as he loosens the towel, allowing the damp cotton to fall to the floor, leaving me exposed. Planting a field of kisses along my neck, he whispers against my ear, "If you ask me to stop, I'll stop. But if we're doing this, I want you to ride me on the couch. I'm sick of sharing you."

Turning to face him, my ass presses against the cool glass as his hand braids into my hair. I know what he needs to hear, and I have no issues with saying it, even with Kold sitting a few feet away at his desk, watching and listening intently. He understands the role I'm playing, and he knows I'll say anything to make Darc happy.

"You don't have to share me with anyone." I run my fingers over the defined lines of his chiseled abs and press my palm against his chest. "I'm all yours. I love you from now until the end."

"Don't say that to me, Valentine. You can lie to me about anything else, but not that." The lights from the party behind me filter through the window and catch in his gaze, turning his blue eyes into a kaleidoscope of color.

"I'm not lying. You know I love you."

"Then prove it." A strained smile plays at the corner of his lips and disappears before coming to fruition. He pulls away from the warmth of my growing need and turns his back on me to walk away, leaving me shattered.

My eyes flash to the desk where Kold is sitting, scrolling through his phone, clearly bored by the night's entertainment. As for Darc, he slips into the bathroom for a second before going to the couch and settling on the center cushion. I can't seem to keep either of them happy. One minute they want the whore, and the next, they want the timeless lover.

I give up. I'm too tired to play. Take over for a little while, but try not to ruin everything. I need them.

Rolling my shoulders back, I straighten my spine and etch a devil's grin across my face. Darc's eyes find mine as I stroll across the room, pausing before him to kneel between his feet. I lick my lips and huff out a breath at the sight of his swollen cock. "I see you've been expecting me."

I suck him down, eager to satisfy my hunger. As soon as the head of his cock hits the back of my throat, I'm soaked and dripping down my leg. The only thing that could make this blowjob better would be having an identical copy of him inside me, but I'll have to put on a hell of a show if I want to encourage that one to join from his seat in the viewing box.

Moving onto the couch to kneel beside him, I take advantage of the new position and work Darc over from a different angle. My legs spread apart as his arm stretches beneath me, and I know it's only a matter of time before he dips inside.

Darc cups my pussy, filling his palm with a serving of my juices before pulling back and drinking me from his hand. "That sweet little cunt tastes so good. Fuck. I need more."

Nothing drives a man like Darc wilder than being denied the taste he craves. I straddle his legs and slide slowly down his cock, making sure to coat every inch. Then I return to my place at his feet, where I lick and suck every drop from his shaft before tonguing down his balls.

"Oh yeah, just like that. You're such a good little whore. Make sure you lick me clean. I love how wet you get from sucking my cock." Darc knots his fingers into my hair, attempting to gain control. "I want to feel you dripping down my balls while I'm buried in your ass."

Powerful hands yank my mouth free from him, leaving me painfully empty. Darc holds me at arm's length and forces me to watch as the lube drips onto the head of his cock. I want to scream with the force of my exiled existence as the hunger returns, burning the back of my throat. "Why would you stop me? I wasn't finished."

"Valentine, be quiet. If you start being disobedient, you're going to get Val punished. Is that what you want?"

"No." I practically growl in response as the muscles in my neck twitch, pulling my head to one side. Darc doesn't know what it's like to truly be denied. These games we're playing are nothing compared to the torture of watching my own life played out at a distance beyond my control.

"Then shut your mouth and come here. I want my turn." He pats his lap and winks as if he's being cute. "You, of all people, should understand that."

I do as I'm told, determined to feel whole again. Darc has a way of filling in all the pieces that are missing. I straddle his legs with my back to his chest and glance at the other man in the room. I don't need Kold's approval, but some part of me seeks it out.

With my attention momentarily distracted, I'm not expecting the penetration. Darc's fingers twist inside me, slick with lube, preparing me for what's to come. I moan and arch and ready myself for more as I drink in Kold's reaction.

Sitting behind his desk with steepled hands, Kold licks his lips in silent encouragement. His gaze is attentive and unwavering. No longer distracted by his phone or computer, he looks on from his position of authority.

I wonder if his dick is swollen with anticipation. Does it throb with lingering memories of moments ago, or was he drained to the point of satisfaction?

"Remember to breathe." Darc's words draw my focus as he eases me in increments down the length of his cock until he's buried to the hilt.

The pain is quick to subside, leaving only the blinding pleasure as my body mirrors the tempo of Darc's movements. I give myself over to him, allowing full access and total control. I belong to him, soul and all, and he belongs to me.

"You feel so good. I wish I could last until midnight."

The lights and sounds of a club full of people, the mounting uncertainty fueled by the disappearing seconds being projected on stage, the man at the desk, and the future we promised each other all fade into static as Darc and I melt into one.

"I want to feel how wet you are for me." His right hand moves from my hip and follows the crease of my upper thigh. Seeking the heat spilling from my abandoned spring, his fingers plunge into my depths as I fall back against him. I'm not certain how much longer I can hold out. And by the way he's working me over, I assume he's close and encouraging me to follow.

"Stop trying to get me off." I attempt to push his hand away, but his fingers curl in response. I'm going to be of no use to him if

I finish before he does. I can barely handle him as it is. "Darc, I'm serious."

I'm not sure how he does it. One second, I'm riding reverse cowgirl as he sits beneath me. The next, his fingers splay across my chest, and he stands without pulling out of me. And then, somehow, I find myself in a new position, kneeling on the cushion where he previously sat, my arms braced against the back of the couch as he fucks me hard from behind.

"I love how good you are at taking my cock." Darc's hold on my body is formidable as he rails into me, driving in the direction of his release. I'm going to be bruised with fingerprint patterns highlighting the curves of my hips.

The sensation fueling my impending orgasm is nearly too much to bear. I close my eyes in an effort to breathe through the agonizing indulgence but find my escape is short-lived. The long strands of my hair have been gathered and gripped, granting the incoming party control of my sight.

"Is this what you plan on doing while I'm away? You're going to let him use you like a whore." Kold's tone matches his name as he growls accusations and assumptions. "You're going to allow him to fuck your body raw while I'm left with my dick in my hand, missing you. Are you going to beg for his cum like you used to beg for mine?"

I want to say *yes*. I want to scream the answer from the top of my lungs, but the word is stolen from me. "I don't know what you want me to say."

"Tell my brother that you belong to him now. That you're his girl. Tell him how much you love him and that he's the only one you want. Convince him. I want to fucking hear the things you say when you think I'm not listening."

I could say *all* that without hesitation if only I could regain control of my mouth, but Kold evokes the side of my soul that knows better. He calls her to the forefront. The part of me that holds him dear renders me in silence rather than risk a loss that neither of us could survive.

"Finish her off! Her body will tell me everything that pretty little mouth refuses to say." Kold untangles his hand from my hair and falls back to sit against the arm of the couch, still watching with fevered interest as the circular strokes of Darc's fingers on my clit send me hurling over the edge without further ado. My orgasm runs parallel with his own as Darc blows a reserve of cum inside me.

"Fuck." Darc collapses onto the cushion beside me, pulling me to his chest. "You did so good. Are you okay?"

I mumble a response, and the pair of us pant with exhaustion as he holds me in his arms. I love the way Darc chooses to stay with me. He's always there, protecting me from the vulnerability that follows the high of our blissful exchange, and I appreciate that he hasn't abandoned me like so many others before him.

"I need to talk to you." Darc's whispered request finds my ear, hidden alongside a kiss on the top of my head. "Let's go rinse off."

A shower makes sense after what we did, but I'm unconvinced that my legs maintain the strength to hold me upright. Thankfully, Darc is sturdy enough for both of us. He carries me in his arms as Kold calls after us. "When you're done, I need to talk to both of you."

Darc nods in response as we retreat into the bathroom.

This time, we wait for the water to warm slightly before stepping into the shower. Normally, I set the temperature to scalding, but the cool droplets feel nice against my heated skin. I wash off another round of sex with the body wash that prompted our venture into anal.

"If I hurt you, I want you to tell me." Darc wraps me up and rocks me gently in his arms. "It seemed like you were enjoying it at first, and then... Maybe I got too rough."

"It's fine. It wasn't anything I couldn't handle. I'll be sore tomorrow, but that's not entirely your fault. Is that what you wanted to talk about?"

"Not exactly." Darc shifts our position and pins my back to the wall. His hands flatten against the tile on either side of me as he leans closer. "I meant what I said when I proposed. I'm in love with *all* of you, not just the parts that love me back. You make me a better man. A man I never thought I could be. And I want to spend my life by your side. I want to make you as happy as you make me. There is no future for me without you."

"I love you so much, I think it might kill me." The water continues to rain on us from either side as I press my palm to his chest.

He straightens and covers my hand with his. "You can't die. You can't ever leave me. I need you too much."

Darc kisses me, taking my breath away and replacing it with his. I remember when I said the same words and told him he could never leave me, and now he's asking the same of me.

"Why are you saying all of this? I'm yours. I love you. I'm sorry I didn't say it. You know I don't want to lose him." The pain in my body numbs, giving way to the emotional agony standing at the front door.

"Sweetheart, I know. I promised you I would never let that happen. You aren't going to lose him."

"I don't understand. What are you not telling me?"

There's a loud knock on the bathroom door before it swings open on its hinges. I half expect the curtain to be yanked aside, but it remains hanging lazily in place. "It's nearly midnight, and we're running out of time! If my fiancée is finished professing her undying love and devotion to you, do you think I could borrow her for a minute?"

Darc stiffens as though he's bracing for a fight. "Take that tone with our girl again, and you won't be breathing long enough to borrow shit from me!"

"Sorry, Val." Kold no longer sounds like the man I fell in love with. He changed on Christmas, or maybe the night before, and I haven't been able to find him since.

"It's fine. I'll be out in a minute." I hold my breath, waiting for the door to close as I take in Darc's expression. His chiseled features are more rigid than usual, having sharpened against the incoming tension. Reaching to turn the water off on my side of the shower, Darc catches my wrist and threads his fingers into mine.

"If he makes you choose, I want you to know I've only ever loved you."

CHAPTER 57

Kold

Val steps out from behind the bathroom door, wearing the clothes I left on the edge of the sink. The long-sleeved thermal and sweatpants hide her body, which has been exposed for most of the evening. I wish I hadn't wasted so much of our time together acting like a jealous boyfriend fixated on the heat of the moment. She didn't deserve that.

When Val walked out alone, I had hoped she would curl up in my lap with her arms draped over my shoulders. I love the feel of her hands in my hair as we talk and the way her eyes brighten when she's about to kiss me. From five feet away, on the employee's side of my desk, I can barely smell the shower on her skin.

"I was told you needed to see me, sir. Did I do something wrong?" The consummate role-playing jokester, Val falls into character as the innocent bartender who got called into the boss's office her first day on the job. If I let it play out, she'd probably suck my dick for a second chance to keep her imaginary job. I'd be lying if I said I wasn't tempted.

"I wanted to speak with both of you. Is he coming?"

"Oh lord, I hope not. That boy's going to pass out from dehydration if he loses any more fluids." Val flashes me a playful grin and sits forward in her chair, speaking as though she's clutching her pearls. "You don't think he's in the bathroom *masturbating*, do you?

We're both laughing when Darc joins us in the office, wearing only a towel. When he moves the chair from his desk to sit beside her, she doubles over in a fit of giggles with tears in her eyes. I love how hard Val laughs at her own jokes and how she smiles when she stops holding back.

"I take it I missed something." Darc's eyebrows pull together as he looks from Val to me.

"We were about to get fired for fucking in the bathroom, and I didn't even give you a hand job. I had to agree to sleep with everyone on the staff in exchange for our jobs."

"What?" The look on Darc's face is priceless. My brother rarely walks into a situation unprepared for every possible scenario, and now he's sitting here confused, wondering if he'll have to fire everyone on the staff. "Did you drug her with something?"

"No. How could you even ask me that?" I'm mildly offended by the implication. I might have even been annoyed if it weren't for Val clutching her side and laughing through the pain.

"Oh my god. Stop. It hurts."

"I leave you alone with her for two minutes, and when I get out here, she's acting like she sucked down half a tank of nitrous."

"Val doesn't do drugs." I shake my head, surprised that he's never seen this side of her.

"I'm certainly not opposed to it! Have you got any? Is that what you're hiding when you're all hush-hush working from your office at The Jakobsson? Are you drug dealers? Is that where all your money comes from? I knew it was something, but I sort of thought you were hitmen. It's smart to funnel it through the clubs."

"Valentine!"

"Okay, sorry. I'll stop. I was only joking around, trying to lighten the mood."

Darc and I exchange a series of looks that convey an hours-long conversation. Val knows we're doing something illegal but doesn't know what it is. And somehow, she figured out that we're cleaning the money through the clubs. Or maybe that was an unlucky guess. While we've never fucked with drugs, we do deal in secrets and dead bodies.

The family business we inherited that's cloaked behind an LLC is a one-hundred-twenty-five-acre cemetery that's successful enough to cover the operating costs. We also accommodate clients willing to pay extra for *discreet* services. Those bodies are buried four feet closer to hell, backfilled with dirt, and capped off by dear sweet Aunt Gertrude. Or whoever happens to be coming in that week.

I'm sure that's where Allen disappeared, even though his jeep, phone, and luggage made it to a bad part of town, two states away.

This isn't the first time Val's *joked* about us killing people, which seems like an odd accusation to make so flippantly. Unless it isn't a joke. Conrad swore up and down that he never told her. He even went so far as to call and beg my mother for mercy.

Fucking coward. I knew he was lying.

My hands might not be clean, but Darc's are fucking filthy. How much does Val actually know, and why is she okay with it? The night is nearing its end, and decisions have to be made, but what am I supposed to say to the one woman who sees the monster and loves me anyway?

"You're being weird as shit. If there's some earth-shattering conversation we desperately need to have, I wish you'd spit it out already. You're all over the place, and I can't tell if you love me or hate me." Fed up with the awkward silence, Val is no longer in a laughing mood.

"Come here one second." I open the contract on my computer as Val steps around the desk. Then I pull her onto my lap, holding her in my arms as she makes herself comfortable. "I'm sorry I've been an asshole."

"Well, I don't think you're an asshole. You haven't been *that* bad. I'm having trouble keeping pace with your mood swings, but I'm sure they're partially my fault. One minute, you're excited about our future, and the next, it feels like you're walking away. You're not even gone, and I already miss you." She lays her head on my shoulder and kisses my neck. "I miss you so much that sometimes it hurts to be around you."

"You haven't done anything wrong. I'm still the guy you fell in love with, but I'm also the guy who doesn't know how to let go. I love you more than anything in this world. That's why I want you to have the final say." I inch our chair closer to the desk, drawing her attention to the document on the screen. "I filled out everything at the top. All it requires is your seal of approval and my name."

"Shouldn't we talk about this?" Val's body trembles.

"Babe, we have. We've talked it to death. And every time we have the conversation, you give me the same answer."

"I know, but..." She swallows hard and looks away.

"Everything's going to work out the way it's supposed to. The indecision has been messing with our heads, but all our plans can fall into place once the contract is signed. You and I are meant to be. We both know that. And Darc will take care of anything you need while I'm away." I pause, giving my brother time to express his disapproval and smile when he doesn't disappoint. Once he's finished groaning and mumbling his displeasure, I continue. "Nothing between the two of you will change when I get back. Darc is still going to spoil you rotten and love you as much as I do because I'm never going to ask you to choose between us, Val. I don't want to leave you, but I agree with every reason we've tirelessly discussed over the last few days. I have obligations to fulfill, but *you* are always my top priority. I'll come home anytime you need me."

"I always need you." Val stands and paces the area beside me, no longer able to sit still. Her eyes sparkle with tears that have yet to fall, and I hate that I'm the reason for her pain. "So, if I sign this, you're telling me there's no chance I could ever lose you?"

I've yet to figure out what she sees in me, but I intend to spend the rest of my life being the man she deserves. "I hate to be the one to break it to you, my love, but you're stuck with me."

"You're stuck with both of us." Darc approaches Val with a tenderness that still surprises me and threads his fingers into hers. "I know that a lowly club owner is a poor substitute for a trending rockstar, but I'll rearrange my schedule so you never feel alone, and once a week, we'll make pizza for dinner."

A smile is exchanged between them, and I know she'll be okay.

The chair pushes back as I stand, and Val's eyes shoot to the remaining minutes being projected behind me. We're running low on time, and we already know what the decision has to be. I extend my hand and pull her close, wanting to absorb every ounce of her grief. "It's now or never, my love. I've tried to sign it, and I can't force myself to hit the keys. I need you to do this for me."

Val's hand shakes as she types with one finger, spelling out my name in the contract's signature box and then adds the date and time. With a shattered expression, she looks at Darc and then at me before selecting agree and hitting submit. A sob racks through her body as I hold her to my chest, feeling her break in my arms. It isn't long until Darc joins the embrace, pressing himself to Val's back. We stand, forever linked, until the overwhelming emotion of the moment begins to loosen its grip.

"You guys are kind of crushing me." Val's small voice appears between us as we step back to offer space. She wipes whatever tears remain in her eyes before fastening a smile to her lips. "Who needs a drink?"

The tour contract has been weighing on me all week, but I realize now that I was never withstanding its burden on my own. My leaving town is laced with benefits and disadvantages, affecting each of us differently. The band's success offers a layer of legitimacy to the life Darc and I lead, keeping prying eyes further from the truth hidden in the shadows. And once I talk Val into visiting me on the road, she'll see I can be trusted. I'm trading booze for books and exchanging groupies for group chats with the people I love back home.

As I shut down my computer and clean off my desk, Val mixes cocktails, and Darc changes out of his towel. Then, it's time to move onto the balcony. This is the end of the night, marking the end of a year that changed our lives forever. We all have an integral part to play in our combined relationship, as unconventional as it may be, and I wouldn't change that dynamic even if it were within my power to do so.

The anticipation in the club builds as the last few minutes slip away and the final countdown begins. With one voice, we count back from ten with raised glasses and renewed hopes. Val sets down her drink and laces her fingers into mine as we shout, "Three... Two... One... Happy New Year!"

Auld Lang Syne plays as confetti cannons send golden flecks whirling overhead. I feel Val squeeze my hand, calling my lips to hers, and we kiss like it's the only thing that's ever mattered. There's no longer an end in sight. No more wavering uncertainty or questionable outcomes, only new beginnings.

As Val turns away to share her kiss with Darc, I lean over the railing and watch as the confetti rains over the embracing couples below. I hope each of them receives a midnight kiss that fills them with happiness.

May our resolutions meet successful conclusions, and may we always find reasons to be better than we are today.

Val has claimed her position between me and my darker half. She's dug in her heels and called that place home, vowing to remain there forever. And I suppose I've always known *we* would stand beside her until the end, filling in her broken pieces with our own fractured soul. The three of us belong together.

And together, we shall stay.

About the Author

Amanda Bryk is a full-time mother and part-time substitute teacher who spends her days obsessing over the characters living in her head. Not sure how to be the *hearts and flowers* type, she writes true-to-life romance, red flags and all. Amanda and her family live in the small boating community of Vermilion, Ohio where they share a home with their boston terriers.

Other books by this author:

Locked Away
(book one in the Locked Away series)

Drifting Apart
(book two in the Locked Away series)

facebook.com/LockedAwaySeries

instagram.com/locked_away_series

tiktok.com/lockedawayseries